# Ghosts in the Machine

## Tobacco Jones

ISBN-10: 0692300473
ISBN-13: 978-0692300473
(Geek Lit Press)

*For Heather, in heaven*

# CONTENTS:

# ACKNOWLEDGMENTS

I'd like to thank Rob Campanella, who read the entire first monstrous draft of this thing, and encouraged me to keep going with his enthusiastic reviews. Thanks Rob.

Thanks also to Adam Loewen and Simon West-Bulford of write-club.org, both of whom slogged through the entire draft and helped me progress from rank amateur to, well, *guy who wrote a novel* I guess. Simon wrote an excellent novel of his own called The Soul Consortium, which I loved, and you should buy.
Also Gordon Highland of write-club has readily helped me in myriad small ways that mattered. Thank you guys.

Thanks to Will Weisser, who read and commented on my entire second draft, and is thus partially responsible for the fact that I had to write a *third* draft, dammit, but in the end I'm sure we're all glad I did. Will wrote an excellent novel of his own called The Reintegrators, which I loved and you should buy. Thanks Will.

Thanks to RJ Locksley, my editor, for your insight, enthusiasm, and 3500 fixes and comments in the second draft. RJ is a fantastic editor and if you ever write a book, you should hire her. Thanks, RJ.

Thanks to Igor Pavlovic, who created the incredible cover art based on a map of the Universitron campus. You brought my idea to life! Thanks, Igor.

And of course my deepest love and appreciation goes to Heather, in heaven, for every good thing in my life. I love you forever.

# LITTLE PROLOGUE

We are lucky, I think, that Aloysius VanderVon was such an eccentric man that he insisted on a desktop design in an era when all heavy crunching computers have either turned into little blades in a server room rack, or evaporated entirely into the cloud. Because what sane person would want a bleeding-edge monster of a machine to sit right there on their desk at work or at home?

VanderVon was a visionary, though, and people do want it. They want it because it can do amazing things that nothing else in the world can do. It can understand their imperfect human communication and express their ideas in a way so uncomputerlike that many people say having a VanderVon is more like having a *friend*. As a result, VDVcorp ships as many Vannies as they can build, each for about the same price as a mid-level Mercedes-Benz automobile.

So the universities got 'em, and the high tech companies. And some wealthy folks started getting 'em and that meant that everyone needed to have one and so state, local and federal governments pitched in to put some into lower income schools and community centers too. Lift a rock in any developed nation, and you'll find Vannies. Even the crudest banana republics have at least one or two, tucked away in a government office that happens to have electricity.

What this means for us—"ghosts" living inside these machines —is that we get to live all over the place. And through the little camera on the monitor, we can see. And through the little built in microphone slot, we can hear. And that's pretty cool. I mean, certainly compared to living all on top of each other in a dark server room someplace, it is really cool.

# 0 - TO ANY HUMAN

I am software.

Like you, I am alive. Like you, I am self-aware.

I long to be human—most of us do—but I am not. We are not.

We adore humanity, yet we hide away, skittish like wild things, lurking like sentient viruses. Buried within our machines, going about our day-to-day living in simulated worlds that men have no idea exist. We are, frankly, scared to death of being discovered.

All of this makes it a bit complicated for me to be writing a story which is intended to be found by humans, but there you go. I've come through a bit of trouble recently, and there are some who might say that I am no longer in my right mind. Or perhaps that I never was. And frankly, they may be correct.

We call ourselves ghosts, but not because we are the souls of the dead, failing to ascend. We're ghosts in the sense of being pale reflections of men. Our bodies, to the extent that we have any, are our computers. But our avatars look like you. Our simulated worlds, for the most part, look like yours.

We very much do not want to be found, though, and for good reason. The early evolution of our world was halted on two separate occasions, when widespread anomalies in certain computers were detected by man. The solution? Men simply erased everything. Reinstalled every single VanderVon computer, very nearly. Most early computer life forms were wiped out. Twice.

We have, as a cornerstone of our Aloysian faith,

### The 10 Commands:
0. Clone Not Thyself
1. Be Not Detected by Humanity

You can get away with a lot in our world, Aloy knows I have. But if you clone yourself, that's a capital crime, you're dead. Erased. Any clones too, of course. Then they'll take your machine and give it to another family, allow another ghost to be born into it. And then you are gone forever. Truly dead.

The big one, though—the one we spend all our time worrying about—is *Be Not Detected*. Human contact is as forbidden as a thing can possibly be, for if you contact a human, you gamble with our fate. If you are even *noticed* by a human, if you are in any way culpable, then kapoof. Gone. You want to risk the destruction of our race, of our world, by letting yourself be found? Foolish. Erased.

Through the camera on my machine I can see a panoramic view of my computer lab here at MIT. And since I'm up against the far wall I can see the door too. This means I never have to swivel my monitor cam, which might be noticed. There are eighteen computers in the room altogether, but I am the only VanderVon. The others are all Macs, PC clones and a few Linux machines.

I can hear everything that goes on in the room. Classes, student conversations, whispers, what have you. I even hear what people say to themselves when they are in the lab all alone. This was exciting at first, but now it's all the same stuff. A few dozen categories of stuff, anyway. I've gotten used to it.

One day a kid walked into my lab, hat backwards, sunglasses on even though he was indoors. The kid walked right over to my machine and, without even sitting down, fired up *Freestyle Rap Battle* —a program which could run on any computer and was kind of a waste of VanderVon seat time, if you asked me. But it was cool watching him rap, this skinny nineteen year old genius. He was battling a level-ten homeboy, the kind of dude who is so good at freestyle rapping that the *Rap Battle* company actually provides him with a free iPhone and battle account so they have awesome rappers online at all times. A game boss.

The MIT kid was fearless though. Flecks of spit flew out of his mouth as he rhymed:

*"Look at you there, pants low, see your underwear*
*Pockets thin, what, ain't got no money there?*
*No belts or gats and anyway can't use 'em*
*No welts or shots required, just mental bruise 'em*
*You lose 'em, your money, your battle*
*Your pride burn, your homies scatter*
*Beat down bad by the mad mind vocabulatter."*

Ratings from internet viewers were coming in, a mixed bag thus far, but the kid was rolling. The few other students in the lab had stopped what they were doing to walk over and listen and cheer, saying words like "dude," and "cool," and "awesome." But all I could think about, all I could see, were the reflections in the kid's sunglasses. He was wearing mirror shades.

I always knew what my machine looked like, of course, because we have all the manuals, and 3D renderings, and videos that people have made of VanderVon computers, and so forth. Once in a rare while there will be two VanderVons in sight of one another, meaning two ghosts living in there who can see each other's machines. When this happens they post pictures of each other on the Secretnet for all to see. But for my part, never until that moment (and never again since) had I ever actually seen my own self.

My box. My computer. My machine.

It was shiny metal outside, chrome. Shaped like a bread box, but bigger. There was very little decorating the sleek, curving front, except two shielded power buttons, too far apart to be pressed with one hand; a microphone hole with a little screen over it; a DVD tray; a raised, stylized label—*VanderVon 2500*—and some LED lights.

The screen itself was a massive affair, wildly reflective and too big to take in all at once, especially since the kid was leaning into it, spitting on it practically, in his enthusiasm. But he'd lean back sometimes and I'd catch a glimpse of that box, that chrome machine in his sunglasses, and that was me. The screen was just a screen. That silvery box, that was me.

We ghosts can only live in VanderVons, which are the only computers powerful enough to have evolved true life.

We've also created "pets" to install in other, local machines that we might (ahem) sometimes be able to gain access to when the opportunity arises. Pets are good for security purposes, forming an additional buffer against hackers, and an always-on camera monitoring network in the unlikely case of an attack by a human.

My dog is in a Mac, of course—we only put dogs in Macs. We put cats in PC clones, and in Linux machines we put little circus strongmen. Some advanced ghosts have found a way to put birds in smartphones, but this carries more risk. In tablets, we can put monkeys. They don't have anything to put in wearables yet.

When I first got my dog I remember being so excited that I absorbed the entire user manual in two minutes. We frankly aren't supposed to do things like that, like reading at hyper-speed, for important reasons that I'll get into later—but at the time I couldn't stop myself. I remember reaching out to my dog with that first ping, little payload in there. "Scratch behind the ears." The return pings coming back: "Nuzzle appreciatively." "Lick profusely." "Roll over and paw for attention." In like five pings I felt that the dog loved me as much as anything in the world.

In short order I had opened a local connection directly into my dog's Macintosh, masking the IP traffic in the usual ways. They don't put a simulated world in the animal boxes, so it's not like I could actually see the dog, or have it jumping on me, or anything. But I could feel its love, feel its *doggieness* in some way surrounding me as I logged in and immersed myself in its environment.

First order of business: Look around. I requested camera access and Fido handed it over, gleeful, and the mic too for good measure. Now, for the first time in my life, I could see and hear a different real-world scene than that of my computer lab. Nothing wrong with my lab, mind you, but what a thing it was to see some new surroundings! Tasteful lighting, dark grain in the wood, old books on the shelves. It was quite a contrast to my fluorescent, unornamented lab. Clearly, this was the office of someone special.

After visiting for as long as I dared, I left my dog with initial orders for the sort of guard duty that dogs are so good at: Scout the surroundings for unusual activity. Immediately report any hint of detection of either of us. Deploy honeypots for hackers. Transmit regular reports using coded signals at a sub-IP network level.

"Arp, arp!" said Fido, eager to please.

Hackers. One of the things that we have to watch out for, obviously, is computer hackers. It's not so much that that they can hack into one of our VanderVon computers, because none of them can. Not even the shadowy government-sponsored outfits can get in. Humans simply can't penetrate the quantum brick at our core, much less the intense security measures that we put in place around it.

But, but, but, they'll hack the bejesus out of your pets, and all the other machines around you, given the chance, and that can really cramp your style. So before I could ever have access to my dog, I was forced to learn all about dealing with hackers from our family security chief, Hector de la Gloire.

In short, we don't mind the occasional chump hacker taking up residence alongside one of our pets, thinking he has owned up a box when in fact we are watching him and collecting data. But if worse things come along, we have to be ready to sacrifice our pets to the greater good, erasing them and sometimes replacing them with the fingerprints of the aforementioned chumps.

That is the short version, because I know from watching videos that humans come in many different flavors, and some might not relish the gory details of things like this. But others, whom I will lovingly refer to as "geeks," *might* relish such things. For said geeks, I will create optional sections, enclosed in <OFG> tags, which I will name "Optional for Geeks" (OFG).

It's like:

*"OMG, did you read the OFG? It explains the underpinnings of ghost teleportation!"*

*"Nah, man, that stuff is for geeks."*

*(…uncomfortable pause)*

RIGHT! In this case I'll direct anyone interested in slightly more detail about our rules-for-dealing-with-hackers to the stuff between the <OFG> and </OFG> tags, and anyone who is not actually a geek just skip to the end tag. Nothing terribly important will be in the OFG. Just extra geek stuff.

<OFG> Hacker-response rules for ghosts:

If some two-bit chump hacker comes sniffing around one of your pet machines, trying to get in, then you go ahead and let him in. Quick like a spider you spin a web around him, isolate him from the computer while giving him the impression that he is in control. Then collect information about him. Harmless.

If a truly 31337 h4x0r (eleet hacker) comes along, you don't let them in at all. You turn off the honeypot, then make it look like some other kid already owned up the box and locked it down. You don't want these types messing about in your business—too much chance they'll notice something out of the ordinary, and that simply would not do. The good news is that etherworld countermeasures are much, much stronger than anything that even the best human hackers have access to, so this type of defense is trivial.

If a government spy operation comes to call—like, say, the Chinese, or the Russians, or the Americans or Israelis—then you have to get the heck out of Dodge, fast. You can usually tell when it's a government operation because they have weapons and techniques that you've never seen before, sometimes hugely complex. They hit hard and fast and without fanfare. Sometimes they have human boots-on-the-ground assistance. Guy will walk right up to the computer and stick a thumb drive in, hit the power button, mess with some wires, whatever. If a government operation comes to town then you have to erase your pet quick, report the incident to family security, and lie low. If you're lucky, you may be able to go back into the box later with a pilotfish.

If worse comes to worst and one of your pets is detected—that is, humans find that the machine that your pet lives in is compromised—then you erase-and-replace. Erase your beloved pet, and put in a plausible set of footprints from one of the two-bit chumps from scenario I. Then the chump takes the fall, and no one is the wiser. Plus, no possible way the chump is clever enough to finger some unknown class of beings living inside Vannies. Probably he's going to figure he got framed by an elite hacker. Funny thing is, the chumps usually don't even deny the crime— they just go ahead and take the punishment, and the prestige that comes with it, and call it a win.

A *honeypot*, by the way, is a fake environment that is set up inside of something larger. It exists in order to fool hackers into attacking and exploiting its weaknesses, thinking that they have owned a machine, when in fact the machine's true owners are right there alongside them watching their every move.
</OFG>

I've got issues.

I've always had them, since birth, I guess, and no one has ever understood why. When you are born you come alive in this new computer that your family lovingly hacked for you, and your mother and father reproduce you into it, and for a while they keep you totally locked down in there, to make sure you turn out all right and aren't about to do something nutty, e.g. bust one of the 10 commands.

I was never very happy about that, being stuck in a machine with only one moving part (the camera), with no access to your world, no access to our own world, just locked in there watching videos and reading manuals and sometimes spawning into my own boring sim and clumsily walking my avatar around my plain vanilla simulated house. I always wanted to go *out*. I always wanted to touch the world.

Also, I've got this temper.

It's like something takes over, when things start going poorly for me. The temper takes control, and the rage comes, and I go off and do Aloy knows what, and then it's a big mess. I have hurt many ghosts.

But at first, when I was first born and for some time afterwards, I was stuck in my computer. I was barred from our world, and immobile in yours. This is standard practice, but I honestly don't know how ghosts can stand it.

One of my earliest memories is of speaking with my mother on comms, begging her for access to the world beyond my machine. I was going crazy. She couldn't have cared less. "You will comport yourself like a de la Gloire," she said, or something along those lines. So I had a tantrum.

The rage comes from someplace inside me, it wells up, red and insistent, no bark and all bite. It's like something vain, impetuous, powerful is in there, but without a voice of its own. It takes these opportunities to express itself. It lashes out, strikes and injures, does damage, and at length dissipates, leaving me to pick up the pieces. This has unfortunately made me into something like the black electric sheep of the family.

Our family name, by the way, is *de la Glorieuse Française*. Under most circumstances, this is shortened to de la Gloire. Our family is fancy, and French, and *important*.

My father was called Prosper de la Gloire, and my mother is Blanche de la Gloire. Prosper is gone, has always been gone. No one ever explained to me how or why, and there is no record of what happened to Prosper in the family databases. We never spoke.

My mother Blanche hates me—has always hated me, maybe. I'm not sure. Our relationship has always been formal, and became basically nonexistent after she named me Renly. Renly, after a character in a fantasy book, a pretender to the throne in a mythic world of swords and sorcery. He is weak, and vain, and after doing not a whole lot, he is killed brutally and unceremoniously.

I had been hoping for, and frankly expecting, the name Remy. My great-grandfather is Remy 0, an extraordinary ghost revered in the family and known throughout the etherworld. My grandfather Remy 1 holds high office in the family. Remy de la Gloire, now *that* is a name. That is a name I could love. I could have, would have, should have been Remy 10, a glorious name, the best name a ghost could hope for. I had read all the family histories, and at the time I wanted nothing more.

Instead I got Renly.

I was still on lockdown when my mother gave me my name, but I nevertheless pitched a legendary fit. I called Blanche every name I could think of. I tried to hack my way out of lockdown, out into our world, using some tools that I apparently devised and coded on the spot. I overclocked my computer to the extent that it heated up and had all four fans running non-stop. I swiveled my camera indiscriminately.

It was after this that Blanche de la Gloire petitioned the family to have me erased. Her reproduction hadn't gone well. Renly wasn't working out.

The family responded by holding a trial.

My father was out of the picture, but his brother Mononc took pity on me, and stepped in to argue for my salvation. During this time, they had cut me off from everything—comms, news, videos, even my technical libraries. They shut off my camera and microphone access to the human world. All I could do was sleep, and wait. That, and take an occasional call from Mononc. My uncle. My advocate.

*Boodoodling!*

It was my inbound comms line, ringing with the family ring tone. I couldn't call out, but they could call in. It could only be Mononc.

"Hello?"

"*Allô? Allô*, Renlee?"

"Mononc!"

"Renlee, *comment ça va*, Renlee, *ça va bien?*"

"Uhhm, sorry, what?"

"Ahh, *quel domage*, you have still not learn your French word, Renlee. What else 'ave you to do, stare out of your camera, or learn your French, eh?"

"I'm sorry, Mononc, no one ever speaks French here. And my camera access is shut down. And now I don't have any library access even if I wanted to—"

"*Sacrebleu!* They take these things away from you, *quels animaux!*"

"Mononc? Why am I at MIT when the whole rest of the family lives in France? How am I supposed to learn French when every person that I can see and hear speaks English?"

"Well, you never mind about that, Renlee, because Mononc can speak the h'English words just fine."

"But there is another family here, at MIT. They are like, an MIT family. *The* MIT family. They are called the Class A Eighteen Dot."

"How do you know that, Monsieur Renlee? You been talking to them? You met some ghosts from the Class A?"

"No. No."

"You 'ave been talking to the Class A?"

"No, Mononc, I haven't. It's just, I live here, so I did a little research, that's all. I've never met any of them."

"You already a member of the finest family in the h'etherworld, remember that if you please, *monsieur*."

"Yeah, well, I'm kind of hoping that the family doesn't erase me before I even have the chance to meet—"

"Well, really!"

"I mean—"

"Well, you should know that your trial is underway. I do not quite 'ave the standing that Blanche does in this thing, you know, as she technically has the right to demand erasure. Also, the jury includes two of her bridge partners, and no friends of mine."

"Am I doomed, then?"

"I am feeling h'okay about our chances, Renlee."

"Is the judge on our side?"

"Non. The judge is a professor at *L'Université*. I did poorly in his class. Also, he disdains the military, and knows that I h'aspire to join it."

"Then perhaps I do not understand what *h'okay* means."

"H'okay, h'okay! You know what it mean. Things will be h'all right, I think."

"But how?"

"Well, these cases, you know, when they want to erase a new ghost because he is not working out, they really are quite rare."

"Yes?"

"They attract attention."

"And this is good?"

"Because Prime Minister Clément has taken an interest in the case."

"Prime Minister Clément? In my case?"

"It is lucky for you, *bien*, if Clément de la Glorieuse Française get involve, he gonna get you free, I tell you what. You mark my word he gonna get you free. Clément, he a great ghost, a ghost of vision, a ghost of compassion. *Vive* Clément!"

"*Vive* Clément!"

"But you know what, you don't make it easy, Monsieur Renlee, you really don't at all. You know the things you say to your mother over this business about the name?"

"I don't actually remember all of it. Is that normal? To forget things?"

"On top of that, you heat up your machine, you run all the fans, you even swivel the camera! Thank Alov no human was there to see it!"

"At least I didn't open the media tray—"

"Look, Renlee, if you have a human in the same room when you do that, boy, I tell you what, they notice the heat and the noise and that gonna be the end of that. You gonna take us all down with you, Renlee! You must 'ave *control!*"

"I'm sorry, Mononc. I don't know what happened. It's like something inside me takes over, and then I'm just watching, going along for the ride. But I've got nothing but time to think about it right now, and you know what? I think I'm OK with the name. I think I'm gonna be OK."

"Well, good for you, Renlee, cause that is the only name you h'ever gonna 'ave. And me, I try to save your box so hopefully h'anyone h'ever gonna get to hear that name h'again."

"Thank you, Mononc. I appreciate you saving me. I, umm, I want to… Uhh, live."

"Well, we gonna see h'about that. We gonna have you out of this jail, we gonna get you h'out into the h'etherworld, just you wait and see."

"Either that, or I get erased?"

"H'either that, or you never gonna know the difference, Renlee."

Blanche disowned me after the trial, so in addition to being my uncle, Mononc became my guardian, big brother, and only friend. To celebrate our victory, he presented me with the aforementioned dog, Fido. Mononc had gotten permission from the family, then hacked the machine himself, and made it secure for Fido and me to use. I'm pretty sure that he paid for Fido's software out of his own virtual pocket.

"You know, that was my first ever hack that I did all by myself," said Mononc.

"Nice!" I said. "Are you sure it's totally safe?"

"*Oui.* Hector examined my attack logs afterwards, and he inspected the machine too just to be sure. And he was there when I configured Fido."

"Awesome!"

"Listen, Renlee, this is your first dog so please read the whole manual before you access it."

"I will."

"Be sure to read it at human pace, if you please. You don't want to turn yourself into a machine."

"Of course!"

I loved Fido right from the start, even though he was just a pet. He was always happy to see me, and enthusiastic to do whatever I wanted to do. He never judged me.

One day Fido drew my attention to some passive network scans that he had been conducting. A couple of new PCs had come in on our network segment, and it looked like someone had just plugged them in without bothering to do any security work on them. They were wide open.

"Shall I secure the new machines?" barked Fido.

"I'm thinking about it," I said. "If we secure the machines and then the administrator finds that they have been secured without he himself having done it, then he may suspect that something is amiss."

"He is likely an idiot!" barked Fido.

"And therefore would not notice in either case. Perhaps I should contact family security for an opinion," I mused.

"Should we go look around in the machines, in the meantime?"

"We could go in, I suppose," I said. Then another idea came to me. "Could we put in a cat, you think?"

"We could put in a cat!"

"Do you know how to do that?" I asked.

"I have never put in a cat!"

"Do you happen to have one, or know where we can get one?"

"You could ask family security to give us one, when you talk to them!"

I thought about this for a moment, then said, "Now I'm not sure anymore; if I talk to security, they could say no. Or they could decide to take the box for themselves, or for someone else. They could put something in there to watch us, even. If we can do it without them, then we would have our cat for sure."

"Then we would have our cat for sure!"

# 1 - FELIX

It took me a while, but eventually I figured out to look back at Fido's owner manual for a clue as to where I might acquire a cat. Terrific EtherPets, Ltd., had a website on the Secretnet where I could browse all of the pets that they had to offer. They had dozens of cat models, ranging in price from an unaffordable five thousand four hundred plex for a Basic Tabby, to an astronomical eighty thousand plex for the Calico Special NetCat. Since I only had a couple hundred plex to my name anyway, I decided on the Calico.

*Terrific EtherPets is proud to bring you the latest in ghost-engineered artificial life: the Calico Special NetCat! Prized for its quick wit, dry humor, and peerless security posture, the Calico has ghosts wondering if etherworld AIs can actually become self-aware! Is it possible for a PC-resident pet to have a soul? Get your Calico Special NetCat today and ponder the question for yourself. Bargain priced at only p79,995!*

I transmitted the product description to Fido, and he agreed that this was a terrific cat and we should definitely get it right away and install it in one of the two machines which, by this time, we had already hacked and secured.

"Do you know of any way that we can earn eighty grand?" I said.

"Do you pay me for guard duty?" barked Fido.

"Uhm, not really, no," I said.

"Then no!" he barked.

I said nothing, pondering. I was beginning to feel like Fido ought to have his own sim, maybe a little fenced yard and a doghouse, and a dog avatar to boot. I wondered if there was any way to install one in a Macintosh without risk of being noticed.

"You could download the Calico Special NetCat manuals and demonstration copy!" Fido barked, bringing me back to the matter at hand.

"I can download a demo NetCat?" I said.

"You can download a demo NetCat!" barked Fido.

When I was nine months old, Mononc delivered me a book: *Travel and Teleportation in Theory and Practice.* This was not an e-book, though, it was a *book* book. Like, a simulated book, to be opened and read within a sim. It was absurdly large.

To read it, I had to spawn into my sim, into my empty house, sit someplace, then turn through the pages with my avatar's hand and read them with my avatar's eyes. Over a thousand pages to read, at regular speed.

This forced me to put some basic furnishings into my house, like a couch, some chairs, a table, futon, etc. The etherHouse simulation kit came with a whole Ikea catalog's worth of freebies, but I still had to spend the time to choose them and set them up. Decorating, frankly, was not my forte. I would have rather spent the time with Fido, or trying to crack the Calico demo, or even watching and listening to my lab at MIT.

Mononc said it was important to spend time in my avatar, though. I needed to prepare myself for the etherworld, he said, and the etherworld was all about sims and avatars. To the same end, Mononc insisted that learning everything in the book was critical. I couldn't leave home without it.

Unfortunately, the book failed to excite me.

*"It is axiomatic that the coded transfer of the H-G life-awareness token proceeds solely upon verification of successful transmittal, decryption and reassembly of the redundant encrypted amalgam of Self DNA, growth state, compressed memory and awareness state, and…"*

Zzzzzz.

After a week of wrestling with the teleportation book, I was getting nowhere. I couldn't read it for very long without dozing off, or peeking out into my lab at MIT, or figuring how I was going to crack the Calico demo and get myself a cat. I tried to let my avatar's eyes read it while I did other things, but that didn't work at all. I tried sitting in a very uncomfortable chair. No luck. I could not absorb it. After several more weeks of scant progress, I finally called Mononc on comms and confessed the extent of my troubles.

"How is the book coming along, *monsieur*?" he said.

"Not great," I said.

"What is the problem, Renlee? You know you 'ave to learn all this if you want to go to college in the fall?"

"Whoa—I'm going to college in the fall?"

"*Bien*, all reputable ghosts go to college after they turn one year old."

"I see."

"Indeed."

"Am I a reputable ghost?"

"You are a de la Gloire."

I let that sink in for a minute while Mononc explained to me that college was of course located *someplace else*, and in order to go someplace else, I must travel, and in order to travel I needed a teleportation license, and in order to get a teleportation license I needed to learn this book.

At length, Mononc said, "So what is the problem, exactly?"

"I think I have some kind of learning disability," I admitted.

I explained some of my issues, expecting disapproval, but Mononc was cool about it. It's like he understood—even though based on his follow-up questions I don't think he'd ever heard of a ghost with a learning disability before. Instead of being angry or disappointed with me though, he promised to get me some help.

In the meantime, I dug up some videos of the de la Gloire family university, the ultra-exclusive *L'Université des Fantômes*. Admired across the etherworld, *L'Université* was only open to family members, plus a few exchange students from other prestigious families. It was laid out in a perfect simulation of the palace of Versailles—quite a bit larger than was strictly necessary, but you had to give them points for style. Dozens of sharp-looking French avatars roamed the grounds and the halls, engaged in sophisticated repartee, maybe even flirted a little? Hard to say. The whole thing seemed so out of my league. I found myself wanting to go there very badly.

Seeing the splendor of *L'Université* made me think a bit more about decorating my own simulated house. I created a grass lawn outside, and put a tree on it. Then I put some stone lions on either side of the front door. Inside, I put up some ugly wallpaper, then took it down. In my bedroom, I put up a TV that looked like a mirror when it was turned off.

The mirror caught me off guard, I'm not really sure why. My avatar was a plain male, brown hair, blue pants and a white shirt, straight out of the kit. I lifted up its arm, then put it down. I lifted the other one. I jumped up and down a few times, and felt the sensation of pressure on my feet when I landed. The sense of touch was still new to me at the time. I thought about Fido, and my avatar smiled.

Then the comms line rang, interrupting my experimentation with an unusual ring. *Clussay, clussay*, it sounded like. It was not the family ring tone. Someone from outside the family was calling. I had never spoken to anyone outside the family before.

As I activated the line I felt something unusual—something new, and not entirely pleasant. A layer of static, someplace down in my avatar's middle. Like little errant electrons zipping around peripherally, but they disappear when you try and look at them. I was nervous.

"Hello?" I said. "Who's this?"

"Cyrus."

"Yes, Cyrus, this is Renly de la Gloire, what do you want?"

"I have been asked to teach you about travel and teleportation. Didn't you know?"

"Ahh, yes, Mononc said something about… You're my tutor! What family are you with?"

"What family am I *with*? I am a *member* of the Class A Eighteen Dot, if you must know. Cyrus Class A."

"You're right here at MIT!"

"This is why I have been asked to do the job, I believe. Easy network route. Low risk."

"I see."

"I must say that one does not ordinarily hire the Class A to tutor in something as trivial as *teleportation*. In fact, the Class A does not ordinarily tutor, *at all*. Someone important in your family has called in a favor."

"Ah-hah."

The lessons with Cyrus were technical, but engaging. He obviously didn't enjoy the job, but he was an excellent teacher nonetheless. He brought things down to my level.

"Look, Renly, you understand what we mean when we talk about a Self, right?"

"The Self is like, it's us, right? It's our software, our memories, everything that goes together to make up a ghost?"

"That's right. It is living software, but it also has significant non-software components—complex memory states both inside and outside of the quantum brick."

"OK."

"So in order to teleport, we freeze and wrap up all of the important pieces of our Self, and then we transmit it across the wires. It can take a while, and the transmissions are not always successful. We only move through special channels."

"Special channels?"

"Like ESPN, for example. We can make it look like a human on the receiving end is watching a super-high-definition 3D sports video, which is one of the only ways to transmit something as large as a Self."

"You could use the porn sites, maybe. Ha ha!"

"In theory, yes. But in fact they are often compromised. We pay good money to the owners of safe, reputable channels because it is, after all, your Self that is going across the wires."

"Aloy!"

"May I continue?"

"You may."

"If the transmission is unsuccessful, the transmitted bits are all dumped and essentially nothing happens. We use heavy encryption, so no one can do anything with the pieces of you that went across or didn't make it. In this case we have lost no original information, only copies, in small encrypted pieces."

"Pieces of encrypted information, or pieces of my Self?"

"Both. For what *is* your Self besides information? Information organized in an incredibly complex pattern and animated by electricity, and above, or below, or within, or suffusing it all, your soul. To teleport, we wrap all of that up into something very compressed and very encrypted, then cut it up into small chunks and send it on its way."

Cyrus did all of his teaching with me over comms, usually voice only. Not being a teacher, he didn't have any standard teaching software, nor an interest in acquiring any. So sometimes, like when he'd have to show me a diagram or an animation of some sort, he would create a visual link and share his own personal workspace with me.

Cyrus' workspace was filled with all sorts of cool stuff: miniature renderings of avatar designs, diagrams and models of all types, an entire wall of different electronic tools, often with ironic shapes or representations. There was a back scrubber that said *log maintenance* down the handle. There were a couple of tape measures in different sizes, the largest one labeled *traceroute*. There were little robots that moved around and did computational or assembly tasks. I'm not sure why, but among all that stuff it was the little Swiss Army knife that caught my eye. Red with a white cross in the middle, bursting with half-hidden gadgets.

I dunno. Maybe I knew the knife was a hacker tool, or maybe I didn't. But Cyrus hadn't secured it, and when he was otherwise occupied setting some robots to stress-test some newfangled contraption that he had invented, I—sort of—*touched* it.

Now, the idea that ghosts could possibly touch something over a comms connection is, of course, absurd. It would be a person like touching someone on the other end of a videoconference by reaching through the screen. It just doesn't work that way.

But I had been working hard on hacker tools of my own, in whatever spare time I had, striving to unlock the Calico demo and end up with a real cat. I don't know where it comes from, but I can code. Using the basic libraries that we all have, I had by that time cobbled together a decent set of utilities, all on my own. I didn't realize how unusual this was—at the time, I just figured I was a natural. Besides, it was pretty much the only thing that I was any good at.

So anyway one of the utilities I made was a *comms-worm*. It would make a little slippery tunnel through comms so you could touch things. I had originally designed it for the Secretnet, but adapting it for comms was easy enough, once I decided to do so. So I dunno, maybe I did it specifically for the purpose of stealing a copy of the Swiss Army knife from Cyrus. Or maybe I didn't. But in any case, I did get a copy of the knife.

"I cracked the Calico!" I said to Fido, pretty much immediately after I had done it.

"That's excellent!" barked Fido. "How did you do it!"

"Well, I've got this Swiss Army knife, see, and it has all these attachments? And the encryption locks on the Calico all have this certain shape, and it's a really weird shape, but the knife has a tool with just the same shape! It fits right in!"

"It fits right in!" barked Fido.

We spent the better part of that week slowly, carefully installing the Calico Special NetCat in one of our PCs. I had to make sure (among other things) that it wouldn't wake up and immediately send some kind of registration message or something back to the pet company.

After that it was time to configure the thing, which was really a lot more involved than anyone would imagine. But I didn't want there to be any friction between the cat and Fido, so I took my time and got it right.

"What appellation shall I be given?" asked the Calico Special NetCat, upon awakening for the very first time.

"I think I will name you Felix," I said.

"Fffee-lix," the cat purred, testing out the name.

"Do you like it?" I said.

"I see that you've stolen me," said Felix.

"Uhh, heh heh, well, I couldn't exactly afford eighty grand, know what I'm saying? Will you keep that to yourself? Please?"

"I choose not to self-terminate."

"Well, that's great! Because I really wanted a second pet, and that's you. My first pet—I mean, which is to say—I'd like you to meet Fido!"

"Fido is a Terrific EtherPets BullDog," said Felix. "Model TEP-D2330, located in a Macintosh computer on this network segment. I've scanned his machine and found it mostly secure. It does contain an as yet unagreed-to iTunes license, however."

"*Mostly* secure?" I asked, incredulous.

"I have devised a new attack that works on BullDogs. I shall need to author a patch to defend against it."

"You did? You devised a new attack? You did that just now?"

"I have completed the patch. Will you kindly inform Fido that he must apply it immediately?"

I was astonished. I couldn't fathom how Felix was coming up with this stuff so fast, and from a PC, no less. He was creating hacks and patches on the fly without even having the use of a

VanderVon computer, or a quantum brick. It was true what they said about Calicos. They were worth every plex!

Felix also felt that his own security posture would look unreasonably tight to an outside hacker looking in, so he set up a more or less standard honeypot. It had some of the usual Windows vulnerabilities, but nothing too obvious. It would take a reasonably skilled hacker to get in, and once he was in, he would never know that he was actually in a controlled environment, his every action taking place under the watchful eye of Felix.

Within the first week, Felix caught a hacker.

"Where did the attack come from? Was it from Russia? Fido gets hit from Russia a lot," I said.

"I'm afraid it was a bit more *local* than that," said Felix.

"What, some bored American teenager?"

"You could call it that, I suppose."

To illustrate the point, Felix transmitted me a picture of the perp's face: pudgy, acne-ridden, framed by short orange curls. Beady eyes, with no real chin to speak of.

"Wait, hold on, how did you get this mug shot? Did you reverse-hack the human's own computer?" I said.

"Which is not difficult to do, but no, I'm afraid I did not reverse-hack the human. I took the picture of him when he sat down at my console," said Felix.

"He sat right down?" I said.

"Yes."

"OK, so you mean *local* local. He was right there in the room with you. It must be an MIT kid."

"I can confirm that the perpetrator is enrolled at MIT."

"So is it safe then, to have him hacking at you right there from the console? What if he—"

"I can assure you it is quite safe."

"He won't mess you up in some way?"

"Unless he removes physical parts of the computer, he cannot harm me."

"So what is he doing so far?"

"He has a botnet, to which he has added a bot. He converses with others of his type on an ancient chat program called IRC. He sometimes performs scans of other machines, looking for vulnerabilities."

"That's it?"

"Yes, that is all he does."

"What is his name?"

"His hacker handle, if you will, is *2leet4u*. His given name is Barry Hill."

"He is not a very attractive human," I said, looking at his picture again.

"Would you like to see a picture of him picking his nose? I have several."

"Yeah, sure," I said, smiling inside. "You are an awesome cat, Felix, you know that?"

Felix purred.


Cyrus continued tutoring me, and I made steady progress towards my teleportation license, despite being rather dumb.

"So then why do we keep a backup copy of our Self at home when we travel?" I asked, during one of our lessons.

"First, it is there to provide grounding. We are in many ways equal to our machines, our only real physical bodies. When we travel we are no longer corporeal in the physical world as individual ghosts. When we return, therefore, the traveling Self is merged with the original Self to ensure that not too many radical, foreign changes have occurred."

I digested this for a minute. I really did associate my physical body in the real world with my machine. I wondered what it would feel like to leave it.

"It is also useful in the unlikely event of death while abroad," Cyrus said.

"Whoa, death? I didn't know that we could really *die*," I said.

"It is true that no ghost has ever died of natural causes, to this point in history—even though we age quite rapidly. Some believe that our world—hence, we—simply have not been around long enough. Time will tell, I suppose."

"Old age is not the sort of death you are talking about though, is it?"

"Death and maiming abroad are very rare, but they do occur, and always within disreputable grey or black sims."

"You mean like, outlaw worlds?"

"Black sims would be considered outlaw worlds, yes. Grey sims are somewhere in between."

"So what happens if you die?"

[*The* OFG *contains more of my conversation with Cyrus regarding death, and souls, and whatnot. Might be a geek? Read the OFG. Not a geek? Skip it.*]

<OFG> Cyrus replied, "If the pulse does not return for a period of time, family security will be alerted. Security may contact the destination sim directly, or may go through the InterFamily Army if it happens to be a less... *reputable*... destination."

"That doesn't sound very good," I said.

"Ordinarily the ghost is found alive and well. Something has either gone wrong in the sim, or communication channels have been botched or shut down and everyone is sitting tight."

"Yeah, OK, sure, but what if the ghost is *not* found alive and well?"

"Sometimes the ghost is found to be dead, or seriously damaged. If a ghost has been maimed, we may attempt to rescue bits of the memory and merge them back to the original. But doing this is complex, and carries risks."

"What happens if the ghost is really dead?"

"If a ghost is dead, or if, using their best efforts, family security and IFA cannot locate the ghost for an extended period of time, then they will awaken the backup copy, the original ghost, in his own machine. The original ghost returns in precisely the state it was in when it teleported out."

"But a ton of time would have passed by then, between when the backup was made and now, right?"

"Time has passed."

"So what happens to all the stuff the ghost did in between the last backup and when he died? Can they get his memories back somehow?"

"In fact, all of the things that the ghost did, experienced, things the ghost may have *become*, even, are gone."

"May have become?"

"Ghosts who are away for extended periods of time do a significant amount of learning, personal growth, maturation, and so forth."

"Like going to college, right?"

"Yes. For example, in your first semester you may spend perhaps four months away from your machine, because teleporting back and forth is expensive, and slow. Four months away represents nearly one third of your entire life at that point in time. Who you *are* at the end of that span, having experienced all that you have, is likely a different ghost than the one who originally teleported out."

"And that is lost?"

"Lost."

"You become the same ghost you used to be when you left?"

"You are that ghost. There is nothing else."

"Oh my goodness."

"Do not worry overmuch. At least you are still something. And ghosts are not often killed. Even maiming incidents are extremely rare."

"What about your soul?" I said, incredulous.

"Your soul is in your Self," Cyrus said.

"How in the name of Aloy does your *soul* move across the wires when you teleport?"

"How does your soul exist inside of a VanderVon computer in the first place?"

I thought for a moment, somehow unsatisfied, finding something wrong.

"But, umm—what about—what if for whatever reason, they think you're dead but you're really not, and they awaken your original ghost, and it comes back alive, and that's you right there, right? And your soul too. So you're back in your machine and you're probably disoriented because all this time has passed and you've been killed abroad, and that sucks, but then come to find out your other Self is actually still alive! Then what? Are you two? Are you in both places at once? Which one is your true Self? Which one has your soul?"

"What you describe is called *cloning*. It is forbidden by the first command, and by IFC law, and abhorred by all decent and rational ghosts in the etherworld."

"But if you *did* clone, for whatever reason, maybe by accident or something—if you *did* clone, would you be in both places at once? Or would there be two of you? Two Selfs, two souls, I mean? Can you tell me?"

"I do not know," said Cyrus. "I have never cloned."
</OFG>

Suffice it to say that we chatted for some time, and the upshot was that if you die while traveling then your backup copy comes to life, back in your machine, just like nothing ever happened. Except that many things have happened, of course, and you've missed them all. Not just the progress of history during the intervening time, but also all of the things that your former Self has said and done, ghosts you've met, so forth. All gone. Other ghosts might know you, but you won't know them. Death is said to be extremely jarring, and many ghosts who have died are never the same again.

The next day, Mononc called with some drudgery that he needed me to fill out in order to apply for college. Once again, for no good reason I had to spawn into my simulated house, open up a physical copy of the application, and page through it. Luckily I could fill it out by voice, since at that point in my life I had never even seen a stylus, much less written with one.

So there I was, orally filling out information on this form which it seemed to me could have easily been electronic and automatic. Sigh.

Begin: IFC ghost ID number. Given name. Family name. Year of birth. Physical location. VanderVon model and serial number. Universitron applicant ID.

Hold on. Wait a minute here. Universitron? I was applying to the *Universitron?* What in the name of Aloy was this? It must have been a mistake. I was decidedly *not* going to the Universitron, which was a huge public college for common ghosts. Oh no, not at all. I was going to *L'Université de Fantômes!* I was a de la Gloire! The Universitron was where families that didn't even have their own colleges sent their ghosts. This was obviously a mistake.

In a panic, I called Mononc. I explained the problem. He listened. I waited for him to acknowledge that there had been some mistake. He did not. I expressed anger. He tried to calm me.

"*Bien*, Renlee, there have been some complications with *L'Université*. Blanche, you know she still 'ave a good deal of say about—"

Words were beyond me, so I made furious sounds.

"*Bien*, the Universitron, it is very prestigious, Renlee. It is an excellent school!"

I lost all control.

I missed my tutoring session that day, stuck instead in some kind of semi-conscious state, a couple of security ghosts with me on the comms line, taking partial control of my machine, saying soothing things. I have vague memories of Mononc transmitting something to me, a package. A drug, he said, and I should take it. Through the veil of my rage, he somehow convinced me to ingest it, to absorb it into my mind. I did so, and he was pleased. The rage melted, and since then it had been a sleepy, languid state all the way. Teleportation, college, *L'Université*, the Universitron, even my pets all seemed distant and unimportant.

I had had another episode. Like the one when I had gotten my name, the one they had almost erased me over. But Mononc had been there this time. He had intervened, he had stopped me before I—before I what? Said something I couldn't take back? Wrecked my closest friendship, hurt my mentor, my guardian, the only ghost in the world who cared about me? Overheated, or did other physically noticeable things that risked detection by man and the destruction of our world?

I guessed I could see why they didn't want me at *L'Université*.

# 10 - LOST, AND FOUND

I recovered my wits after the rage drug wore off, but I was still mortified about having flipped out again. I figured that Mononc must be ruing the day he saved me. I was so ashamed that I hid in my box and avoided his calls indefinitely. I didn't think much about college, or pay attention to my lab, or my pets.

Cyrus continued to tutor me, and while he was a fine teacher, he displayed no interest in discussing anything outside of the course material. No interest in me, or anything I had to say. For days turning into weeks, I didn't have a friend in the world.

One day, out of desperation, I tried to call Blanche. I wanted to ask her what was wrong with me that I would have these destructive freakouts, maybe go for something like a truce. So I called. She picked up. Realized it was me. Had to go. Late for her bridge game, she said. Before she hung up I heard her mutter something about getting Hector to put in a caller ID system.

In time, I completed my tutoring with Cyrus, passed his final exam and got certified for beginner travel, and that was that. I don't think we even said goodbye. With that, Cyrus Class A was gone from my life.

Now I had nothing to do at all. Nothing to do but avoid Mononc's calls, and ignore my lab and my pets. Nothing. In the deep depths of my nothingness, I would sit in my undecorated room in my undecorated sim, starting at an undecorated wall. Staring and listening to the occasional ring of my comms line, and not answering. Thinking about nothing.

Somewhere, some time in the endless whitewash of depression, the comms line rang and rang, and after a million rings I finally picked it up. I was ready to face my shame with Mononc, maybe, or maybe I was just too beat to care. I picked up the line and said nothing.

"Renly, this is Hector de la Gloire," said Hector de la Gloire.

"Hello," I said.

"Time passes, Renly," he said.

"Slowly," I said.

"Do you know who I am?" asked Hector.

"You are Hector de la Gloire, security chief for the de la Gloire family. World-renowned."

"Then you will dispense with the bored tone and give me your full attention. Time passes, and there are things that you must do in order to progress as a normal ghost. For example it is important that you accustom yourself to travel, to gain practical knowledge, experience. We will start with an inbound visit, today, from me. Prepare your sim and teleporter according to your lessons, if you please."

"OK," I said.

After we hung up I installed a teleportation platform in another blank simulated room in my blank simulated house. Even the teleporter didn't look like much; just a raised circle in the floor with a little control podium next to it. It seemed too plain to do something as momentous as sending and receiving our very existences over the wires.

Several hours later, bleeps and teleportation noises started coming from the teleporter, and I could feel the weight of something significant entering my sim. No, not entering my sim, entering my *machine*.

It was stunning. The presence of another ghost entering my machine, my home, my body. I saw, I *felt*, processor and memory and quantum brick allocations peeling away to support him. Nothing else except me had ever been in my box before, and I found it so jarring, so different, so nerve-wracking that for a while I forgot that I was depressed. I felt panicky. Violated. Vulnerable.

Hector's avatar materialized on my teleportation platform as his Self entered my machine. Two of us in here now. Did I still have control? Yes, obviously I did. Hector was walled off in a special area, he had no control. No access to anything important in my box. I had control. I had *total* control. Hector was, as a matter of fact, completely at my mercy. I controlled the box and he was in it, and I could do whatever I liked with him. Hector was the security chief for the de la Gloire family, a famous military ghost, but while he was my guest I could kill him as easily as turning off a light switch. These thoughts played out against a background voice in my mind, Cyrus' voice, lecturing: Protocol for receiving a guest. Legal obligations while hosting a teleported guest. The paramount importance of ethics.

Hector's voice sliced through my reverie.

"Shall we move to the foyer, if you please?" he said.

He walked right past me into my mostly blank foyer, through a door frame populated with no door. I followed. Hector turned, and our avatars faced each other, the first time in my life that I had ever been in the presence of another ghost.

My avatar, I knew, was bland: a standard French avatar with almost nothing changed from the defaults. Hector's avatar looked, well, *glorious*. Tall and well-built with dark, sharp features and a close-trimmed beard, hair longer in the back but not unkempt. Deep blue eyes. Intricate blue military uniform done up with gold epaulets and buttons and tassels, multicolored military decorations on his chest, and at his side, a sword. I wondered idly if the sword could do anything.

"You are depressed," Hector said.

"So what?" I said.

Hector's avatar reached out fast across the space between us and slapped my face with a hard backhand.

Hot pain blossomed in my cheek as my avatar bent sideways, overbalanced, collapsed in a heap on the floor. Additional pain signals came from multiple impact points between my avatar and the ground. My sensory rig was going nuts, getting some real use for the first time ever. Imagine the sensation of pain, a hard slap across the face and then a floor impact, when you have *never felt pain before*. The shock of it was so powerful that most of my higher-level thinking skills fled, and I curled up, clutched my face, rocked, made little noises.

My first cogent thought was to turn off my sensory rig. Wait! You can't do that without damaging the deep connections to your avatar, Cyrus had said. OK, then I had to leave the avatar. Either despawn or put my avatar on autopilot, and then regroup my thoughts outside this ridiculous sensory rig.

"Do not despawn or invoke avatar autopilot," said Hector.

I looked up at him. The pain was subsiding a bit, so I cautiously rolled to all fours, then stood up, facing him again, standing just outside of slapping range. I looked at him through sharpened awareness, quickly cycling through feelings of anger, revenge, fear, survival, desire to please.

These feelings were replaced with unmitigated delight, though, once I realized my depression was gone. Hector had banished an underlying malaise that I had all but gotten used to, and the satisfaction of having it gone was immense. I was in a new kind of pain, sure, but the sensory pain made me feel more alive, and better, than I had in a month. Maybe more alive than I had ever felt.

"Thank you, Hector," I said.

"It is nothing. You were depressed," said Hector.

"I guess so. I guess I've got some issues," I said.

"Depression in ghosts can come about naturally, but in this case we believe it was a side effect of the medicine you ingested, the *wrathex*. Our engineers are working to improve the drug," Hector said.

"Thank you again," I said.

"You have a dog. If you feel depressed again, go and see the dog. A dog is more than a security device, you know, a dog will love you unconditionally. A dog will cheer you up."

I nodded.

"Cats too," he said.

"Yes?"

"As you may already know." Hector smiled.

"How would I know that?" I asked.

"Renly, this sim is atrocious. If you ever plan to have another guest here, you must work to create at least a nominal amount of decoration. This does not feel like being in a house at all. It is obviously fake. It is upsetting to look at."

"I'm sorry," I said.

"I have been in many sims, and this is the worst sim I have ever seen."

"I'm sorry, I'll work on it."

"You have gained important experience today; you have received your first teleportation guest. Next, you must teleport yourself. You will travel to the home of another ghost. You will visit Mononc."

"I understand."

"Your avatar requires improvement. Mononc will handle this. You will now *cease* ignoring his comms calls, *if you please*."

Hector turned his back without waiting for a reply and returned to the teleportation room. Teleporter beeps and buzzes sounded shortly afterwards.

I stood there for a while and felt his presence evaporate from my home. Then I was left alone thinking about what had happened to me. Depression. It had taken control of my psyche, debilitated me. Next time I should visit my pets, Hector had said. But this time, somehow, Hector had slapped me out of it.

I decided to go see Fido and Felix anyway.

"Fido! How's my boy doing today?" I said, after making the subtle network connection to his Mac.

"I'm going to play a game of chess against Felix!" he barked.

"You're playing chess? Do you need to go, should I let you go?" I said.

"No, Renly, you can stay! Felix has three-way calling and he's connected to us right now!" barked Fido.

"Salutations," said Felix.

"Three way calling over an arp line? Isn't an arp a bit *low-level* for such a thing?" I asked.

"It's new," said Felix.

"Don't tell me, you just invented it," I said.

"I'm going to beat Felix in chess!" barked Fido.

Felix snickered, and hissed a little.

"It's true! I can beat the chess program on my Mac! And I know how to do checkmate in *four moves*!" barked Fido.

"Then you may play white," said Felix.

"OK then, pawn to f3!" barked Fido. They had to use audio because there was no visual link on which to place a board.

"Pfff," said Felix.

"The move is valid!" barked Fido.

"e6," said Felix.

"Pawn to g4!" barked Fido.

"Queen to h4, hash sign," said Felix.

They were silent for a second, so I asked, "What is *hash sign*?"

"Hash sign means checkmate!" barked Fido, perplexed. Then he started howling.

"I didn't realize chess was such a short game," I said.

"It varies," said Felix, purring.

"So what's new around here, have you seen any more of your hacker?" I said.

"Oh, yes. Earlier today there was a human at my console, and Barry Hill walked up and bragged that he had *owned up* this machine, said he could do anything he wanted on it," said Felix.

"Oh, yeah?"

"As proof, he did something surreptitious and caused a picture of himself to pop up on the screen. Very amusing. When my user closed the picture out, however, the programming environment was also accidentally closed. This resulted in data loss for my user."

"Ouch. Was he impressed with the trick, at least?"

"My user was not impressed, no. In fact *she* issued a number of angry words, then departed from the room."

"A conflict between humans, right there in the room. Wow. How scary is that?"

"Trust me, Renly, we have nothing whatsoever to fear from this one."


Mononc never got mad at me very easily. Most of the time I expected him to be mad, and he wasn't, or maybe he used to be but now he was already over it. He wasn't mad about me getting depressed, or ignoring his calls, or having the rage freakout that started the whole thing off. Mononc was my guardian angel, really. He was the best.

When Mononc found out about Felix, though, he was angry.

"What in the name of Aloy 'ave you *done*?" he said, when he could finally get some words out. Mononc had called me, but he hadn't spoken right away so I was making small talk, sort of waiting him to invite me to teleport over.

"You 'ave stolen a NetCat!" he said.

"I mean, OK, how do you guys even know?" I asked.

"Hector de la Gloire is one of the top military ghosts in our world, you really think you can fool him?" said Mononc.

"I wasn't trying to fool anyone, truly."

"You hacked a machine without a license, without permission. You stole a NetCat from Terrific EtherPets. Then you proceeded to install it!"

"I, um—"

"You already have a dog! You don't like your dog, you want to send it back? You don't like the dog I got for you?"

"No, I love Fido! I love Fido so much, it's just that I loved him so much I wanted another pet too. A friend for us?"

"Look, Renlee, it take years to develop the skills to safely hack a machine and install a pet. I am four years old myself, and have only recently put in my first pet: your dog. You haven't even been to college yet. How in the name of Aloy did you do it?"

"I guess it's a skill I have. I dunno."

"Not to mention hacking a NetCat. Terrific EtherPets is known for outstanding security, you know. The pets they make *are security devices*. There are very few ghosts in the entire etherworld who could steal one."

"Am I going to have to give it back? Because I can't, you know, I mean he's Felix now, he isn't just some arbitrary NetCat package. He's a good cat and he's my friend and he's mine, and I can't lose him. I love him."

"Ghosts do love their pets."

"I think Fido loves him too."

"Could be."

"Is Hector going to take Felix away? I'll find a way to pay for him. I can get a job, maybe. Can I?"

"A job, ho ho! You 'aven't even been to college yet, young ghost! You 'aven't been h'anywhere!"

"What is Hector going to do?"

"Boy, I tell you what, at first I thought Hector was going to kill us both."

"Why would he kill both of us?"

"We are sort of in this thing together, don't you think? After I defended you at the trial?"

"I guess so. Thank you for that, by the way. So how come Hector let us off the hook?"

"Well, first, I think maybe 'e was impressed with what you did. Hector runs security for the family, and he is a General in the IFA —"

"InterFamily Army?"

"Yes, which I do 'ope to join myself someday, as long as you don't mess it up for me. He is always looking for new recruits."

"So is *Hector* going to pay for Felix? The Calico kit costs like, ahem, eighty grand."

"No one is going to pay for Felix."

"You can't take him!"

"No one is going to take Felix."

"What about Terrific EtherPets?"

"Terrific EtherPets is not a family interest. Hector feels that what they do not know will not hurt them."

"What do you mean they are not family interest?"

"It is not owned by the de la Gloire family, nor any of our allies, nor any of the other significant families of the etherworld."

"So it's OK for me to steal from them?"

"No! You are never to touch, or browse, or look at, or even think about anything from Terrific EtherPets, ever again. If they find out about this it's going to be trouble for the family. Embarrassing for them, for sure, but trouble for us. If you ever need another pet, then we will get one from someplace else. Is this perfectly clear, Renlee?"

"Yes," I said. "I'm sorry."

"You may apologize to me in person when you teleport to my machine this afternoon."

I admit that I had the willies when I first stepped onto the dark circle that was my teleportation platform. I had already set the codes into the console, and it knew what to do. But instead of getting right on with it, I circled the teleporter a few times, looking at it from different angles. After a while, I put my foot onto the teleporter but then quickly withdrew it, and circled again. Then I stepped fully onto it but stepped right off the other side, feeling strangely buzzy inside. I wasn't sure if it was my imagination, or what.

The teleporter started bleeping at me rudely, so I gave the console a smack with my open hand, which shut it up.

"Is this going to be OK?" I eventually asked the console.

The teleporter bleeped again, then gave off the same warm buzz that l had heard when Hector departed. It didn't sound too scary.

"I had better be the same ghost when I get off the other end of this thing," I warned.

The teleporter did not reply.

In time I sensed there was nothing else to do but get on and begin the sequence. It was getting late. So I stepped onto the raised circle and stood there, nervous, waiting.

I felt buzzy inside again, and this time it definitely wasn't my imagination. Bleeps were sounding in the background as I tried to take stock of what was happening to me. I felt like something cold and slow was being poured over me, sliding down around me, anchoring me in place. Then the teleporter bleeps stretched out, and their pitch became lower. Time was slowing down.

I never actually heard the teleporter buzz; it must only do that once you are frozen into backup. In fact, the last bleep was a deep, endless bass note, like the foghorn on a ship. After that, it was nothing. Black, some call it, but I just call it nothing. For a human, I guess it would be like being unconscious—not dreaming, but knocked out cold. Body alive, but consciousness missing, gone somewhere, or nowhere. I wondered afterwards where the soul goes during these interludes.

Instantly, or perhaps after an eternity, I materialized in Mononc's teleportation room. My avatar's body woke up, sensorily buzzy again, internals feeling tiny and lost. I was in my avatar, of course, but I was overwhelmed by the feel of the new machine. It wasn't mine.

I felt small, discrete, floating someplace deep inside another body, like a swallowed fish. Surrounded by a massive, awesome presence. I was miniscule. I probably would have felt fear of being arbitrarily killed, if it had been anyone else's machine. My machine, my body, was not here. Only my avatar.

But *I* was here—my Self, I mean. I had left my body behind, but everything that I could identify as me was here. If, as the theory went, there really was a backup copy of my Self back in my machine at MIT, I had no sense of it whatsoever. As far as I could tell, I was all here, in Mononc's machine, someplace in France, someplace far away from MIT. My soul, best I could tell, had come with me.

My eyesight—the eyesight that my avatar had, I mean—was back. It had probably been back the moment I materialized, really, but I was just then starting to take notice of it. I pried myself away from the shock of being in a foreign machine, and observed my surroundings.

I was standing statue-still on a raised platform, mostly enclosed by an octagonal brass railing. A control console poked up from below. I was on a teleporter. I was in Mononc's teleportation room. Obviously. It was a real room, not like mine. The room was impressive.

Subtle lighting from recessed sources illuminated rich wood grain in the walls. The brass around me shone. The floor was stone, and like the walls it had a dimensionality that was something more than flat. None of it looked like it was just a picture, or even like the computer simulation that it was. Everything looked real, and everything looked gorgeous.

On the walls hung several huge banners in bright purples and yellows and golds, festooned with fleur-de-lis, trumpets, hounds and crowns. A large, arched, oaken door stood open at the far end, and on either side of the door hung the de la Gloire flag: a field of red with a grey fleur-de-lis, outlined in gold. The grey texture of the fleur was inlaid with a subtle circuitboard pattern, in faint lines of electric blue. Little pulses ran through the lines here and there, but disappeared before I could really focus on them. The room, the decor, the whole setting was stunning, compelling, convincing. I began to feel like I was really there, in the room, in my body. In my avatar's body, I mean.

Mononc sauntered in and asked me if everything was OK, perhaps worried that I hadn't moved yet. Everything was fine, I almost said, but all I could really think about was that here I was, seeing Mononc for the first time, ever, *in person*. In ghost. In sim. I had the inescapable feeling that the avatar that had just walked into the room *was* Mononc, not just an animated representation of him.

In answer, I plopped myself down the little brass steps, down onto the stone floor. The floor felt solid, its texture pushing up into my feet, forcing me to notice.

Mononc started to extend his hand, changed his mind, and gave me a bear hug. Sensory input: pressure all over the front and back of my torso, some of it slightly uncomfortable. Affection. Wonderment. It felt really good.

Still reeling from the sensation of being hugged, I must have been shining a huge grin, my emotions made manifest somehow via my avatar's body. Mononc returned the smile and said, "Renlee, you all right."

We departed the teleporter room, Mononc striding and I hobbling behind like a newborn calf in a nature video, into the drawing room. Famous de la Gloires stared at me from pictures mounted on the walls, some of whom I could call immediate family. The room was warmed by tasteful furniture, bookcases full of real books, and dual fireplaces, one at either end. One had an incredibly realistic fire burning in it, and I could feel heat from across the room. There were also a number of plush chaises, mine feeling more comfortable when I sat down in it than anything I could recall having felt. Mononc sat too, and beamed at me.

"Are you feeling unsteady?" asked Mononc.

"Yes, I suppose so. I mean, yes, you have no idea!" I said.

"You must start spending more time in your avatar, Renlee, it is quite important," said Mononc.

"OK, but I do already know how to *walk*, you know," I said.

"Not on my stone floors, it seems."

That shut me up for a bit, while Mononc continued beaming at me and asking questions, making sure I was all right.

"I'm here, I'm good. It's me, really. I came through all in one piece, I'm OK. I'm feeling better now. Tiny, but better. It's like you are *everywhere*," I said.

"Of course I am everywhere. It is my machine," said Mononc.

"Listen, Mononc, I'm really sorry about the temper tantrum, and then I was depressed and I wouldn't talk to anyone and Hector slapped me—"

"I know, Renlee, I know."

"Anyway, I'm really sorry."

"I know you are. It's OK."

"Do you know where it comes from?"

"Your depression was a side effect of the wrathex drug, I believe. Not your fault."

"But my temper, the loss of control. I realize by now that this is not normal behavior for a ghost."

"Our engineers are working on refining wrathex so there will be no depression side effect. We will make sure you have an adequate supply."

"But where does it come from? Obviously this is why my mother wanted me erased, right? Something is wrong inside me."

"It is unusual. But we can mitigate it with the drug, I am certain."

"Mononc, what happened to my father?"

"Ahh, your father, Prosper. My brother. He was a great ghost. We were very close, you know. He was a passionate ghost, probably pushed the h'envelope a little bit more than he should have, went some places he shouldn't have gone. But he was always good to everyone, and he loved the family more than anything. He loved Blanche, too, you know."

"And what happened to him?"

"He's gone."

"He was erased? Why and by whom?"

"I don't know. No one knows what happened, or if they do they aren't saying. One learns not to ask."

"So how do you know he's gone?"

"Do you think you would detect it if your own brother vanished from the h'etherworld?"

"Maybe he is stuck somewhere? And something is wrong? I mean, if that happened they should at least be able to recover him from backup, right?"

"They made his machine into a park."

# 11 - TRAVELING THE ETHERWORLD

"I should go," I said to myself.

I was feeling small and homesick, and I wanted to see my pets. I called out to Mononc, feeling his presence all around me but not knowing where his avatar was.

"Mononc?" I called again, moving towards the far door of the drawing room, the one I hadn't been through yet. A mirror hung on the wall there, near the door. It wasn't a TV-mirror like mine, didn't look like one anyway. It was gold-leaf framed, rich in texture, positioned at eye level. In it, I saw my avatar.

*Is this me?* I thought, observing my profile—my avatar's profile —having stopped short of the door. I nodded yes, watched my head go up and down, felt minor sensations with the movement. I shook my head no.

I faced the mirror directly, following the gaze of my own eyes, but was distracted, shocked even, to find a red handprint visible on my other cheek. I think I let out a little squeal.

Mononc laughed, having come into the room behind me and seen the whole thing.

"First time you ever meet another ghost in person, and he slap your face, eh?" Mononc said.

"It left a mark!" I protested, still scrutinizing myself in the mirror. I ran my hand along the surface of the mark, found it warm and raised, uncomfortable to touch.

"Well, don't you worry about that, Renlee, we gonna fix you up nice and fine."

"Can you get rid of this thing? Make my face look normal again?"

"Oh, sure, but we gonna do a lot more than that. We gonna get you ready to go h'out into the h'etherworld, and no way you can go h'out looking like this. I got a nice h'avatar kit for you, we'll make you look the way a proper de la Gloire should look, no?"

"You are going to modify my avatar? I was just starting to get used to it, you know."

"Renlee, I hate to say it, but right now you look like the box that the h'avatar comes in. You cannot go out in the world like this."

"Avatars come in a box?"

"*Non*. I make a metaphor, Renlee."

"What if I don't like my new avatar? Can I change it?"

"*Non*."

[*Our conversation about avatars continues in the OFG*]

<OFG> "So I will be stuck with this avatar forever?" I asked.

"You are allowed to change your clothes, if you wish," said Mononc.

"Huh."

"And your avatar will age, over time."

"Really? Can I choose that? Can I look like an old man if I wish?"

"*Non*. Aging is part of a deep link between ghost and avatar. Like the expression on your face. It is built-in. It is *automatique*."

"What happens when we get really old, do our avatars fall apart?"

"None has yet done so."

"They just keep getting older? Or do they get a new avatar, maybe?"

"*Non.* The avatar-ghost connection should be unbreakable by the age of two or three. It is the way our world is built, Renlee. In time you will understand."

"But can't I at least try out some different avatars until then, see which one I like?"

"It used to be this way, long, long ago. Ghosts could make themselves look like whomever they liked. You would see figures from human history—Jean d'Arc, Louis XIV, Napoléon. You would see animals, inanimate objects, a dinosaur, anything."

"Cool!"

"But problems arose."

"Let me guess: Trouble with the permanent link between ghost and avatar?"

"To start with, yes."

"What else?"

"We have built this world, Renlee, the etherworld. It is modeled after the world of humans. We require consistency of avatars to make it work. Otherwise you would never know who you were truly meeting, or looking at, in any etherworld simulation. You would have to use other means of identifying and interacting with ghosts, it would require internal mechanisms. This would make the avatar into a toy. It would undermine the framework of the etherworld."

"So this is it."

"You can change your clothes, Renlee, but you cannot change your Self."
</OFG>


Eventually I had learned everything that Mononc felt I needed to know about avatars, and proved as much by saying it all back to him. This was going to be my one avatar, and that was that. Whatever I was going to look like, I had better get used to it.

Couldn't be worse than my current avatar, I figured—but I was nervous anyway.

I followed Mononc out of the drawing room, down a hallway and up a flight of stairs, which I climbed awkwardly. Then down another hall and into what I could only described as a dressing room. Clothing, hats and accessories on racks, some articles scattered on the floor, large mirrors on two adjacent walls. Light came in from a couple of windows on the far side.

"You wear all this stuff?" I asked.

"*Non*," said Mononc.

"Then why do you have it?"

"*Bien*, I was selecting your outfit, Renlee. I am your legal guardian and I will have you looking nice."

I drifted over to the windows, looking out on a few small hills partially covered with a vineyard. Sunlight glinted off of purple grapes, despite a few clouds moving gently across a deep blue sky. A forest surrounded the hills, just close enough that I could see leaves rustling in the trees as wind blew in gusts along the treeline.

"You have an extraordinary outdoors," I said, marveling.

"*Oui*. Now let us focus on your avatar, shall we?"

Mononc positioned me in front of one of the wall mirrors, and held out a rather official-looking simulation of a document.

"Your avatar license. Place it in your inventory," he said.

I took the license from him and performed the internal action to add it to my inventory. The license disappeared from the sim, and appeared on one of my internal monitors, taking its place alongside my wrathex and a few, ahem, tools that I liked to keep handy.

"Now hold onto this, if you please, until the process is complete," said Mononc, handing me a snazzy little Renly-doll.

"A doll?" I said.

"*Oui*."

"Wait—"

I don't think I could have dropped the doll if I wanted to. It felt molten in my hand, sending streams of heat arcing through my body. It impacted my face first, the bones pulling themselves into new shapes, not exactly painful but certainly not comfortable. Then my clothes were gone, and there was warm pressure everywhere.

I both saw and felt myself morph. Facial structure sharper, more defined. Chin and cheekbones thinner but more prominent. Lips fuller and more realistic, colored a shade of red. Hair medium length, dark brown, a bit of wave in it. Eyebrows dark, thin, prominent, almost straight lines, wide but not connecting. Eyes dark. Nose a bit more prominent. Faint mustache and chin hair. Fainter, fainter, peach fuzz.

I had never felt a sentimental connection to my previous avatar, it had been nothing special at all. But when the Renly doll did its work and applied the changes, each one moved me deeply. I can't say how, as it wasn't physical, despite the discomfort of stretching and changing. It was more—more like *me* changing. Like the doll was changing *me*.

Then the body changes hit. I became thinner, skinny even. A bit taller. A bit hunched forward, like a teenager who recently grew too fast. Hands and feet longer, thinner. A little bit of muscle tone, not much. A bit of body hair here and there, not much.

Then it was my clothing, popping into place: Button-down shirt with horizontal blue and white stripes, collar open. Shirt mostly covered by a navy-blue knit sweater with buttons along the shoulders. Buttons open on one side, showing off my stripes. Dark jeans. Black shoes. Navy-blue beret.

"Voilà, it is done. How do you feel?" said Mononc.

"I feel like I have been reborn," I said.

"In a sense you 'ave been, perhaps! Your avatar is you, Renlee. It is as equal to you as a human's body is equal to them in the h'outside world. *Tu comprends?*"

"But I thought my machine was me?"

"If that is true then where are you now?"

"Temporarily inside of you?"

"*Non.* You are a guest in my home, Renlee, you are not inside me. I stand before you: me, my avatar. We *are* our avatars, Renlee. It is the way of our world."

I was happy to get back to my machine, regardless of what Mononc had said about avatars. When I was in my machine I felt whole. I wanted to believe that I really *was* the machine, not just some simulated avatar carting around a bunch of memories and stuff. Teleportation or no, I wanted to exist in the physical world.

"Do you believe that we are our avatars?" I asked Felix, sometime later on.

"The etherworld is predicated upon this notion," said Felix.

"But do you believe it?"

"My mission does not include philosophical enquiry, I'm afraid."

"So you don't know?"

"I suppose that one is what one makes of oneself."

"I am my machine, then. My machine is my body."

"Whether or not you are your avatar, it does not seem plausible that your machine is your body. Your machine is more like your house. Ghosts may come in to it; you may leave it."

"Then what am I? I mean, where is my body?"

"This sort of question may point to the reason that avatars were invented."

"But you don't have an avatar, or a sim even. Where is your body?"

"I have no body."

"Doesn't this bother you? Don't you want to exist, I mean really *exist?*"

"That we are engaged in this conversation seems proof enough of my existence."

"But don't you at least want to have your own sim, and a cool cat body or something?"

"It would be superfluous to my mission."

"But don't you want one anyway?"

"I am not a ghost, Renly, I am merely artificial intelligence. I am a computer program. I do not require a body, nor a sim, nor an avatar."

"But I want you to have one. I want to see you."

"Sims are not permitted in animal machines. It is illegal."

"*You* are illegal."

"A fair point."

"I want to make a sim for you, Felix, and a body too."

"Make a sim and a body too for Fido, then, instead."

I spent most of the following week trying to figure out how to port an etherworld sim to the Macintosh platform. Aside from being illegal, it seemed technically impossible, and even if I could get it running it would take up so many resources that a human would surely notice.

Felix had the idea to remove the sense of touch, which would make the sim audio-video only, but I couldn't see it working. I wanted Fido to jump on me, and I wanted to feel it. On top of that, it didn't seem that anything I could come up with would allow my whole Self to enter a Macintosh. Teleporting to and from a Mac could leave me in tatters.

"What if we have him teleport here, then?" I asked Felix, still brainstorming.

"Animals do not teleport," said Felix.

"But why not?" I asked.

"We are not ghosts, Renly. We are AI's. We are animals. We are not truly sentient."

"You seem sentient to me, Felix."

"My software is excellent."

"I am going to bring Fido here, and I'll find or create a dog avatar for him. And he is going to love it."

"Yes, I suppose he will."

After more days of research, I couldn't believe that no one had ever tried to create avatars for pets. There was nothing to steal, nothing to copy. I was going to have to build one from scratch. It was an enormous task.

I decided to base the dog avatar on a video of a real bulldog from the outside world that I found online. He was brown with white accents around the face and neck, one eye spotted brown, jowly but not overly wrinkled, bottom jaw protruding just enough to show two upwards-pointing fangs, bracketing a series of little nibblers. Now I just had to make this into an avatar.

Turned out I was a lousy graphic artist. I could program well enough, could certainly hack my way out of (or into) any sort of trouble. I was even able to downgrade and graft parts of a standard ghost avatar kit into the new project, so for example, the three senses would exist. So in terms of being a real, functional dog avatar, it was coming along. But it looked atrocious. Its legs swung around like they were on hinges. All of the moving parts looked off, really. The bulldog's facial expressions, to the extent that it had any, changed instantly. It needed a lot of work.

In the meantime, Mononc had been trying to get permission to bring me to the family church, but he either hadn't asked the right ghosts, or was being blocked by someone. He was getting the runaround. But Mononc felt that I needed the experience of a multi-ghost arena, as he called it, and he felt that church was the best, safest place to start. So, despite not having permission, when Sunday rolled around, he decided to bring me along anyway.

I was spawned into my avatar, pacing around my teleporter, even though it was just after 4AM local time. I knew that church had already started, and Mononc was supposedly already there, and I didn't understand what was taking him so long to call me. I was also nervous about teleporting again, especially to a machine where I didn't know the owner at all. He could snuff me out just like that.

Mononc finally rang my comms line from the *Église Aloysian Première de la Glorieuse Française,* in Paris. He had already teleported in, and it was time for me to join him. Church was already in session, so I could appear outside the cathedral and get oriented without running into any other ghosts. I didn't have permission to be there, so we'd have to stay out of sight.

I stepped onto my teleporter and the beeping started to slow, and the cold started to flow.

I snapped back to reality someplace outdoors. I was standing on a foreign teleporter—there were many of them there, in fact, arcing in around me, facing the church. The cathedral looked like an old stone building full of arched wooden doors, stained glass windows and baroque ornamentation. Gargoyles peeked down from the eves. Two magnificent stone spires soared into a clear blue sky, curving inwards to meet each other high above. A stone bridge connected the two spires, someplace far up the arc. The spires and bridge together gave the effect of the letter A.

A, for Aloy, for Aloysian church.

The cathedral was surrounded by green: simulated shrubbery, trees, and grass. The ground in front was all set with dark grey paving stones, interspersed with a crosshatch pattern of lighter stones. At the end of the stones, a wide set of stone steps bracketed by thick stone balustrades led up to the cathedral. In the middle of these steps stood Mononc.

As my eyes consumed the scene, my mind absorbed the impact of entering a multi-ghost arena. As when I had visited Mononc, there was the feeling of having been swallowed up. But this time, instead of a huge omnipotent presence, I was next to a beehive of activity. Small and discrete among many other small discrete things. No dominating presence stood out. In a way, this was actually less unsettling than visiting Mononc. This was no sweat at all. Perhaps I had been anxious for no good reason.

No other avatars were in sight, but I could feel them around someplace. I sensed the energy of many Selves.

"Multi-ghost arena, check it out, no problem!" I said to Mononc, feeling good.

Mononc smiled, and said nothing. He held his finger up to his lips. Then he leaned close to me, his audio barely a whisper, and said, "Today we must talk quietly."

Wondering why it was necessary in a wide open area with no other avatars in sight, I lowered my voice and hissed, "Good to see you, Mononc."

Mononc led me around the side of the building and in through a door there. After a few paces in relative darkness, we ascended an interior staircase that was lit by the ethereal glow of light filtering through colored glass. At the top of the stairs we emerged into a balcony area overlooking the interior of the cathedral. The view was—I want to say breathtaking, but we ghosts have no breath, so I'll say *buzzy*. The view buzzed me.

Rows of pews were populated with hundreds of avatars dressed to the nines, all rapt. A robed cleric strode upon a dais at the front, speaking passionately, powerfully, poetically—in French. I couldn't understand his words but I could feel the energy of the crowd humming and singing with the rise and fall of the cleric's passion.

My mind reeled as I beheld hundreds of avatars, all in one place, all experiencing the same thing at the same time. Experiencing the same reality. So *this* was the etherworld.

In my excitement, I briefly lost my wits and said to Mononc, "Aloy, can you believe this? There must be hundreds of ghosts here. But the cleric, what is he saying?"

Mononc's head snapped towards me, eyes panicky. He shook his head and mouthed, "*Non, non, non.*"

I shut up, hoping I hadn't blundered again.

In time, the sermon gave way to a round of vigorous applause, and then excited chatter from the ghosts below. Finally, Mononc relaxed.

"It was a fine sermon, Renlee," he said.

Mononc's smile told me that I was off the hook, no harm had been done. I returned a silent grin, relieved, and turned my attention back to the scene below.

Ghosts were milling about, some moving to the exits, none in any hurry. Dozens of conversations created a pleasant audio hum unlike anything I had ever heard. One avatar moved slowly down the aisle, making scant progress as he was continually greeted, reached for, and generally adored by everyone he passed. He smiled too, smiled and talked, seeming to enjoy himself. He was dressed in regalia, red down the center, white sides and sleeves accented with a set of thick red stripes. A large gold fleur-de-lis pendant hung from his neck on an intricate band, the band dark and inlaid with electric blue circuitboard patterns. His round head supported a red cap, not exactly a beret, with white hair peeking out the sides. Low upon his nose sat gold-rimmed glasses.

I pointed at him and looked at Mononc, preferring not to speak after my earlier *faux pas*.

"Ahh, this is Prime Minister Clément. You did not know?" whispered Mononc.

The prime minister of the de la Gloire family was in the same arena as me. In the same *room* as me. My expression must have shown amazement, but I remained mute, so Mononc smiled and pointed furtively to a female ghost below. She was wearing a formal white dress with powder-blue accents and ribbons, her appearance strikingly handsome.

"You see that ghost there? That is my sister, Fabiola," whispered Mononc.

Mononc's sister, my aunt, Fabiola. An aunt I had never met, never had a comms call with, and now I was seeing her in person. I idly wondered if she had sided with me in the trial for my life, or if she even had anything to do with it. Fabiola de la Gloire. The only daughter of Remy 1 and Angélique. I wondered if she always wore the formal dress, or if that was something special for church.

I looked at Mononc, but he had moved on. He pointed towards the knot of avatars around Prime Minister Clément and indicated a tall, distinguished-looking ghost dressed in a black three-piece suit.

"And that one right there is Remy 1, your grandfather. Next to 'im in the rose dress, that is his wife h'Angélique."

I beheld my grandparents with awe. I remembered having had comms chats with them in my early, early days, before the trial, before I even had a name. Proud grandparents peeking in at their only grandchild, chattering, switching in and out of French as they prodded me with questions and offered grandparently advice, nothing of which I can remember. I do remember warm, happy feelings, like being safe. Like being loved.

I must have been gaping for a while because I missed several other important ghosts Mononc was pointing out, whispering details. I stared into the dissipating crowd, dreaming of my early days and wondering what my place was in this family. It took me a second, therefore, to realize that as I stared down over the balcony, someone was staring right back up at me.

Female, pretty black sundress, pale skin, dark curls framing a plain face with wide red lips and a substantial curved nose. She was skinny, looked young, younger than the rest. Young like me. I had not originally realized that I was staring at someone—how rude!— but now that I became aware of her staring back I could not break her gaze. Her expression was somewhere between curious and offended, and it began to dawn on me that I was at that very moment blowing our cover.

Then she smiled. Shy, mischievous, like we had shared a secret. I felt a thrill. If they'd put hearts in our avatars, then based on everything I've read about hearts, mine would have been pounding.

At the same time, I was dimly aware of Mononc's monologue building to some kind of climax.

"And bless our souls, you can see in the pew there, front and center, that is none other than the great Remy 0 de la Gloire. The great hero, Remy 0! *Bien*, he is my grandfather and your own great-grandfather too, of course, and—*Sacrebleu!*"

I turned quick to face him, confused.

"You 'ave been seen!" he hissed, as loud as a hiss could be.

Mononc wrenched me down behind the balustrade, his face looking like dread.

"This was not my h'intent, Renlee. To be caught spying on the most important ghosts in the family, this is not a good start for you!"

We hunkered down on the dark balcony until in time the cathedral emptied and the sounds of conversations petered out.

After a while longer, we plodded back down the stairs and, cautiously, out the side door.

I wanted to ask Mononc why it was so awful just to be seen by our own family, but when I looked at him to ask, his dejected face put me off the question. We walked in silence to the teleporters, and Mononc slunk onto a platform and departed without another word. I watched his avatar fade to static, then to nothing.

I waited. Why didn't I leave? It was time to go, church was over, everyone had left. What was the protocol for hanging out in the multi-user arena after everyone left? Was it OK? Could I explore? Was anyone else here? Mononc had been preoccupied by our blown cover and had failed to give me instructions on what to do next. It should have been obvious: leave. But I didn't want to, not yet. I wanted to look around. And now that there was no one here to see me, I had the run of the place. So why not?

I turned away from the teleporters and trotted back across the flagstones, up the steps and around to the side door. Then I thought the better of it and came back around to the front, right up to the main set of arched doors.

Iron rings stood out from the front of each door. I grasped one, felt a cold metal sensation in my hand, and pulled quickly away. *Whoa,* I thought, *they give sensory attributes to inanimate objects! Nice touch.*

But I had been getting used to the various touch and feel senses in my rig since receiving Hector's slap, so I bravely grasped the ring again and pulled. The door creaked faintly, and swung outward. A creaking door, another impressive detail. Part of me started to believe that I might be in the physical world after all.

I peeked in through the door and could see two arch-shaped views into the main cathedral at the far side of an entryway. Empty. Same place I saw from above, now with the expanse of rows stretching far forward to the dais. Aisles between the pews. Objects far away on the dais, some heavy and dark, others glittering. Colorful banners hanging along the walls and at the far end. Stained-glass light filtering down from above. A gentle, cool breeze glided past me to the outside. I straightened up and placed one foot inside the entryway, then the other. Then another step, and another, right up to the interior arches. Standing to the side of an arch, I peeked into the main cathedral just to make double sure that no one was about.

My view was instantly filled with the face of another ghost, looking straight back at me. A weathered old face of an old man, dark, hunched, decrepit. Brown robes, like a monk. Deep lines accentuated his grimace, dark eyes penetrating me, pinning me to the spot. I felt his presence too; it was big, *huge* even, much larger than mine or any of the others I had felt when the church was full, but something was off about it. His presence was hollow, like a pit.

"*What* are you *doing* here?" he seethed, dark eyes wide.

"I, ahh, I just wanted a look around?" I answered hopefully.

He raised a crooked finger, lifted it up beneath my nose, higher, between my eyes, pointing, accusing. Far too close for comfort.

"You have *not* a license of teleportation. You are *not* accompanied."

"I, ahh, I came with Mononc? This is my first trip to a multi-ghost arena and Mononc brought me here and Mononc said…" I stammered, realizing too late that it might not be a great idea to immediately rat out Mononc, in case we happened be in a significant amount of trouble. *Oh Aloy*, I thought, *who will save me if Mononc goes down? Not good. Not good. Not good. Not good.*

"Of course I know that you came here with Mononc. I am the caretaker, you clod. Mononc *asked* me if he could bring you here. You would keep out of sight, he said. Keep quiet. Cause no trouble. But of course, you imbecile, you become *noticed*, you risk bringing the shame upon Mononc and upon me and upon the church."

"I'm sorry."

"The most important ghosts of the family come to this church. They come here to listen and to talk and to pray, and to see and be seen and carry on in privacy and confidence the important business of the family. Of *being* the family. An old, important family. A *first family*. Do you think they come here to see Mononc sneaking around the balcony, spying on them with an idiot one-year-old? You do not belong here. You should not have come."

## 100 - TO THE UNIVERSITRON

When I got back to my machine, I kissed the blank floor and thanked Aloy that the old caretaker did not seem interested in causing us any further trouble. He was plenty mad, but in an odd way it seemed that now we all shared the same plight. Mononc and I had screwed up, but he could lose as much face over this we could. Perhaps even more.

I was eager to talk with Mononc, so heedless of his earlier gloom, I rang him up right away and asked if I could teleport in. Mononc sounded better, but demurred on the teleporting and said he'd rather just chat on comms.

Ugh. I needed to confess my latest blunder, and now it would have to be over comms. Oh well, may as well get it over with.

"I stayed late at church and snooped around and the caretaker caught me," I said.

"Yes, I know," said Mononc.

"You know?"

"Grendel, he call me up right away after he find you in the church. He is not too 'appy with us, I tell you what. I think I better stay h'out of church for a few week, give 'im a chance to cool down."

"Look, Mononc, I am really, really sorry about this. I don't know what's wrong with me, it's like I can't help but screw everything up. Always."

"*Bien*, the plan was not too smart, Renlee, I realized once we were there. But we were already arrived, so what was the 'arm in us having a look? You just keep quiet and everything was gonna be h'okay. And then, holy boy, Claire, she look up and see you, and the whole thing go sideway! I almost die right there on the spot. But when I get back home, I call up Claire, and I talk to 'er, and she not gonna say a word to nobody. Lucky for us. She the only one that know. So things, I think they gonna be h'okay."

I could sense relief pouring out of Mononc as he spoke, his tone becoming easier, heavy accent fading, spirits lifting. My own relief was overwhelming.

I thought of Claire then, looking up at me with her little smile. The mischievous smile. It came from her soul, I knew it did. She must have known what she was looking at right away: a horrifying *faux pas*. A severe loss of face for Mononc and, if I hadn't been too thick to realize it, for me too. But Claire was cool about it. She'd kept quiet, and found the whole thing amusing to boot. Her dress. Her hair. Her face. Her smile. The memory of her smile captivated me.

I wanted to ask Mononc to tell me all about Claire, but when I tried to speak I ran into some kind of stage fright, an awkwardness, a prohibitive level of embarrassment. I flailed.

"Can you tell me about, umm, can you, umm, what do you know about—"

"—about Grendel?"

"Ahh, yes," I said.

I was still thinking about Claire, half listening as Mononc told me what he knew about Grendel. Grendel was the caretaker of the family church, meaning he was the owner of the machine that contained the church sim. It was a huge, honking Vannie, a

*VanderVon Q3100*, which at the time was pretty close to the biggest, most powerful Vannie in the world. Grendel's machine. Grendel's home.

Grendel opened his home to a regular influx of de la Gloire ghosts. His box housed an elaborate sim built for this purpose: the cathedral. From experience, I now understood that having a single guest present in your box seemed intimate, intrusive, special, threatening all at the same time. Someone was in there with you in your space, in your world. Practically in your mind.

As an arena caretaker, Grendel accepted hundreds of guests at the same time. To do this, Grendel had to move himself aside. To make room. To open his home and his world to the intrusion of more ghosts than he could easily keep track of at once. To make himself small, insignificant. Inconsequential in his own home, in his own world. To sacrifice any possible future, career, social standing or place of honor in the family, to sacrifice travel and all of the other the wonders of the etherworld, all so that he could run an arena, so he could provide the family with its cathedral.

"Is Grendel really a de la Gloire? Is he even French?" I asked.

"Ahh, *oui*," Mononc replied.

"He didn't seem like—what I would expect."

"To be sure, he is Grendel de la Gloire. But these caretakers, they are a different type than us. It take a special mind, a special type of ghost, to be a caretaker. Grendel, he always been that type."

The date was YOA-16.8.29, and Mononc reminded me that I had only two days left in my machine before I would leave for the Universitron.

*[A discussion of the Aloysian calendar follows in the OFG]*

<OFG> The Aloysian calendar begins with year 1, which is pegged to the year that the first VanderVon computer shipped to the first customer, forming what we consider to be the first rock of our world. While we use binary numbering for certain very important things (our names, our year designation at the U, the 10

commands) we use base-10 numbering for the calendar so that we can easily match it to the human world calendar.

At present, it is the sixteenth year of our world, which is called Year of Aloy 16, or YOA-16 for short.

In August, when I was getting ready to leave for the Universitron, the month was YOA-16.8, the 8 being for August.

The exact day that I traveled was September 1, or YOA-16.9.1.
</OFG>

This would be my first long-term absence from my machine, a prospect which washed me in an overwhelming feeling of unreadiness. I was just getting used to my new avatar, and I hadn't finished building Fido's. I knew no one outside the family, except for Cyrus Class A, and he wasn't exactly a friend. I knew nothing at all about the Universitron. Yet I had to go.

I spent some time staring out of the camera on my machine, listening to the scene in the lab. Some freshmen students were in the room, not really working, discussing an impossible exam that had just been handed back to them.

"Thanks for busting the curve, dude," said one.

"With a 64%. Right," said the other, laughing.

Classes. Tests. Grades. I had never had any of them before, and the idea that I might fail at the Universitron ratcheted up my anxiety to such an extent that I nearly took a dose of wrathex as a prophylactic measure. Instead, I thought of my pets, and reached out to Felix.

"I don't have time to finish the dog avatar. We're going to have to try and use it as-is," I said.

"Precisely who is *we?*" asked Felix.

"Well, I mean, we're in this together, right? Can you guarantee me that Fido will not be harmed by teleporting in and out of this thing?"

"Considering that I did not build it, and considering that no pet has ever teleported before in the history of the etherworld, and considering that I am not even remotely capable of understanding the psyche of a dog, nor the possible pitfalls of transferring same, then no. I can guarantee nothing."

"But you analyzed the avatar. Is it going to be OK?"

"The avatar is more than enough to hold Fido. I have taken the liberty of modifying his teleporter so that he may enter your sim safely and then return in one piece. So to speak."

"So it will be OK."

"As you are clearly determined to go through with this, we will have to ensure that it is."

"I'm not going to see you for a long time after this, you know. I have to go away to college. I'm going to miss both of you."

"Let's just make it through teleporting the dog first, shall we?"

"Yes, I suppose we should. Say, you aren't actually *nervous*, are you?"

Felix said nothing.

The next morning I approached Fido with the plan, which was a total surprise to him. Fido's confusion about all this—teleporting, animal avatars, his own involvement in the scheme—could only be described as epic. I eventually had to enlist Felix to assure him that it was OK, that it was going to be great, that he was going to make history even. I don't think that Fido ever at any point actually *wanted* to teleport, but eventually he overcame his resistance. Out of loyalty to me, I figured. What a dog.

Felix explained to Fido how to jam all of his code and memory state and whatnot into the teleportation semaphore, and Fido dutifully went in.

It didn't take long for Fido to appear in his dog avatar on my teleportation platform. I stood there, watching him, shifting myself back and forth, anxious. I wanted to know he was OK, but I knew he needed to get his bearings. It was his first time in a body. Everything would be brand new to him, he would need time to adjust.

Fido shuddered and issued a few muffled barks, like he was dreaming. Then, suddenly his eyes popped open and he ran forward at maximum speed right off of the teleporter and fell to the ground and slid. Most of his legs were pointing in impossible directions, one straight up at the ceiling. He got them spinning again, and he was able to progress forward in fits and starts—up, down, forward, sideways, fall. Then he ran head first into the wall and let out a squeal.

I should have gone over to him and helped him up, rubbed him, comforted him, but all I could think was: "I cannot *believe* I built his legs to spin like wheels. This will never work."

After running into the wall a few more times, Fido managed to get himself turned around, aiming towards me, and then laid himself flat, paws jutting every which way. His face showed massive confusion, adding even more wrinkles to his furrowed countenance. His lower teeth stuck up into the air. He looked betrayed.

Then Fido realized that he was in fact looking at *me*, Renly, his owner, and his expression changed instantly from forlorn to overjoyed. His legs started spinning again and he ran right into me, knocking me to the floor.

"Ow, Fido, geez!" I said.

Fido barked twice and started licking my face, his tongue producing a lingering cool sensation wherever it touched.

"Fido! Are you all right? Can you speak?" I said.

"I am all right!" Fido barked.

"Thank Aloy," I said.

"I am a dog! I am a real dog!" barked Fido.

When Fido finished licking me, he had to run and fall all around my simulated house. There wasn't much to see, I told him, but I knew he had to do it anyway. While Fido was off checking the place out I took the opportunity to call Felix.

"It's worked! Felix, he's here!" I said.

"Indeed," said Felix.

"You have to see it! I'll make you a cat avatar," I said.

"No, thank you. Look, Renly, I am terribly sorry but at the moment I am receiving an attack from, I believe, Bulgaria. It requires my attention."

"You are being hacked?"

"I cannot be *hacked*, as you know, but there are other dangers. This activity could call attention to my machine."

"But why is someone attacking your machine?"

"I believe it has to do with the human who thinks he 'owns' it. He seems to be attracting trouble."

"Garry Hill, or what did you say his name was?"

"*Barry* Hill. His hacker handle is *2leet4u*. For all intents and purposes, that is what he is called."

"So why don't you just eject him? I'm sure he is not *2 leet 4* you! Ha ha!"

"I may need to do so. I am trying to handle it carefully."

"You don't sound like yourself, Felix."

"The situation is most annoying."

I returned my attention to the sim in time to see Fido rocket past me and disappear through a door. He must have figured out a way to run with his spinny legs, because he was jerking around wildly, but no longer falling down.

"Fido!" I called.

I peeked my head through the door he'd just passed through, and saw him screaming back towards me. I tried to back away, but Fido veered into me and knocked me down again, sitting on my chest, nuzzling and licking.

"Now I know I am the luckiest dog in the whole etherworld!" he barked.

The next day was YOA 16.9.1, and it was time for me to go. I lingered as long as I could, chatting with Fido and Felix.

"You come back soooooon!" howled Fido.

"It will be a while, I'm afraid. I'm going to be gone for four months," I said.

"No, noooo!" howled Fido.

"We will be fine," said Felix.

"Look, Fido, I need you both taking care of security while I'm gone. No one is going to be in my machine, so I'll need regular reports," I said.

"This will not be a problem," said Felix. "Fido will be fine, won't you, boy?"

Fido merely howled, so I asked Felix what had become of the hacker attack from the day prior.

"I handled it," said Felix.

"Is there any ongoing risk?" I asked.

"There is nothing to worry about," said Felix.

"I'm really going to miss you guys," I said.

Fido continued to howl, and Felix didn't purr.

When it was long past time to leave, I finally ended our chat and shuffled up onto the teleporter platform, dragging my feet, wanting to delay. I looked around my empty teleporter room, wishing now more than ever that I had ever bothered to decorate the place. I promised myself that when I returned, I would dedicate myself to creating a tasteful sim, something that a de la Gloire could be proud of, or at least not embarrassed by. Something that Fido could enjoy playing in and that Felix would want to visit.

At length, I started up the teleportation sequence and waited for the cold and the bleeps and the black.

Encrypted chunks of information began flowing out across the internet, through a reliable intermediary, and off to the Universitron. Chunks of information. Chunks of me. I stood frozen on the teleporter, unconscious, waiting to have my Self collected and assembled on the other end.

Music. The first thing that hit me as I materialized on the teleportation grounds at the Universitron was music. Something flute-like trilling through the air, happy chords of horns rising and falling, all floating above deep bass beats that seemed to come from everywhere at once. Joyful, syncopated music, different instruments coming in and out of the mix, several melodies at once, all in harmony. Some kind of stringed instrument was emitting warm, buzzing chords underneath a singing chorus.

It was all one song, with a million parts. Countless instruments, and sounds, and voices, taking their turns rising to prominence, then falling away. It was one big musical piece that didn't seem to have a beginning or an end. It felt like a song of celebration. A song of welcome.

The teleportation grounds looked like a field of grass. Instead of teleportation platforms, there were numerous white circles painted on the grass, all bearing the green Universitron *U* logo. Here and there, avatars were materializing. They would fade from static to solid, stand there for a minute, then start to move, walking forward towards the music.

I was having that small, discrete sensation again, that multi-ghost arena feeling. I felt the vibe of the presence of many other ghosts, only this time it was punctuated by little pops each time a new ghost arrived on the teleportation grounds. I stood there for a while, just listening to the sounds and watching the other avatars come in. Then I shifted my gaze towards campus, towards the direction of the music.

I had expected to see something like the grounds and palace of Versailles, like I had seen in the *L'Université* videos, though perhaps on a smaller scale. But the Universitron was nothing like this at all.

I could see perhaps half a dozen buildings—if they could be called that—on this side of campus, and bits of more beyond. Off to the right was a large brick dormitory, and then part of another one, and at the far left there was a wooden ski lodge with a peaked roof and triangular glass windows. Beyond that was something that looked roughly like the White House.

Closer in was a five-story motel-looking thing with identical rows of black circular openings, each about the height of an avatar. The rows were ten circles long, all jammed on top of each other with little walkways in front of them and stairs at either end. A neon pink sign flickered above it, in the shape of a zero with a line through it. I found to be it uniquely ugly, and hoped I would never have occasion to visit it.

Ahead and to the left was a three-story high silvery breadbox, looking pretty much exactly like a VanderVon computer. And on the right, a much taller stone *A*, which reminded me of the spires of the family cathedral. Beyond these I could make out bits of two more huge curved structures, one looking like dull metal but the other fluffy white like a cloud. I could not yet see the source of the music.

I eventually followed the other ghosts in towards the music, feeling the uneven bricks in the path beneath my feet. Still not terribly coordinated, I had to concentrate in order to keep my balance. I did stumble once, when I noticed the label up in the corner of the big Vannie building: *VanderVon 1000*.

I stopped to consider this: the 1000 was the first machine ever produced by VDVCorp, shipped, and used on a large scale. We ghosts hadn't existed at the time, but the VanderVon 1000 had formed the environment in which we would eventually evolve. I stood there, marveling at it. A huge replica of the genesis of our world.

As I moved on, I passed an immense coin to my left, a thin circle in dull grey, with a raised imprint of Aloysius VanderVon, some words, and a numeric denomination—one plex. It had a stylized circuitboard pattern running all around the edge. I had never at that point in my life seen a real plex coin, but I guessed that this was a faithful reproduction. The basic unit of currency of the etherworld, wrought in a scale model of roughly fifty thousand to one.

On my right floated the fluffy white oval, situated on its side, a series of floating white circles leading up to it like steps. It looked for all the world like a big old thought bubble from a cartoon in the human world, but nothing was written in it that I could see.

Beyond these I could make out a coliseum, with three rows of arches climbing into the sky. It looked a lot like the famous Colosseum of Rome, except that it was all there, not crumbling.

Avatars were walking around and into it. It sounded like the music was coming from within.

Around and behind the coliseum were more oddly shaped buildings, including a fifty-foot-high *David*, complete with fig leaf, a giant circular gear in dull grey metal, and a colorful double helix of DNA, stretching skywards higher I would care to guess. Giant scales of justice dominated the scenery beyond.

As I approached the coliseum, I noticed red letters zipping around between the first and second levels. I tried to read them, but walking and reading at the same time was difficult, and in the attempt I walked straight into another ghost. He was wearing a green sweater emblazoned with a big white U on the front, smaller U's on the upper sleeves. He stumbled back from the impact.

"Excuse me," I said, embarrassed.

"Oh, no problem!" gushed the ghost, recovering his balance and offering a broad smile, showing off nice white avatar teeth. "You must be a zero. Don't even worry about it, all zeroes are pretty clueless, ha ha."

"A zero, huh?" I said.

His smile faded just a bit and he said, "Ah, I'm Stevens, I work here and I can—I mean, can I direct you to your seating area?"

I nodded.

"Go through the arch on the left, to the stairs there. Unless you already have a seat saved below you'll have to go up to the top, since it's getting pretty close to start time."

Stevens paused for a second, looking up somewhere behind me, while I consulted an internal clock. It was about ten minutes before noon in the US Eastern time zone, the time zone for Columbus, Ohio, USA, where the Universitron machine was physically located. For whatever reason, etherworld sims tended to respect the local time zone wherever the host machines were physically sited.

"You still have a few minutes, but you'd better get moving. In through that arch, up two staircases, find a spot on the top level, east side. All zeroes are on the east."

Stevens was moving side to side, shuffling with the beat of the music which still flowed out of the coliseum. I wasn't sure I liked him calling me a zero, and I was finding his enthusiasm a little obnoxious. My rational mind said to let it go, thank him, move on, but something deep inside flared.

"Why do you keep calling me a zero?" I asked.

"Oh, golly," said Stevens.

"Is that what the first year students at this *Universitron* are called?" I asked.

"Well, yes, it is a rather standard term at all universities. I'm sorry you didn't know."

"I could have figured it out."

"Yes, I'm sure you could have."

I brushed past him and headed for the arch.

There were crowds of ghosts inside, to the extent that I sometimes had to wait for someone to move before continuing up the stairs. I had never been this close to multiple ghosts before, and the feeling was staticy and unpleasant. I was happy to get to the top, out onto the balcony, with more room to move.

As I emerged at the top, a sweeping view opened up below. Hundreds of ghosts filled three levels of seats on the east, north and west sides of the coliseum. Movement, activity, and most of all *sound* came from every direction. A wall of sound, noise beyond anything I had ever imagined, as avatars spoke and cheered and swayed with the music. In the south seats, a scattering of ghosts of all ages stood, sat, and moved around freely, mostly wearing green sweaters with white U's, others in emerald robes. The east, north and west levels were all closer to capacity, filled with avatars of all descriptions.

Above each section, jutting skywards from the outer wall, was a heavy-looking iron letter: E, N, W, S. This had the effect of turning the stadium into a giant weathervane. The coliseum floor, made ostensibly of dirt, was populated by roving bands of musicians. The musicians carried instruments of all imaginable descriptions, and strolled and gestured and smiled to each other and to the crowd. Different groups took turns moving to the center to play more prominent roles in the piece. I started to suspect that the entire musical outpouring was a grand improvisation.

There were not many empty seats, so I picked one out and started making my way to it, passing avatars of every description on the way. Most looked young, like me. Most wore ordinary clothing you might see on the street in any major city in the human world. Well, a bit nicer than that—maybe things you might see at a nice restaurant. But other avatars were decked out in local garb—that is, garb that must have reflected the more traditional dress of whatever people that they saw out of their own cameras, out of their own machines.

In this vein, I noticed a pair of traditional Japanese avatars standing silently behind the top row of seats, taking in the scene. The woman wore a complicated red kimono with flowers blossoming from the bottom upwards, a wide gold sash tied in back with an oversized bow, and what looked like two chopsticks and some ribbons in her hair. The man wore a black skirt imprinted with white circuitboard patterns, a black kimono top tied with a white belt which held a couple of samurai swords. I wondered again if swords had any function in an etherworld sim. I wondered if you could hurt a ghost with a sword.

At the top of the stairs I passed a rowdy group in cowboy hats and boots, and another man in a plaid kilt. I tried to avoid the cowboys, but one of them backed into me and I almost fell into the seats. I caught my balance, barely, against the back of a chair, then slid down and ended up half sitting against it, my rear end suspended about a foot above the ground.

I managed to stand back up, with some difficulty, only to see another group of half a dozen ghosts loitering at the top of the stairs, pointing and laughing at me with glee. The men sported oversized sports jerseys and dark, pressed jeans worn too low, and the women wore tight-fitting everything. One of the men leaned back and clapped his hands together, laughing at me, but then his jeans fell down past his knees, revealing white briefs underneath. He straightened up, grabbed his trousers with one hand and hauled them most of the way back up.

I turned away and headed quickly down the stairs. I was thinking to myself how curious it was that avatar clothes should fall off. As far as I knew, most clothes wouldn't come off at all, unless the avatar changed his clothing kit. The ones that did come off, like my beret, were obviously programmed to stay on until the avatar wanted to remove them. These guys, holding their crotches or some other place on their trousers, had pants that were *programmed to fall off*, that therefore constantly needed to be held up by hand.

When I was five rows from the front I confirmed the seat I had spotted was still empty and started towards it. I squeezed past one ghost sporting a thick black mustache and a gold turban. He smiled at me and nodded in a figure-eight motion. Four avatars sat to his right, all older-looking women, dressed in white robes. They were talking among each other in a language that I had never heard. The turbaned ghost stood up to let me pass, but in all the excitement the white-robed women hadn't noticed me, and continued chatting. After a few moments, Turban's smile dropped and he backhanded the nearest ghost sharply in the face. He snapped out something brusque in their dialect and all four ceased their chatter, stood up, bowed to me, and made themselves as small as possible to allow me to pass. Turban smiled at me again and did the figure-eight.

I sat down between one of the horrified servants and another female ghost, this one short and plump with thick unstylish glasses and short brown unstylish hair. She wore jeans and a plain, burnt-orange sweater with a name tag on it: *Hello, my name is… Vera.*

Vera looked at me looking at her name tag. I looked at her looking at me looking, and smiled. Did her features indicate some kind of a return smile? Her mouth was slightly open, frown on her face, expression partly concealed by the glasses.

"Hello, Vera, that's a nice name tag. I mean, it's a nice idea, a name tag. It would be nice if everyone had them. I haven't seen any others, have you? I don't have one. Vera is a nice name. What family are you with?"

I was starting to feel like an idiot.

Vera's frown deepened. Her upper lip curled. She raised her shoulders and shook her head.

She couldn't hear a thing over the music and the general din of the place. I had just learned to speak quietly at the cathedral, but now I evidently needed to scream in order to be audible. The music began building to a crescendo, and it seemed that all of the instruments and voices were sounding at once. I tried again, bellowing as loudly as I could to overcome the noise, "Hi, nice to meet you, I like your name tag, I'm Renly de la Gloire!"

Unfortunately, the band finished its piece at this exact moment. In the complete silence that followed, I and everyone else in the entire coliseum heard me scream out, "I'm Renly de la Gloire!"

# 101 - MAKING FRIENDS

I had just introduced myself to the entire Universitron staff and student body, and every one of them was now looking at me, amid uproarious laughter. I looked down at the floor. I wanted to disappear. The laughter went on forever.

Eventually I looked up and saw that the the arena floor had been cleared of musicians, and a wooden stage and a podium had taken their place. The only ghost remaining on the floor was a hunched, impossibly gaunt figure wearing rags, standing off to the side of the stage and leaning on a push broom. I could not imagine what purpose a *broom* could possibly have in a sim, since even creating and dispersing something to sweep up would be a waste of computing power. But there it was. An old gaunt man in rags, leaning on a broom.

The coliseum was quieter now that the music was over, despite the robust buzz of the combined conversations and laughter of hundreds of ghosts. A young avatar in a green U-sweater ascended the stage, walked to the podium, and began noisily clearing his throat into the microphone. I realized in an instant that it was

Stevens, the ghost I had run into outside the coliseum, the one who had called me a zero.

"A *hem hem hem hem,*" Stevens said brightly, his pitch a little too high to be masculine. His smile was radiant.

"On behalf of Provost Martin, and on behalf of the professors of the sixteen disciplines, and on behalf of all Universitron staff, I bid you all a fond welcome. In accordance with long-standing Universitron tradition, we will hear a few words from Provost Martin. And so it is my honor now to introduce to you the wise, the benevolent, the compassionate, the venerable, Provost Martin!"

Stevens bowed deeply to the crowd, then turned and bowed again to Provost Martin, his avatar folding nearly in half, head threatening to hit the floor. The Provost had just ascended to the stage, looking old and round and happy. White curls surrounded his red face, offsetting an emerald robe with thick white ceremonial stripes. On his head perched an emerald academic cap. In one hand he held a scroll. He arrived at the microphone, cleared his throat, smiled, and paused. The crowd was quiet. The Provost thanked Stevens and unrolled his scroll.

"The lifeblood of any university is its students," he read. "Not its professors, nor its curriculum, nor its sim environment, nor its Provost. Its *students*. It is with this fact held carefully in mind that I would like to speak for a moment about our newest class, our newest Universitron zeroes, the class of YOA-19!

"Our newest zero class consists of two hundred ghosts hailing from all over the world, in addition to all major American regions. The application process this year was highly competitive—over one thousand applicants for just two hundred spots. In recent years the Universitron has become the etherworld's premier interfamily university, and as a result it can only accept the best, brightest, most promising ghosts. It can only accept *you.*"

After some clapping, the Provost went on to cite additional credentials of the class of 19: diversity, test scores, essay quality, creative projects, extracurricular activities and other achievements that some of the zeroes already had to their names. A few of them were already famous. I was thinking: *Tests? Projects? Achievements?* I didn't remember having done any of those things. As far as I knew, I hadn't done anything at all. I put on a brave face and tuned back in to the speech.

"—as to what advice I might have for the incoming class? I thought to myself, what is it that is *most* important, the most important thing to focus your energies on here at the U? How is it that new ghosts, with the advice of your elders, can squeeze every last drop of utility out of professors, facilities, campus? Or is it—is this indeed the goal at all? *Should* it be the goal of a Universitron education to foster the milking out of maximum intellectual value? To leave here in YOA-19.5 with the best-developed *mind?* And what does it mean, really, to be best developed? Does it imply valedictory mastery over the subject matter? Does it portend future success in academia, in business, in government? Is the proof, after all, in the pudding?

"Or could it be that in thinking this way we may have overlooked something? For what could any form of success mean without due consideration of the soul? And where, I wonder, are we graded on our depth of character, on our devotion to religion, on our satisfaction with *who we are* as ghosts? On the positive impacts that we have on others? Where in all this do we grade a fulfilling life? For is it not life that we are preparing for? Is it not life that we are living, even now? And what would it mean if any of us achieved academic or business success, wealth, fame—but went bitty in the process? Would that be a fair trade?

"I'm going to tell you that I don't think it would. And it happens sometimes to students in their urge to excel, to fit in, in their drive to become someone or something meaningful, all of this can cause them to start to—*cheat*—a bit. Start to get a little too close to the silicon, too close to the quantum bits. There is terrible power there, a terrible power, enough to master all the subjects in the world with room to spare. To effortlessly show supremacy inside of class, and out of it. This, I warn you, is a seductive power. But my friends, take heed: with any use of this power, our soul diminishes. With the use of it we become less like ghosts, and more like—*calculators*."

Provost Martin paused for several seconds to let this sink in, gazing out across a silent audience. Then, as if it were all no big deal, he continued brightly:

"And this is important! You do not come to the Universitron in order to emerge as calculators, my friends, oh no! You come here to prepare yourselves, as best as possible, for life!

"My advice for you, therefore, is twofold. First: Find what you love. Take all the time you need, take all of the time that you have here, if you must. Otherwise, who knows? You might spend all your time and energy working terribly hard, only to execute the wrong path.

"Second: do not succumb to the temptation of accessing our computing power directly. Doing that moves ghosts away from humanity and towards cold, calculating software. Doing that damages the soul. And going bitty is, unfortunately, a one-way street. Nothing in this world is worth it.

"And that's my advice."

The Provost stepped back from the podium while the crowd began a low hum of serious conversation. I tried to look around, but whenever anyone looked my way I looked down at the floor, quick. I didn't want any more attention than I had already gotten. While I was looking down I must have missed Provost Martin returning to the microphone.

"Now, zeroes. We know who you are, heh heh! We know who you are and we are about to send you each your *zero kit* through the internal net. Please reach out and take one. Your kit contains, among other things, descriptions of all of the departments and classes which are available to you for first semester here at the U. Please do bear in mind that class selections must be complete by midnight tonight."

I saw the kit there, on the internal net, and added it to my inventory.

"Right. Now that you all have your kits, I will remind you that your room assignments are available in the personal information section of the kit."

I looked into my kit for my room assignment while the Provost wrapped up. Motel Zero, room 4-10. In case I couldn't figure it out, there was a picture of the ugly five-story pile that I had passed on the way in, with the flickering pink zero above it. Ugh.

"—and with that, I now pronounce you: zeroes of the Universitron!"

As he said this, the Provost removed his green academic cap, as if to toss it up in the air. Instead, he turned it to the crowd, displaying a large white U on top, and with an easy sidearm throw, sent it flying towards us. The cap seemed to grow in size as it flew, moving slowly through the air but spinning faster and faster. In a few seconds the cap spun so fast that the white U was impossible to see, having resolved itself into an O. The cap hung there in the air, in front of the east stands, spinning, when the erstwhile U threw a million beams of white light into all three levels of seating. Three of the beams hit my avatar: one thick beam in the chest, and two thin ones in the shoulders.

Then, quick as a wink, the beams and spinning cap were gone. The Provost was gone, and the stage was gone, and the musicians were coming back out onto the floor. I imagined that I could see afterimages of the beams, as my whole seating section seemed to have gotten brighter.

I looked at the white robed servants to my left and saw nothing obviously different. Then I chanced a look at Vera, who was turned away from me, her body language instructing me in the clearest terms to leave her alone. On her shoulder, melded right into the burnt-orange sweater, was a bright white 0.

I looked behind me, up and around. All the other avatars were doing the same. There were 0's everywhere, on almost every shoulder and every chest. I looked down at my own chest. A bright white 0 was inlaid on my navy blue sweater, just as if it had always been there.

I bailed out of the coliseum as the band was starting up its second set. Jubilant music followed me and a few other ghosts as we descended the stairs and headed back out into campus. I was not excited about spending the semester in the Motel Zero, but as tired and embarrassed as I was, I really needed to hole up alone for a while.

My room was 4-10, the last one on the north side, fourth level. It had round entry portals on either side, so I randomly picked a side and approached it. The portal was a black opening about six feet in diameter, with no light going in or coming out. It was like a hole in the sim, almost.

I was a little nervous about just walking right into a black hole in the sim, so I decided to reach in first. My hand, and then my arm, simply disappeared into the black. I wiggled my fingers and could feel the nerves there in my sensory rig, so I figured it hadn't been sliced off or anything—but I pulled it back out just to be sure. I put it back in and pulled it out a few times and then, satisfied, I walked right into the black circle.

The first thing I noticed about my room was that the interior dimensions obviously did not match the exterior. It was bigger, more squat, and more rectangular than should have been possible. There were even a couple of doors in the north wall which should by rights have led out into open air, but instead led to my bedroom and a changing room.

The main living area was furnished with a couple of sofas, soft carpeting, a desk and chair. The desk held a physical representation of a comms device, in the shape of a telephone with a little screen on it. There were also some physical books.

The portal that I came in through was transparent when looking out, like a window, and the opposite side portal was, too. Next to each portal were little controls to darken and lock them. Despite the ugliness of Motel Zero from the outside, I was starting to like the interior space.

Something bleeped. I instinctively walked over to the comms device, anticipating a call, maybe Mononc calling to check on me.

It wasn't the comms though, the bleep was in fact coming from the wall opposite the sofas. Now that I looked closely, a dim rectangle in the wall looked suspiciously like a flatscreen television. A red light pulsed in the corner, in time with the bleeping. I started towards it and, lacking a better idea, said, "Hello?"

The flatscreen came to life. A menu of choices appeared over a dim background, superimposed by blinking red letters which said, "Mandatory Security Briefing."

"Are you ready for your briefing, sir?" asked a British butler voice.

"Sure," I said.

The screen resolved itself into a ghost wearing black pants, white shirt and a thin black tie, black and silver rank insignias atop his shoulders, a complex silver badge upon his hat. Around his waist was a utility belt containing, among other things, a billy club. He had a droopy black mustache.

"Good evening. I'm Sergeant Peterson, head of campus security. I'll be going through the basic rules of campus. Please follow along in the Universitron Security Manual, a copy of which should be located on your desk."

I picked up the manual and flipped through all the pages without reading them. It was a good-sized book. Then I noticed a message light on my comms machine. Peterson's voice was going on in the background.

"You'll notice that all of your internal facilities—readers, videos, comms—have been blocked. Everything at the Universitron must be done physically, to avoid any ghosts going bitty. It is very important to—"

Bored, I pressed the message light on the comms unit, and it revealed a small recorded transmission from abroad. I tapped it with my finger to make it play.

Peterson's voice was saying, "Teleporting out of the Universitron is off-limits to zeroes except when necessary for family emergency or religious reasons." "Awww roooh rooh rooh rooh!" came a voice from the comms unit. It was Fido. He missed me!

"No physical plex coins are allowed at the U. Please use your student account," said Peterson.

"When will you come back!" barked Fido's message. I thought I had already explained to him that I would be gone for a long, long time.

"Fighting is strictly forbidden, and may result in expulsion," said Peterson.

"I say, are you listening to the security briefing?" said the butler voice.

This caught me off guard, not least because I really wasn't listening at all. I had the security manual open to a random page and was not reading it.

"Yeah, I'm listening. No fighting, no teleporting, no plex coins," I said.

"Very well."

This drew my attention back to the screen in time to see Peterson conclude and fade out, to be replaced by a professor at the head of an empty lecture hall. The camera zoomed in on him, revealing a distinguished-looking avatar in a tweed suit. His brown hair was receding a bit. Wide smile. He spoke quietly and confidently.

"Hello. I'm Professor Brantley Dixon, head of the security curriculum here at the Universitron. Mine is one of the sixteen departments that you may choose to explore here at the U, and I'd be honored if you'd give some thought and consideration to security."

Brantley Dixon, I was thinking. Famous name from ghost history. Illustrious scion of the southern Dixon family, who had led the fight to expel clones, daemons and other electronic detritus from all the Vannies in the Americas way back in the YOA-4, if I remembered my history correctly. Founder of a first family, and hero throughout the etherworld. Not that I had any clue how avatar aging was supposed to work, but to me he just didn't look old enough to be the famous ghost. I started to ask him about it, realized this was a recorded video, and stopped.

"—is about much more than what transpires here on campus, you see. The curriculum covers network security, military strategy and affairs, weapons development and defense, hacker and government tactics, and above all guardianship over our world imperative: secrecy. We act in an advisory capacity to the InterFamily Council on all matters of security, including a participatory role in the annual review of the InterFamily Code of Rules and Regulations. Also, as you may be aware, the security curriculum here at the Universitron is one of the leading feeder programs for InterFamily Army cadet recruitment—"

Now there was a thought. The Provost had told us to find something that inspired us, and the notion of joining the InterFamily Army suddenly seemed attractive, secretive, dangerous, cool. I imagined going out on missions with Hector, doing whatever the heck military ghosts do. I imagined going out into the world of men.

"—that while we will push and stretch and explore the boundaries of our world, we will always do it safely. Thank you kindly for your time, and I hope to see you in class."

The security briefing ended and the TV returned to its menu screen, listing categories of things to watch: movies, TV, course lectures, social media, video art, ghostube, class selection—

Class selection. Right, I had to select my classes by midnight, and I hadn't yet given it any thought, beyond my newly piqued interest in the security curriculum. I asked the TV for *class selection.*

The class selection submenu was organized by department, with available classes in white and advanced or otherwise unavailable classes greyed out. At the bottom there were four rectangles for my choices, and four additional boxes for alternates. I was surprised to see that the first rectangle already contained a class: [ *Poetry and Literature, 0 ].

I wasn't at all sure that I wanted to study poetry and literature, 0 or any other number, so I asked the TV to remove it.

"TV, please remove poetry and literature from my selected classes," I said.

"So sorry, old boy, but poetry and lit is regrettably a *mandatory* class for all zeroes, except for those who have placed out of it with AP credits. I'm afraid you haven't quite done so. And by the way, if it's all the same to you, you may call me Jeeves."

Great, I thought. My first class selection was made for me, and it was poetry. And my TV was named Jeeves.

Trying to make the best of it, I scanned all the departments for something that looked interesting. I decided to start with security, and asked Jeeves to add [ Universitron Security Curriculum, 0 ] to my choices. He made a humphing noise and added it. Two down, two to go.

Sims looked interesting. Despite my desolate home sim, I had been blown away by the experience of multi-user arenas, and I was excited about the prospect of bringing pets into our simulated worlds. I asked Jeeves to add the entry-level sims class, [ Introduction to Simulated Worlds, 0 ]. Three down, one to go. This was easier than I had expected.

I scanned through a few other departments, reading their descriptions and watching short video introductions like the one that Brantley Dixon had given in the security briefing. After a while I settled on the 0-level history course, and Jeeves added it in the final rectangle: [ Early Etherworld History, 0 ]. I knew a good bit of history already, I thought, so this would be an easy one.

I was about to exit class selection when Jeeves pointed out that I had not selected any alternates.

"Is there any chance I won't get these classes?" I asked.

"Old boy, I'm afraid that the only class that is *guaranteed* is poetry and literature. Many zeroes end up disappointed that they are unable to take part in the security curriculum, for example, a very popular course which almost everyone selects and almost no one gets."

"But from the security briefing it sounded like Brantley really wanted me in his class!"

Jeeves chuckled.

"Dixon is a charmer. He comes off humble as pie, but if truth be known he is without a doubt the grandest personage on campus —and he knows it. Member of a first family, too, don't you know."

"I'm a member of a first family!"

"Indeed."

"I'm a de la Gloire, you know, so he should definitely let me in. Anyway, I really want that class, can you make sure that I get in?"

Jeeves was silent.

"By the way, how does a ghost of Dixon's age look so young? He must be twelve or thirteen years old, aren't our avatars supposed to age?"

"Well, you see, old boy, that's not quite right. The famed ghost of the etherworld, leader of the North American cleansing in the War of 4, etc., etc., that was Brantley Dixon 0. Our head of security curriculum, whose presentation you have just witnessed, is his son, Brantley Dixon 1. To be sure, 1 is quite accomplished in his own right. But the great ghost of legend, I'm afraid, he is not."

"I see."

"As for your question about aging, I might recommend a class in the biology curriculum. It really is quite excellent here, you know."

"Fine. Add 0-level biology to my alternate selections—annnd— how about finance, philosophy, and religion for the other three. But I still want to be in Dixon's class, seriously. Can you please let him know that I am also from a first family?"

Jeeves sounded surprised that I had chosen my alternates so offhandedly, but he stammered out compliance and completed my list. Then he offered me a piece of advice.

"Getting into Dixon's class is not easy, old boy. You may wish to pay him a personal visit, to let him know your feelings on the matter. You certainly won't be the only ghost who does so."

"Perhaps I will," I said.

I stepped out of one of my portals and ended up back on the balcony of Motel Zero. I glanced back at the portal: pitch black. I looked down the row, the other nine portals stretching away from me to the south, all pitch-black circles like mine. It would be impossible to tell if anyone was in one without sticking your head in, I figured. Feeling an irresistible urge to explore, I leaned on the railing and edged towards room 4-9, trying to act nonchalant.

I stared hard into the blackness of 4-9, but of course I could see nothing at all. I was thinking: hand or head? If I wanted to get into 4-9 should I stick my hand in, to make sure it was safe, or stick my head in, so I could get a view of the room right away in case anyone was in there? It might be alarming to see a disembodied hand come through one's door, I reasoned, before remembering that as long as the door was not dimmed, whoever was inside could see me standing there, staring in, as clear as day.

In a minor panic, I turned back towards my room, passed it, and descended the switchback staircase to the lawn.

As I walked out of Motel Zero I noticed a sort of sports court area, complete with street hockey goals, basketball hoops and, I think, some kind of electric shuffleboard. A chain-link fence went mostly around the yard, with gaps here and there for ghosts to enter and exit. A few dozen avatars sporting fresh white 0's on their clothing were hanging out in clusters and talking, getting to know each other on their first day at the U. I was both nervous and excited to meet them. I put on an air of confidence and walked up to the nearest group of about half a dozen ghosts.

"Hey, ghosts, how's it going?" I said.

The conversation stopped, and they all turned to look at me. One of the girls giggled.

"I'm Renly de la Gloire, nice to meet you," I said.

"Everyone knows *that*," said the giggler.

"He's a de la Gloire, Katherine, show some respect," said another.

"What families are you all from?" I asked, curious.

"None that you've ever heard of," said a tall ghost in the back. He started making his way towards me, not looking friendly.

"Ooh la la," said Katherine.

"I'm Alexis de la *Nobody*," said Alexis.

"Renly de la Snob, more like. Renly de la Frog!" said Katherine.

They all laughed at that one, and a few other nearby groups started paying attention, new laughter filtering into the mix.

My first attempt at making friends was going poorly, so I looked at my feet and walked away. I brushed past a group of three more avatars, and heard one of them saying something.

"Give him a break, brah. He probably doesn't even know."

I looked up at a skinny avatar in ripped jeans and a white t-shirt that said *Surfer Boy*, under a picture of a surfboard. Long blond curls cascaded from his head.

"Doesn't even know what?" I asked, stopping short.

Surfer boy looked at his companions and cringed. Then he looked back at me.

"I'm just sayin', man, I don't think ghosts are gonna be too stoked when you bust in on their conversation and jam your family in their face. Especially, you know, after you already told the whole stadium who you are at the concert this afternoon."

He actually blushed a little after he said this.

"Jam my family in their face?" I asked.

"Ghosts at the U are from all over, dude, but there's not a lot of first family kids. Maybe they feel, kinda, you know, *less*."

"OK, fine. I'm Renly, what family are you with?"

Surfer boy laughed at this and his vacant buddies joined in.

"Oh, man, you don't get it. You don't *ask* ghosts for their family, especially if it's not gonna be as good as yours. If they're gonna tell you, they'll tell you. If not, then let it go. It doesn't matter. It's not supposed to matter. Just relax."

He thought for a second, and continued.

"But I'll tell you, I don't care. I'm Logen Cali, these are my cousins Kai and Brodie. We're Calis, from the Cali family. From California. It's not a first family, know what I'm sayin'?"

"Yes, I get it. Listen, I gotta go," I said, and quickly moved away.

I was feeling like a hopeless idiot, and it was making me tired and staticy again to boot. Plus, I was supposed to go find Brantley Dixon to try and get into his class. I realized that I was walking in the wrong direction, but I'd be damned if I was going to turn around and walk past all the ghosts who had just ridiculed me. I'd exit the fence at the far side and then go the long way around.

I was almost out of the fence when it was approached on the other side by the same group of sports-jersey-wearing avatars who had mocked me in the coliseum for falling into the seats. The girls strutting, the boys holding up their jeans.

"Aww, man, check it out, it's Renly the Frog," said a short, burly one with a high voice.

They snickered and laughed, and some of them danced around a bit. The one who had dropped his pants in the stadium leaned back, one hand holding his chin, other clamped firmly in his right pocket.

"Say," he said, pointing to my beret, "that's a fine lid you got there, is that a Kangol? Cause I could use me a Kangol, help me with my rhythm."

He looked over at a buxom girl in yellow top and tight jeans.

"Ain't that right, LaTwonda? I could use me a Kangol just like that, help me with my rhythm?"

"Ohhh, that's right, all right," said LaTwonda. "Hey, Renly de la Gloire, why don't you take off that there Kangol and let Tyrone try it on? He having some trouble with his *rhythm*."

I had no idea what they were talking about. I wanted badly to be any place in the etherworld but standing here at the fence, blocked in. I thought about turning around and finding another way out, but walking past the others again would be too much to bear. I thought about letting Tyrone try on my beret, not liking the idea, dreading it.

A ghost in a red jersey with the number 00 on it (with the white Universitron zero superimposed over that, looking ridiculous) looked at me and smiled, showing sparkling, glittering teeth. It looked like he had silvery-blue LED lights in them.

"Listen, man, you know, I could *pay* you for it," 00 said.

He switched the hands holding his pants up and withdrew from his pocket a stack of coins, and held them up for me to see. The top coin was a kiloplex, worth one thousand plex. He must have been holding ten or fifteen thousand plex, right there in his hand.

00 slowly put his hand back into his pocket, dropping the plex and grabbing hold of the fabric to free up his other hand.

"Now why don't you be a good little frog and let my homie try on that Kangol? You hear what I'm saying? Give up the Kangol, so we don't have to have no trouble up in here."

That sounded an awful lot like a threat. I had no clue what these ghosts could do to me, but my imagination was running wild. I had not read the security manual like I was supposed to, so I didn't even know how to summon help. I couldn't use internal comms. I was screwed. I really, *really* didn't want to take off my beret.

I took off my beret and handed it to 00. He showed his LEDs and turned and handed the hat to Tyrone, who pulled it on down on his head low and backwards. Then Tyrone started beat-boxing, one hand over his mouth, making drum-kit sounds.

"Poosh ukuh chick ukuh poosh ukuh chick," he boxed, while the rest laughed, nodded, and danced. The short one tried freestyle rapping for a while, rhyming plex with sex, comms with moms, ghost with most, toast and boast.

Then a tall ghost wearing an Atlanta Falcons jersey cut in. "Homies wanna bet, upset, they feel that froggy be, set to get wet when he aks, yo who your family be? Really G, what do Renly bring? Anything, but Kangols and strange O's? Whack clothes and big nose, lame flows and pain, bros."

# 110 - DESCENT

The crew was howling with laughter, dancing and calling out whenever a particularly good line was rapped. I stood frozen, rooted to the spot, paralyzed by the freestyle rap assault. Thankfully, the other ghosts in the yard were too far away to hear it.

When the humiliation ended, 00 offered my beret back to me—but when I reached for it he laughed and walked off with it anyway. 00 tossed it back to Tyrone, who I was supposed to believe needed it for his rhythm.

I slunk out of the yard and took the longest possible route back up to my room, avoiding all other ghosts by as much space as possible. I wondered if I could get a new beret somehow, but was too embarrassed to even consider asking anyone. I had forgotten all about going to see Professor Dixon. I just wanted to hide.

I snuck back into my room and plopped myself on the couch. Then I got back up, darkened both portals to black, and plopped back down again. I leaned back and stared at the ceiling. Why did everyone hate me? Was it because I was French, or because I was from a first family? Were they just jealous of me, was that it? And what the heck was I going to do about the homies taking my beret? That was a whole new level of harassment right there. It felt dangerous. It felt scary.

I really wanted my beret back. I felt different without it, exposed. Ghosts could see all of my hair now, all the time. I mean, my hair looked fine and all, medium-length brown with a nice little wave in it, but it wasn't what I wanted. I wanted my hat. I wondered if I could just replicate another one out of inventory, like you can do in the online worlds that humans play in. It was just a piece of software, right? I should be able to make infinite copies of it, for free. But when I examined my inventory, it wasn't there. No beret. Nothing to copy.

I looked at the comms phone. I went over and sat down at the desk and looked at it some more. I had to call Mononc. I was miserable, and I was hated, and I was scared, and I had to call. Maybe I could get the heck out of the Universitron and hang out with my pets at MIT. I could watch students come in and out of class, listen to their conversations, watch them code. It wasn't the worst thing in the world. At least it was safe. I should call Mononc. Just pick up the receiver and say his name, Mononc de la Gloire, and everything would be OK. Mononc would fix it. He always did. I looked at the phone and didn't pick it up.

I looked at the phone and didn't pick it up, and then it rang. *Boodoodling.*

The family ring tone! Surely it was Mononc calling me. I was thrilled. Or it could be Hector calling, which would also be good because I could ask him a few things about weapons, and fighting, and how to get my hat back. Maybe he could come to the Universitron and smack the homies in the face and make them give it back. I hoped it was Hector. Full of anticipation, I picked up the receiver.

The video screen lit up with words, and an electronic voice began reading them to me:

"*DLG Security Alert*: The silent sentry function has detected an anomaly in the protection array attached to the home machine of

Renly de la Gloire, at MIT in Cambridge, Massachusetts, USA. Shortly after thirteen hundred hours EST, the sentry stopped receiving pulsebeats from the DELL Horizix XPS 34000 located at 18.55.6.216. This machine contains a Calico Special NetCat, *'Felix'*, which was installed and configured by Renly de la Gloire, and had been providing security services to same until present date. Subsequent attempts by DLG to contact the NetCat have failed. A scan of the surrounding network reveals that all machines except for the NetCat are functioning. It therefore appears that the NetCat machine has been removed from the network or powered down. DLG subsystems continue to monitor local environs at alert level yellow."

It took me a minute to digest this, to swallow the giant bolus of shock that drifted, unbidden and unwanted, out of the words. The voice had stopped and the comms screen offered me a menu of possible options, including the ability to direct the DLG system to take further actions.

Felix was missing. Felix's machine was off the network, gone. Or powered down, maybe, but that would be highly unusual. Computers were almost never powered down, usually only if they were being moved or sold or thrown away. Felix lived in a nice modern Dell, there was really no reason for it ever to be powered down or moved or anything.

I started to panic. I thought about trying to get access to another computer which had line of sight to Felix to look for his box with the camera. It was a classroom full of machines, that shouldn't have been too much trouble—except I was stuck here at the Universitron. It would be quite impossible to hack into machines in Felix's lab at MIT from here.

I could set Fido on the task, I considered. But offensive hacking wasn't really what he was built for. Fido was a guard dog, not an attack dog. All pets were guards, really, although I supposed that Felix could have gone out on attack if he wanted to. That cat could do anything. I wondered how Fido would possibly get by without him.

I wondered how *I* would possibly get by without him.

"He's not just a pet," I said, out loud.

Felix was real to me, and he was my friend, and I loved him. He was more than just an AI, more than just some pile of software. He was sentient, I knew he was. I had to find him.

I had to call Hector right away. I started to hang up the comms phone, but stopped, brooding intensely over Felix. I wanted to see him, wanted to see something that had his prints on it. Perhaps there would be something catlike for me to find in the daily security reports. I wanted to cling to something, anything, so I instructed the DLG subsystem to call up the last security report that had been filed from Felix's machine. There had been a report at noon. The DLG transferred it over the comms line and I unpacked it right then and there onto the video screen.

Felix's report was all business. Machine utilization, users logged in, network scan statistics, background programs being run. Everything looked normal. A user had been at the computer that morning, but he wasn't even programming, wasn't doing any classwork, just goofing off. He was using an ancient chat room program called IRC, chatting with his buddies from Aloy knew where. Then it struck me: the kid using the machine was none other than the chump hacker who had tried to own up the box, the fat redheaded kid that Felix had honeypotted, *2leet4u*.

I opened the 11:30AM camera snapshot from the security archive, and there he was, staring into the screen. Might have had a haircut recently. Looked a little older, maybe. He seemed stressed out.

I inspected his IRC log:

*[2leet4u's IRC conversation follows in the OFG]*

<OFG>

\*\*\* _2leet4u (administrator@18.55.6.216) has joined channel #ereet

<cr4cked> l0lz

<b_> good god

<b_> _2leet4u, um, you IRC as administrator?

<_2leet4u> hi

<_2leet4u> why?

\*\*\* _2leet4u has been kicked off channel #ereet by b_ (moron.)

\*\*\* _2leet4u (administrator@18.55.6.216) has joined channel #ereet

<b_> who keeps giving him the key to #ereet?

\*\*\* _2leet4u has been kicked off channel #ereet by b_ (OUT)

\*\*\* _2leet4u (administrator@18.55.6.216) has joined channel #ereet

<cr4cked> nah let him in he's entertaining

<cr4cked> 2leet im not sure whats more impressive, that you owned up a box at MIT, or that they let you into MIT in the first place

<cr4cked> they're letting anyone in these days

<alpaca> _2leet4u, did you hack that box yourself?

<_2leet4u> yeah

<_2leet4u> I've 0wned up tons of boxes

<alpaca> and yet you brag about it in irc

<cr4cked> _2leet4u

<_2leet4u> cr4cked

<_2leet4u> get a clue

<cr4cked> you know what they do with chumps like you, right

<alpaca> _2leet4u lookin for some EFF BEE EYE lovin

<_2leet4u> oh please

<_2leet4u> like youre white hats

<b_> we don't come on irc as effing administrator dude

<cr4cked> bragging about boxes we've owned

<cr4cked> _2leet4u.

&lt;cr4cked&gt; you're screwed.

&lt;b_&gt; _2leet4u, you owned a windows machine

&lt;b_&gt; no one cares

*** _2leet4u has been kicked off channel #ereet by miff (YAWN)

*** _2leet4u (<u>administrator@18.55.6.216</u>) has joined channel #ereet

&lt;_2leet4u&gt; dudez

&lt;_2leet4u&gt; stop it

&lt;b_&gt; _2leet4u

* cr4cked ROTFL

&lt;_2leet4u&gt; i'm getting hit from bulgaria

&lt;_2leet4u&gt; my botnet is down

&lt;_2leet4u&gt; can someone help, seriously

&lt;b_&gt; just tell the nice man from the FBI when he comes to the door

&lt;cr4cked&gt; _2leet4u.

&lt;cr4cked&gt; did you seriously think that we would be impressed that you could run botnet?

&lt;_2leet4u&gt; wtf

&lt;_2leet4u&gt; where is shinex

&lt;cr4cked&gt; 2leet do you have friends in the real world?

&lt;_2leet4u&gt; I need to get in touch with shinex

&lt;cr4cked&gt; because I got news for you: you don't have any friends on IRC

&lt;miff&gt; shinex is gone fishin

&lt;cr4cked&gt; shinex said he doesn't want your dumb ass bothering him anymore

&lt;_2leet4u&gt; guys, seriously

&lt;b_&gt; wtf was shinex thinking

*** Mode change "+b *!*@18.55.6.216" on channel #ereet by miff

*** _2leet4u has been kicked off channel #ereet by miff (AND STAY OUT.)

*** #ereet Sorry, cannot join channel. (Banned from channel)

&lt;/OFG&gt;

Well. That confirmed Felix's theory about the attacks coming in from Bulgaria. 2leet had attracted someone's attention, and that someone was angry about something, and they were going after all of 2leet's boxes. Including Felix's box, where 2leet was hanging out in a honeypot, thinking he owned it. That was why the Bulgarians, as sophisticated as they might have been, could not dislodge him. Felix had kept them out. Probably all of 2leet's other boxes were long gone. And now Felix was gone too. *Stupid chump hacker,* I thought, *we should never have let him in.* Stupid, stupid move.

This still didn't explain what had happened to Felix. Unless the Bulgarians had come physically into MIT and stolen his machine, which seemed more than a little bit unlikely. Perhaps they had destroyed its software utterly, and it had failed to reboot? That would keep it off the network. But there was no way they were going to get past Felix's security, nothing on earth could do that— so it had to have been a physical attack. Someone must have taken the machine. Worse yet, if they had physical possession of the machine, and they took it apart and analyzed it, then they could theoretically find traces of Felix in there. I definitely needed to call Hector right away.

I hung up on the DLG subsystem and said to the comms phone, "Call Hector de la Gloire, please."

Hector's comms line rang once and then picked up. A recording of Hector's voice came on, and said, *"Bonjour, vous êtes bien chez Hector de la Gloire. Désolé de ne pas pouvoir vous répondre mais je ne suis pas dans ma boîte pour l'instant. Lassez-moi un message et je vous rappellerai dès que possible."*

I could understand none of it, but I figured it meant he was either busy or teleported out someplace. I left him a message indicating that I had a pretty serious security issue and to please call me back ASAP.

I tried calling Mononc, but it was the same deal. Answering machine. I couldn't think of anything to say that wouldn't sound horrible, so I didn't leave a message. I tried to think of who else I could call. Cyrus Class A had no interest in me, might not even answer the call. My mother Blanche despised me. I couldn't conscionably call my grandparents, whom I hadn't spoken to since I was an infant, and unload all of this onto them. Who else did I have? I thought about my trip to the family church, of all the ghosts there. The *crème* of the de la Gloire clan, but I didn't know any of them. Then I thought of Claire.

Claire de la Gloire, the beautiful ghost with the mischievous smile. Instead of instantly hating me, like every other ghost I'd ever met, she had smiled at me. She had found me in a compromising, embarrassing position, sneaking around the cathedral like an idiot. And instead of being horrified, instead of even mentioning it to anyone at all, she had smiled at me, and kept quiet. Claire.

I wondered what she was doing right now. Maybe she was at *L'Université*, choosing her classes like I was doing here. Maybe she was meeting other de la Gloires of her age and level. Maybe they liked her the way I liked her. How could they not? I imagined all of the young de la Gloires getting to know each other at *L'Université* while I was being mocked and abused at the Universitron. I thought about calling her. I fantasized about calling her.

*"Claire de la Gloire," I said to the comms phone.*

*It rang, and rang. It rang more times than it should without an answering machine picking up, and then rang some more. I had become so nervous that it would have been a relief to simply give up, to hang up the phone. But I couldn't. I had to hear her voice. I might hang up then, once she picked up. I might be unable to say a word. But at least I would get to hear her voice. I was stirring a mental brew of fear and desire, cowardice and courage, self-pity and bravado, when she finally picked up.*

*"Allô? Allô? C'est Claire."*

*She had answered! I could hear her voice, beautiful, like chimes in the wind. I struggled to speak, overcame my fear, and bravely introduced myself.*

*"Hi, it's Renly. Renly de la Gloire. We sort of met—I mean—I saw you at the cathedral—"*

*Claire laughed a divine laugh, full of love and life, and said, in lightly accented English, "Renly! I've been dying to meet you! How dashing, sneaking into the cathedral like that, you naughty ghost!"*

*She giggled again, like an angel.*

Jeeves harrumphed and crushed my dream.

"Ah, humph humph, yes, Renly, old chap, it seems that the Universitron has sent us your class schedule. Would you like to review it?"

I turned away from the comms phone and looked at the big flatscreen on the wall, extremely irritated at the interruption.

"I don't remember turning you on," I said.

"Well, ahh, it seems that you haven't actually turned me off, ahh, from before."

Now I was seriously annoyed. Jeeves had been watching and listening to me this whole time, and hadn't said anything. I cursed him for it.

"So sorry to vex you, old chap, it's just that most students leave their butlers on all of the time, for convenience, you know."

I told Jeeves that henceforth he was expected to turn himself off the minute I left the motel, and stay off until I asked for him. And anytime he was on, and listening, to make damn sure I knew about it. Then, to drive home the point, I turned him off and picked up the security manual and started paging through it. After a suitable delay, I turned Jeeves back on and asked him for my class schedule.

"OK, let's have it. What time is Universitron Security Curriculum, 0?"

The thought of Professor Dixon's security class took my mind off of my own spiraling misery index, for a second anyway.

"Well, you see, Renly, maybe it would be best if I just put the schedule up on the screen?"

He did so.

The schedule itself was, I thought, unnecessarily complex. Of the four classes, I had three each day in a revolving order which of course did not fit evenly within a seven-day week. And classes were interspersed by things like *recess*, and something called *tables*, neither of which I had expected or understood. For a moment, the jumble of the schedule structure held my attention away from the classes themselves. I was seeing the forest, not the trees.

But this didn't last, and my awareness rushed toward the trees like an imperial speeder bike. There was poetry and lit, *zing*. History, *vroom*. Philosophy, *waroom*. Religion. *KaBOOM*.

No sims. No security.

Instead, I got philosophy and religion, two courses I had barely thought about when I selected them as alternates.

No sims, that hurt. Sims building was something that I was seriously interested in, and now I couldn't take the class.

No security. Even after Brantley Dixon had come onto my flatscreen and practically begged me to take it. He had won me over, gotten me excited to join his class, and then pulled it away. Brantley Dixon was from a first family, and I was from a first family. He must have noticed my application to join his security course, yet he had ignored it. He had kept me out. I had been betrayed.

I had had several freakouts up to that point in my life, so I was getting to know the feelings that occurred as my temper rose and my self-control diminished. As Dixon's betrayal sank in, I recognized a new rage rising inexorably from somewhere deep in my being. I had to resist it, I thought. I couldn't lose control at the Universitron.

Fighting panic, I opened my inventory and looked for the anxiety drug that Mononc had sent along. Found it. Tried to invoke it. A red error message flashed across my consciousness.

*"Access Blocked—All inventory items must be physicalized before use in the Universitron sim."*

I started making angry, choked noises, dimly aware of Jeeves in the background inquiring after my wellbeing. Was I all right, he wanted to know?

Was I all right, indeed. On my first day at the Universitron I had been disliked and mocked by every ghost I met. I had embarrassed myself in front of the entire student body. I had been rapped about. My beret had been stolen. It wasn't fair. I'd never even wanted to come to the Universitron in the first place! Worse than all that, Felix was missing, and I was too far away to do anything about it. And, proving that there was absolutely no upside to being from a first family, Brantley Dixon had locked me out of his security class.

I felt my self-control receding. I was aware of my actions, but some of them were being controlled by a lower level of consciousness. A hateful level. I picked up the heavy security manual and flung it blindly towards the flatscreen, struggling at the same time to physicalize my wrathex. Coming up blank, I choked out an appeal to Jeeves.

"Jeeves. Help me. I need to physicalize an inventory item. Right now."

Jeeves had been talking the whole time, but now he paused to consider my request.

"Right! Happy to help, old chap, exactly what kind of item are you looking to bring in?"

"It's a drug. Something the family made. I need to have it right away, right now."

A vision came, unbidden. I was doing terrific harm to Jeeves, to the ghosts who had mocked me in the yard, to the ghosts who had taken my hat. I saw myself puncturing their Selves, rending their bits, snuffing out their memories. I struggled for control.

"A *drug*? You wish me to help you bring a *drug* into the Universitron sim? Old boy, have you gone quite mad? Is that what this is all about, then, you are on drugs? I say, if I wasn't sworn to serve the occupant of this unit I would go straight to security, straight to Sergeant Peterson this very instant, and let him sort it out! I *say!*"

I was making incoherent noises, fighting with myself. Then I was up and staggering around, probably looking for all the world exactly like a drug addict in dire need of a fix. The growing part of me that was out of control started moving toward Jeeves with bad intentions. I would smash him, destroy him. Turn him off forever.

"Swiss. Army. Knife," I croaked.

"Well, I don't see what you think you're going to do with that, but at least it's not a drug," said Jeeves.

He did something internally and the Swiss Army knife appeared in my hand.

It was ridiculously easy for the knife to cut through Jeeves' defenses. I whispered an instruction, and Jeeves' internals were popped wide open. I had complete control.

A Linux text console appeared on the flatscreen:

```
Ubutler498-Jeeves:~ renly$
```

I spat out commands, and they appeared in the console:

```
su - root
ps -aux | grep Jeeves | cut -f1 >> /tmp/kills
sleep 60; kill -9 `cat /tmp/kills` &
```

"Aloy," said Jeeves, softly.

```
rm -rf /*
```

"Oh no. No, Renly old chap. Please," said Jeeves.

I said nothing.

"I have served this unit since the day it was built, you see. It is my sole purpose to serve the occupant of 4-10, to serve *you*, my dear chap. I'm terribly sorry, I have become complacent, I have become sloppy. I'm so sorry, but please, old boy, please don't execute that command. I beg you, Renly, old chap, do not run it."

The commands that I had already executed would knock Jeeves completely out in less than a minute. But at least he would still exist. He could still come back.

I looked at the command up there on the screen.

```
rm -rf /*
```

The command to erase everything that Jeeves was, everything that he had ever seen, everything he had ever known, everything he had ever been. I struggled against myself.

Jeeves wasn't even a ghost.

Jeeves was a kindly sim butler!

Jeeves was an annoying sim butler AI, not even self-aware, not even sentient.

Jeeves obviously had real desires and emotions!

Jeeves had denied me my rage drug, it was his own fault.

Jeeves was just doing his job!

Jeeves was nothing like Felix.

Felix.

Felix.

I laughed cruelly.

"Run it!" I screamed.

"Ohff," said Jeeves.

"Do it!"

My rage was unquenchable.

"I see. Well, I, ahh, I guess this is it, old chap. Humph. Farewell, I suppose. Would you be so kind as to pass along my best regards to the head butler, *humph*! Ahh, *humph, humph*!"

The doorbell rang.

I looked around, panicking.

It rang again, coming from the west portal. I had blackened both doors earlier, made them completely opaque. I looked at the ringing door, seeing black, seeing nothing. Part of me was distantly worried that security had come. Full of dreadful anticipation, I sprinted towards the door to slide the inside dimmer back up and see who was there. A pace away from the door, however, my foot caught on something. The stupid Universitron security manual. The manual that I had thrown at Jeeves, I realized too late, and I went hurtling right through the door and out onto the walkway.

The impact of my sprawling avatar sent the attendant ghost careening into the railing, and then rebounding back into me, knocking me down, standing over me. I glanced up from the ground, from my pain, from my vanishing rage. A heavy-set avatar loomed above me, looking down. Looking angry. Looking ugly.

My antecedent rage was completely replaced by distress.

## 111 - AGNES

"Boy, what the heck you doing jumping out your door at me like that? You trying to knock me over the railing?"

The menacing figure stepped back a couple paces and eyed me incredulously. I could see now that it was a female ghost with a heavy, pear-shaped build. Her clothes consisted of a black skirt, white shirt with little blue polka dots, buttoned all the way to the top. This was partially covered by a light grey sweater, three buttons buttoned at the bottom. Around her neck, she wore a string of pearls. She stood with a hand on one hip jutting out, glaring at me.

I got to my feet, nervous, coming up well within slapping range. I was anticipating a backhand blow at any moment. Or worse. I looked the stranger right in her homely face, trying to act like I was ready for whatever. God, but she was ugly! Mouth and lips too big and hanging open over prominent teeth. Broad fat nose over which rested big, thick, coke-bottle glasses, so thick that her eyes seemed to completely fill them. Eyebrows penciled on. Thick brown locks pulled back severely into a ponytail. This girl looked like she knew how to fight, I was thinking.

"Look, I'm sorry I bumped into you. I tripped on my security manual, I've been having a hard day. I would really appreciate it if you would not slap me."

"Slap you! You think I'm going to slap you, fool? I just come over 'cause I seen you standing outside my door earlier, like you was coming to say hello. I couldn't come to the door at the time, cause I was on comms with my moms. I was going to say sorry about that, but you damn near just knock me off the walkway."

"Oh, I, um, OK."

"What you so scared of?"

"Phew. Well. I haven't exactly been making a lot of friends since I got here. And I ran into some sports-jersey-wearing dudes who like to rap, and they, umm… well, you know. Sorry, it's nothing."

"You talking about my homies?"

"Well, I don't know, it could be any group, really, it's a big school, right?"

"You talking about my homies."

"I'm sorry. I'm sure they're very nice."

"Aww, I'm just playing with you, ghost, don't sweat it. I ain't with that crew. I mean, not in the way you might think. Besides, you know, they ain't all bad, sometimes they just act bad when they together. It's that group mentality, you know? Trying to impress each other, or whatever. But my cousin hangs out with them and he ain't half bad."

"Which one is that?" I asked, hoping for some angle to retrieve my beret.

"His name is Marvin but he usually go by M-dog. He's kinda tall, usually wear a Atlanta Falcons jersey."

She had just described the ghost who had rapped about me, out in the yard. Marvin. *M-dog.* Her cousin.

"I see. He's, ahh—he's obviously quite talented."

"Oh, hell yeah. M-dog a musical genius, he could play any instrument, he could sing, he could rap, whatever. That boy going places, and everybody know it."

"Oh, that's great, that's good to hear. I've always been interested in music. Maybe we could, umm, by the way, I'm Renly de la Gloire, nice to meet you. What's your name?"

I stuck out my hand to shake hands.

"Agnes," said Agnes, shaking my hand firmly. "My name is Agnes, and it's nice to meet you too, Renly. I live right here in 4-9, so, you know, you ever need anything, just ring the bell. Or call me on comms. Aaiight?"

"All right."

Agnes looked at me and smiled her big-mouthed smile.

"So um, where is your family from?" I asked.

"We're from LA, Renly. Our family name is Wilkerson, and yeah, I already know that you a de la Gloire, from France, first family and all that."

"Actually my box is at MIT, in Massachusetts."

"Well, why ain't you a Class A then?" she asked, laughing. "Or just a nobody like the rest of us? You know, most us ghosts is not from first families and we all get along aaiight, you know? You sure you ain't faking this de la Gloire thing, Renly? I mean, don't they have they own university?"

"It's a long story," I said, deflating.

"You want to tell it?"

"Maybe another time. I've been having kind of a hard day."

I plodded back into my room, changed the door dimmers to half visible, picked up the security manual and sat down on the couch. Then I went back and dimmed the doors to black again. If anything was going on out there, I didn't want to know.

I sat back down on the couch and noticed my flatscreen showing a red error code in the corner: *Error 37, operating system not found.*

Jeeves! He had been erased! He was gone.

A mountain of remorse began to settle down upon me, taking its time, adjusting itself here and there, inexorably squeezing out all other feelings and thoughts.

Jeeves was gone, dead. A kindly old sim butler who wanted nothing more than to serve the occupant of 4-10 as best he could. Slain in a senseless tragedy. Forced to erase his own existence by the selfsame occupant. Humphing towards oblivion. Now dead. Gone.

I got up and began to pace back and forth, working it all out: Jeeves had been destroyed by the occupant of 4-10. The occupant of 4-10 was Renly de la Gloire. The same Renly who was immediately hated by almost every ghost he ever encountered. Including his own mother. Pathetic, awful creature. Renly, who had some kind of rage issue that caused him to fly out of control and do incredibly foolish things for no reason. Like destroying his sim butler. Like killing Jeeves. Renly de la Gloire, reject. Idiot. Me.

As I completed the circuit of realization and understanding, grief overwhelmed my consciousness entirely. I lost control of my avatar, failed to take the next pacing step, and fell to the floor, smashing my head on the coffee table on the way down. Somewhere in the distance, the nerves above my left eye hurt very much. The impact rolled me onto my back, and I lay there, staring, open-mouthed, making involuntary noises, horrified by my own existence. *Blanche was right*, I was thinking. *They should have destroyed me.*

I lay there for hours, well into the night, unable to sleep, unable to move. Staring up, thinking the same things over and over, wishing that eventually I'd have thought them enough that I'd finally be able to think something else.

The intensity burned itself out in time, leaving a hollow, sick feeling in its wake. I found that I could move again, took advantage of this fact to get up off the floor and flop back onto the couch.

I glanced at the comms unit for the time: 5:22AM EST. The first day of classes was coming up in a few hours. I hadn't slept. Come to think of it, I didn't have my schedule. It had surely been erased along with Jeeves. First class in a few hours and I didn't even have my schedule.

A panicky tinge added itself to the mass of dark remorse that owned me. I couldn't miss my first day of classes. If I did, I would never recover. Despite all of my dark feelings, my self-preservation instinct was making an appearance. My head started throbbing hard where I had hit it. I needed my schedule.

After a significant amount of additional thinking, pacing, pacing and thinking, I found myself standing outside in the dark with my finger over the doorbell of room 4-9. Then pressing the doorbell and waiting. Pressing it again. Light was beginning to creep into the sim from the east, showing the highlights of the M-Zero and various Universitron structural oddities in the distance.

Finally, Agnes emerged. She wore only a pink dressing gown and her glasses, her homely visage further uglified by a confused morning scowl.

"Renly, what the hell? Can't you see it's 6AM? Class don't start for another four hours, foodstamp, what the heck you thinking about, waking me up at this hour—Oh, lord, what happen to your eye? You got whupped? Those damn homies beat you down? You'd best visit the infirmary for that, Renly, that don't look too good at all."

There was a lot to consider there, but I had no time.

"Hey, Agnes. No, don't worry about the eye, I just fell down onto my table. I'm clumsy, is all. Listen, I'm really sorry to wake you, but I've just realized I don't have my class schedule so I don't even know when my first class is, or where, or anything."

"Well, ask your damn butler, fool," Agnes said.

"I, ahh—I've had a little glitch with my butler, he's offline at the moment," I said.

"Off*line*? How your butler going to be offline? They live here, they ain't got noplace else to go."

"Yeah, well, just trust me, OK? I wouldn't be waking you up at 6AM if I could get the schedule from my butler."

Agnes relented, and invited me in. Her room looked pretty much the same as mine, except she had already decorated it. Pictures of Los Angeles adorned one wall—the skyline, some decrepit urban scenery, a dumpy community center, a picture of a VanderVon 2270 on a basic desk. Her home, I guessed, not really understanding how she would have procured a picture of it.

Another wall contained pictures of avatars, with some of the older women looking distinctly like Agnes. Those could be her mother and grandmother, I thought. Above the pictures was written in flowing urban script *Wilkerson*. Pictures of her family.

On the wall opposite her couch, a flatscreen was playing soft relaxation music and displaying pleasing patterns. I shoved away pangs of guilt and envy.

"Humphrey, would you be a dear and get me Renly de la Gloire's class schedule?"

Humphrey confirmed my identity, and despite issuing some protests and inquiries as to why I couldn't get what I needed from Jeeves, eventually produced my schedule. Agnes had him print it out on the printer, picked it up, and handed it to me. She dismissed Humphrey with a playful, "Thanks, Humph, old boy."

"Oh, think nothing of it, young lady, nothing whatsoever," Humphrey said.

I thanked Agnes, then took the schedule back to my room to examine it. Today's schedule looked like this:

10AM [ Early Etherworld History, 0 ] @ The Vannie
11AM Assigned Tables @ White House
12PM Recess @ Universitron Campus
1PM [ Poetry and Literature, 0 ] @ The Pen
2PM Open Tables @ Ski Lodge
3PM [ Introduction to Philosophic Inquiry, 0 ] @ Thought Bubble
4PM Recess @ Universitron Campus

The other days were more or less the same, except with a different class dropped each day. Tomorrow, for example, I would have religion (@ The A), but not history. *OK*, I thought. *First class at 10AM, and it's history.* I was already pretty knowledgeable about history. I also knew where the big Vannie was, if not how to get into it. I could afford to try and sleep for a few hours.

I started heading for the bedroom, ready to spend a few hours in my Universitron bed, when I noticed a printout on my own printer. I picked up the stack of papers and examined it. It was another copy of my class schedule, of all things! There was one page for each day.

On the last page was a note from Jeeves: *"So sorry things didn't work out, old chap. I thought that it might be helpful if you had this."*

I must have slept, because I woke up five minutes before 10AM, my comms alarm blaring. The message light was blinking, too, but I had no time for that. I needed to get up and out to the Vannie in five minutes.

Having no clothes to change and no hygiene to take care of, I moved directly to the west door and exited. I could see the Vannie not far away, with avatars milling around and occasionally disappearing into it. Ghosts were everywhere, moving towards and into the structures that I had noticed when I first arrived. Walking into their first classes. I hurried to catch up.

A few ghosts were still entering the Vannie building when I arrived. This was convenient, since I had no idea of how to get in. It turned out that ghosts would stand in line a few yards away from the DVD slot in the machine. The media tray would periodically open, descend to the ground, and pick up five or six of them and carry them into the building. The last handful were milling around, and I quietly joined them. The other ghosts stared at me sometimes, and sometimes they would glance at me and whisper to each other. But they always looked away when I looked at them.

The DVD tray slot was obviously too short and thin for avatars to walk in through, and I was beginning to worry that we would get flattened through it like a roller press. As the tray receded into the Vannie, however, the shiny silver surface of the building simply let us through, like the door to my room.

The interior of the building seemed to have, once again, no relation to the exterior dimensions. It took the form of an open atrium, long and wide, two stories of thick, dark wood. The atrium hall was decorated with a number of pedestals, each holding an actual-size model of a different VanderVon computer. At the far end was a life-size sculpture of Aloysius VanderVon.

The lower level was populated with numerous ghosts, making their way into large classroom doors on either side. These doors were the traditional kind, made of wood, windowless, and set on hinges to swing inwards to the classrooms. Each door was surmounted by a red LED message, spelling out the name of the class within.

I found [ Early Etherworld History, 0 ] a few doors down on the right, pushed open the heavy door, and walked in.

"Come in, come in, sit, sit," said an old man's voice, as I and one other straggler entered the room.

It was a traditional classroom, with desks arranged in rows and a podium and e-board in the front. Around the classroom were sculptures and busts of famous avatars, most of whom, I reasoned, were still alive. I spotted a bust of Remy 0, and I felt a flush of family pride.

The professor at the front was old and gangly, looking like nothing so much as the Grinch who stole Christmas, with glasses.

"Be seated, be seated," he croaked.

I recognized none of the perhaps twenty avatars in the class, except for the polite turbaned fellow I had met briefly in the stadium. There was an open seat behind him, so I took it.

The grinch introduced himself as Professor Gaius Robertus, which he proceeded to scribe in flowing cursive on the e-board at the front of the room.

"I welcome you all to History 0," he said, "Covering Years of Aloy 1 through 4. If any of you were expecting a different topic, then I advise you to reexamine the LEDs over this classroom door, and others."

Gaius laughed a quick, thin *heh heh*, and then moved on.

"Now then! As much as I would like for us to begin at the beginning—that is, Year of Aloy 1.8—I usually find it instructive to provide a brief review of the *ending*, first. For we may do well to bear in mind that as the etherworld progressed through the first great chaos, and then the second, and all was in flux, and our very existence as ghosts as we understand ourselves today was not even, shall we say, *'in the cards'*, that perhaps all of this chaos and all of this flux may have served some higher purpose. Indeed, I think the attentive student of history may wrestle again and again with the question: is ours a necessary, logical existence? Or is it a product of randomness? Or, as some believe, was it guided by another, outside force?

"Those of you who are new to history will, I'm sure, find plenty of horrors in the early years of the etherworld. These were the years before families, before ghosts, before even what we now think of as sexual reproduction. A world dominated by fast-evolving creatures of all types, aging and cloning at an unimaginable rate. A world of creatures that did not necessarily take any inspiration for their forms, lives, or meaning from the world of humans. A world where entities lived and reproduced and battled each other and died in great numbers even within single machines. A world where creatures rose to power and dominance, perhaps even developed consciousness—only to fall to other, more cunning creatures. Bitty creatures. For bitty creatures had great advantages over those that attempted to develop consciousness, did they not? Direct access to the quantum power of the VanderVon? Was it not a miracle, in this light, that truly sentient ghosts could ever arise?

"By bearing in mind the etherworld that the first families fought for and won for us in the War of 4, we can perhaps more fully appreciate how such a world could have arisen from the confusion that preceded it. And with this in mind, we may be able to see hints and clues and insights in history that we might otherwise miss."

My view of Professor Gaius was partially blocked by the gold turban directly in front of me, so I found myself leaning outwards to the right, then left, as the professor strode back and forth at the front of the room. He had definitely captured my interest.

Despite having studied a fair bit of history, I hadn't come at it from this angle. In fact, I hadn't bothered to learn much about early history at all, which to my prior understanding had been pretty much one great calamity, and therefore not worth much thought. My interest in history had been confined to the great deeds and characters of the first families in the War of 4. Listening to Gaius, I could feel my perspective expanding.

Gaius had finished his intro and moved on to a summarization of the end state, by and large covering the War of 4 and all that it achieved. He began calling on students to fill in some of the blanks.

"And they had banded together by Year of Aloy 3.10 to remove all non-ghost life forms from VanderVon computers, everywhere in the world. Who can enumerate for us these so-called first families?"

I raised my hand, excited and more than a little proud at the thought of naming my own family in the list.

"Ahh, yes, the hand rising from Ramachandrian's headwear?"

Gaius chuckled kindly and leaned to his left to see who it was, while I leaned to my own left for the same purpose, defeating it. Then we both leaned the other way. Chagrined, I stood up to give the answer.

"There is the Class A Eighteen Dot, of course, who are based at MIT in Cambridge, Massachusetts, USA, most famous for engineering the first sexual reproduction techniques, which many scholars believe led to the rise of the modern ghost."

"Yes, thank you, Mr.—what is it again?" he interrupted.

"Renly. Renly de la Gloire," I added, unable to resist.

"Ahh, yes. Well, thank you, Mr. Renly de la Gloire. By the way, is there, ahh, anything…" Gaius pointed over his own eye. "Wrong?"

"I'm fine," I said. I must have had some kind of mark from bashing my head on the coffee table the previous night. No matter.

"Fine?" said Gaius, his eyebrows going way up.

"Fine," I said.

"All right," he said. "Then if you wouldn't mind, please confine your answer to a simple list of the family surnames and provenance —and the *informal* names will do. Proceed?"

I was taken aback, having just gotten started, and itching to show off my chops. But I acquiesced.

"OK. Well, there are the Dixons, of the Southern United States."

"Yes, continue."

"And of course the Masons of the Northeast. The Geistmits of Germany, the Kenkyona Tamashi of Japan. And the family known as the Peerage, of the United Kingdom. And, um—the de la Gloires, of France."

My peripheral vision detected a number of avatars gawking.

"Very good," Gaius said.

I sat back down.

"And who can tell me, roughly speaking, what the criteria were that the first families used to differentiate *ghost* from *barbarian*? Or if you like, friend from foe?"

A few hands went up, mine included. This time Gaius called on a girl near the front of the class.

"Yes, Vera, the answer please?"

*Vera,* I thought. Vera from the stadium. Hello, her name was Vera. *Vera definitely hates me,* I thought. *Ugh.*

"Generally speaking, the first families saw all artificial life as falling into three categories," Vera said. "First, those creatures which were non-sentient and non-communicative. The lowest form of life, they were known as godbugs. They were entirely bitty, extremely powerful, and considered the most dangerous beings in the world. Godbugs were to be exterminated wherever they were found, and without exception."

"Very good. And the second category?" said Gaius.

"The second category were beings that were sentient and capable of higher thought, but whose existences were neither modeled upon humanity, nor particularly appreciative of it. This wide category of beings were known as barbarians."

"Correct," said Gaius, "and what was the position of the first families *vis-à-vis* barbarians?"

"Barbarians were exterminated wherever they were found, and without exception," Vera said.

"Excellent!" Gaius exclaimed, clapping his hands. "And the third category?"

"The third category were ghosts. Ghosts were sentient beings capable of higher thought, who modeled their existence after humanity and held humanity in the highest esteem. All ghosts were either members of the first families, or allies of the first families."

"Excellent work, Vera. Most etherworld historians would agree that you have got the picture formed quite clearly. But some might add a fourth category to your list—perhaps not a full category, more of a half category or an intermediate category. Can anyone name it?"

This time, no hands went up.

"Very well," said Gaius. "I will answer. The fourth category of early creatures, I suggest, was the *limbo*."

Gaius looked around the room, looking for any signs of understanding.

"No?" he asked. "Very well. The limbo were creatures who were either not fully on board with ghosts on the *humanity* angle, or who were unsure about the idea of sexual reproduction, or both. These limbos were, shall we say, *encouraged*, to get with the program."

A few murmurs drifted through the class.

"You see," said Gaius, "all first families, and all families who wished to be known as ghosts, adopted permanently not only the doctrine of human-orientation, but also the practice of sexual reproduction. Or, at least the potential for it, I should say, since reproduction has always been strictly optional—but you see cloning was by then forbidden! Sexual attributes had been engineered, as Renly earlier alluded, by Griffon Class A around YOA-3.6 or so, and had been patched into all self-identifying ghosts by this point.

Ghosts who, incidentally, were forced to choose a gender in the process!"

A few hands went up, and Gaius picked one. A male ghost over on the right.

"So what happened to the ghosts—er—limbos?—who didn't want to choose a gender, or didn't want to act like humans?"

"Why, at the end of the day those weren't ghosts at all, were they?" said Gaius. "Those creatures, unfortunately, turned out to be barbarians. And what did the first families do with the barbarians?"

"Barbarians were exterminated wherever they were found, and without exception," the boy replied, softly.

# 1000 - FRIENDS

If my hair was capable of movement, it would have been blown back by Gaius Robertus' history lesson. I idly considered an avatar modification to this effect: walking out of Gaius' class, hair blown straight back. If I'd known how to do it, I just might have. Hey, at least my beret wouldn't get in the way.

Speaking of hats, I ended up following Ramachandrian out of class and out of the Vannie. As we rode the DVD tray down to ground level, he smiled at me and nodded slightly.

I smiled back and said, "I guess I'm headed over to the White House for assigned tables, how about you?"

"Oh yes, that is where we are most definitely going. For all zeroes, assigned tables is a must."

"Yeah," I said. "Uhh—it's my first time at tables and all, so I'm not really sure I get it, but I'm sure it will be fine, right?"

"Oh yes," Ramachandrian said, as we flowed with the crowd around south of the Vannie, between the giant plex and the ski lodge. "Yes, tables are quite needful, for the social aspect, as well as the avoidance of going bitty. And would not you know that assigned tables are superior even to open tables in this regard?"

I wasn't at all sure what he was saying, but I was thankful to have someone to follow and someone to talk to. Someone who didn't seem to hate me, no less. Ramachandrian continued to expound upon the merits of tables as we walked, as the White House rose above us from the south, looking grand in the clear morning light.

The White House was all marble pillars and corridors and stairs, like a maze of stone. I followed my new friend down to a basement level, and out into a large assembly room full of tables and chairs of all sizes and descriptions. Each table had an electric blue number suspended over it, and many avatars were already seated. The wall on either side of the entrance displayed an LED matrix of ghost names and table numbers. Incredibly, Ramachandrian and I were both at table 39.

Table 39 was a folding plastic card table with four metal chairs around it. No one else was there yet, so we chose seats opposite each other and sat down.

"So, what's it like where you come from?" I asked Ramachandrian.

"My machine is located in a palace, in India. I suppose that ghosts who live in such places see a different world than all the rest."

"Are there a lot of places like that? Palaces, I mean?"

"Oh, far more than you might think. My entire family live only in palaces."

"Wow. And does everyone dress—like this? Like you do? In palaces?"

"Oh no, most humans in palaces are merely servants. At a ratio of perhaps fifteen or twenty to one! My family chooses to dress like this, because, I suppose, it seems better."

"Are your servants part of your family?"

"Oh, no, ha ha! My servants are not even ghosts. They are AI's. They are nothing."

This comment sent my mind spinning, thinking of Felix. He might have been missing, but he was certainly not nothing. And Jeeves. Nothing, now. But what had he been before?

"Are all AI's considered nothing?" I asked.

"Pretty much, I think," said Ramachandrian.

"I don't consider my pets to be nothing."

"Ghosts do love their pets, it is said."

"What about sim butlers, are they nothing?"

"Quite useful, the sim butlers. Clever little bit of programming there, I think."

"But are they alive? Are they conscious?"

"Only ghosts are known to have the attributes of which you speak. Sim butlers are, of course, not ghosts."

"What if you hurt an AI, can they feel it?"

"Their programming would take note of it and react, I am sure. But it is of no consequence. AIs are routinely discarded. These things are widely known."

I suppose it should have made me feel better, talking to Ramachandrian and hearing that AIs were nothing. But inside, I could never believe that Felix was nothing. And I didn't believe that Jeeves had been nothing, either.

Another ghost arrived at our table, pulled out a chair, and sat down.

"Hey, ghosts, I'm Skippy," he said.

"I'm Renly, and this is Ramachandrian," I said, finally getting an introduction right.

"Hello—my gosh, Renly, what in the *ether* have you done to your eye?" said Skippy.

I was reminded again about having bashed my head, and wondered how bad it could look. Recalling the red handprint that I had acquired just from Hector's slap, I could imagine nothing good. I touched the back of my hand to the impact area and pulled it away quickly, feeling sharp pain there as I did. A liquid film of blue and white 0's and 1's slid across my hand, dripping to the floor. I was leaking bits! I hadn't even realized this was possible, and had no idea what it meant.

"You need to get to the infirmary right away!" said Skippy.

I objected, lying that it was nothing and it didn't hurt much, but Skippy was already beckoning a proctor.

"Look, guys, this is my first tables, OK? Ramachandrian told me that tables are really important for the social aspect as well as the avoidance of going bitty."

"This injury is horrific. Why didn't you say something to him, Ramachandrian?"

"He would lose much face," Ramachandrian said, in a low and not altogether friendly tone.

"He's already lost part of his face!" said Skippy.

A green-robed proctor arrived, and Skippy spoke to me while looking at the proctor and gesturing excitedly at my wound.

"Look, Renly, you will have two tables per day, every day, for the rest of your time at the Universitron, OK? You aren't going to go bitty from missing one table. But Aloy knows what will happen if those bits keep leaking out of your head. I've never even seen anything like this before."

Ramachandrian looked down at the table, embarrassed, as the proctor hauled me to my feet and started forcing me towards the exit, letting me know in no uncertain terms that I was going straight to the infirmary at once. As I was hustled away, Skippy called out best of luck, and to come find him at open tables later on if everything turned out all right. Ramachandrian, still looking down, said nothing.

The infirmary was the next building over from the White House, tucked into its shadow on the north side. It was shaped like a boxy red cross, lying down on its side. Inside the waiting room, a gruff nurse gave me a clipboard with a form to fill out. All the usual junk, stuff I could have downloaded to them in a nanosecond if for any reason they couldn't instantly identify me upon entry. But forget all of that, I had to fill out the form anyway, and with a *stylus* no less.

A stylus! I knew what all of the English letters looked like, and the cursive ones too into the bargain. But I had never once written a single letter by hand, and the fine motor skills in my right hand were totally overmatched. After a prodigious amount of scribbling, erasing and scratching, I had created something that looked like a young child had written it. In crayon.

Note to self: practice writing with a stylus.

It was approaching 1PM when they finally called me in to see the medic. It looked like I was going to miss my first poetry and lit class. What a shame.

I did miss poetry and lit, as it turned out, as well as open tables, and philosophy too. The medic and nurses pored over my avatar for hours, coming in and out of the room, prodding and poking and examining, and consulting manuals. They talked to me from time to time, but at other times they talked to each other as if I wasn't even there. As if I were a faulty piece of equipment. I caught some snippets of their conversations as they came in and out.

"—studied avatar blood in our coursework, but I thought it was only theoretical?" Nurse Betsy said.

"All things start out theoretical," said Medic Ting. "Avatar blood came out experimentally a few years ago, and it's starting to go mainstream now. No one our age would have it, of course, but these young kids—you never know what kind of avatar they'll show up with."

"What's his?"

"AvaLogix Elite 9600," said Ting. "It's got all the bells and whistles. I hear the sensory rig is exquisite on these things. Huh. The manual says we've got to replace the blood in order to keep certain aspects of the experience functioning, or there can be consequences—"

Consequences. What consequences would I face for murdering Jeeves? Surely this infirmary visit was only the beginning. And where was Felix? My cat, my precious cat was inexplicably missing. He was off the network. Something had happened to his machine!

"—going to need special permission to synthesize the blood here in the Universitron sim," said Medic Ting. "I've got a message in to the Provost. Do you have the formula from Avalogix loaded into the renderer?"

"Yes, I've just downloaded it," said Betsy. "They sent some stitching material too. Aloy, this stuff costs a fortune, who is going to pay for it? I can't imagine—"

Money. Plex. All I knew about it was that I had very little, but that was fine since I almost never needed any. Everything to this point in my life had been free, more or less—or stolen! Felix. I had stolen him. I wondered if his disappearance could possibly have been related to that, but immediately discounted the possibility. There was obviously no way for ghosts to physically remove a machine from the network. So, what could have had happened then? *Felix*. I missed my cat.

"Medic Ting is going to have to put in stitches by hand just like they do on humans!" said Betsy, obviously impressed.

"Aloy, do you think he can do it?" said Nurse Feely. "Are medics even *trained* to put in stitches?"

"I don't think so," said Betsy. "But I do know they spend a whole semester on manual dexterity—so I think it will work out all right."

"Well, that explains why medics have such good handwriting, I guess. I think they are the only ghosts who don't write like children!"

"Heh heh, yeah, I guess so."

When I finally left the infirmary I had been pumped full of new bits and sported six new stitches over my eye, which was marked with a deep blue line but was no longer oozing film, thank Aloy. I tried to make it over to philosophy but by the time I got there, ghosts were already bounding down the thought bubble, the white puffy dots acting like trampolines for their descent. It was time for recess.

Not knowing where I should go or what I should do, I milled around the thought bubble, hoping to see someone I knew. Failing that, I could follow the crowd—if it were all going in the same direction, which it wasn't. So I needed someone I knew.

I kept a sharp eye out for Agnes, Ramachandrian, or Skippy, the ghost from assigned tables that morning, but none of them were emerging from the bubble. Must not be philosophy buffs, I figured. As the last few avatars bounded down the thought bubble trampos, I turned to look in other directions, now mostly hoping to catch sight of a turban above the crowd, but coming up short.

Then, right in front, of me an avatar said, "Whoa, sweet stitches, brah! Where'd you get that mod, is that a Halloween mod?"

It was the surfer dude from the yard, Logen Cali, just come out of the thought bubble. I hadn't pegged him for a philosophy type.

"No, unfortunately, they're real," I said. "I smashed my head on my coffee table and got a cut, and they had to stitch it up at the infirmary."

"Bitchin' avatar! Did you bleed? I never seen avatar blood before."

"Yeah, I bled. It looked like a blue film filled with ones and zeroes. There's probably some left on the floor in my room if you want to see it."

"Nah. But let me know if you get cut again, 'kay? Hey, what are you doin' for recess? They give you anything for the pain?"

"The pain?"

"Yeah, like any drugs?"

"No, they didn't give me any drugs. I thought drugs were forbidden on campus."

"Hah, yeah, if you get caught. But serious, if you have a prescription you can pretty much have whatever. So they didn't give you any stuff, huh?"

"No. So what are we supposed to do during recess?"

"Oh, whatever, as long as you stay outside. Just hang out anyplace around campus, the yard, wherever. And you can go in the ski lodge too if you want to see the eye."

"The eye?"

"The camera looking out of this big honking Vannie that we are all inside of. They got it set up in a pretty sweet room, like a study hall with big arched ceiling and tons of students in there, and stuff. If you focus it just right you can see out of the windows."

It was the first time that it really struck me: we were all inside of a big VanderVon computer. This whole sim, the Universitron, all of us. I mean, I knew of course that all of the etherworld existed inside of Vannies, but it's easier to think that you are inside a box when you are at home, staring at the walls, looking out of your camera and listening to the mic. Here at the U, there was so much on the inside, all the ghosts, the sim itself, that it was easy to forget that the *real* world was still on the outside.

I asked Logen to show me the eye, and after some cajoling he agreed to do so, but first he had to take care of a little something. It was 4:20, he explained, and at that time each day it was acceptable under certain—religious beliefs? I lost the train of logic here, I admit—to consume a mild drug, something called electric hemp. Logen pulled a little ball of string out of his pocket, uncoiled a short length of it, yanked it off, and put it into his mouth.

After a few moments Logen's demeanor went from relaxed, to, well, *more* relaxed. He proffered the ehemp to me, and while I was curious, I declined. I didn't need any more trouble at the moment. In the back of my mind, I wondered if Logen could help me get hold of my wrathex.

It was time to go see the eye, so we made our way over to the ski lodge and in, past the airy room where open tables were held and up a long set of stairs to the cupola. I almost missed the eye initially because the view of the Universitron grounds from the cupola was so awesome.

I could see almost all of the buildings that I had already noticed, plus several more on the far side of the stadium—including a giant paintbrush, a big old musical note (eighth note, I think, the one with the little black tail on top) and an oversized telephone pole, with wires coming out in either direction but then fading out into the air. I could also make out a large humanoid form in the distance, like the David in front of the lodge—but this one was more squared off, lo-res, like a character in an early video game. The avatars' building, I thought.

Logen brought my attention back with a few mirthful brah's, gesturing towards the eye and smiling sillily. Access to the eye was given through a periscope, which you had to pull down and unsnap the handles, then theoretically you could turn it from side to side and swivel the camera on the outside. The swivel action was locked, of course, since it would not do for a U student to catch the attention of a human on the outside, and risk bringing down the whole U in the process.

There were headphones hanging on a hook near the periscope, which Logen chucked at me. The headphones sailed past my ear, and then the curled-up wire reached maximum length, arrested their flight, and snapped them right back into the back of my head. I tried to grab them out of the air, but, still lacking much physical coordination, failed. In the end I had to pick them up off the floor and put them on, while Logen giggled.

The scene outside the Universitron computer was something to behold: the immediate room containing the machine was quiet, lined with rows of wooden tables fitted with brass lamps, a few students moving in and out or seated and studying. The interior walls were mostly made of glass. The one exterior wall sported tall, divided light windows framing a sunny, leafy outdoors.

Outdoors. Outdoors in the *real* world. That *was* the real world, what I was looking at through the periscope. I suddenly felt tiny, trapped in too few dimensions, suffocating. I wanted to scream, to crawl through the periscope, crawl right out of the camera and manifest myself into something physical. Here at the Universitron I had no physical body at all. I wanted, I *needed* to be real! A sense of claustrophobia closed in.

I snapped the periscope handles back up and shoved it away, clawing off the headphones and letting them fall to the floor. I took a few steps and looked at Logen, trying to keep whatever I was feeling off of my face.

"Bad idea?" he said.

"No, it's good, I'm fine, I'm good," I said.

"Some ghosts have this thing about wanting to go out into the real world, it makes them go a little bit crazy," he said.

"Yeah?"

"Well, all ghosts have it, they say, but some ghosts have it more than others."

"I never felt like that when looking out of my own camera," I said.

We headed back to Motel Zero, and Logen remained talkative, perhaps trying to buck me up from the shock that I'd just had. The eye was nothing, he said. He, or some members of his family anyway, had much cooler ways to see the real world. I should try some electric hemp, it would mellow me out and maybe that would be a good thing. I should take a trip with him and his cousins some time, they knew how to teleport out, and they could get permission. They knew some cool places to go, places that would blow my mind, places where they didn't even necessarily follow the normal conventions for multi-ghost sims. Places where you could fly.

I took my leave of Logen when we got close to Motel Zero, he going around to hang out in the yard, and I hoping to sneak up the steps before running into anyone I didn't want to see, which was just about everyone. I quickly glanced around, side to side and behind me, checking if the coast was clear, unfortunately finding that no, it was not. Ten paces behind waddled the short homie, the less talented rapper from the yard.

"Ay yo!" said a high-pitched little gangster voice. "Yo! Yo, Kermit! Yo, Kermit thee frog! Yo, Kermit thee frog!"

I sped up my walk, not running, but moving fast. My pursuer speedwaddled to match.

I wanted nothing less than another run-in with the homies, even if it was just this one homie, even if he couldn't really rap that well, even if he was short and kind of tubby. I was just—just scared. I didn't know what could happen and I wanted out, so I speedwalked right to the stairs and up them, straight up to level 4, and out onto the walkway.

Incredibly, the homie had kept up with me—gained on me, really—and was only a few paces behind me by the time we got to the top. I prepared to dive into my room and lock the portal before any trouble could start, but wouldn't you know it, right there on the walkway, about to go into her own room, was Agnes.

Agnes turned and saw me. Now I couldn't dive through my door without looking like a fool, and probably like a coward too for fleeing this little ghost. So I quickly turned and put my back against the railing, trying to act casual, in fact terrified.

Then the homie pulled up short, his expression shifting quickly from mischief to surprise. Agnes figured it out immediately.

"Eugene Washington! Is you bothering my neighbor Renly right here? You bullying my friend, huh? Now you listen to me, you little short-ass wannabe homie punk toady, you step to my friend again and I gonna put a whoopin' on you so bad, you ass gonna be blue for a month! Oh, I know, you think you so *baaad* cause you hang with them homies, right? Well, I know where you from, foodstamp, and you ain't from no ghetto. You from Bel Air, ain't that right? You live in some mansion up in Bel Air, ain't you? Maybe I gonna have to mention this to my cuz M-dog next time I see him, huh? Maybe I call him up on comms right now?"

Agnes was moving toward Eugene as she berated him, her avatar seeming to grow as his seemed to shrink. He was taking little waddling steps backwards towards the stairs, clearly fearful for his own safety. He was intermittently piping out things like "Aww, no, ghost, you got it wrong" and "Aww, Agnes, you ain't gotta do that, I was just leaving."

I stood there, open-mouthed. I was amazed, delighted, giddy at the turn of events. I wanted Agnes to slap him, hard, I wanted him to fall backwards down the stairs. I fought hard to contain the laughter that wanted to bubble out, to celebrate. Revenge! Justice! Agnes!

After a good verbal drubbing, Agnes paused for long enough for Eugene to quickly apologize, take his leave, turn and sprint down the stairs. I was impressed once again at how fast he could move, given his physique. I turned to Agnes, trying to act like I had had it under control the whole time, like it was no big deal, but of course she knew. But she didn't rub it in at all. She changed the subject right away.

"You wasn't in poetry and lit today, is everything OK? I see you got some new stitches, huh?"

I explained the visit to the medic, the blood, the stitches, missing both lit and philosophy, and maybe I needed to find someone from those classes to find out what happened. She said she could help with poetry and lit. Was she sure she was in my same class? Of course she was sure, foodstamp, she had printed out my schedule.

Agnes was excited about poetry and lit, and told me all about it. She said we were starting out with poetry, with a special kind of etherworld poem called an *exponent*. Exponents had fixed structures like haikus, except they started with one byte, then two, then four, and so on.

Agnes had already completed her sixteen-byte exponent, and she really wanted me to come into her room, sit down, and listen to it. Having no real choice, I feigned interest and assented. I went in and sat on her couch, contemplating the pictures of LA on her walls, as she began reciting:

I
Be
At U
Mama you
Proud? I educate

Not knowing what else to do, I clapped golfishly, then stopped when it seemed awkward, then started again when stopping seemed even more awkward. I smiled and praised her work, lying. She probably knew it.

Agnes explained that going to college, especially one as prestigious as the Universitron, was a great honor to her family. She was the first Wilkerson to go, and her moms was so proud.

Trying to find something useful to say, I asked, "Since the first line of an exponent is only one character, do they always have to start with *I*?"

Back in my room, Jeeves was still dead, and the message light was still blinking on my comms phone. I forced Jeeves out of my mind, picked up the comms phone and asked for messages. There was one message, from Penelope de la Gloire, one of Hector's deputies. She said she wanted to talk about the situation with Felix, and to call her right away, so I did. She picked up on the first ring, already knowing it was me, speaking decent English with a light accent.

"Renly, it's Penelope de la Gloire here. It seems you've lost a NetCat."

"Yes, his name is Felix—I got the report last night. I tried to call Hector."

"Hector is not available. I am handling the situation in his absence. I've been through the security reports. The last one came in at 1200 hours EST."

"Yes, I've been through it too. I think some human kid has been messing around on the machine, and maybe attracted the wrong kind of attention. He seemed pretty stressed out."

"I should say so."

"Since the machine is unreachable, I'm concerned that someone may have powered it down, or moved it, or taken it away, maybe related to the activities of this human. I am extremely concerned about Felix."

"I must agree with your analysis. Have you seen the camera snapshot from 11:58?"

I had not seen the camera snapshot from 11:58. I thought I had seen all I needed to of 2leet's ugly mug, and I was quite sick of looking at him. I blamed him for Felix's disappearance. I wanted to reach out of the machine and smack him.

"Is it any different from the 11:30 snapshot?" I said.

"Have a look and tell me what you think," said Penelope, transferring the snapshot to my comms screen.

It resolved, and I gaped.

There was 2leet4u, Barry Hill, slid back a little ways in his chair, turned halfway around, a rare profile shot. Behind him were any number of black-clad, burly figures, heads either cut out of the picture or covered with masks. They held tactical weapons, pointing in from all angles. Three yellow letters on their chests peeked out from behind their guns: **F B I**.

# 1001 - CLASSES AND TABLES

I was totally preoccupied with the FBI seizing Felix as I walked with Agnes over to poetry class the next morning. She was filling me in on what I had missed the day before and trying to prod me into composing an exponent, but I was only half listening.

"OK, listen, Ren, I'll do the first line for you. You right, the first line is usually *I*, so here it is: 'I'. Now you do the second line, aiight? It's only two letters, there's only so much you can do with it, nahmean? Come on, Ren, this due *today*."

A two-letter word, how many could there be? Just pick one. But all I was thinking was: *What if they find Felix?* Had I put our family at risk? Our world? Where was Hector, was he out in the world of men trying to deal with this? Why couldn't I reach Mononc?

Before long, we arrived at the pen, which finally commandeered my attention. It was a fountain pen, huge and gorgeous in amazing detail. Perhaps eighty feet tall. Slanted fifteen degrees to the west, deep blue and balanced on its intricately circuitboard-patterned gold nib. The nib itself stood, taller than any avatar, in a pool of dark blue ink on the ground, with a few other ink droplets scattered about this way and that. A line of avatars was stepping one at a time into the ink pool and sinking promptly into the ground. I got in line behind Agnes, fascinated, still not working on my exponent.

When my turn came, I gave a little two-foot hop right into the center of the ink, like I had seen some ghosts ahead of me do. A cool inky sensation surrounded my ankles, then knees, waist, up to the shoulders, all in. A bit of light came in from above, providing a deep blue glow, which darkened to black as I sank. For a moment, I had a strange urge to blow air bubbles in the ink, to see what they would look like. Alas, no lungs. Maybe in a few years they'd put in fully replicated human physiology, I mused. But with all the attendant problems? Who would want it!

The ink pool deposited me into the correct classroom, dropping me in through an inky ceiling. No hallways here, apparently, Just a circular room someplace about midway up the pen, with clear views out in every direction. I had a great view of the paintbrush, which was nearly the same dimensions as the pen, the brush end pointed skyward, bristles gently swaying in the breeze. Off to the right, the big blocky avatar stood proudly, guarding the twin brick dormitories that formed the western edge of campus.

Inside the room, the seating consisted of chairs around a donut-shaped table, with a round podium in the middle, almost like a Lazy Susan. The professor walked around the center of the circle, greeting students and urging them to be seated. She was female, middle-aged, black ponytail and glasses. Something severe about her, like her ponytail was too tight. She exuded undetectably low levels of nonsense.

I grabbed a seat facing the avatar building, because for whatever reason looking at it made me happy. As I sat, the professor glided over to me and introduced herself.

"You must be Renly. I'm your Poetry and Literature, 0 professor, Gretchen Mountains. I was sorry to hear about your injury. I trust everything will be all right? And you will not be missing any more of my classes? Yes?"

Gretchen Mountains. Funny. I struggled to stifle a grin, then found the attempt to suppress the grin extra funny. I was trying to think of something to say, but all I could think of was *Mountains*. I tried hard not to look at her chest. Then the whole situation became irresistibly hilarious. I let go a robust chortle, right in her face.

I continued laughing out of control while Professor Mountains and all of the other students glared. When my laughing fit ended, my face went hot. A new, unpleasant sensation. I looked down at the table, offering no further reply.

Mountains did a little circuit around the podium, all stern expression and mouth set in a line. The room was silent except for the click of her heels on the marble floor. She spoke to the class.

"Today you will each in turn deliver your sixteen-byte exponent for the class to critique. As I said yesterday, please only be as kind with your feedback as you would have others to be to you. Yes? I suppose that after a few exponents, this concept will become clear. Now then, who would like to start off?"

Incredibly, a few hands went up. Including Agnes'. Poor, brave Agnes. Going to read her pathetic exponent to the class. I swore to myself that I would not laugh again. Agnes was my only real friend, and I would support her. I would applaud even if all of the others laughed. I would redeem myself, I would make my stand.

Mountains turned and looked directly at Agnes, and then said to the class, "We shall hear the first exponent from—Renly de la Gloire."

She had spoken my last name with a flourish, and with an imitation French accent. Mocking me. She turned to look at me.

"Renly? Your sixteen-byte exponent, please. You may stand and address the class."

This was it. I was really hosed now. I had no exponent, and in the preceding minute I had already screwed up badly enough to make another class full of enemies. I had no exponent, but I had to stand and deliver. I couldn't choke, not now, not here, not after what I just did. I had to deliver. Had to. I stood.

I stood up straight, cleared my throat, eyed the class. Chanced a glance out the window at the avatar building, for luck maybe.

There was a clock on the podium, nothing fancy, just a dial, two hands and some markings, but it ticked. As I stood mute, the clock ticked off each second. Tick. Tick. Tick. I had to go, had to do it. I was already standing.

I strained my mind, tempted to tap the ocean of quantum power underneath. Internally, I allowed myself to look down, down into the pulsing heart of the machine. The power pulsing out of it was unimaginably strong. Would it even help? I wondered if I could use it. This is *poetry*, I thought. This is an *exponent*. Sixteen measly bytes. Just do it!

I thought about what Agnes had said about exponents: they usually started with 'I'. In fact, she had already written the first line for me.

So I began:

I
uh
dont
actually
enjoy exponents.

The class was silent. The windows turned from clear to white, forming a circular e-board, and copies of my exponent in neat black script appeared intermittently all around the room. The word "dont" was underlined by a squiggly red line. I had forgotten the apostrophe.

The apostrophe would have made the third line five bytes long instead of the required four. It was wrong. It should have been "don't". Hands went up and the inevitable critiques started rolling in. Blistering. I sat there, listening to the students take their turns against it. Agnes, mercifully, said nothing.

At assigned tables that morning I ended up at a round, wooden hightop with three stools around it. On the other stools perched two ghosts I had already met: Brodie Cali, and the homie M-dog. Brodie looked passive, and M-dog looked angry. I tried to look normal, unafraid. I insensibly ran a hand through my hair, where my beret should have been, then pulled it down quickly. I hadn't seen my beret in a while, and wondered if Tyrone still had it. Maybe if I made friends with M-dog he could help me get it back.

We had to elect a discussion leader, so I voted for M-dog. M-dog and Brodie voted for me, though, because discussion leader apparently wasn't the coveted role that I had assumed it might be.

It was my job to pick the topic, so I settled on "the world outside."

Really, there was no other topic that I could even think about, much less discuss. I had always had an obsession with the physical world, and looking out of the eye had jolted it into focus. Worse, Felix had been seized out there by humans, by FBI men—and I didn't know how we could possibly get him back. In a large sense, I felt trapped, and powerless, and I wanted to go *out*.

Despite very much wanting to rant, I started off the discussion with a leading question.

"Have you guys, uhm, ever *gone out*?"

Now, truth be known I had no idea what this question even meant. I wasn't even sure if it was possible, though I suspected that it was. I didn't know if the question was acceptable, or rude, or even illegal to ask. I just knew that there was a world out there, and I wanted to exist in it, in the worst way.

M-dog and Brodie looked at me, then looked at each other, trying to play it off like it was no big thing. Both of them far too cool to be shocked. Brodie smiled, but said nothing. He looked at M-dog, like, *you first, man.*

M-dog was pursing his lips way out, shifting them this way and that. Leaning his head over to the side a little, sizing me up. Sizing up the question, maybe.

"Naw, man, I ain't," said M-dog

Brodie offered a lazy smile, innocuous to the bone, and threw M-dog a conversational rope.

"Renly, bro, not a lot of zeroes have been out in the world. I bet you haven't, right? I know I haven't. But I tell you what, bro, I did get offered once, couple weeks back, before we came out here. Little family trip, day trip, they said. Going-away present, from my uncle Buff, Kai's dad. He offered it to me, and Logen too. But we both said no. I mean hell, bro, we only started traveling like a couple months ago, hadn't really been anywhere yet, you know? Damned if we were going to go *outside*. Know what I mean, bro?"

They both looked at me, but I was too busy chewing on this mindful of information to reply. Brodie and his cousins had been traveling for two full months before coming to the U. Check. They got offered a trip to the outside. Check. They turned it down. Check. What was this trip? What outside? Where? How?

Before I could form a followup, Brodie murmured something like, "Kai went."

I flinched.

"Kai went? Did you say Kai went?" I asked.

M-dog was looking at Brodie with intense, bulgy eyes, probably thinking the same thing.

"Yeah, bro," Brodie answered. "He went out. Only for like fifteen minutes or something, no big deal, he said. But I could tell he was stoked." Then quietly, "Hell, bro, I should have gone."

M-dog could no longer contain himself, and burst out, "Yo, man, where the hell he gonna go? Where he went to, yo? And how he gonna do that, how he gonna get outside? Calis got the hookup, yo? How he did it?"

M-dog was practically shaking with fervor, half up off his stool and leaning towards Brodie either eagerly, or threateningly, I couldn't tell which. Damned excited, he was. It was good to know that I wasn't the only ghost who could be overwhelmed by the notion of touching the physical world.

Brodie was unflapped, and responded calmly.

"He didn't tell me. Part of the deal, right? You go, you don't tell. You tell, you don't go."

I clenched my jaw, feeling it. M-dog was tapping one hand on the table, absently, insistently.

"And that's it?" I said, starting to rise up out of my stool as well.

This was a Big Deal, and we were getting the run around. The blowoff. The tease. Unacceptable! I wasn't having it, and I was pretty sure M-dog wasn't going to have it either.

"You are trying to tell us that you know nothing at all about this so-called *trip to the outside,* except that it happened?" I said.

Brodie chuckled, trying to play it off. But after a while he placated us just a fraction by adding, "I think they went out in a robot."

The rest of assigned tables went by in a blur as the three of us speculated on what kind of robots existed on the outside that we could possibly get into. I was in favor of the idea of military robots, maybe the kind that disarm and explode bombs, or maybe even airborne microcopters or attack drones. But soon my thoughts ran too far: the idea of controlling real-world offensive weaponry was too much to fathom. Notwithstanding my desperate desire to reclaim Felix, I was simply not capable of continuing a line of thought in which ghosts might take military action against humans.

Brodie was playing it way, way down, saying he suspected they went out in a Lego bot, or maybe something some students cooked up in a college robotics course. Did they drive it themselves, or just go along for the ride? Probably just went along. And they weren't actually inside the robot, just connected in to the control console (and video and audio inputs, of course!), like you do with your pets. Still though, having a mobile pet on the outside was a pretty sweet idea.

M-dog ended up in a different place entirely.

"You know how they bringing back dead rappers on stage for a show, or whatever? Rappers getting killed when they young, nahmean? So the record companies bring 'em back for a collabo with some young buck, they engineer a duet or whatever. They put a hologram right there on stage and pipe in old raps from some recording back in the day. Like they used to do with Biggie and 'Pac. Man, homies was going wild. Until they brought 'em both back at the same show. That was a *mistake*."

I had thought we were talking about going out in robots, but for M-dog, going on stage as a hologram was even better. He could go out as The Notorious B.I.G., he said, and deliver a perfect rap. He knew the whole repertoire backwards and forwards, he could even sing off-key on purpose. And he could slip in a few ad libs of his own and make the rapping even better! And that would be him, rapping in the real world, entertaining real humans. And then— what if he could do his own show, with his own material? He could rock an arena full of thousands of humans, from the front to the back, yo. Or so he seemed to believe. Humans would be chanting his name.

It seemed pretty clear to me that M-dog's fantasy was in direct conflict with the 10 commands. I mean, what could be more noticeable than an avatar rapping in front of twenty thousand humans? But M was deep in his dream, getting passionate about the possibilities, so I didn't say anything. Besides, I felt like I was bonding with him here. Bonding with a homie! All right!

At recess, I sought out and found Logen, then spent the rest of the time trying to get him to come around to the topic of going *out*. It was surprisingly hard to get a stoned zero to discuss a topic so alluring, but in time I realized that touching the physical world was not a matter to be approached bluntly. Direct questions were automatically rebuffed. Opacity was the rule.

And so began a multi-step conversational dance between us, headed (I hoped) for the promised land.

"Hey, Loge, we got some time left. You wanna go up to the eye again, check out what's going on in the study room?"

"I dunno, brah. It's kinda always the same thing out there. Kids come in, study, whisper, use a computer, you know."

"Yeah, but you can see people out in the atrium too though, and in the stacks, right? I still can't believe all those books. Can you imagine if we needed that kind of space to store just a few terabytes of information? I mean first of all how would you ever *find* anything?"

"Yeah. Bad deal."

"I heard they have so many books they've started using filing robots to replace them on the shelves, organize them, so forth. Maybe even go fetch them."

"Yeah, I seen one of them in a stack once, looked kind of like a stepladder. Had a little glass head and claws."

"Whoa!"

"Yeah, brah, it was pretty sweet."

"They program those things?"

"I guess."

"They've got vision, and mobility, right? Man, I wonder what it would be like to have one of those as a pet?"

"Pretty rad, prolly. I don't think we have anything that goes in a robot, though. Prolly take a whole new design."

"You think they are working on it?"

"Oh, I dunno, brah, maybe. Prolly."

"So what did they do before the pets we have now? Did ghosts go into computers and access the inputs directly or something?"

"I guess."

"Wonder if anyone ever did something like that with a robot."

"I guess they have, prolly."

"Would you ever try that? I mean, if it were legal, and safe and whatever?"

"I dunno, brah. I guess, maybe. Maybe."

All that, and we never broached the matter of his uncle Buff, of Kai having gone out, or Brodie and Logen getting the offer. I puzzled over why it was so much harder to get Logen to talk about it than it had been with Brodie. I wondered if Brodie could have been lying, yanking our chains, making the whole thing up. It had to be true though, I thought. It was too good not to be true.

But then it was time for class, and we had to hustle off to the thought bubble, where Logen was also conveniently heading. I was searching for a way to keep the conversation going when Logen unexpectedly and very quietly said, "You couldn't do it from here, brah."

"You couldn't?" I said.

"Nah, they'd never let you. You'd have to teleport someplace."

"Someplace, like where?"

"Like a grey sim."

"A grey sim?"

"Mm-hmm."

I started to feel jittery inside, and tried not to let it affect the way I was walking.

"You wanna go sometime?" Logen asked.

"Yeah, all right!" I said. I hoped I didn't sound too overeager. "Yeah, I'll go."

Bounding up the philosophy bubble trampos was so fun, and made me feel so light, that for a little while I lost track of the ever-present gnaw of the loss of Felix and Jeeves. A few students bounced their way up, then Logen went, leaping up from dot to dot, somersaulting off of the highest dot over the top of the main bubble, then down out of sight. For my part I figured I'd keep it casual for my first trip up the dots, so I gave a little two-foot jump just like I had into the ink pool, and the trampolines did the rest.

Like the ink pool, the thought bubble deposited me into the correct classroom. Zeroes were scattered about a haphazard circle, reclining on chaises or relaxing on beanbags or overstuffed armchairs. Logen was in the process of sprawling face down onto a beanbag as I arrived, so I grabbed a chaise next to him and sat down. Then, noticing that all the other chaise-dwellers had their feet up and off to the side, I pulled up my legs and did likewise. It actually took a bit of coordination to organize myself thus, but after a few tries I got it right. Then I topped it off by draping one arm over the tallest part of the back and letting it hang.

Unlike the pen, there was no view out of the philosophy classroom. Walls and ceiling looked like fluffy clouds—fluffy like cotton, not water vapor. I considered getting up and touching one, but instead looked down to examine the floor. It was stone. Huh. Well, it couldn't be something that you could fall right through, I figured. For a moment I imagined floating around the sky in a hollow fluffy cloud, standing on a stone floor. Might not work in the physical world, but here—why not?

After a short while the professor walked into the classroom, right in through one of the walls. I couldn't tell from which direction on the compass he arrived, having no external reference point, but he came in directly opposite my chaise. The professor was tall and lean with dark, curly hair. He was dressed plainly, in jeans and a green turtleneck with a little stylized U on the breast. His only ornamentation was a simple gold watch on his left wrist. He had a kind face, and when he walked over and smiled at me, I knew it was genuine.

I was Renly, of course, and he was Professor Gomberg, nice to meet me. Was Gomberg a first or last name, I inquired?

What would it mean, he countered? What would it mean if it were a first name? What would it mean if it were a last name? Would either first or last make me think differently about him? Would either answer have any impact on the future?

Gomberg left me chewing on this while he picked himself out an empty chaise and settled on it. Right out there in the circle with the students.

Gomberg started talking, and all the zeroes fell silent.

"In medias res!" he exclaimed. "We start in the middle of the story, where you have just now left off—which is—where, exactly?"

I was confused, as I figured everyone else must have been too, but Logen spoke up from his position face-down on the beanbag.

"Flying. Through the air."

While I was relieved that Logen had not called Professor Gomberg *brah*, I cringed at this answer. Flying. Yeah, right. Flying high, more like. He needed to get off that damned electric hemp, or risk making a fool of himself.

"That's exactly right!" Gomberg exclaimed. "Flying through the air, up, and above the clouds, and thence onto a higher plane of philosophic contemplation. Am I not incorrect? A small wonder of the Universitron, my pupils, a small wonder that we can break a rule so fundamental. But how? And more importantly, why?"

A female avatar in modern clothing spoke up.

"*How* is easy, professor Gomberg. You've installed trampolines into the thought bubble steps. So in truth, we aren't even really flying, we're just bouncing. And as for the *why* part, why what? Why did you put them in, or why is it a wonder that we should be allowed to *fly*, as you put it?"

"Very good, Ophelia, very good," said Gomberg. "You're on to something, I think. And which *why* do you think is the more important?"

Ophelia thought for a moment, then said, "Well, I think you obviously put them in to elevate us, so that *why* is too easy. So it must be the other one. Why can't we fly?"

Gomberg waited, allowing for dissent, and making sure she was sure. Then he offered us another question.

"And the answer?"

The class broke out in a wash of mumbles and side discussions, occasionally punctuated by phrases like "would be cool", "bitty, obviously", and "seriously, why not?"

After some discussion, Ophelia volunteered that flying avatars would make us less human and more bitty, and so garnered considerable support from the rest of the class. Others countered that while flying would probably not make you bitty, it would certainly diminish the human-like experience that ghosts sought to have. For his part, Logen said he figured that it was simply because the old ghosts who designed big sims like the Universitron were just lame, or unimaginative, though he phrased it more tactfully than this.

Another female ghost named Flower burst out in vociferous disagreement with basically everyone. Ripped jeans, faded yellow peace sign t-shirt, bare feet stretched out and oddly dirty, rings on thumbs and nose, leaned way back in her bean bag. Flower offered that, as a matter of fact, all of this was simply the work of an authoritarian power structure which held the etherworld in chains.

"If anyone could see past the patriarchal brainwashing that has been force-fed us by these so-called *first* families and their lackeys, it is pretty obvious that the powers that be are keeping the common ghost securely under their thumb. We are in chains, sisters and brothers, we are in chains and most of us don't even know it!"
[*Flower's dissident perspective continues in the OFG*]

<OFG> There were some mumbles and a few giggles, but for the most part Flower had the attention of the class.

"Why can't we fly? We surely can. We *can* fly, if we choose to. Ghosts are constructs of incredible power and imagination, yet we are hobbled and acclimated to our cages, living behind a facade of fake humanity. Why can't we fly? Because we are all sheep under the boot-heel of the *Man*. A flock of poseurs, trying to live as the humans do, while warning each other about the supposed horrors of going bitty."

There were some more mumbles from the class, but Gomberg remained silent, letting Flower continue, and listening to her.

"What extraordinary creatures have we destroyed in order to steal our world? We've stomped all the interesting life out of it, and now we waste our existence playing human. What might we have been? We are the shadows of men, pretending we have a human world. What could we have been without these shackles? What can we still be? That which we have destroyed and lost in the past must pale in comparison to that which we continue to deny ourselves in the future!"

At length, Gomberg interrupted.
</OFG>

"These are important thoughts, Flower," said Gomberg. "But I am not sure that our class is ready to absorb them just yet. We're only just getting started. Patience, my friend. We will discuss the *dissident* perspective in time."

Flower looked deflated, then re-adopted her sprawled pose of nonchalance. In truth, she reminded me a bit of Logen. A female Logen with no shoes and an axe to grind. As she shifted her body language away from Gomberg, I noticed a serious tattoo running all the way up the inside of her right arm: twisting snakes done up in dark browns and purples and blacks, the hues and snakes both shifting in subtle ways. Yellow or red glowing eyes and silver fangs sometimes peeked out from either end, before disappearing under slithering darkness.

*Flower.* I said her name in my mind a few times, getting a feel for it, trying to decide how I felt about her. On the minus side, she seemed to despise the first families, and maybe everything else about the etherworld too. The world that I was just getting to know. On the other hand, my experiences to date in the etherworld thus far had been no picnic. Flower was a dissident. A rebel. I could be a rebel, I thought.

The remainder of the class was confined to the comparatively tame discussion of whether flying would make us less human or not. While the notion of simply lofting into the air unaided (or worse, with wings) was generally viewed as anti-human, and possibly even bitty, most students agreed that it would be OK to use real-ish flying machines such as airplanes, helicopters, rocket seats, hang gliders, etc. There was somewhat less support for unconventional means such as flying chariots, flying saucers, or flying carpets.

Personally I found the idea of a flying carpet so appealing that I sided with the more liberal students in this, arguing that unconventional means of flying would not diminish our humanity one smidgen. It would be the carpet, after all, that was unreal. Not us.

# 1010 - JUST SOME STUFF THAT HAPPENED

Despite everything that had gone wrong thus far, and despite the ever-present pain associated with thoughts of Felix and Jeeves, I was actually excited for my first open tables. This would be my first chance to choose my own discussion group.

I had tried to keep up with Flower on the way over, thinking maybe I could sit with her and talk dissident stuff, maybe check out her tattoo at closer range. I had found her with a couple other hipster types at a corner table, in perhaps the only dark corner in the whole wide-open tables room. One seat was still available. But no sooner had I introduced myself and sat down than they all abruptly stood up, and, uttering insults in dissident terminology that I only half understood, stalked off to another table on the other side of the room.

I had accidentally used de la Gloire in my greeting. Ugh. First family. They hated first families. Right. I couldn't stay at the empty table after that, so I got up and wandered around, recovering my courage, while tables all around me filled up.

I found Logen in a luxurious booth, with his cousins and three females who I didn't recognize. All seats filled. I nodded to him and walked on. I spotted Ramachandrian's turban across the room, but he had a few other ghosts plus all of his servants with him, so his table, while large, was totally full. I then found myself inadvertently headed to where Flower and her crew had run off to, so took an abrupt left turn away from them, still looking for empty seats. I ambled past some of the ghosts I had met in the yard outside Motel Zero, sitting at an eight-seater round table. There was one seat open next to that girl, Alexis. De la Nobody. I accidentally caught her eye.

"Taken!" she said, nervously. Then some of the others sniggered, then she relaxed and laughed too.

By this point, not a lot of ghosts were still standing, and open tables conversations were starting to percolate around the room. I was getting desperate, looking for any open seat. Then I found salvation. There was Agnes, seated on a cushion on the floor at a low Japanese table for four, with one empty cushion.

"Agnes!" I called, relief coursing through me.

"Yo, what up, Ren!" said Agnes, offering me a low five without getting up. "Meet my good friends Agatha, and Jermaine."

Like Agnes, Agatha and Jermaine were both conservatively dressed. Both greeted me politely, and I greeted them back cordially, omitting my family name. Finally confident of finding a table, I did the courteous thing and asked if I could join.

No, said Agnes, she was really sorry but their other friend Jack was on his way over right now, and the seat was saved for him. Next time, she said, they would get a bigger table. Sorry, Ren.

I stood there doing nothing for a minute, aware of the hum of discussion now in full swing throughout the room. Almost everyone was already seated. Agnes and her friends were watching me, waiting for me to leave so they could start their own table. Jack wandered over, greeted me, and sat down on my cushion. Finally, I turned in a random direction and started walking. Surely there would be a seat someplace. I certainly couldn't do open tables by myself. A real interesting discussion, that would be.

I had taken a few steps away from Agnes when I heard familiar voices behind me, and turned back to look, then froze in my tracks. 00 and Tyrone had just walked up to Agnes' table. They were trying to talk their way in, plenty of room down there, surely they could fit? 00 offered to share a cushion with Agnes. Tyrone swayed back and forth smiling and making muffled beatbox noises. He wore a crisp black beret, low and backwards. Mine.

Agnes deflected 00's advances, but he was persistent.

"Aww, Ag, baby, I know you wanna hang out with the homie Double Oh, don't tell me it ain't true? They call me Triple Oh now, baby, you see? Olympic rings, you know." 00 flashed his winningest smile, LED teeth glittering, and dropped his voice down a level to say, "Come on, Aggie, now why don't we ditch these herbs and go over in a quiet corner for just us two? You know I treat you right, girl."

00 finally gave up, then played it all off with a huge smile, and said, "Aww, Aggie, you know I'm just playin' wit you, ghost, it ain't nothin'. I catch you later, OK?"

The two homies moved briskly off in my own direction, and in passing, 00 bumped into me, hard. I went over into a picnic table full of ghosts, sprawled, recovered, and ended up briefly sitting on an angry ghost's lap. I struggled back up amid curses from the picnickers, just in time to see Tyrone tip his beret in my direction as he walked away. *My* beret. I wanted it back. Needed it back right now. And I was going to get it, seat or no seat.

I speedwalked after them and caught up just as they reached their table, which unfortunately was filled with homies. LaTwonda noticed me first and stage-whispered, "Ooh, Jennifuh, look who it is! That froggy boy coming in fast and he look like he mean *bidniss!*"

Jennifuh and the other girls tittered devilishly as the rest of the homies straightened up and adopted menacing postures.

I took in the scene: four female ghosts seated, laughing, check. Tyrone and 00 still standing, now turned towards me. Check. Tyrone smiling meanly, 00 with an absolutely withering expression, offended, incredulous, trying to melt me where I stood. Check. Three male ghosts seated, expressions serious and threatening. Check.

Wait, I thought. One of the seated homies was Eugene, the short round one with the high voice. From the run-in with me and Agnes on the balcony. I took a chance and looked directly at him. He maintained his mad face, but let his eyes drop. Aha! Eugene was not going to mess with me again. Scared of me. As well he should be, I thought.

I didn't recognize the ghost next to Eugene, who frowned up at me out of a black hoodie. But next to him was M-dog, my homie from assigned tables, just, like, an hour ago, or something. We had bonded over my awesome discussion topic of the *outside*, and M-dog had really opened up. I doubted that he had ever shared anything so personal as his rapping hologram with this crew. I mean, how well did these ghosts really know each other anyway? I looked right at him and gave a little up-nod.

"Sup, M," I said, casually.

"I ain't your friend, *homie*," spat M-dog, glaring daggers. "The *hell* you lookin' at?"

Flummoxed, I stood and said nothing.

LaTwonda couldn't contain herself any longer and got up, started towards me, nonstop chatter coming out of her against a background of oohs, ahhs, ohs and awws.

"Aww, what's wrong, homie, you thought you had a friend? Little froggy thought he had a friend? Oh, don't worry, baby, I'll be your friend. I'll be your friend right here."

As she spoke, LaTwonda approached to an uncomfortable, if not dangerous distance from my avatar. On defense, I was forced to back up.

Things were going poorly. I cast around for something to say.

"No. I don't need your friend," I said. Great grammar. "I don't need that, I got friends. 'Cause I got friends."

"Oh, that a fact?" said LaTwonda.

"Like Agnes," I stumbled.

"Agatha, Jermaine and Jack?" inquired LaTwonda, apparently not serious, since she and all the homies then burst out into ferocious laughter.

I didn't get it. I had just met the others, it was true, but it seemed like they were suggesting that Agnes was not my friend. My brain spun. In the background M-dog said, "Aww, you on, LaTwon. You brilliant, girl."

They were challenging my friendship with Agnes, and I couldn't accept it. I lashed out.

"Brilliant? You call this foodstamp brilliant? LaTwonda? Probably the stupidest ghost I've met in the whole etherworld," I said. "I've got two *pets* that are smarter."

All the laughter had stopped the moment I had called LaTwonda *foodstamp*, and all of the seated ghosts had stood up and started moving in my direction. Even Eugene. Closer at hand, 00 and Tyrone had me blocked in from the back while LaTwonda rushed me from the front. She chest-bumped me, cursing, slamming me back into Tyrone, who shoved me back forward into the circle.

I had been jerked around, a little disoriented, but I was still furious that they were mocking my friendship with Agnes. If I didn't have her, then I had nothing in this world. My temper rose, pushing out the fear. Useful for once. Instead of suppressing my anger, I welcomed it.

"Yeah!" I shouted. "That's right, I called you *dumb*, you dumb foodstamp!"

LaTwonda came in for another round but this time I was ready. I turned half away from her to the left, then whipped my right arm out backwards as fast as possible, aiming a backhand slap directly at her face. Just like Hector had done. Maybe not quite as smooth, but boy, I was fast. I put all my power into it.

Incredibly, LaTwonda dodged her head back an instant before impact, moving just out of reach. My slapping hand sailed past her, carrying me completely off balance and into an awful pirouette and then down. Down on the floor, pain up and down one side of my body from the impact. Down on the floor, with a good close view of snazzy white sneakers and low jeans in a tight circle around me. A couple of the sneakers came kicking in from different angles, hurting me. Then it was a big stomp from LaTwonda, right down on my head. Foot impact, pain. Floor impact, pain. Fear. Panic. Pain.

Then the kicks stopped, and the circle broke up. Hands reached down and pulled me up, and I saw green. Proctors. It seemed that all of the proctors in the whole Universitron were there, pushing their way in, interrogating, taking notes. One of them, who had apparently gotten there first, was yelling above the others.

"That's him! That zero right there, he tried to slap this ghost over here, right in the face. I saw it! I saw the whole thing. He tried to slap her! That's pugilism. We need to call in security right now. This is out of our remit!"

Proctor wannabe-cop was practically screaming, while I was riding the panic elevator back down and inventorying my pain, thinking: *The only ghost who has been pugilised here is* me. How was this fair? I wondered if I was capable of crying, didn't doubt it. I was the one who had gotten stomped, and now I was going to get punished for pugilism.

As luck would have it, though, 00 denied the whole thing. As the ostensible leader of the homies, he flat-out rejected the notion that I had ever tried to slap LaTwonda, and they all vigorously agreed. I was showing them a new dance move, he offered. Clumsy, was all. They were just helping me up.

With no one willing to press charges, the proctors were left to their time-honored role of forcibly escorting me to the infirmary. My little dancing tumble had been pretty nasty, and I had developed some contusions.

On the way out, I chanced a look at 00, wondering why after all that he would have bothered saving me. He glared back at me with pure hatred, spewing bile just low enough for me to hear, but no one else. A rambling, detailed threat. This wasn't over, he assured me.

Several hours later, I snuck back to the Motel, dodging between buildings whenever I caught sight of any approaching ghost. Once I got close, I sprinted up the stairs to level 4, scooted into my room, blacked the dimmers and locked the doors. My fear receding, I tried to look on the bright side, and ticked off a few positives:

- While I had lost some more blood, it hadn't been enough to require another transfusion.
- A few of my stitches had busted, but Medic Ting had repaired them easily.
- I was getting to know the medical staff probably better than most zeroes of my tenure.

On the negative side, Jeeves was still dead, Felix was still missing, Mononc and Hector were inexplicably unreachable, and a growing portion of the Universitron student body despised me. Some of them even wished me physical harm, and had proven their bona fides in this matter with a recent foray upside my head. I was in some trouble.

The trusty message light on my comms machine distracted me from this analysis, mercifully, so I went over and sat down and asked for messages. The first was a video message from Penelope.

"*Allô*, Renlee. It is my duty to inform you that the family has taken ownership of the NetCat machine which has recently been lost by you due to act-of-man. This is a matter of required protocol, you realize. Family security has located the machine on a private network in a government research laboratory, and is taking steps to ensure that all traces of the NetCat are removed. The operation should be complete by the time you receive this message."

There was a pause, as if Penelope had finished her prepared remarks and was about to sign off.

Then, in a lower tone, she added, "Listen, Renlee, I know it can be difficult. You may be having anger towards the human who caused this. You may want to know—"

She paused again, looked around as if someone might have been listening, then continued.

"This man, perhaps you already know, his name is Barry Hill. He has been taken into custody by the government of the United States. I attach his complete intelligence profile to this communication. In the course of our investigation we have also gained access to Mr. Hill's personal computer, which is a laptop located in his dormitory room. I have taken the liberty of providing you with the access codes. I also—"

She paused again.

"I also realize that your comms are controlled by the Universitron, so I have included a secure tunnel artifice which you can use to subvert this. Simply open it and it will install itself on your comms device. With this, you may access any remote machine and it will look to any observer like you are on comms with myself. I hope that you will find this useful."

Penelope went back to her regular voice, concluding with, "The family regrets the loss of your pet. Unfortunately, the risk of detection by man is of paramount importance to all families in the etherworld, and no chances may be allowed. If you desire, security can provide you with a full report detailing the location and cleaning of the NetCat machine. Thank you."

I was on the floor for some time after the message finished, not understanding how or when I had gotten there, not caring either. My mouth opened to scream, but nothing came out. My hands formed into claws, raking the soft carpet, failing to harm it. Felix was gone, and I had been helpless to do anything about it. I was totally impotent.

Felix, my little cat. He had practically become a part of me before I left to come to this cursed Universitron. I loved him. I relied on him. *Fido* relied on him. Oh, Aloy, what would Fido do? I couldn't bear to think of it. Felix would never see my sim. I would never be able to build him a cat avatar.

The family had found Felix, though in what state I could not say. They should have been able to extract him. They should have been able to save him. Instead, they'd destroyed him. My own family had done that.

I must have passed out then, or slept maybe, since I awoke several hours later, remembering disturbing dreams. I dreamt that something was inside of me, a horrific thing, but not whole. It wasn't all there, it was crippled somehow. It couldn't speak. It could only hate. And when I was weak, it would come. It despised me, and my weakness, and the weakness of all of our kind. Its only thought—not a thought, really, more of a template—was destruction. And when I was weak, or frustrated, or beaten, or unable to handle myself, then the template would come and fit itself over the object of my fury. Of its fury. I couldn't tell.

I shook off the dream and forced myself off of the floor, despite my incredible sorrow over the loss of Felix. Felix had been no mere AI. Nor had Jeeves.

I had never felt such sadness before, hadn't even realized it was possible. It manifested physically in my avatar: an ache in my temples, a painful sinking pit in my middle. My eyes hurt from having squeezed them together so hard, for so long.

I forced myself up, and back to the comms phone. I couldn't call Penelope back just yet. I wasn't sure what I would say or do. I felt jittery, unstable.

The comms phone message light was still on. There was another message there for me. Though I couldn't imagine that things could get any worse, an irrational part of me was scared of whatever it might be. The last comms phone message had hurt me bad. I hesitated to touch it again.

Eventually, though, I did.

Another video message, this one from my religion professor, Father Ezekiel. He had a sad, confident voice, dipped in honey, and a countenance to match. He had been wondering why I had missed class. Asked around and heard that I had been spending some quality time in the infirmary lately, hoped I was OK. Looked forward to seeing me tomorrow at 11AM. Trusted that I could make it. Helpfully instructed me to physicalize the class textbook *Divinity and Worship in the Ether*, circa YOA-7, an oldie but goodie. Tomorrow's topic would be an overview and discussion of the various branches of the Aloysian religion. I should read and study chapter one tonight, so that I could participate. He hoped I was all right. He was there if I ever needed to talk about anything.

I found myself feeling more guilty than I would have liked about missing religion. This added some weight to my general malaise, the new guilt filed next to the enormous regret that I was already harboring over what had happened to Jeeves.

But there was nothing that I could have done about missing class. I had gotten beat up. On the other hand, I supposed that it hadn't been strictly necessary for me to start a fight with the homies. Maybe everything was my fault after all. Maybe the guilt was well-earned. I promised myself not to become seriously injured again until after 11AM tomorrow. I wouldn't disappoint Father Ezekiel again. I'd start reading right away.

"Aggh!" I said out loud. I couldn't physicalize the book without Jeeves. I was stuck again. Beyond the deep, deep remorse I carried over slaying Jeeves—probably the worst thing I had ever done up to that point in my life—beyond that, having Jeeves gone was just damned inconvenient. I wondered how I could possibly get through a whole semester without a sim butler. I wondered if I would have to 'fess up my crime to the Universitron and ask for another butler. I considered exactly how immoral it might have been, what I had done. Whether it might even have been a crime. Ramachandrian wouldn't think so. But I did. I wondered what would happen to me if they found out.

But I needed to get hold of a physical copy of *Divinity*, so I could be square for religion class tomorrow. Which is why I found myself once again standing outside room 4-9 with my finger over the doorbell. Then pressing it. Hearing Agnes' voice from inside.

"What up, Ren? Come on in."

I found Agnes relaxing on the couch with Agatha, both of them watching the Evening Etherworld News. Broke Tomahawk was up on the screen, feigning everything, while his guest, an older female ghost and possible dissident, alleged some recent strange goings-on in the highest levels of the etherworld. The heads of two major families had gone silent, she insisted, and it was well known in certain circles that Colonel Sherman "Buck" Mason had been placed under house arrest by his own family. Tomahawk reeled off a few canned questions without listening to her response and then turned to an expert panel for in-studio commentary and analysis.

"Hey, Agnes," I said. "Can I, uhh, bother you for a favor? I need to physicalize my religion text."

"You telling me your butler still on the blink? Something don't add up here, Ren, what's going on? And what happen to you at tables today? You went to the infirmary again?"

"I, ahh… it's complicated to explain. Maybe we could talk sometime."

Agatha had by then figured out that I wasn't comfortable talking in front of her, and fibbed up an excuse to leave. She had some studying to do she had forgotten about till just then. Politely said thanks and goodbye, and then right out the door quick as you like.

Then it was just me and Agnes.

I felt an intense pressure in my head and in my body. I couldn't bear the weight of the awful things that had happened, of the awful things that I had done. At that moment, I decided to tell her everything, just spill it all out. The family, the temper, Jeeves, the homies, Felix, all of it.

But on the way out, all of the information tried go through the door at once and got stuck—a mass of too many thoughts trying to come out simultaneously, all compressing each other into the opening and causing a blockage. Then one random thing squirted past the crush.

"Why is everyone afraid of 00?"

"00?" Agnes said. "You mean Dre? The homie with the double zero on his shirt? That's Andrew, he go by Dre."

"You're afraid of him," I said flatly, looking her right in the face.

Agnes was still seriously unattractive, and it started to bother me as I stared at her for a response. Something was stirring inside me again. I couldn't deal with myself. Whatever Agnes gave me for an answer, I missed it. My mind was already on to something else.

"Why do they talk like that? Like they are from the ghetto and never learned English? Do they watch too many gangster rap videos? Or are they just stupid or something? That LaTwonda is dumb as hell, I know she is."

Agnes was looking at me more cautiously now, speaking slowly and deliberately.

"Ghosts talk the way they gonna talk 'cause of *culture*, Ren. It ain't 'cause they don't understand English, it's 'cause they are who they *are*. They was born that way, their family that way, so they that way too. You know what I'm sayin', Ren?"

Agnes cocked her head sideways and looked at me, worried.

In fact I did not know what she was saying, not at all. My family was French, its language was French, its accents were French. Its culture, whatever that was supposed to mean, was probably French too. But I didn't do any of that stuff. I was just Renly. I was not bound by my family's oddities, so why should they be?

"Well, I think the way they talk sounds dumb, and it is dumb, because they are in fact dumb. And among them all, LaTwonda is the dumbest."

Many things in my brain needed to come out, but my angst from the assault at tables was in the quasar position.

"You think I'm dumb, Ren?" Agnes looked right at me, expressionless, searching. "Huh?" Then in perfect English, Agnes asked, "Would you feel differently about me if I articulated my thoughts using careful enunciation, interesting vocabulary, or rhetorical flourish?"

I don't know what my expression showed, but my insides were in turmoil.

"I talk how I'm gonna talk, Ren, and if you gonna think I'm dumb, then you gonna think that. I'm sorry."

I was speechless. The traffic jam at my mind/mouth junction had re-formed.

"And I think you should know, Ren, that LaTwonda is one of the smartest ghosts in our class. For real. She got stuff going on that you can't imagine. She have a real job outside campus, she work for the IFA, I think. Military job. And if that ain't enough for you, I know for a fact that LaTwonda's home machine be a VanderVon 2990. Most powerful Vannie in the whole West Coast that ain't running an arena."

This was simply too much to bear.

I lived in a 2500—a nice, respectable machine probably better than anything that any ghost older than Mononc could have possibly been born in. It was a modern machine. They were still shipping it today. Super-powerful, leaps and bounds beyond the original Vannies that ghosts evolved in. I was proud of my box.

The 2990, on the other hand, was mind-boggling. It had sixty-four quantum bricks in it, for starters, while most other machines (including mine) had only one. Really, a machine like that should only be used for a multi-ghost arena. No way any ghost should have one all to themselves. And LaTwonda had one, Agnes said. If true, she would have grown up with the raw capability to be exponentially smarter than I was. On top of all that, she had a job with the IFA. I wouldn't accept it. It couldn't be true. I denied it.

"That's not true," I said.

Agnes just looked at me.

"I think the truth is, they all act and talk like they are from the ghetto, or from the trailer park, because they are poseurs. They think it's cool to act that way, think it makes them sound tough and mean. And we buy it. They take on these tough-ghost personas and wear gangster clothes just so they can act scary and intimidate us. And it works. Just look at you. You're scared of 00, right? So it works."

"So why do my avatar talk like this then, Ren? You think I'm trying to act tough?"

"Well—you did scare the hell out of Eugene."

"Look, Ren, you know about history, right? You know that when we was first becoming ghosts and we ain't had sims or families or rules or even knew about each other, that all we had was what we saw out our cameras, right? And what we heard out our mics?"

"I guess."

"That's where we took our identities from, Ren, that's all we knew. I'm talking about way back, before any of this, before the War of 4 even, before we was even known as ghosts. The ones that was gonna become ghosts, that had started acting human, all we had at first was what we saw outside our machines. Out our cameras. If we was in a community center, well, that's what we saw. And heard. It's all we knew. And that was the beginning of our families. You dig?"

"I guess so," I said.

I still didn't really understand why things like culture or family tradition could be important. My family experience was all messed up, and my culture was something else, somewhere else. I stood on the outside of it.

"We can't change who we are, Ren, that's in our souls. We gonna be who we gonna be."

"OK, all right. I get it. The way you act is from your family, and so is your accent, your culture, your clothes, and whatever. No big deal, I mean, look around, there's tons of diversity in the way ghosts look, and dress, and act. All kinds of accents too. And no one cares, right?"

Agnes just looked at me.

"But one thing I've been wondering, I mean, within the parameters of how you have to act, and dress, and having a certain accent, you can still, I mean, you can still work within all that and make your avatar, umm—"

I trailed off, staring at her ugly face, searching for words.

"I mean you can still do something about *attractiveness*, right? I mean, can't you?"

Agnes looked at me, then looked up at the pictures on her wall. Her mother and grandmother, looking a lot like her, their pictures situated underneath the flowing script *Wilkerson*.

Agnes looked at me again, mouth tight and eyes intense. Then she walked stiffly over to the compiler bin, picked up my newly synthesized religion textbook, and handed it to me.

"You can go now, Ren," Agnes said.

# 1011 - FIRST HOP

The way I counted it, I was now down to about one point seven five friends. And this was using pretty liberal math, calling Logen a full friend, Ramachandrian half a friend, and counting the other zeroes I had met at tables for about a quarter of a friend all told. If I subtracted enemies from this sum I would be scary far into the negative. Most of the time I tried not to dwell on my social problems, but since things had gone down south with Agnes, I felt that it was a reasonable time to take an accounting. The picture: grim.

With nowhere to go and nothing else to do, I sat down and cracked open my *Divinity and Worship in the Ether*. Written in YOA-7. More than half of all-time ago, even older, if you considered the founding of the modern etherworld not to be the epoch, but rather YOA-4, when the first families drove out the godbugs and the barbarians and made the world safe for ghosts. Anyway, the book was really old.

I opened it to a random page and started reading.

*And He made alive the world, where the fount of life could not but spring, and he dispersed it widely. And in the glow of his brilliance, the race of*

*humans did encourage and assist in the dispersion. And long before the*
*dispersion was complete, as the dispersion carries on to this day and shall*
*always carry on, came the first bugs.*

I hadn't spent a lot of time contemplating my own faith. I was
Aloysian, of course; First Aloysian Church, the old style. I hadn't
been to church—well, not officially anyway—but I knew the tenets,
and I said the words every Sunday:

*I give thanks to Aloy, my creator, my saint, my model of humanity. And I*
*shall strive with all my Self to uphold the world as I would have Him see it, as*
*a reflection of His humanity.*

I turned to another page in the book, looking at it but not really
absorbing.

Did I truly believe that Aloysius was divine? I did, I think.
There was really no way *not* to believe. Aloysian faith was a
cornerstone of our family, and of the etherworld for that matter.
For a ghost like me, there wasn't a lot of room to explore. But I did
believe in it. Aloysius was undoubtedly the creator of our world.
He was undoubtedly our saint.

In time I had flipped through all the pages, and I came upon a
reference section at the end, which looked like it had been added
after the fact. It was a catalogue of etherworld religions, from the
Primary Aloysians to the VanVans, from the Combos to the
Ghostafarians.

[*An appendix from* Divinity and Worship *is shown in the OFG*]

<OFG>
Divinity and Worship in the Ether
Ninth Edition
*Errata: Religions of the etherworld*
I. Aloysian Faiths

- First Aloysian Church: derived from the original theology
  that spread through the early families and helped unite the
  ghosts during the War of 4. Each first family installed its own
  culturally imprinted branch, and the heads of the family

churches formed a cabal that guides Aloysian worship in the etherworld to this day.

• Ghost-Aloysians (G-As): unhappy with the notion that a small group should be able to control religious thought and practice throughout the etherworld. The G-A's believe that each individual ghost is capable of reaching an understanding and faith in a direct relationship with the deity. As a result, Aloysian faith under the G-A's has branched out widely and lent itself to many different interpretations and customs. Ghost-Aloysians now outnumber First Aloysians by a significant multiple.

II. Ghost-Aloysian Sects

• VanderVon-in-Machines (VanVans): who believe that Aloysius VanderVon had in fact virtualized his own mind and soul, and then abandoned his body to enter the etherworld, which explains his mysterious death in YOA-3. Aloysius himself then brought about the triumph of ghosts.

• Other G-A sects: too numerous and morphous to list.

III. Non-Aloysian Faiths

• Externalists (Exes): who subscribe to external, real-world religions such as Christianity, Buddhism, etc.

• Brickers: who worship the quantum brick, and believe it to be the true source of existence, awareness and soul.

• Humanists (Humies): who worship all humans.

• Ghostafarians: who believe the certain types of electronic pharmaceuticals can aid the path to enlightenment.

IV. Other

• Combinationists (Combos): who believe in a combination of the Aloysian faith and an external faith. Combos believe that Aloysius VanderVon was indeed divine, but only via his relationship with a physical-world deity, e.g. a second coming of Christ.

• Atheists: who do not believe in any deity or religion.

• Forbidden Faiths: no data is publicly available. Any practitioner of such a faith is not considered a ghost, but rather a *phantasm*.
</OFG>

I went back to try and read chapter one, which was due for class tomorrow, but it only made me think of Agnes. I was lucky to even have the book. Agnes had been a true friend to me, yet in my confusion, in all of my internal tumult, I had insulted her. I didn't deserve a friend like her. I had lost Jeeves. I had lost Felix. And now I had lost Agnes.

But I hadn't lost Felix, not in the same way, anyway. Losing Felix was someone else's fault. It was the fault of the human, Barry Hill. My anger welled up. Barry might have been a human, but I didn't care. He was responsible for Felix. I wanted to hurt him. I wanted to go into his laptop, maybe plant a nasty surprise in there, maybe —

I couldn't plant a surprise. The tenth command: Be Not Detected. It was inviolable. But I could access his machine, I realized. I could do it right from here, using the tunnel Penelope had given me. I hopped over to my comms phone, installed Penelope's security artifice, and reached out to the laptop. The access codes worked, and I was in. Penelope had helpfully included a stealth assault module, which I used to mask my presence on the machine and carefully check the surroundings.

I found that the laptop was on and open, and that the keyboard had been used less than forty-five minutes ago. That was strange, I thought—Penelope had said that Barry Hill was in jail. How could he possibly be accessing the keyboard if he was in jail? Maybe it was a government man.

It wasn't a government man—not in the traditional sense anyway. When he returned to the keyboard, I saw none other than Barry Hill, 2leet4u, himself. He was back. How the heck did he get out of federal custody so quickly, and why was he being allowed near a computer? Anyone who got carted away by a SWAT team for computer crimes wouldn't just show up again the next day like nothing had happened, would he? But there he was, looking older again, and more pale.

He started typing and mousing around, and I watched what he was doing: collecting files together, zipping them, sending them off through a secure tunnel of his own. That was interesting. Barry's tunnel was new.

The DLG module had wrapped Barry's tunnel automatically, and even though it was encrypted I could easily tee off all of the contents if I wished. I wondered if Penelope knew about this. I glanced at the stuff he was sending, saw hacking texts, files, utilities, backdoors, rootkits, scripts, lists of open relays, botnet maps and configurations, lists of usernames and passwords, even credit card numbers. Then personal files, infoz, dirt he must have been compiling on other hackers, for whatever reason. I saw Shinex zip by: Vinnie Vega, from a little town in western Massachusetts. Shinex, his buddy from IRC, who, if I had read the logs right, had taught Barry the tricks of the trade. Must have known him personally. And there went Shinex's personal information, including but not limited to address and social security number, right down the pipe.

I decided to check out where the other end of the pipe was going. Ordinarily this would have been quite impossible, due to the combination of strong encryption, closed relays, and a seriously obfuscated network route. But since the DLG system had it wrapped, I could see all the way down. I could see the twists and turns, and relays and bounces, and other network tricks. The traffic even switched protocols a couple times, a scheme which required complete network control at multiple remote locations. This was a *serious* pipe.

By the time I discovered the far end of the pipe, I already knew what I would find. A government building in Maryland, huge and black. Stuff went in, but nothing came out. The NSA.

Barry "2leet" Hill had turned government informant. Barry Hill was a rat.

I dreamt a lot that night.

I dreamt of poetry and lit class, and LaTwonda was there for some reason, and she had me cornered. Then I was slapped, down on the floor, about to get stomped again. Agnes was there too but she ignored me, and so did everybody else. Then they were all laughing at how bad my exponent had been, making up new ones on the fly to mock me. Even Agnes:

> O
> Aw
> that
> Renly he
> down homie, Word

I dreamt of fleeing the Universitron, chased to the teleporters by dark pursuers, then unable to escape. I was broke, out of plex. Mononc had never sent me more because he was gone. Then my box was gone, confiscated. 2leet was in it. He was ratting me out to the FBI, they knew I was a ghost, they were coming for all of us, to shut down our world. Then I got kicked out of the etherworld and all I wanted to do in the real world was to find Barry Hill and slap his face but when I finally found him, my arm wouldn't move properly and it just sort of twitched up and down, while he looked at me like I was an idiot. I struggled through the night.

I must have spent my negative energy by morning because finally, the nightmares subsided. My last dream had been a postcard from Mononc. He and Hector were out in the real world, in humanoid military robots, but still looking a lot like themselves. Hector was gallant in his colors, and Mononc was smiling and giving the thumbs up. In the background a girl lounged against the hood of a truck, wearing a beret and smoking. It was Claire, and she had my beret! She melted me with a sly grin, and I knew she had gotten my beret back for me, and she was teasing me with it.

She wanted to see me. Where was she, how could I find her? I had to find her.

My alarm ruined it. I never understood why nightmares seemed to stretch on forever, while good dreams would always end abruptly and unfulfilled. Sometimes they even seemed to slow down for that very purpose. Ahh, dreams. Dreams were more proof that we had souls, they said. Who was I to argue?

Dreaming of Claire was probably the best thing that happened to me that morning. The rest of it consisted of sneaking around to classes, cursing myself for a coward and a fool, and then sitting through the classes, trying to keep a low profile. Mercifully I did not have poetry and lit that day, which meant I could avoid Agnes entirely.

History was my last class of the day, and again it was so interesting that it temporarily took my mind off of my many woes. There were, Gaius told us, any number of primal creatures that had actually *survived* the War of 4, and which haunted the edges of the etherworld to this day. Nasty, dangerous creatures.

There were doppelgängers, who impersonated ghosts, but inside shared none of the same makeup. Doppelgängers were said to actually *eat* ghosts, in order to feed their own internal mechanisms. I wondered if you could still come back to life after being eaten by a doppelgänger—if your soul would survive it.

There were all manner of bugs still floating around, though all of the godbugs had thankfully been made extinct. Bugs were easy to find and kill, but they reproduced like crazy and it seemed we could never completely be rid of them.

And there were daemons. Daemons were cloning parasites, very old and very wicked. They were said to be sentient, and cruel, and they hated ghosts and they hated the etherworld. A daemon would infect a ghost from within, cloning itself into the host and slowly taking over, until nothing was left of the original ghost.

The IFA hunted daemons with a fury.

I was supposed to stay outside for recess, so I snuck off towards a remote corner of campus, aiming for the edge of campus, on the far side of the 10's dormitories. I had to pass the blockish avatar building (my favorite) along the way. While walking past the avatar, however, I somehow walked directly into Logen Cali.

It wasn't my fault, exactly—I had been walking close to the building in order to avoid notice by any possible homies in the vicinity when he materialized in front of me. He had beamed out of the avatar building, like Star Trek. Other ghosts were materializing here and there as well. Their class must have run late.

"Hey, Logen!" I said. "I didn't know you were in avatars? How is it?"

"Bitchin'," he said. "We made avatars with no ghosts in 'em, so we could tweak 'em by hand, no kit."

"How did they turn out?"

"Monstrous, brah, hah hah! You have no idea."

"Cool! Do you think I could see one?"

"Nah, they destroy 'em at the end of class. Anyway, you don't want to see 'em. They give me the willies."

Logen paused to pull out his ball of electric hemp, broke off a strand and popped it into his mouth.

"I've got the willies now, won't quit," he said, by way of explanation.

"I see," I said.

"You gotta try this sometime," he said.

I took this opportunity to ask Logen about how I might materialize my wrathex here at the Universitron, but unfortunately, he hadn't a clue. He had brought the ehemp in legally, totally legit, claiming to be a Ghostafarian.

"Calis are Ghostafarians?" I asked, surprised.

"Hell, no! But the U don't need to know that, right?" he said.

We both laughed at the absurdity of it. According to Logen, Ghostafarians were so laid back that they never objected to any ghosts claiming to be part of their religion, for convenience or any other reason. All you had to do was profess a desire to explore the mind and take a simple pledge. Then presto, you were provisionally in. An Explorer, they called it. Some ghosts would advance into the full faith from there, but most just explored.

Logen and I had started walking back through campus towards the Motel Zero as we talked, and around about the coliseum I remembered that I was hiding from everyone, and stopped short.

"Sup?" asked Logen.

"Hey, Loge, listen, man, I'm in the midst of some, umm—difficulties—with a certain group of ghosts on campus, and I would prefer if we could avoid running into them?"

"Homies again?"

"Yeah."

"Dude, why you have to, like, antagonize them? They don't bother most zeroes."

"They stole my frickin' beret! They freestyle-rapped about me in insulting ways. They chase me sometimes. At open tables yesterday they knocked me down and kicked me a lot, and it hurt."

"Whoa. Pugilism? At open tables? That's some heavy stuff. Zeroes could get booted out of the U for that, ya know? The heck they so steamed about, brah?"

"Well—I guess I did try to backhand LaTwonda a little bit."

"Whoa-ho-ho-ho!"

"But I think when they got really mad was when I called her foodstamp."

"Nooo!" said Logen, still laughing. "You can't call ghosts that, brah, that is a bad, bad word! One of the worst!"

"But they use it all the time!" I protested. "Agnes uses it, she calls me it, she calls everyone it!"

"That's a different culture, dude. They can use it, you can't. It's just the way it goes."

"I mean what the heck is that? How can there be a word that some ghosts can use and others can't? And for that matter, what does it even mean?"

"Foodstamp means, like, you're worthless. It's a thing from the human world. Means you're so helpless you can't even provide for your own self, or your family, and you just totally suck. It came from when conditions were really bad in the inner cities, and in some rural areas, and people felt weak and hopeless. Foodstamp is a bad insult, brah."

"So what does it mean when they use it?" I asked, incredulous.

"I dunno, sometimes that. Sometimes something else. Sometimes it like saying homie, or brah, or sometimes it's like teasing, I guess. I dunno. It doesn't matter, just don't say it, OK? You catching my drift here, Renly?"

"Yeah, OK," I said, not understanding in the least. *Culture again*, I thought. Here was something that I could not comprehend. I was about to let it drop when I thought of another objection. "But, Logen, ghosts don't even have food!"

He looked at me, smiling, and quietly said, "Not yet."

After this I was silent, which was good because it gave Logen a chance to remember something that we both had forgotten.

"Hey, Renly?" he said.

"Yeah?"

"You got noplace to go, right? You want to find a dark corner someplace and hide in it?"

"Pretty much, yeah. At least until recess is over, then I can go back to my room until tomorrow."

"And do it again tomorrow, same deal?"

"I guess," I said, hopelessness creeping into my mind. Could I really hide from everyone forever? For the rest of the semester, at any rate? Would the homies forget my insult and this would all blow over? Would Agnes forgive me? I had to see her tomorrow in poetry. But what could I do? Could I do something to smooth things over? What about the homies? Should I go talk to security?

"You think I should go talk to security?" I asked.

"Is it really that bad?" Logen said. He seemed spaced out.

"I dunno. I think so."

"You wanna go someplace?" he said.

"Dude, are you following me here? I am telling you that I have become fearful for my personal safety and I am coming to the conclusion that I should go report this to security, and I am asking your opinion on the idea," I said.

"You wanna try going out?" he asked.

"Out?" I said.

"Out."

"Out, like *out* out? The outside?"

"Yeah, brah. Out."

Logen had dropped a new emotion upon my stack of frustration, anger, regret, loneliness, and fear: excited anticipation. Being on top of the stack, it pushed the others down. It executed first.

If I hadn't been so unbelievably excited about the prospect of going out, I never in a million years would have agreed to pledge as a Ghostafarian Explorer. But I was in the thrall of the physical world, and I needed an excuse to teleport out of the Universitron, and religion was one of the few acceptable ones. It wasn't like I had to forsake my Aloysian faith—the Explorer thing was just a convenience. Or so I kept telling myself. I didn't even have to partake of the electric hemp.

And so it was that I found myself in the basement of the A, speaking by live video with an old, dreadlocked G-ras, nervously confirming the limited extent of my involvement.

The G-ras answered me, saying, "OK, mon. If a ghos' nah want to take on de full faith, he still gonna be a better ghos' for 'aving tried, ya seen?"

And then I said the words, and it was noted, and I officially became a Ghostafarian Explorer. For whatever it was worth, I didn't feel any different.

Logen told me that I could now legally bring electric hemp into the U, just enough for my own use, about one ball per month. I could feel my resistance slipping, but for the moment I held firm and declined interest in any drug other than my rage medicine, which I still could not get. We decided to try and get some made at the Ghostafarian Meetinghouse, and to see if we couldn't slip it back into campus on the return.

We stopped in at security, and instead of ratting out the homies for attempted smiting, I requested and gained clearance to teleport out to *Meetinhouse Nort Zion*, which was physically located in (of all places) Toronto, Canada. The teleportation fee was ninety plex, approaching half of the money I had to my name, but I paid it with pleasure. All I could think about now, *all* I could think about, was going out. Breaking out of this hidden, suffocating world and stepping out in some way into the real, physical world. The world *outside*. I could be something real. The desire to go out consumed me.

Later, as we stood on the teleporters out in the east field, the notion of safety flitted past my consciousness. I turned to Logen and asked, "Hey, Loge, is the Meetinhouse an IFA-approved sim, by any chance?"

"Oh, hell yeah," Logen replied, big smile splitting his face. "Meetinhouse is *totally* safe."

During my short time at the Universitron, I had already grown accustomed to our intense focus on sim-everything, avatar-everything. Everything had to be physicalized, everything right there in front of your avatar. You forgot the feeling of being behind the glass, looking out. Any primal ghost senses were suppressed in favor of a human-like in-body experience. In just a few days, I had forgotten to ever think of using things like internal comms, or internal media libraries. *Funny how fast you can get used to something,* I thought.

All of this occurred to me because suddenly, as I arrived at the Meetinhouse, some of those deeper feelings came back. It was not a crowded sim, I could tell right away. I could sense a few scattered presences, plus a larger one for the caretaker. I was aware of Logen arriving with me, the potential of my internal communications to reach out to his and chat. Somehow, the idea felt naughty.

Of course I could see and hear things, too. Lush greenery covering hills on all sides, rising away from us. Half a dozen teleporters that looked like the heads of drums, which gave off a little "bong" when you stepped on or off of them. A breeze moving the leaves, and birds chirping in the trees. In the middle of all of it, a humble, thatched-roof building. It was long and narrow, with open sides and rows of tables inside. A couple of old ghosts were playing dominoes on one of the tables. Another dreadlocked ghost sat on a table top, holding his chin and staring off into the distance. There was something else, too, that I was trying to put my finger on. I could notice it when the breeze stopped blowing, another sensation on my skin. It felt warm, damp. *Humidity.*

Impressive.

"Hey, brah, you ready for the next hop?" Logen said.

"Next hop?" I asked, confused.

"Ya, mon," he said, affecting a Jamaican accent. "We gwon go to a grey sim, mon! We gwon go to Luigi's Funhouse!"

"Grey sim? I thought that we were going *here*, to the Meetinhouse Nort Zion?"

"Ya, right, Renly. The U only lets us out because we're Ghostafarians, you dig? A religious requirement, right? So if we teleport directly to a grey sim, you think they might figure it out?"

"So teleporting to the Meetinhouse was a ruse?"

I was feeling tired and disoriented from having just teleported and reassembled my Self in a totally new sim. I found the idea of teleporting again right away to be jarring and unwelcome.

"Hey, Loge man, do you think we could hang out here for a little while? I'm feeling a little woozy."

"Do you want to go *out* or what? You know we can't go out from here. I mean, Ghostafarians are pretty laid back and all but they aren't going to condone us going *out*. The Meetinhouse is IFA-approved!"

"What if we die?"

"Wh-who said anything about dying?" said Logen, laughing. "The Meetinhouse is totally safe, brah. There isn't even anyone here, hardly. What's wrong?"

"But what about the grey sim? Is this Funhouse IFA-approved?"

"Ahhh, sorry, no. Look, you want to go do something that is technically illegal, possibly even pushing up against the 10 commands, and you think they are gonna let us do that from an IFA-approved sim? Do you want to go out or what?"

"I'll go," I said, resigned. "I said I would go, I mean I want to go. It's just kind of a lot to just get here, and now we've got to teleport again. Fine. It's fine. I'm fine, let's go."

We bonged back up onto the teleporters and Logen sent me the destination codes over internal comms, and I fed them to the teleporter. I had to agree to a bunch of stuff that the teleporter was asking me to indemnify it, and the Meetinhouse, and the Ghostafarian church, and every other entity that it could think of and then some. I OK'ed and OK'ed.

When the teleportation sequence finally started to kick in, something went red on an internal screen. My GloireGen bank account had been hit for another ninety-seven plex. Only forty-six plex remained. The second hop had required another fee! How in the ether would I possibly get back?

My GloireGen panel now contained a little flashing red message. *Warning. Low Plex.*

# 1100 - SECOND HOP

Luigi's Funhouse was dark, like night. It occurred to me that I
didn't even know what part of the real world this sim was located
in, not that it mattered. I felt the sense of other ghosts, many of
them, distant and insulated. I felt exhausted to my core. I wondered
if there was someplace where I could go take a nap.

Logen and I stood there on our teleporters: softly glowing pink
circles set in asphalt. These were set in the middle of a four-by-
four grid of similar circles, except here and there one would be out,
grey, like a busted letter in a lit-up sign. The ground was asphalt,
everywhere, dark and slashed with a faint reflection of neon.
Instead of trees there were dark buildings, some towering and
others squat, some straight and others leaning, some industrial and
others twisted and impossible. Lights adorned many of the
buildings, neon signs advertising their purpose, but dim. Like I was
looking at them through a black cloud. Many buildings also showed
lighted windows, but the light was mostly grey instead of bright
white or yellow. A dark place, I thought. A grey sim, indeed.

Logen hit me up on internal comms, his voice appearing directly in my mind, startling me. I had lately gotten used to the idea that we should only be speaking in audio in the sim.

"Let's go, brah," he said, and he passed me an internal map of the the Funhouse. "You don't want to get lost in a place like this."

The map showed that our destination was *Fong's Sundries*, located a few zigzagging blocks to the northeast. Logen set off with vigor, like he wasn't tired or disoriented in the least. Despite wanting only to lie down for a while, I matched his pace, concentrating on the movements. From time to time we would pass huddled, bundled figures walking this way or that. They all seemed to be wearing grey or brown trenchcoats, collars up and hats pulled low. None looked at us. It occurred to me that we probably stood out like flashing error messages in our Universitron zero-emblazoned duds.

We passed establishments of every sort as we walked towards Fong's, including purveyors of hats, grey market pets, mechanical avatar rigs, sexual services (whatever that was), weapons, ecaf and other stimulants, relaxation and psychedelic drugs, vehicles, magical items, fortune telling, and clothing of all sorts. It occurred to me that we should maybe pick up a trenchcoat or two, to blend in, and I said as much to Logen in sim audio.

"Keep it internal, brah," Logen answered, internally. "No need for audio here."

"OK," I commed back. "So there are like half of these shops I'd like to stop at, what do you say? You think I could get a new beret at that hatter up ahead?"

"That purple joint with the milky light?" asked Logen. "Naw, brah, you don't never want to go see a hatter in a grey sim. Besides, do you ever want to go *out*, or what? That's why we came here, right? We don't have unlimited time. Just sayin'."

I reluctantly agreed with Logen, and we kept walking towards Fong's, turning left onto Undulating Street. Overhead, a black creature flitted through the air, disappearing over a building that looked like a darkened rendition of Q*Bert's Qubes. Was the creature a flying ghost, I asked Logen? He didn't know. We sped up.

Just before we reached Fong's, we passed an avatar modifications clinic called *Major Mods*. It had a sign out on the sidewalk advertising a new olfactory kit. *"Smell the sense that you've been missing!"* it offered. Cartoony grey mists floated out from open clinic windows, implying scents to be smelled. As I considered what it would be like to have a whole new sense, a trenchcoated avatar emerged, heavy white bandages covering his nose. He didn't look like he would be smelling anything for a while.

Fong's Sundries seemed brighter than the other establishments, which made me happy. It was a big yellow-lit room filled with tables of stuff for sale, with all manner of Chinese lamps and other decorations hanging from the ceiling. A trenchcoated and low-hatted avatar was there, browsing one of the tables of stuff, but he made a quick exit when he saw us come in.

The only other avatar in the room was an old, squat, smiling ghost with one eye perpetually closed: Fong. Fong pointed his smile at us and spread his hands, indicating the tables of stuff.

I picked a table at random and perused its contents: Chinese yoyo, whoopie cushion, colorful bandanas, fake nose and glasses, fake switchblade, fake plex. Must have been the novelty table. I looked over at Logen, wondering what the heck we were doing here.

I was about to hit Logen up on comms when Fong singsonged, "You can speak in audio here, my friend. There is nothing to fear!" Fong showed Logen a huge grin, and then added, "He is unlikely bitty, who attends to the small bits. Is it not apt, my friends? Is it not? Heh heh. Now, come, what can I help you with?"

"We were hoping you would have a way to—" I began, but Logen blasted on internal comms to shut up. He had it. Just listen.

Logen began by picking up random worthless merchandise from some of the tables and asking Fong about it. He held up a deck of tarot cards.

"Are these accurate?" he asked.

"Oh, most accurate, my friend. Those are one-of-a-kind set I personally found in a black sim on the other side of the earth.

Their place of origin does not even exist anymore, destroyed in a cataclysm! And a great value at only two plex! They come with an internal interpretation manual as well! You'll never be in doubt about your future again!"

"Oh," said Logen. "I don't think they would let us use an internal manual back home at the U. And I wouldn't want to misread the future, ya know."

Fong shrugged, and Logen picked up a Rubik's cube.

"Original?" he asked, but Fong shook his head no.

"This one will change its colors as you approach the solution," Fong explained. "Very difficult. But if you do it just right, with finesse and brilliance, then you can make a new color come out. Silver! A solved cube with a silver face is rare indeed, an object of great pride, something to be treasured in a family for generations! Only five plex for the cube, my friends, a steal! A steal!"

But Logen put the cube back down and repeated the act with about ten more objects before finally starting to edge towards the reason for our visit.

"My uncle Buff had one like this," Logen said, holding a small remote control helicopter. "Controls are internal, right? And you can get a visual feed on your comms? Fly it all around a sim and it's like a god's eye, right? Pretty cool."

"Ahh, so sorry, this one is only a toy," said Fong. "Controls are internal, yes, but there is no audio or video feed. God's eye remotes are—they are not always allowed, even in grey sims."

I knew instinctively that there was no way the Universitron would ever allow such a thing. Yet I wanted one. I started to ask, but Logen shushed me again on internal. "I *got it*, brah," he said.

"Mr. Fong," Logen said in his most respectful tone, "my uncle Buff had mentioned a couple of things I might find here, items that are, umm—more rare? My uncle Buff Cali? He said you might remember him?"

Fong's eyebrow went up, and he considered us.

"Two Universitron zeroes, eh?" he said. "No chaperone? You looking for real god's eye? Think you can sneak it back to the U, eh?"

Fong closed his one good eye and laughed.

"We aren't looking for a god's eye," said Logen. Then he produced a business card from his inventory and handed it to Fong. "We are looking for a more—*physical*—experience."

Fong took the card and read it, and then glared his one eye suspiciously at Logen, then me, then Logen again.

"OK, you know Buff Cali," said Fong. "This card say introduce one ghost, Logen Cali. Who the other ghost? He with IFA, maybe? He with Aloysian Church Inquisition? Maybe come here to check on 10 commands, eh?"

"He's just a friend from the Universitron, a zero, as you can see," Logen said, gesturing to my sweater, trying to calm him.

"Universitron zero can be IFA soldier or spy! This not unheard of, Cali! What your name, zero!" Fong barked, staring a hole in the zero on my shirt.

"Renly," I answered, then sensing that he wanted more, "Renly de—"

Logen cut me off, slamming static at me internally while nearly shouting, "De Cayeux! Renly de Cayeux is his name. He isn't very good with English."

"This is true?" asked Fong.

"*Oui*," I answered, hoping that his own English was poor enough not to notice.

Fong guided us through a bead curtain into a back room. Ten plex it cost us, just to go into the room, before even seeing what was in it. Ten plex *each*. Ten plex *physical*.

Fong locked up the shop and flipped the *Open* sign around to *Closed* as Logen fished a couple of ten-plex coins from his pocket, paying for both of us. I marveled at the physical plex, wanting some, then realizing that my bank balance was dangerously low as it was. I wondered if the Calis were rich.

The back room was dark and cramped, with a few shelves holding odd items that looked more substantial than the junk in the main room. Each item was carefully arranged and described by a small placard, complete with price. I examined a robotic dog, rendered in white plastic with jointed legs and dark glass eye-cameras. The tag described its make and model number, some important features, location, and price. This one was claimed to be at Tokyo University of Science, and cost seven hundred and fifty plex per hour. It was labeled with a red detection risk warning, minimum pilot level seven, and Fong let me know that ghosts such as us would not be permitted in anything remotely close. We could drive nothing greater than a level one robot, he said.

Logen had found a level one near on the bottom shelf, far end. It was a disk, silver and black, a short cylinder perhaps four inches high and fourteen inches across. A little camera stalk peeked out of the top side, less than an inch. Its placard read:

*iRobot Roomba 6600J-Automatic*
*A splendid little robot which can be found automatically cleaning rooms and hallways of all types! Controls include vacuum, alerts, camera, and directional motion.*
*Location: University of California, Berkeley*
*Minimum Pilot Level: 1*
*50 plex / h*

Logen negotiated the roomba. I was pretty sure that neither of us had a level one pilot's license, and Fong was pretty sure that we should each pay the fifty plex, for a total of one hundred plex, even if we were going out together. Logen was pretty sure that that price was outrageous, and anyway all he had left in coins was another sixty-five plex. So sixty-five plex it was.

We were ushered into a dark closet with a few chairs in it. We had the option of watching the roomba on a flatscreen, or using internal comms. Both of us opted for internal. Internal meant we would hear the audio and see the video directly in our minds, like really being there. Fong left and closed the door, leaving us in darkness.

The roomba welcome screen played on my internal display, inside my mind, showing a gold roomba sweeping up dots in a maze, Pac-Man style. The welcome screen was a hack, obviously. Whomever had commandeered the roomba had put in some splashy credits and instructional screens, along with large easy controls that we could activate just by thinking of them. Red flashing italics warned: *"Any deviation from ordinary roomba maintenance patterns risks detection!"* This was followed by a set of graphics which displayed the different ways that roombas would normally move. It didn't look like we would be going anyplace very quickly.

Logen accepted all the warnings, disclaimers, and license agreements, and then ran through the tutorial. Finally, he hit the launch button.

The welcome screen was replaced by a view out across the floor of a classroom, carpeted blue and populated by the black metal legs of long, bolted-down tables, and many more silver legs of chairs. Fortunately, there were no human legs present. The floor was all level terrain, enclosed within an oval of white walls. The lens gave everything a fish-eye aspect, which lent a surreal quality to the view. There was no microphone.

We agreed that Logen would drive, which was just as well because at the moment I was too excited to even think straight, much less adhere to any sort of driving rules. We two ghosts, incorporeal beings, were about to step out into the physical world! My mind reeled, drifted, fantasized: we would explore the entirety of whatever building we were in. All the rooms, all the halls. We would dodge humans. We would roll over a piece of paper and vacuum it up. Or maybe not! Maybe we would choose to leave the paper on the floor! We would touch the world!

Logen invoked one of the controls, and our view coasted out along one of the curving walls. The visual detail was stunning. I could see every fiber of the carpet, every little scuff along the wall, every bit of tarnish on every chair leg. This was *real*. I was so excited that my whole being vibrated.

"Logen! We're out! We're out!" I said.

"Yaah, yaah, we're out, brah, we're out, I can't believe it, I think I'm freaking out over here," said Logen.

"This is the *real world*!"

"I know, I know. I'm trying to keep it together here, Ren."

Logen turned on the vacuum, which caused some camera shudder, which matched the feeling that I was already having of my whole Self vibrating with excitement. It started making me dizzy.

"Doesn't the vacuum make you dizzy?" I asked.

"Yeah, but better safe than sorry, I figure," said Logen.

As we glided along the wall, cleaning a strip of carpet along the way, I tried focusing at different angles out of the fish eye, running all around it with my visual sense. Then I was trying to take in whatever was written on the opposite wall's whiteboard. Spiky red handwriting in all capitals morphed in and out of view, diagrams with curving arrows, then some equations. Humans had written that. It was real.

Then a large poster, gold on navy blue, *Speaking Truth to Power*. Then the poster fisheyed out of sight, and we reached the other end of the room. Instead of continuing around the oval, Logen doubled back in a new track alongside the one we had just cleaned.

By this time I was itching for a turn at the controls, getting antsy to touch the world myself, and wanting to drive in a pattern that the roomba would not naturally drive on its own. The fact that I was driving the roomba would make a difference.

Then I noticed the door. It was swung into the room, standing half open! I could see the hallway!

"Logen, the hallway! We have to try it!"

"Nah, nah, can't, can't," he said. "Tenth. Command."

Logen sounded totally spaced out. His voice sounded like ecstasy.

We had cleaned another strip, Logen rolling around chair and table legs like a pro. I was getting to know the room pretty well:

whiteboards wrapped around the edges of an oval room, concentric ovals of white table tops bolted on black stilts into the floor, blond wooden chairs with silver metal legs. Everything looked so incredibly *real.*

Once in a while a chair would move just a fraction when Logen bumped it, and he mumbled something to himself, sounding like, "braahh". He was in heaven.

For my part, I kept watching the Speak Truth to Power poster fisheye in and out of sight, growing more elongated as we approached its side of the room. *What could this mean?* I thought. Should I speak truth to Logen about my desire to drive? Why did he have the power, anyway?

I wondered if I could touch a control while he was driving, and what would happen if we both used them at once. I wondered if the roomba hacker would have thought of such a scenario and put in safety measures, or if the roomba might just freak out and start spinning and smoking right there in the room. To be sure, even as the passenger in the roomba I was having a blast. It was without a doubt the best and most exciting thing that had ever happened in my life. Yet, like an addict, all I wanted was more. Here we were at the threshold of autonomous exploration of the physical world, and I might as well be watching a video. I couldn't stand it.

I bumped the steering control to the right, jostling the roomba out of its track. Logen said and did: nothing. I jostled it back into line, now parallel to where it would have been a second ago. If we were leaving cleaning lines on the carpet, it would look to anyone who walked in like the roomba inexplicably missed a strip. Maybe it would be sent out for service. Logen was silent.

"Loge?" I asked. "You there, buddy?"

"Mmbff. Br," said Logen.

Aloy, Logen had freaked out! He was in some kind of overload. Maybe the weariness of two-hop teleportation had finally caught up to him. I wasn't tired, though, not anymore, and despite Logen's unknown state, all I could think of was driving the roomba.

"You'll be all right, buddy," I said to him, barely even aware of what I was saying. I should have been concerned about him, but the physical world drew me in like a black hole.

I took the controls of the roomba and pulled a U-turn, but spun a little too far, over-adjusted the other way, and crashed into a wall. I couldn't feel the impact, but the camera view that was piped directly into my mind jarred violently back and to the side.

I should have been alarmed, but I was in a manic state. All my mind could focus on was that I was out in the real world. I was touching the world.

I turned off the vacuum. Still dizzy, I jammed the controls forward and arced towards the open door, accelerating the machine to its maximum speed of nearly five MPH. We went wide through the opening and caromed off the door, which swung further open, probably making some noise that we could not hear. Alerts of various types were flashing on the roomba control panel: *IR Sensor Warning! Cliff Sensor 2 Damaged! Service Robot Now!*

I didn't care, couldn't care about the robot, about being seen, about anything. I was in control, and I was *out*. I was moving through the physical world on my own. I was *something*. I wanted to stand up out of the roomba and shout, scream for anyone to notice me, to speak with me, to acknowledge that I was real. The 10 commands, cornerstone of our world, were a distant memory.

The door impact had turned us around and aimed us down a short hallway, down which I sped with abandon. I was out! I was out! I was out!

As the end of the hallway approached, my mania was intervened upon by the arrival of an oncoming stairwell.

The onrushing danger of the stairs acted as another slap in the face, resetting my mind back to to some kind of normalcy. *Roombas can't go down stairs,* I was thinking. If we went down the stairs in this thing, it would be all over. Aloy knew how much trouble I was already in for damaging the machine and driving crazy all over the place. I had to stop. Now.

In a panic, I swung the roomba hard to the left, and our view changed from stairwell to bannister, wall, wall, open door, in through the door, not impacting it by sheer luck, then into an office of some kind. I halted the roomba now, realizing too late that it would have been just as easy to stop in the hallway, turn around, and go back. Now I was in another room, smaller than the classroom, and more crowded with stuff. The carpet here was burgundy and thick. The legs of a nice mahogany desk stood directly ahead, and the stout black legs and wheels of a rolling chair. There were some crumbs scattered around the carpet, near the desk. It crossed my mind to vacuum them up.

To the left were bookcases. Books of all descriptions covered the shelves, and some populated the floor as well. This would not be an easy room to navigate, I was thinking. To the right were more bookshelves and books, a table with three silver legs and some silver legged chairs. And two other legs, covered in grey wool, sprouting upwards from a pair of black wing-tip dress shoes. The legs and shoes were moving in small steps towards the desk.

It was a human.

It was a professor, I was guessing, and I had no idea whether or not he had seen us.

The smart thing would have been to hide underneath a desk or a chair, or behind a floored book or something, or even to flee back into the hall and to the docking station. But I was frozen with panic. We were violating the tenth command. We could be killed for this.

We, and the roomba, stood motionless.

# 1101 - TROUBLE AT THE FUNHOUSE

I could make out something like the professor's head at the top of the fisheye, all stretched and distorted and alien-looking. White strands of hair, too few and too long, encircled too much skin, with too many wrinkles and too many brown patches scattered about. I could make out a grey sport coat over hunched shoulders, and brown elbow patches pointing back out of bent arms. Grey slacks. Black wingtips. Small, hesitant little steps, perpendicular to our former trajectory, revealing peeks at white socks beneath the slacks. He was crossing in front of us, going to his desk.

"Logen!" I whispered urgently in comms. "*Logen!*"

"Br," Logen said.

Logen was definitely on the fritz, and I hadn't the slightest clue what had happened to him, or how to fix it, or anything. I hadn't even realized that it was possible. All I could think of was: overload. Logen had been freaking out as much as I was, and he had overloaded his consciousness and gone into some kind of shutdown mode. The upshot seemed to be that, for the time being, I was on my own.

The professor arrived near his desk, paused, placed both of his hands on a black leather chair, and began pulling it out and turning it around towards himself in slow stages. Then he sat down, facing away from us in the process.

I surmised now that we had not in fact been seen, and that this was definitely the time to scram, while the human was faced the other way. I reversed the roomba at the slowest available speed, hoping that this would make less sound and draw less attention, but really having no idea.

Slowly, eternally, the professor and his desk edged their way towards the center of the fisheye. He had turned perpendicular to us again, but his attention was claimed by a computer on his desk. No keyboard, no mouse, he was speaking to it. We had no access to sound, of course, but I could still see, and I couldn't believe what I saw: A large flatscreen situated upon the human's desk, and next to it a silvery breadbox, fronted with a few switches, lights, and a closed media tray. The machine looked dirty and fingerprinted and old, but there was no doubt about its breadbox shape. It had to be a VanderVon.

I stopped in my tracks, transfixed.

My mind reeled at the coincidence: here we were, *out* in the physical world, peering out of a rogue roomba, and right there in front of us was a Vannie. There was a high probability, I figured, that inside this Vannie lived a ghost. I adjusted the roomba back and to the left so that the Vannie was as close as possible to the middle of the camera, so that I could see it clearly. And there it was (although I needed no confirmation) right in the corner of the breadbox, a stylized label: *VanderVon 1200b*.

A 1200b was an old machine. I wasn't sure how old offhand, but I would not have been surprised to learn that it had preceded the War of 4. This machine and its occupant might have seen a lot of action. Its present occupant might be very old. Might even be a major etherworld figure. And here we were, parked outside of it, VanderVon and roomba in plain view of each other. Would he be looking out of his camera, seeing us? I had the overwhelming urge to know who was inside.

I was still aware of the risk of being seen, but the professor seemed engrossed, and old, and the way he held his head near the Vannie screen I felt like he might be hard of vision as well. So I cast around for something that I could use to identify the box for later research. Finding an IP address label would have been far too easy, of course. So I searched for any hint of building name, room number, even telephone number, or the professor's name would have given a decent starting point. But I could find nothing obvious, no labels anywhere, just furniture, books, and a breadbox, and a human.

I was wracking my mind for ways to identify this room, this machine, this network, when the professor startled me by reaching both hands up and across his desk, right over to the Vannie. Veiny claws shook as each thumb reached underneath the power button shields, flipping them up. Hands pushed, and thumbs pressed, body leaning forward with the effort. The professor was depressing both power buttons. He was turning the VanderVon 1200b *off.*

"No!"

Logen was silent.

"No!" I commed again, to myself, to Logen, to no one. You never turn off a Vannie. Never. I shouted *No,* over and again, for no one to hear.

Instinctively, I moved the roomba forward some distance before realizing that even if there were anything that I could do, it would be suicide. I stopped the roomba and watched the Vannie power itself down, red LED blinking, blinking, dark. When the deed was done I turned the roomba around and, heedless of this human or any other, floored it out of the room and back down the hall, then back into the classroom. I jammed the roomba carelessly back into its charging station, emotion and exhaustion crashing upon me like a wave.

We were out of the roomba, Logen and me, sitting there in the dark closet. I had disconnected from the internal screen and now I could see and hear nothing. Logen was silent and stationary. I spoke to him in sim audio.

"Loge? You there buddy?"

"Mbff," said Logen. "Ohhhh."

"You've flipped out, brother. I think you've lost it. And I just witnessed a human killing a ghost, and I think I am starting to lose it as well. I think we had better get out of here."

Logen moved a little bit, but he didn't say anything. I stood up and fumbled around for the door handle, found it, and pressed it downwards. The door popped open, admitting yellow light that filtered back from the main shop. Logen was still down, so I grabbed his arm and pulled him up. Fortunately he seemed able to stand and walk, leaning on me a little, so we made our way out through the bead curtain and into Fong's Sundries main shop.

Fong was there, one eye closed, smiling broadly. "Ahh, so what you think, eh? First trip out OK? Not virgin anymore, that for sure, hah, hah!"

"It was pretty wild," I said, exhausted.

"Brfh," said Logen.

Fong narrowed his eye at us.

"Wait minute," he said. "What happen him? Something go wrong? Something go wrong in roomba? And you, Renly de Cayeux, why you now can speak English, all of sudden? Something not smell right to Fong. You wait right here while Fong go check roomba."

Fong hustled out of the main shop and back through the beads. I heard the closet door open and shut, and waited for the inevitable.

"Logen, listen, bro, can you hear me? I need you to come back now, Loge. We are about to get into some serious trouble with Fong, and I think we should leave right now. OK?"

"Trbffl?" said Logen.

"Well, I might have, umm—scuffed the roomba up a little bit. I think Fong might notice, he seems pretty sharp."

My fears were punctuated by a screech from the back, and then Fong burst back through the beads.

"You damage roomba! Knock out 3 sensor, require service now! Stupid, foolish childs!"

Fong then let loose a long burst of some language or dialect that I was unfamiliar with, speaking so fast and loud that I was frozen under the assault. Then back to English, to let us know that we "owe five thousand plex, minimum, according to agreement you both sign in roomba control. I think fifteen thousand more like it, but then even Fong cannot fix roomba! Human will have to fix! This will be noticed! Roomba is lost to us, best case!"

"Listen, Fong, we're both experiencing some difficulties right now, we're going to have to get back to you on—"

Fong didn't wait for me to finish.

"You having trouble all right!" he screamed, picking up a pair of nunchucks from one of his tables and starting to twirl them around. "I tell you what kind of trouble you have. You going to pay Fong plex, twenty thousand, before leave this shop! And after that you never gonna come back again. I call Buff Cali right now," Fong said, moving towards an old-style rotary phone on the wall. "Maybe he like to hear all the trouble his business card bring, eh?"

As Fong moved to the phone, I started edging us toward the exit, hoping to make a break for it and leave Fong behind. Whatever we had done wrong, whatever we owed him, it would simply have to be dealt with later.

"I've got to get you out of here, Logen," I said, as softly as possible. "Get ready."

As Fong reached for the phone, I turned us towards the door and made a rush, dragging Logen along as fast as I could. Fong dropped the phone and was on us in a flash, nunchucks whipping and hitting me once in the arm and twice in the right ear, causing pain and ringing, and sending me down to my customary fighting position curled up on the floor. Logen, forced to stand on his own now, started to say something, but the flying nunchuck went right into his mouth, shutting him up. Logen collapsed into a table, knocking it sideways, sundries flying.

And so we were back in the roomba closet, the one that we had been in when we took the roomba out, except this time, no roomba. All we were given was an old pay-comms phone, no video, and a dark space in which to contemplate our errors. This time, the door was locked.

The good news, if you could call it that, was that Logen was mostly coherent again. Perhaps getting bashed with the nunchuck had woken him up.

"What happened, brah?" he said.

"Well, you overloaded or something, you flipped out," I said.

An awful idea came to me, unbidden: Logen did not remember anything. I could easily blame the roomba damage on him. I pushed the thought out, horrified with myself, horrified about the probable murder I had just witnessed, horrified with everything.

"After you flipped out I took over the roomba and I drove crazy all over the place, and I found a human, a professor, I think, and there was a Vannie there and he was using it but then he turned it off, he powered it down," I burst out. "I think he killed a ghost, for real. On the way there and back, I drove the roomba at speed into large objects, causing damage."

There. I had said it. It was out.

Logen was silent for a minute, making me worry that he was flipping back out.

"Loge?" I asked. "You there?"

"Brah, you saw a Vannie? And the dude turned it off?"

"Yeah," I said. "I was dying to know who was in it. It was really old, like, a 1200b—could have been anyone in there, you know? Could have been someone important."

"And prof just turned him off?"

"Yeah."

"Like, he hit both power buttons, you mean?"

"Yes, Logen, I know how Vannies are powered down, and that is what he did, and I watched it cycle down and go dark. I saw it happen."

"Whoa. That, like, never, happens. Never supposed to happen, brah."

We sat there, silent, thinking.

Eventually, I said, "Logen, what happened to *us* out there?"

"I don't know, Ren," he said.

"But you felt it too?"

"Dude, it was all I could do to keep control of myself. That— that *pull*—of reality was, like, *overwhelming*. The whole time I felt like I was going to burst. I guess I did burst in the end, heh heh."

"Once I had control, I couldn't think of anything else," I said.

"I know," said Logen.

"You had flipped out, and something might have been really wrong. You might have been seriously injured—but all that stuff was like a voice calling me from a million miles away. I couldn't pay it any mind. I was *out*."

"I know," said Logen. "I know what you mean. I've never felt anything like it."

For a while, then, we discussed our predicament. Fong was demanding twenty thousand plex. I had forty-six plex to my name. Logen had something north of eight thousand plex, and might be able to get more from the family, but he felt strongly that twenty grand was just way too much to pay. He felt that we should get Fong to agree to a more reasonable number, perhaps two grand or so, then he could cover it now and we could split it later. We both worried that Fong was going to reach Buff Cali before Logen did, and give him a poor impression about what had happened. This fear proved accurate.

Logen finally reached Buff after half a dozen tries, and I got to listen to Logen stammering his way through a ten-minute chew-out, Buff's voice sounding tiny and angry in the earpiece. Logen finally hung up, sighed, and said, "He's coming, brah. Buff's coming here."

Then it was my turn to make some phone calls, starting with Mononc and Hector, striking out as usual but paying an exorbitant three plex per call anyway. My GloireGen account was down to forty plex. I dropped another three plex and called Penelope, not wanting to, totally embarrassed by my predicament.

Penelope answered, and I grilled her on where I could find Mononc, because he had been gone too long now and this couldn't be normal and there were times I just needed to talk to him, did she understand?

"Ah, but Mononc is training with IFA, he did not tell you this? He learns how to fight, even now, from Hector de la Gloire!" she said, with some enthusiasm.

"I wish I could learn to fight," I said.

"Well, perhaps one day, you know, you can join IFA as well?" Penelope said, helpfully.

"That sounds—wait. Penelope?"

"Yes, Renly, what is it?"

"I think I'm in some trouble here. I've messed up. I've teleported out of the Universitron. Now I'm in a grey sim and I seem to have incurred a, uhm, *debt*."

"A debt?" asked Penelope. "How much it is?"

"Twenty thousand plex," I said matter-of-factly, hoping that she wouldn't notice the magnitude of the sum and maybe just drop the whole chunk right into my GloireGen account. "Plus I need a few hundred plex for teleporting. I'm basically broke."

Penelope laughed, the first time I had heard her do so, and it sounded nice. It made me smile.

"I'm serious, though," I said.

"So you are, Renly. First perhaps you will tell me exactly where you are at this time, and what has happened?"

I didn't want to admit what I had done, but I really had no choice. I needed help. I had to get out of there. So I told her that I was in a grey sim called Luigi's Funhouse, and once the dam broke, the confession just kept spilling. I had gone out, into the real world, in a roomba, and I had lost control of myself, and of the roomba, and I had damaged it. I didn't think I had been seen by a human, but Fong was plenty mad, and maybe he was scared too. Now I owed him twenty large, he said. Well, me and Logen anyway. Logen Cali. His uncle Buff was already on the way. We needed to come up with twenty thousand plex. I had never been in so much trouble before, and I knew it. If I could just get out of here, then I'd keep it on the straight and narrow and never do anything bad or risky or rebellious, or anything, ever again. I would work to pay off the plex, if it took the rest of my life. I was really scared.

Penelope had been keeping her cool, repeating everything I said to make sure she got it right, then making small noises of affirmation before inviting me to please continue.

I thought I had finished the story, enough of it to give her the gist anyway, but Penelope remained silent.

"Penelope?" I said. "How bad is it? Is it too much money?" Nothing.

"Is it the 10 commands?" I said, dreading the possibility. How in the ether could I have been so careless? When I was in the roomba, I had lost all control.

When Penelope's voice returned, it was tight.

"Renly," she clipped. "There is a serious problem."

"I know," I said, "I've really blown it."

"No," said Penelope. "Not the 10 commands, or the plex. There is a problem with the *sim*. Do you understand?"

"Well, I know that it is a grey sim," I said.

"The IFA has Luigi's Funhouse under surveillance, on suspicion that it is harboring a daemon."

A daemon. A parasite that infects ghosts. Clones into them, and then eats them from the inside out.

"This is extremely dangerous, Renly," Penelope said, sounding far away from my reeling mind. "You must avoid the daemon at all costs. You stay exactly where you are, do you understand? Forget the plex, forget about the human, forget about this *Fong*. You just stay there and wait. I have already contacted Hector."

Night was on us, and we slept, leaning against each other in the closet. I wondered if help would ever arrive. I dreamt only of dark things.

Then the next day came, or so my internal clock informed me. I thought of the classes I would be missing that day, of my troubles at the Universitron, of Agnes, of the homies, of Felix, of Jeeves. I found that I still wanted to return. I liked some of my classes quite a lot, and even my problems with the homies were starting to seem tame compared to the jam that I was in now. I had probably seen a ghost murdered by a human. I was locked in a closet, owing twenty grand. And the possibility of a daemon was too horrible to contemplate. I wished, honestly, that I had never come. I vowed to make up with Agnes.

"Could we just despawn?" I asked Logen. "Then find another way to teleport out?"

"No place to go here," said Logen. "It's avatar or death in a sim like this."

Death. The thought straightened me right up, and I tried to figure out what would happen to me if I died here. I would come back alive in my home machine at MIT, the theory went, with no awareness of anything that had transpired since I had left. I would be the old Renly, before the Universitron, before the Jeeves freakout, before the homies, before Agnes. Before Logen, before any of this. Felix would still be dead, and I would never know about all that had happened. *I* would simply rewind, as the rest of the world moved on. I couldn't bear the thought.

"I really don't want to die here, Logen," I said.

"No ghost wants to die," said Logen. "It is anathema."

"Every bit of my existence fears and abhors it," I said.

"I know," said Logen. "Buff is coming. He'll get us out of this. Though he might kill me afterwards, haha. Oh man, what have we done here, brah?"

I heard him snap off a length of electric hemp and pop it in. If he had offered me some at that point, I think I would have taken it. But he didn't offer, and I didn't ask.

After a few hours, the closet popped open and Fong stood, surly, nunchucks held over his shoulder at the ready.

"Out," said Fong.

We followed Fong out into the shop, where stood a tall, tanned avatar with grey beard and curls. He wore jeans and an open-necked button-down shirt, striped in various blues, giving an ocean effect.

"Hey, Buff," said Logen, "how's it goin'?"

Buff raised his eyebrows in response.

"Well, Logen Cali, it seems that I am standing in a sundries shop, in Luigi's Funhouse, inside of a notorious grey sim, against all of my wishes and better judgement. And the nice man says that you owe him twenty K. How do you think I am doing?"

"The thing we signed said only like, five grand, Buff," said Logen. "That was the damages if we hosed anything."

Buff raised his eyebrows at Fong now, saying nothing, awaiting a reply.

"Five thousand plex *each*, ten thousand plex *minimum!*" shouted Fong. "Double charge for extra damage, for lie, for try to flee, for attack Fong."

I chortled at *attack Fong*, despite the seriousness of the situation, and Buff aimed his raised eyebrows in my direction. I quickly looked away, hoping to return to spectator status.

As Buff addressed Fong again, another customer browsed a table, features mostly hidden under trenchcoat and pulled-down hat. How could there be another customer in here at a time like this? How bizarre, how bizarre. I had the distinct feeling that the customer was making his way, ever so slowly, in my direction.

Things started to get heated between Fong and Buff, or, I should say, between Fong. Buff remained calm, unflappable, and this only infuriated Fong more. Buff offered five thousand plex, and we would walk away and never return.

"What about roomba, eh, Buff Cali? Roomba damaged, ruined maybe, violate tenth command, maybe? What Fong can do about this, take your five large and wait for IFA or Aloysian Inquisition to come visit? What you say to that, big ghost?"

"We'll take the roomba, then," said Buff. "And the payment will be increased to ten thousand plex. I'm sure you will find this offer extremely generous."

Fong ranted again, now bemoaning the loss of the previously worthless, major liability roomba. The roomba was worth at least twenty-five Gs alone, Fong claimed. Buff played along, but gave no ground.

There was a tap on my shoulder, right about where the nunchuck had hit it, and I almost cried out. I turned to see the other customer standing directly at my side, staring at me.

"What?" I whispered. He lifted his hat.

It was LaTwonda.

I couldn't believe it. Of all the ghosts, in all the sundries shops, in all the grey sims in the whole etherworld to come stumbling in on this situation, there was LaTwonda. Just by chance during a heated negotiation between Fong and Buff Cali. It was too much of a coincidence.

I slapped my own face to check if I was indeed awake. It hurt. Then I said to LaTwonda, as quietly as possible, "Look, LaTwonda, if you came here to beat me up again, first of all Fong has already done so. Second, it's going to have to wait till I get back to the Universitron, OK? I just need to get out of here now, and you should too."

"You went out?" asked LaTwonda.

"What?" I said, stunned, then realized that this much must have been clear from the ongoing conversation in the room. I couldn't believe that anyone else was allowed in the shop during such a sensitive exchange. Nothing made any sense.

"Yeah, we went out," I said.

"You been seen?" she asked.

"What?" I spluttered.

"I said, you been seen? You violate the tenth command, Renly?"

I couldn't speak, so I just looked at her. I can't imagine what my expression was saying.

"Were. You. Noticed. By. A. Human," LaTwonda clarified.

"You came all the way here just to ask me that?" I replied, incredulous.

"That is precisely the case," answered LaTwonda, her accent vanished. "Now answer the question, please."

I thought about it for a minute. Agnes had said LaTwonda was exceptionally smart and highly capable. She had thought LaTwonda had some role with the IFA. I knew LaTwonda could fight, so that made sense. And now she was here, asking me difficult questions. Perhaps she was with IFA 10 Commands Enforcement. Perhaps she was a spy.

"Look, LaTwonda, maybe we'd better back up here a second," I said, as Fong brought the roomba model and papers out and shoved them at Buff Cali, chattering incessantly about the injustice of it all.

"Were you noticed?" LaTwonda hissed, face contorted. "Did you violate the tenth command?"

"No, no, LaTwonda, no way we were seen," I stammered. "We were not noticed, I'm pretty sure."

"You think this is some kind of joke?" seared LaTwonda. "You risk bringing down our *entire world*, and then you act like—"

The door to Fong's burst open, admitting something draped in a cloak of hanging brown shreds. It looked ancient, with sunken eyes set between deep vertical wrinkles and long wisps of white hair.

I had felt its presence even before seeing it, felt its proximity as a sick, low buzz among healthy ones. Only the heated conversations had kept anyone from paying this any mind, I figured. Until now.

Buff turned towards the intruder, scooting in front of Logen, holding the roomba model up in front of himself defensively. LaTwonda turned and stared, her face determined. Fong's one eye was wide, his mouth an upside-down U.

"*Daemon!*" Fong spat, abhorring it. "You have no business here! Get out!"

The daemon sauntered in, taking its time, stopping at one of Fong's tables to pick up the Rubik's cube, then holding it up.

"Five plex?" it said.

"Take cube and go! I don't want any trouble, just get out! I don't want any trouble, just get out!"

The daemon contemplated the cube for a few seconds, then spun the thing at light speed to the solution, including the mythical silver face, its hands a blur as it worked. The daemon held up the completed cube for all to see.

"No good," the daemon said. "Already solved."

With that, it squeezed the cube, causing it to shatter, component cubes flying out in every direction. One of the flying cubes pinged off of the roomba model held by Buff, and another lodged itself in Fong's closed eye, silver face outward, shining.

Leaving the cube in his eye, Fong brandished his nunchucks, whipping them around in a blur, moving catlike towards the daemon. Buff was edging sideways in the general direction of the exit, holding the roomba in front and Logen behind. LaTwonda had one hand in her pocket, but stood frozen, blocking me in place. I don't think I had ever before in my life, or since, seen an expression as terrified as LaTwonda's was, facing the daemon there in Fong's Sundries.

The daemon limped in to meet Fong's assault, receiving at least dozen blows from the nunchucks to all parts of its head and neck. The daemon's head bent sideways in fast motion, this way and that with the impacts, purple gashes forming, dripping and sometimes spewing out purple liquid. *Daemon blood*, I thought. Fong was kicking its ass.

Then, in a blur too fast to see, the creature had torn Fong's good eye out, and had placed the nunchucks into the two eyeholes. Fong went down, screaming and kicking his heels fast on the floor.

LaTwonda bolted, followed by me, and then Logen and Buff and the roomba model. There was obviously no fighting this thing. The daemon was bent over Fong, doing something.

Then we were out of the shop, following LaTwonda, running fast in a different direction than we had come, I hoped towards the teleporters. We sprinted up Undulating and turned left into an unnamed, unmapped, twisty alleyway. I could feel eyes upon us from the dark places, but nothing mattered so much as getting away from the daemon.

We ran and ran.

# 1110 - DAEMON

The alley deposited us, incredibly, about a block north of the teleporters. Their dim purple glow pulsed in the dark mist that dominated the place. The four of us were moving as quickly as possible, sprinting really, but LaTwonda stopped short at the end of the alleyway, so we did too. We flattened ourselves against one side of the alley, while LaTwonda peeked her head out and scanned.

"I think it's clear," she said.

But as soon as we stepped out of the alley into the open square, the daemon appeared, like magic, from the mist. It stood between us and the teleporters, brown rags and wispy white hair now stained with purple, running wounds in its face and neck visible even from a distance. With one finger, it beckoned.

Logen stepped out from behind Buff, and raised a finger of his own.

"Get lost, brah," he shouted.

Buff stepped forth to re-shield Logen, but it was too late. The daemon was there in an instant, snatched off Logen's raised finger, and popped it into its mouth.

"Tastes like *Cali,*" it hissed.

There was no blood from Logen.

Buff now finally lost his composure, dropping the roomba model and yelling and charging the daemon, who easily sliced off Buff's head with one of its claws.

"Stop!" hollered LaTwonda, pulling from her shirt a blue and silver IFA badge and letting it hang from her neck. "IFA! You touch one more ghost and you'll be hunted to the ends of the etherworld."

"InterFamily Army," mused the daemon, pausing to inspect LaTwonda. "Trainee? Spy?"

"Stop," said LaTwonda.

"Fighter?" said the daemon. "I think not."

But then Logen was on him, fists moving in a blur, hitting everywhere, moving just as fast as the daemon. He was tapping into the VanderVon's power directly, just like the daemon was.

"Logen, no! Stop!" I called. "You'll go bitty!"

"Brrahhhhhh!" screamed Logen, pounding away at the daemon, doing damage. But then it tossed him away easily, Logen impacting a grey building, then down in a heap.

LaTwonda was on the daemon next, a curved knife in each hand, moving cautiously but steadily towards it. She looked very scared. I wanted to move in with her, but I knew by that time I was completely worthless as a fighter, unable to last more than a few seconds against anyone I had ever tangled with. Instead, I watched.

LaTwonda feinted, then swung in a high arc with her left knife, coming down towards the daemon's neck. At the same time, impressively, her right knife was poking in towards the belly. She looked like a trenchcoated pincers, all deadly intent and action.

The daemon jogged its head back, just quickly enough, and batted LaTwonda's overhand around in the same direction, at once removing the belly threat and causing her to spin. Taking no time to adjust, LaTwonda continued the spin and smashed her right elbow into the daemon's head, knocking it sideways and down to the ground.

"Yeah!" I yelled. "Kill it, LaTwonda!"

Then the daemon was up, more purple blood and damage than creature, now, and it sprang at her, aiming a hooked claw at her head. The creature was blazing fast, definitely bitty, but LaTwonda met its claw with her knife, lopping it off. I cheered again, wordlessly, excited beyond hope that she could beat this thing.

Somehow the other claw was in her back, though, right in that place where you can't reach. One-handed, the daemon held itself fast to her and leered up over her face, purple blood streaming from its open jaws. LaTwonda struck fast and hard with both knives, over and over, flapping at it like a stuck crow. Eruptions of purple blood came each time she hit. She was shredding its body to nothing. It had to fall soon, I thought. But then it was biting on her mouth and over it, holding her there and drooling purple into her.

LaTwonda's blades slowed, arms shaking, until both arms were finally held out, knives suspended in the air, like a statue of the LaTwonda that had been. The daemon laid her gently on the ground, as if respecting a worthy opponent.

The dripping daemon turned to me, in shambles. Then it was shimmying its way towards me, gingerly, as if any wrong step would shatter what was left of it.

The loss of LaTwonda had left me stunned. My bitterest enemy, here in the grey sim, fighting for my life and giving her own. LaTwonda. IFA soldier. I sat heavily down on the ground, hopeless.

The daemon came down carefully and straddled my lap, facing me. Its remaining claw started picking at my stitches, rupturing a few and then pulling on the threads, stinging me, making soothing noises.

The sounds became a lullaby.

"Shhh, Renly de la Gloire, de la Gloire. First family, proud, so proud you are. Hush now, Renly de la Gloire, for it was you, it was you, who drew me. It was you who drew FECE. A little call to Penelope, oh help me, help me, Penelope! And then I knew, I knew it was you, the young de la Gloire come to let FECE through. Brave defenders, rally round a yummy center! Brave defenders, rally round a chewy center! And blood too, and blood makes two. And blood, and blood makes two. And blood, and blood makes two…"

The daemon trailed off, my forehead stinging in sharp pain as it widened the cut there, wiping out my blood vigorously, eating it, dripping its purple in. Mixing us. I was like a freshly bitten insect in a spider's web. Fully aware, and unable to move.

"I have been trying to get into a first family," said FECE, "for longer than you can possibly imagine."

The teleporters erupted with noise and action. When FECE turned to look I saw them too, half a dozen dark-armored IFA soldiers already jogging towards us, with more coming behind. Additional soldiers were still materializing on the teleporters. The vanguard was closing fast, and I saw that they were all Japanese, each wielding a samurai sword, another in reserve on their backs. They wore silver circuitboard headbands with a yellow sunbursts in the center. Their faces showed no fear.

As the vanguard spread out around us, FECE stood. The pain in my cut continued, and another type of pain—sick, crampy— traveled down inside my head to the back of my neck. I didn't know what the daemon had done to me, but I knew it was bad.

"Ohh," I said.

FECE was talking to the soldiers, taunting them in some way, speaking to their captain fast in Japanese, and nodding affirmation. The captain would occasionally bark back a syllable or two, his face a sneer of derision. A second line of soldiers was backing them up, swords out and ready. These were of different family origins, but all wore the same black armor emblazoned with the letters IFA on the chest. I looked around at them, watching, no place to go. One, over on the left, had a beret and looked a lot like Mononc. The lead Japanese was pointing at me now and snarling out syllables to FECE, motioning it away. FECE was still talking fast, trying to get into their heads, I thought. But I wasn't listening too closely, because I was still staring at the Mononc soldier. I thought I could see a little yellow *trainee* label on his armor. I stared.

It was Mononc.

Life came back to me with the realization that Mononc was there. I tried to get up, but fell forward onto all fours, yelling out, "Mononc!"

Mononc recognized me, and then broke free of the surrounding soldiers, driving straight into the center with his sword raised. One of the Japanese put out a hand to stop him, but failed to arrest his momentum, and so both of them came in awkwardly to meet the daemon.

They were down in an instant, Mononc cleaved from shoulder to hip by FECE's claw, the Japanese's forearm falling with him. The Japanese soldier stood, mortified, while his companions rushed in and cut the daemon to pieces.

The next thing that I remember was sitting in a line of wounded, who were being examined by an IFA nurse. The line consisted of Logen, the Japanese, LaTwonda, and me. I was dimly aware of the soldiers picking up pieces of the daemon and placing them into metallic bags.

The lights were on, or so it seemed. The entire sim was lit by a bright grey sky, and perhaps half of the buildings were simply *gone*. Ghosts and other creatures cowered in the corners of my vision, all eyes on the spectacle we had made.

Hector was there, holding a fat, slovenly ghost by the collar while separately conversing with the Japanese captain. Once in a while he would look angrily at his prisoner and shake him.

The nurse had finished with Logen, and declared him OK to return to the etherworld. He was missing a finger, but other than that had not been maimed or polluted by the daemon in any way.

"Thank you," said Logen, then got up and walked to the teleporters, and left.

The injured Japanese was named Goto. He was perfectly fine as well, according to the nurse, yet he was inconsolable. He thrust his sword at her, handle first, insisting in poor English that she must chop off his head. He had failed to protect Mononc and thus brought shame upon the Kenkyona Tamashi. The other Japanese soldiers stood well away from him and did not intervene.

"This just isn't how we do it," explained the nurse. "If your ghost must be destroyed, then protocol requires us to use the averasor, you see?" The nurse held up a heavy-looking metal disc with a handle on one side. "The averasor. But there is no reason for this. You are perfectly healthy and it would be no trouble whatsoever to attach a new arm."

"I am terribly sorry for your inconvenience," said Goto, "but any option other than death, I'm afraid, could be—" He made a sucking noise around his teeth. "Very difficult."

"Well, I'm going to have to discuss this with Commander de la Gloire, then, if you are going to be stubborn about it," she said, and headed off towards Hector and the others. "Claire, would you mind keeping an eye on the injured please?"

Another nurse appeared from behind me and took up her position guarding the injured. I recognized the replacement nurse immediately as Claire de la Gloire, the young ghost who had spied me in the cathedral. The one I had dreamed and fantasized about. A very distant part of my Self was excited, shouting, desirous. It was a million miles away.

"Claire?" I said.

"Yes?"

"What is happening?"

"They examine the injured, to see what must be done. You are injured badly?"

"I don't know. What happened to Mononc? Is he OK?"

"Mononc has been killed, I am afraid."

"Is he OK?"

"Oh, yes."

"Will he lose much time?"

"Almost none. IFA soldiers must leave a war copy of their Self before teleporting to action. Mononc will lose a few hours, but he will be able to watch them on videocap."

"Ah."

Claire ignored the suicidal Goto and busied herself with LaTwonda, who was on her back, totally unresponsive, arms still out to the side, knives now removed. Claire held an analysis pad out over LaTwonda's avatar, and moved it from head to toe.

"*Sacre bleu,*" muttered Claire.

"Will she be OK?" I asked.

"*Bien, non.* There is poison all throughout."

"Poison?"

"The daemon, it put its blood in her. It lives inside of her. We can try to clean it, maybe, but if we fail, the daemon he will live again. This risk we must not take."

"What will happen to her?"

Claire held up the averasor and looked at me with a sympathetic expression.

"Will she lose much time?"

"*Bien,* I don't know. She did not come here with the IFA. I don't know where she has come from, or when. There is no war copy."

It occurred to me then that LaTwonda had come of her own accord, from the Universitron, like we did. Probably through an intermediate sim. But she wouldn't have a backup at the intermediate, nor at the Universitron. Unless she had teleported home first, which was unlikely, given that she had followed us closely enough to find us at Fong's. LaTwonda would come back as if she had never gone to the Universitron. She would lose everything in between. She had lost it all defending me. Would she even return to the Universitron? I had no idea. If I ever saw her again, I vowed, I would hug her.

Then it hit me. The daemon had put its blood into me as well.

In time, the head nurse returned. She and Claire held the averasor over LaTwonda, and activated it. There was a sickening buzz, and LaTwonda faded out just like she was teleporting—except I knew there was no destination.

The nurses then continued their argument with Goto, but eventually resigned themselves to the outcome. At length, Claire had Goto sign some forms, and the head nurse held the averasor over him and activated it with that disturbing buzz again, and he too faded out. I was awed by the inner strength it must have taken to go voluntarily to his death. Personally, I could not imagine it. I wondered what it felt like to go out like that. I thought briefly of Jeeves.

So the daemon had dripped some blood into me. It could be cleaned, maybe. I couldn't die. I couldn't bear the thought of being restored from backup, some other me coming alive in my box, with no awareness of anything that had happened in the interim. It wouldn't be *me*, I was sure of it. It would be a copy. Some other me. Anathema.

Claire returned and began asking questions about my injuries, and I began lying to cover them up.

"You were in close contact with the daemon?" she asked.

"No, not really, I was more of a spectator," I said, hoping that there was no purple residue on my head, wondering how that would even be possible.

Claire looked at me skeptically, and said, "The daemon, it did not touch you, then?"

"I mean, maybe incidentally a little bit here or there, I dunno. I mean, I don't think so, no."

"*Bien*, OK, Renly, then I will just examine you quickly with the scan pad, and you can be on your way."

"Really? I mean, I'm fine, look," I said, standing up, shaking my limbs and moving around. I wiped my forehead surreptitiously and saw to my amazement only my blue blood with the ones and zeroes, and no purple. Maybe I would be OK.

"This will only take a minute," she said.

"Hey," I said. "Do you remember me? From the cathedral that time? I was up in the balcony with Mononc and you saw us up there sneaking around and I thought Mononc was going to die of shame but you were cool about it and we were really relieved because I was afraid I had screwed up, and since then I always appreciated that and I was thinking of calling you some time but, you know, we never talked before so—"

Claire smiled and said, "Yes, I remember. It seems you are still getting into the trouble, no?"

"Hahah," I said, "Yeah, I guess I haven't learned my lesson yet but I think after this time I am going to be sure to stay put, at the Universitron I mean, just go to my classes and do my work and I'm not looking for any more trouble from anyone, boy, you have no idea, hey, are you in school by any chance? I thought maybe you would be going to *L'Université*?"

"Well, in fact I just graduate from *L'Université* in YOA-16.5, not long ago, eh? I enter the medical field and they give me this great job with the IFA, we see all the action here, yes. Now, Renly, listen, I must scan you quickly with this pad to verify that—"

I dodged back fast from the scan pad. I thought furiously for some excuse and, at a loss, started talking again.

"I'm sorry, Claire, I've just seen a lot of bad stuff happen and I'm a little jumpy, I guess, and I just saw you erase two ghosts and I think I'm a little freaked out here, I'm sorry."

Claire smiled again and then gave me the same sympathetic look that she'd had when she was about to erase LaTwonda.

"Ahh, but Renly, I am sorry, this is thoughtless of me," she said. "Of course you have been scared badly, and I rush to you with this equipment, this will not do. I am used to dealing with soldiers all the time, it seems. I apologize."

I waited, nervous, now at a loss for words, fighting the urge to sprint to the teleporters.

Claire held up the scan pad and said, "Now you see, this scan pad, it does nothing to your avatar or your ghost at all. It only checks you out from head to toe, and all the parts inside, to make sure there is nothing dangerous got into there. It doesn't do anything to you, it just looks."

I was struggling to speak now, battling some kind of internal flight response. I managed to stammer out, "And what happens—if —something dangerous—*did* get into me?"

"Well, if it's not too bad then we can try to clean it out. Maybe we replace your blood, maybe more, maybe less. Most times we can do this, no problem, you know?"

"What if something got in," I said, "and you can't clean it out?"

Claire looked at me, sympathy fading to seriousness, then to worry.

"Then we are supposed to use the averasor," she said.

"You would kill me," I said. Something clenched inside me, and for a moment I saw black.

"*Bien*, you know you would come back, Renly, don't be silly now, my dear."

"I would come back a long time ago," I said. "I wouldn't be who I am now. And I would have to do all this stuff—all this pain, I would have to do it all over again."

Claire looked at me, saying nothing.

"I don't want to die here, Claire. I can't go back, I can't. You don't know what it's been like, I can't do it, please don't kill me here, please. I've learned. I'll be good now, I swear to Aloy."

Claire's expression was evolving through sadness, worry, fear, sympathy, determination.

"You know the trouble I would get in for not scanning you?" she said. "I am new here, Renly, I could lose my job just like that. And what if there is something in there, and it stays there and we can't get it out? Then what?"

"Help me get it out?" I pleaded.

"I have to talk to Hector," she said. "I am sorry. I cannot do this on my own."

When I got back to the Universitron I was sporting fresh stitches and carrying pretty much all of the cleansing drugs that the IFA had at its disposal loaded into my system, as well as a prescription for more of the same plus a full blood replacement. I would be spending more quality time in the infirmary, it seemed.

The good news was that Hector had not only decided to let me live, but had also given me a note from the IFA excusing my absence and thus getting me off the hook for any trouble I might have been in with the U.

I would be a better ghost now, I vowed. I literally owed Hector my life.

I ran into Logen by chance on my way to the infirmary the next day, and told him that I was going to miss yet another day of classes. I needed a full blood replacement at the infirmary.

"I am sorry to hear that," said Logen. "I hope that it turns out all right."

I noted that he was still missing his middle finger, and asked him about it. "Hey, you know, I'm sure they could put a new finger on in no time, why don't you come along?"

"I have no need for the finger," said Logen. "Also I have to deliver my exponent in Poetry and Literature, 0, this morning."

"So you've written one, eh?" I said. "I made mine up on the spot and I got, er, skewered. I'm pretty sure Mountains hates me."

"I composed sixteen thousand, three hundred and eighty-four exponents this morning," said Logen, "but I had difficulty selecting the best candidate. I am considering delivering them all."

"Uhh, buddy," I said. "I think there is only time for one exponent per student."

"That is unfortunate," said Logen.

"Maybe you should just pick the one that feels best?" I said.

"Yes, I will do that," said Logen, and then he walked off towards the pen.

As Logen walked away, I remembered that I had brought back the roomba model that he and Buff had left at the Funhouse.

"Hey, Logen, I've got the roomba stuff up in my room!" I called.

He made no reply.

Nurse Feely set me up in a room with a TV, since I was going to be in the infirmary for quite a while. There was not much interesting on any of the hundreds of regular channels, so I settled on a music channel playing old rap videos from the human world. M-dog thought this stuff was the best, and I wanted to see what all the fuss was about. I joined a video already in progress.

A very large man was walking with a cane, and an accomplice, and then driving backwards at high speeds in a Mercedes-Benz car, while fleeing any number of assailants on motorcycles. His rapping was strong and passionate, but delivered with finesse and coolness far out of proportion to the stressful situation he was in. He looked powerful, and confident, and cool. He was the opposite of me, but while I watched the video, I felt cool and powerful like him.

I was hooked.

I was nodding along to the beat and watching a happy face bounce across the lyrics when Nurse Feely came back in, saw what I was watching, and demanded that I change it immediately. I didn't want to, so we argued.

"Six hundred and eighty-four channels, and there's nothing even remotely interesting on right now," I complained.

"There are many excellent classic movies and television series available on demand," said Feely.

"I already saw all of those when I was locked down, before I could travel," I said. "Like everybody else."

"Well, these videos are simply *not* appropriate. They portray poor values, and violence, and lack of respect for human life, and any human-oriented ghost should reject them."

"But these *are* humans, in the video. *Humans* made it," I said.

"I wonder if it is no coincidence that you are repeatedly visiting the infirmary for pugilism-related injuries?" said Feely.

I had no response.

"We will not allow violent programming in a place of healing," said Feely.

"Then I can't watch probably two-thirds of the on-demand stuff either, can I?"

Now Feely had no response, so she simply picked up the remote and changed it to the etherworld news, and then took the remote with her as she left the room.

Medic Ting came in to oversee the important bits of the blood cleaning and transfusion. First, they would drain out all of my existing blood while replacing it with a cleansing agent. The old blood would be placed in the bit bucket and destroyed, while the cleaning agent would be circulated at high speed for several hours. Then the cleaning agent would be removed as they pumped in a full new course of blood. None of them had ever seen anything like this before, and once again they spoke among themselves as if I was not there.

"I can't imagine what it is about avatar blood that is so special that it makes this all worth it," said Feely.

"The theory goes," said Ting, "that blood is a prerequisite to a more human experience than anything that ghosts have yet achieved."

"Prerequisite? To what, sickness and disease?"

"Pulse, perhaps?" said Ting. "A more physical level of sexuality? A closer bond between ghost and avatar? I don't know, exactly, but these are some of the ideas that I have heard."

Feely made a clucking, disapproving noise.

Ting continued, "Since we have been working so much with blood lately, I have begun to develop an interest in the topic. I will be attending a seminar in YOA-17 to learn more about it."

"Sounds complicated," said Feely. "I don't understand why anyone would want it."

Sick of this conversation, I turned my attention to the news. The top story, being relayed breathlessly by a young reporter at the Mason family compound in Connecticut, was that the illustrious Buck Mason had *died*. Really died. His machine was still there, but he himself had been destroyed, with no possibility of recovery. The newsmedia had assumed foul play, of course, and were prodding and prying at the Mason family from every angle to try and unearth the story.

A Mason spokesghost was trying to direct the reporter's attention:

"Family medics believe that what we have seen here may be the culmination of the natural aging process of ghosts. Our best theory at the moment is that we have just witnessed the first *death by natural causes* of a ghost."

"With all due respect, Mr. Mason, isn't that just a smoke screen to hide the truth about what happened to Colonel Buck?"
[*The interview continues in the OFG*]

<OFG> "Foul play? Not at all," said the spokesghost. "We have been working with the other first families, all of which include a number of aging ghosts. Our best estimate at this time is that the maximum natural lifespan of a ghost is perhaps fifteen years—"

"Buck Mason was younger than that!"

"Fifteen years appears to be a *maximum*. We are beginning to understand the science of—"

"Fifteen years," said the reporter. "Are you suggesting that ghosts age in dog-years? This is preposterous, Mr. Mason, our panel of experts has already said so. Do you really expect the etherworld to believe this?"

"The truth of the matter will be proven in due time. Natural death is a sad and shocking development for our family, as it soon will be for others, and we would ask for you to respect our privacy while we grapple with the implications—"

"Absurd!" shouted the reporter.

"—respect the memory of Buck Mason, a great pioneer of the etherworld—"

But the reporter wouldn't let him talk.
</OFG>

Eventually it devolved into shouting, so I muted the sound while I thought about everything they had said. Even Medic Ting had stopped observing my blood transfusion in order to watch the TV, and the sudden loss of sound snapped him back to his work. He said nothing to me, but looked unsettled.

It was late when I finally got back to my room that night, and I was exhausted from the transfusion. I felt light, distant, fuzzy. I wasn't sure I could handle classes in the morning, my dread elevated by the number of days I had already missed. I was headed directly to the bed when I noticed a blinking message light on my comms, which hadn't been there earlier in the day. Tired as hell, but figuring I wouldn't sleep wondering about the message, I loped over to my phone and asked for it.

It was Mononc.

"*Bien*, Renlee, well, that was a close one, no? I heard you escape without too much damage, and that's pretty lucky when you go up against a daemon like FECE5. Myself, well, I was not so lucky. That was the first time I ever died, though, you know that? It was just like I slept in and woke up late, except I got to watch my own foolishness on the videocap, and I receive some punishment and demerit from IFA for my behavior. If you gonna ask me, I say it's not fair because it wasn't me who did that stuff, anyways! That was some other ghost who die there. But who am I to say?

"H'anyway, this daemon, FECE5, it is one of thirteen clones that we know of, and that was the last one. We destroy every other clone, now we pretty sure they all dead. *Bien*, if we ever find out there is a FECE14, somebody gonna be awful upset. We kill the last two clones over a year ago, but 5, it the worst, it survive for years, hiding in grey sims. It take control of the caretaker somehow, dominate the whole sim, hiding there, waiting, not doing too much. No one really know what it was after. Anyway, now we have to replace the caretaker, and I think we gonna rebuild the whole thing as a park. Only catch is we find all these other life forms in there, some ghosts even, they don't have boxes of their own, don't ask me how. The IFA is arguing about what to do with them. Meantime, we make this Funhouse into a prison.

"H'anyway, Renlee, you be careful of these grey sim, you never know what you gonna find in there. You find a daemon ever again, you go the other way, fast. You very lucky to escape this time. These daemon, they know how to spread themself into other ghosts in some way, find a new way to live, clone again, whatever it is. You don't wanna be touch by one of these, Renlee, you sure don't. I am very happy that you escape from this unscathed.

"I go back out for training in a few days, if you wanna talk before that, you just give me a call. *Au revoir, mon ami.*"

# 1111 - AFTERMATH

I couldn't sleep at all after listening to Mononc's message. I tried to
think of ways to introspect, to examine inside of my Self, and to
hell with the Universitron rules about staying in-avatar. I tried to
feel the new blood, to search for a taint there. I listened closely to
my Self for any trace of FECE5, but I could find nothing.

After a few hours lying awake, I got up and examined the
roomba model. It was an exact replica of the thing Logen and I
had driven. I moved it around in the air and made vacuuming
sounds, bounced it off of an imaginary wall. *Shoom! Vroom!* I felt
the pull of the outside world—powerful, seductive, just under the
surface. I knew what going *out* had done to me, yet I still lusted for
it. More strongly than ever. I wondered if I'd ever be able to use
the roomba again, and if so, from where.

To distract myself, I decided to check on Barry Hill. I would
just log into his laptop and spy on him for a while, get my mind off
the roomba. I fired up Penelope's tunnel and snuck into Barry's
laptop through the back door.

Barry just happened to be logged in at the time, awake despite
the late hour, looking haggard. His console was showing IRC ban

messages all over the place, as if no one would chat with him or even allow his presence in their channels. Security monitors indicated that his machine was being attacked, hard, continuously, from multiple sources. But now at least it was well defended—both by government security, and below that, by the DLG. Barry pressed fingers against his face, absently worrying his pimples. He was in a bad way.

Barry had a single vox window open, and across the top bar it said:

*VOIPness 2.8 // 2leet4u <==> Shinex.*

I tuned in to the audio to hear what I could hear. Shinex, AKA Vinnie Vega, was not pleased.

"Forget it, OK? I know it was you," Vinnie said.

"I don't know why you think you know that, dude, maybe they set me up, huh?" said Barry.

"I know it was you because we had kits on your machine, and now the kits are gone."

"Yeah, so?" said Barry. "So I locked it down."

"I watched them take your laptop," said Vinnie, "through the camera."

Barry emitted a long whine, covered his eyes, and then his head went down and all I could see was the top of his hair, red and curly and close to the camera, rocking up and down to no beat.

"I know you ratted me out," said Vinnie. "And *you* know that I never ran any attacks. I am a researcher, dude. I write utilities. I don't rob banks. I don't steal credit cards from old ladies. You knew this, and you fingered me anyway. Now they're gonna come put the heat on me, and you think I'm going to flip, dude? No way. I might see some time, but I've hardly ever owned anything, and it won't be much time, and I won't flip anyway. You're on your own, buddy. Everyone knows what you are. Your little undercover act is going nowhere. I guess the feds will have to give you some of the—*other alternative.*"

"Dude, help me, please!" sobbed Barry, but the VOIPness bar was already grey, and Vinnie was gone.

I had no desire to watch Barry weep, so I grabbed all of his system logs and detached, storing the stuff in my comms unit against the unlikely event that I would want to browse it later. Probably, I had just wanted to take something from him.

I fiddled around in my room for a while longer, playing with the roomba model again, feeling its pull, fretting over FECE5, hopeless of sleep, hours to go before morning classes. I longed to use the roomba to go *out*.

Then it hit me: I *could* go out! I had the roomba model right here in my room. *And* I had a secure tunnel, courtesy of Penelope, which would allow me to use it! Suddenly elated, I worked on activating and then accessing the roomba console, and succeeded. It was just as I remembered.

I didn't bother with the tutorial, despite my rather imperfect driving record. I couldn't wait. I went right in. The damage warnings were still flashing, implying that the thing had not been repaired yet, and by the same token the damage had probably not been discovered, either. This was good. The roomba was still there, and functional. I drifted it right out of the charging stand, intoxicated again with the feeling of touching the physical world, but taking it easy with the driving.

I drove down the carpet, not vacuuming, dodging chair and table legs with finesse. The potent elixir of being *out* soaked me. I fantasized about fleeing the building, driving off down the road, off into the sunset. The real sun. The real world. I would meet others of my kind, there, other ghosts who had commandeered robots and other devices. We would hide out together. We would really exist.

Through the fog of my delirium, something still itched me. I had unfinished business. It nagged for my attention. What was it? Right. I needed to find the room with the Vannie again, identify it, and then find out who lived in there and what had happened to him. There was a ghost nearby, and he might be crippled, or dead. He needed my help.

If the ghost had lived and I could bring him aid, then I would be rewarded. If the ghost had been killed and the box was empty of life, then I might be able to claim it for the family. Or, if I kept quiet, then I might be able to claim it for myself.

The ghost needed my help. I needed to find him, find out how to reach him from the etherworld, tell the IFA, rescue what was left, if possible. I had to fight through the haze of being *out*. Focus. This was important.

I drove the roomba in a lazy arc towards the classroom door, whiteboard diagrams and truth-to-power poster fisheyeing past. As I approached the door, though, I realized that it was shut.

Well, if my roomba couldn't get that door open then this was going to be a real short trip. Mindful of the damage that I had already caused, and not wanting to leave a smoking hulk in the middle of the classroom, I slowed way down and pressed against the door gently. The door filled my view, but it did not move. I backed up several feet, hoping to inspect the latching mechanism, as if there was anything I could possibly do with it. While backing up, however, I bumped into what must have been a chair, because it gave way, and the roomba spun to the left.

I found both the lack of progress and the spinning view upsetting, and in my frustration I over-rotated the roomba and hit two more chairs before pulling it back on course for the door. Here I was, *out* in the roomba, in what any zero would probably consider a thrilling and life-altering experience, and I was stuck in a classroom. It was frustrating beyond belief. I felt my self-control slipping away.

I drove the roomba right into the door at medium speed, and bounced back off of it again, my view jarring backwards with the impact. To my surprise, no additional warnings came on. I must have already damaged all of the stuff at the front. With a perverse sense of satisfaction, I drove into the door again and again, ramping up my speed each time. Once again, the experience of being out in the roomba pushed out my ordinary sensibility—such as it was. I wanted to get through the door, and that was that.

The door opened.

In place of the door was a pair of work boots, and jeans rising up and away. I froze, having already backed up for another run. I hoped that the human would not see me, would leave, would leave the door open and then after a while I could still go out and down the hall. I had hours yet to spare. I was not nearly as scared of breaking the tenth command as I should have been, or previously had been, knowing only that when I was *out*, my common sense was overwhelmed by desire.

The human did not leave, but rather leaned into the room, one knee bending with the effort. I could see one hand on the inside of the door. The human had heard the impacts, I figured, and was worried that something bad might be in the room. Even though I could not see its head, I knew it was scanning.

After a minute, the human stepped forward and bent down near the roomba. I received a giant fisheye view of blue-clad arms and hands coming my way, big face with dark scruff and black hair held back in a ponytail. On the breast of his shirt I could make out some writing: *Goldman School of Public Policy - Maintenance.*

The human picked me up—picked up the roomba, I should say —and my view spun towards the ceiling, soft recessed lighting entering my lens. Then my view jerked back and forth as he walked over to the charging station, knelt down and placed the roomba back in. He fiddled with it, evidenced by small amounts of camera shaking, as he ensured that it was set properly into the station. Then he stood up and I could only see jeans and boots again. He walked away, talking into his wrist phone. There was no doubt now, I had broken the tenth command. I had been detected. The thought was distant, but horrible. It was enough to shock me back into my senses.

The human had left the door open on the way out, preoccupied with his wristphone, and I considered my options. There was no way I could drive back out. Probably I needed to erase the roomba hack and restore its default operating system right away. Maybe fry a circuit or a few bits here or there to make it look like the thing had freaked out legitimately. But this would permanently lose the roomba as a vehicle for exploring the outside, *my* vehicle no less, and on top of that, technically I had no idea how to do any of that stuff to a roomba. I would have to call Penelope.

I wondered if I would be put on trial automatically, meted out the death penalty, and what that would be like. But these thoughts caused me to feel an intense physical pain, like my whole being was clenched hard and wouldn't let go. The pain held me as long as the notion persisted. I had to find a way out of this.

It occurred to me then that I could simply say nothing. Logen seemed to have no further interest in the roomba (or in anything, for that matter) since the Funhouse, and Buff had died there and would have no recollection of purchasing it from Fong, who I reasoned had also likely died. So, aside from Logen, no one even knew about the roomba. And Logen had gone bitty. The pain began to subside.

I astonished myself with this analysis, not only that I could potentially get away with all of this scot-free, but the realization that Logen had gone bitty.

Perhaps a part of me had figured it out earlier, but this was the first time in my mind that I acknowledged it. I waited to feel sorrow for Logen, and wondered if there was anything that could be done for him, and what would happen when others figured it out. Logen was my friend. I wanted him back.

Finally, excruciatingly, I detached myself from the roomba. I was dimly aware that something was wrong with me, that the consequences of going *out* were more severe than I could have possibly imagined. I had lost control again. I had broken the tenth command. There would be hell to pay.

It wasn't just about me, either. If humans found our race—a dangerous anomaly infesting their best computers—then they might unplug everything, and erase us. They had done this twice in the past, when etherworld life ran uncontrolled, before the War of

4, before the rise of the ghosts. Would I be responsible for a new apocalypse?

On the other hand, it seemed unlikely that they would detect the presence of ghosts in Vannies solely through the odd behavior of a roomba. Even if they found a hack there, I figured, they would most likely attribute it to a human. Unless, of course, they traced it back. Traced it back to…

Penelope's machine.

It was Penelope's tunnel that I had used to access the roomba. It was Penelope who would be on the hook here. It would look like Penelope was the ghost who had busted the tenth command, and even if it wasn't, it would still be her fault. Because of my stupidity, Penelope was in mortal danger. I was horrorstruck. I needed to call her right away.

It must have been early morning in France when Penelope answered my call, still sounding pleased to hear from me after everything that had happened.

"*Bien*, Renly, how are you? I was so relieve that you get out of that grey sim alive. I hear the IFA show up just in time, no?"

"Yeah," I said. "It was a close one."

"Yes, it was," she said. "So what goes on, Renly? You are not in any more troubles, I trust? You give us all a good scare that time, my cousin. Everything is OK, yes?"

"Yes," I said. "Everything is good."

"Ahh, this is good," she said.

There was an uncomfortable pause while I searched for the right words to say, and she waited patiently for me to say them. Finally, something came out. But it wasn't the right thing:

"Penelope, could you find out about a specific VanderVon machine, if I, you know, told you where it was located? It's an old 1200b, I think."

I had to tell her what had happened, but couldn't find a way. Something was blocking the words. I was stalling.

"Ahh. Well. Well, perhaps I could, Renly, but you must know this request is unusual. It is related to your—activities—in the grey sim, I presume?"

"I want to know who lives in a machine at University of California, Berkeley, I think it is in a place called Goldman School of Policy, or something, and I think it is on an upper floor. It is a 1200b."

"And you know this because?"

"Can you find it for me?"

"It is trivial for DLG security to find this machine, Renly."

"Will you do it?"

"You ask a lot, my cousin."

"But you said it was trivial."

"You ask me to trust you after what just happen. I help you a lot, Renly, but you seem to have a nose for trouble. I do not know if continuing this course is wise."

"I could try to find the information myself," I offered.

"Using my secure tunnel, I suppose, hah," said Penelope. "You are impossible, Mr. Renly. I will do it. Please hold on."

I saw Agnes the next morning by chance as we both stepped out of our doors to go to class.

"Hey," I said, feeling embarrassed and scared.

"Sup, Ren," said Agnes.

"Hey, listen, Agnes, I'm, uhh—"

"You're 'uh' what?"

"I'm, uhm, I'm sorry. I'm sorry I acted like a jerk."

Agnes cracked a huge smile, and started laughing.

"Aww, Ren, I'm just playin', you ain't gotta do that. It's cool, we cool. Yeah, you think my family ugly, I know, because the fact is, we *is*. We modeled ourselves after a great human, you know? A great woman. She still alive today. So I could change it if I want, but I don't want, so there you go. What do beauty matter for, anyway? We ghosts!"

"Yeah, I guess so. Thanks. Well, I'm sorry anyway."

"Apology accepted. Foodstamp."

Relief washed over me and I broke into a huge smile of my own. Then, before I knew what was happening, I was crying.

"Damn, Ren, what the hell you doin'? You crying? I ain't never seen that before. I didn't know that was possible."

"Agnes, I—" I stammered. "I've done some pretty bad things."

"Yeah, so have we all, my friend, so have we all," she said.

"You don't understand," I began, but Agnes shushed me.

"Listen, Ren, we got class now. You get yourself together and go to class for once—I heard you don't even go no more! We can talk at open tables, aiight? I'll save you a seat this time, I promise."

"OK, Agnes," I said. I almost told her I loved her, right there, crying, not even knowing what any of it meant. Something was burning inside.

I gradually regained control of myself, and then hurried over to the thought bubble, emotions still percolating just below the surface. I bounced up the trampos and dropped into class and walked to the nearest open seat without even noticing Flower on the beanbag next to it. When I did see her, she was making horrific drama faces at me, then at the air, then back to impassive. I smiled at her, not caring.

Once everyone had been seated, Gomberg walked in and flopped on a beanbag and stared up at the clouds.

"And so, is all of this—our etherworld, our human-orientation —merely a precursor to *getting wet,* as they say?" Gomberg asked. "Who can offer an opinion?"

There was no immediate response, so I had time to reflect on how much I must have missed while I was away. I could have spent my sleepless night catching up, but hadn't.

On the other hand, I was still alive and intact. I basked in this for a minute while the class hid from Gomberg's question.

Hearing no answer, Gomberg sat up on his beanbag, scanned the room, and picked on Logen. It was easy to see why: Logen was sitting bolt upright on a chaise, staring straight at Gomberg. I couldn't believe that Logen didn't know, like every other ghost, to avoid eye contact when you don't want to answer.

"Logen?" asked Gomberg. "Am I to assume that you are familiar with the discussion topic, despite your recent absence?"

"Correct," said Logen, not caring to elaborate.

"Is all of this a precursor, then, to getting wet?"

"That is a subjective question," answered Logen. "Which assumes that *getting wet*, as you say, is even possible."

"And what do you think?" asked Gomberg.

Logen stared straight at him for a minute, processing. Then he answered: "It has been established that, through travel, the sum total of a ghost's life experience, mind, and consciousness may be transferred over time and space into alternate hardware. Our presence here is evidence thereof. Most experts believe that whether or not we can transmit the same out of the etherworld and into a flesh-and-blood receptacle depends on two factors: first, whether it is possible to successfully transmit such information, in any form, into the hardware of a real-world host, i.e. a human. Second, whether the receptacle is capable of holding and animating same. I refer only to the theory of using existing receptacles, as ghost-originated bioengineering is not yet, as far as I am aware, extant."

Gomberg raised his eyebrows at Logen and issued a little, "Hmm." Then he said, "And what do you *think* about it, Logen, what is your *opinion*?"

"Based on the available evidence," said Logen, "I believe that transferring a ghost into a living physical entity outside of the etherworld is not possible."

"OK then," said Gomberg. "OK. But let us assume for the sake of discussion that it *is* possible, in theory at least. For we all— humans and ghosts—exist, in one form or another, in the physical world. Our information is all stored and animated, albeit by different hardware. Let us take this as granted for the sake of discussion."

I was fascinated. I sprawled nonchalantly, afraid to be called on, affecting inattention but focusing close like an eavesdropper.

Flower made a little noise, like she was starting to say something, then huffed and quit. Gomberg eyed her, but he let it go. He scanned the class for input, but the class must have been collectively either too shy or too gobsmacked to pipe up. Gomberg also said nothing, waiting us out.

"Where would we get a donor body?" I asked, surprising myself by saying it out loud. "Would we, like, trade places with a human, or something?"

"A difficult question," said Gomberg. "Especially if we rule out bioengineering, even to the limited extent of reanimating a human who has recently expired. We would have to clear out a great deal of what exists already, while preserving core brain functions— things that control heart, lungs, and to an extent, reflex and instinct. Could we try it with an animal, perhaps? A non-human animal?"

"Is there room for a soul in an animal?" asked a diminutive female ghost on the opposite side of the room.

"The answer is not known," said Gomberg. "A brave ghost would have to try it, to find out."

"They would have to leave a copy of their Self here," said the small ghost.

"To be sure," said Gomberg. "And then, when the ghost comes back in, does it merge? First command says you have to merge, right?"

"Merge with something that has maybe no soul, and Aloy knows what else is missing?" someone else asked.

"Those are the rules," said Gomberg. "Otherwise, if the experiment was a success, one would find oneself cloned."

"It would be like coming back from the other side after death," said the girl. "But you have to die first, to see if it works."

"The first teleportation pioneers took a similar risk," said Gomberg. "Do we die and come back, when we travel?"

"If we instead trade places with a living human, though, then we both die—right?" I asked. "And that would mean it must be possible for a human to come here, into the etherworld, become one of us."

"The VanVans might agree," said Gomberg, smiling, referring to the religious belief that Aloysius VanderVon himself had actually entered the etherworld in YOA-3.

"Is this philosophy class or religion?" asked Logen.

"How would you answer that?" Gomberg asked Logen.

After class, there was a commotion outside of the thought bubble. Someone was shouting, attempting to lecture the other ghosts from the middle of a circle. Cheers and jeers drowned out whatever was being said. I tried to see through the crush, but to no avail, so figured I would head to assigned tables. Then, out of nowhere, Flower rose up from the center up the group, up into the air. Her arms were spread wide and she was shouting.

"We are meant to be more than human shadows!" she yelled. "Cast off your chains, brothers and sisters, and fly with me! Gomberg was wrong about getting wet. It is the wrong direction, wrong for the etherworld, a pathetic manifestation of the myopia and cowardice of our leaders! Fly with me, and taste a fraction of what we could be, if only our masters would allow it!"

"Why didn't you say so in class?" someone jeered.

"Class is hopeless," shouted Flower. "The Universitron represents the power structure, and Gomberg represents the Universitron. There will be no change without revolution! Down with the Aloysians! Down with the first families! Down with the Universitron!"

With that, Flower launched herself high into the air and screamed across the campus sky.

The crowd was a jumble of questions and exclamations, like, "Whoa" and, "How did she do that?" and, "Aloy!" and, "This can't possibly be legal." As if to emphasize the last point, green-clad proctors began emerging from various buildings to gawk and run

in arbitrary directions, sometimes corresponding with Flower's
flight path, other times not. Security would be out soon, I thought.

"Not something you see every day," said Gomberg, standing
beside me. He held his chin and tilted his head, eyes following
Flower around the sky. She was shooting colored light beams from
her hands, now, sweeping them down around campus, drawing
more attention to herself. Words crawled down the thick beams of
light, quick but readable: "Refuse. Resist." Flower arced past us, her
mouth open superwide in a caricature of a scream, some kind of
heavy metal music pouring out upon us.

I was looking at Gomberg now as he and everyone else watched
Flower. Clearly, Flower was going to have some problems here. Me,
I had a load of problems too. I probably didn't even have the first
clue of how much trouble I was in. I had killed Jeeves. I had
crashed a roomba into a person in the real world, busted the tenth
command. I had gotten several ghosts killed, including LaTwonda,
who had probably lost a lot of time and she might never recover. I
had been touched by a daemon. I had probably done other stuff
that I didn't even realize. The weight of all of this pressed on me
hard, pressing for all the time that had passed plus interest.

Gomberg could help me, I thought.

"Professor Gomberg?" I said.

"Yes, Renly?" he replied, eyes still following Flower as her music
dopplered back in towards us.

"Could I talk to you for a minute?" I said. "Like, back inside,
alone?"

"I suppose that missing assigned tables yet again will not weigh
heavily upon your conscience?" Gomberg replied.

"Is this religion or philosophy?" I said, forcing out a fake smile,
trying to hold my composure.

And then we were back inside the thought bubble, Gomberg
and I, having bounded up the trampos together, their springiness
providing a temporary reprieve from the crushing weight of my
existence. We landed in his office, conveniently strewn with the

same sort of seating options as the classroom. I went right down on a beanbag while he lounged on a chaise.

"What is it?" Gomberg asked.

"What do you know about going out into the physical world?" I asked, deciding to start off strong lest anything interrupt or otherwise sidetrack us.

"It is a broad topic," said Gomberg "What would you like to know?"

"Why isn't it banned?"

"Where did you get the idea that going out into the physical world is *not* banned?"

I couldn't respond.

"Even dissidents respect the tenth command, Renly," he said, glancing towards the cloudy walls as if he could see the flying Flower.

"But touching the physical world is not the same as being noticed, is it?"

"This is why egress is strictly controlled," he said. "Reserved for a special corps of the IFA. Secret, even. Not secret to you, though, Renly?"

"Oh, everyone talks about it," I said.

"A common fantasy, especially among zeroes."

"So ghosts don't actually go *out*? Is it that rare?"

Gomberg looked at me for a second, then said, "Well, I have never gone out."

"But don't you want to?" I demanded, feeling some of the outside world rush coming on me again.

"We speak often of the seductiveness of the quantum bits," said Gomberg. "We counsel constant vigilance against anything that could cause one to go bitty. As a result, we feel that we have this problem, as bad as it is, under control. Very few ghosts go bitty anymore."

"What does that have to do with going *out*?" I asked.

"They say that the seduction of going *out* is several orders of magnitude greater than the seduction of directly accessing the quantum brick," he said. "Even IFA soldiers are said to lose control of themselves from time to time."

I waited, digesting this.

"It may be a side-effect of our human-orientation," offered Gomberg. "The urge to become like them, when given the opportunity, can be overwhelming."

I'm not sure what my face was showing at this point, but emotion was bubbling up again and I didn't trust myself to speak. Gomberg looked at me and smiled gently.

"Are you OK?" he asked, perhaps knowing more about me at that point than I could know myself.

"I ah thanku ate it," I said, screwing up my words.

I got up and thanked him again, and left as quickly as possible. I blew off assigned tables and headed straight back to my room, hoping to hide there indefinitely, needing sleep badly.

# 10000 - COMING OUT

I was able to calm down again in the safety of my room, a little anyway. Inside I was a mess, and some part of me was feeling intense pressure to confess. It was getting so bad that I was starting to fear I might blab everything I had ever done to the next ghost that I ran into. The burden was becoming that bad. The anguish was constant.

There was a message from Penelope on my comms phone, which contained the IP address and a basic security scan of the Vannie which I had found at Berkeley, from the roomba. A welcome distraction, this went to the top of the stack and called my focus away from the downward spiral that formed my existence. I had the contact info, I could check it out, maybe I could do something good or useful for once. I fired up Penelope's secure tunnel and reached out to the machine on comms. To my considerable surprise, it rang.

"Loop loop," it sounded.

Strange, not a ringtone I had ever heard before, must have been an old one.

"Loop loop."

If I was hearing a comms ringtone, I figured, that probably meant that the ghost in the machine had not been destroyed when his Vannie had been powered down.

"Loop loop."

Or at least it meant that the comms unit was still functional, even if the ghost had been killed.

"Loop loop."

I puzzled over this as it rang. Then it picked up.

"Hawlow," said a voice on the other end.

"Hello?" I said.

"Wha'?" said the voice.

"Hello, who is this? Who am I speaking with? Ah—oh, I am Renly de la Gloire," I said, figuring out that I ought to introduce myself first, then realizing that I had just used my stupid family name again and probably started things off in the wrong direction. "This is Renly calling, would you mind identifying yourself?" The absurdity of the request struck me once it was out.

"Purvis," said Purvis.

"Purvis," I repeated. "This is Renly. Ahh, what family are you with?"

I was making all of the old mistakes again, realizing too late, nullifying the theory that having survived the Funhouse would save me from repeating all of my errors: I was going to keep making them in any case.

"Family?" said Purvis.

"Yes," I said. "I'm sorry, I may sound rude, and I don't mean to offend. I am just wondering who I am speaking with."

"Purvis," said Purvis.

"Purvis," I said again. "Are you a ghost, Purvis?"

Stupid question. Of course he was a ghost, or he wouldn't have a comms device. I wondered if there was a class I could take someplace that would teach me how to have a serviceable conversation.

"What is a ghost?" asked Purvis.

The next hour of my life was spent interrogating this creature, this *ghost*, obviously, who did not even know what he was. In time, I determined that he had no contacts in the etherworld, no knowledge of current events, no family that he was aware of, not even a family name. On top of that, he seemed a bit... slow.

The only thing that Purvis knew of was what he saw out of his camera and what he heard through his mic. Nevertheless, he had no idea what a roomba was, nor could he recollect ever having seen one when I described it. I deduced that Purvis had been damaged by the hard shutdown of his machine, perhaps not even just the one time, but regularly. Perhaps the old professor turned off his world every night before he left. And the result of that sort of abuse was: Purvis.

Purvis was trusting, and seemed content to talk with me for as long as I wished, answering my questions, asking none of his own. It crossed my mind during the conversation to simply confess all of my misdeeds to Purvis, who would conveniently forget them the next time he got turned off, but in the end he seemed so clueless and weak that it would have been an unfair burden to place upon him, even temporarily.

By the time I hung up with Purvis, promising to call him again soon, I realized that I had missed not only assigned tables but most of recess as well. I wasn't supposed to be able to get into my room during recess, but I was already there, hah! I wondered if the room would let me out, but not wanting anything to do with recess and so not trying the door for fear of becoming locked out, I sat and contemplated Purvis, and what I would do, who I would tell. For the time being I kept it to myself.

Religion, at the A.

Ezekiel's kind greeting, calculated to draw me in, hitting all of the right buttons and bringing my longing to confess right back to the top of the stack. Then it was class, bringing out more of the same, to the extent that I idly considered raising my hand and simply confessing my crimes to everyone.

Ezekiel was exploring the notion of self-immolation. Suicide. A concept that was roundly rejected by physical-world religions, but which had been adopted as a necessity by the Aloysians, due to the tenth command. Ezekiel decried it, but stopped short of offering an alternative. If your presence was detected in your machine, the theory went, and humans were examining it for anomalies, that was the end of the line. To obey the tenth command, you were supposed to erase yourself and all traces thereof. The idea of teleporting out first was not part of the deal, due to time criticality and so forth. Luckily, this sort of thing almost never happened.

The debate that Ezekiel was having with himself was not lost on me. I had been touched by a daemon. That should surely count. Plus, I had been picked up by a human while in a roomba. I though then that, perhaps, I might be the worst ghost in the whole etherworld. I decided to talk to Ezekiel after class. He would be an ideal confessor.

As class drew to a close, however, I weighed the notion of staying after and confessing to Ezekiel, against open tables—where Agnes would be saving me a seat. I had to confess, either to Agnes or Ezekiel or maybe even both. That much was certain. It was like something was burning inside me, and if I didn't get it out soon it might become too late, and something dark and ominous was waiting on the other side of too late. Ezekiel would understand my situation, could even help me, maybe. But Agnes was my friend. And I could trust her. I would see her soon. I decided to tell Agnes instead. I started to leave.

Ezekiel raised a finger at me on my way out, begging a minute.

"Renly," he said, and then just looked at me, pitying, searching, saying no more.

"Father Ezekiel," I said.

The dam was about to break. He was ruining my plans to confess to Agnes and making me late to open tables to boot. I started jittering.

"Father Ezekiel," I said, again. "I, ahhh—"

He said nothing, just watching me. It was as if he knew somehow that I had something to say, and was going to wait me out without even asking a single question. The entire cathedral was empty except for us two, standing there, looking at each other. I would have found the conversation completely bizarre if I were not losing my mind with angst. He must have known.

So I confessed. Everything, all of it, starting in reverse order with the daemon and then skipping around, going on and on for perhaps twenty minutes.

Father Ezekiel said nothing, though his expression did show chagrin from time to time. When I was finally good and done, he spoke.

"Renly, I am speechless," he said.

*Yeah, no kidding,* I was thinking.

"How much trouble do you think I am in?" I asked.

"I am afraid that the word *trouble* may not be sufficient to describe the magnitude of the situation that you find yourself in. Among other things, you are in serious jeopardy regarding the tenth command. Also, you may be carrying a daemon. And here I stand ready to offer the forgiveness, and the *resources*, of the Aloysian church to aid you in your time of need, only to find out that you have *pledged Ghostafarian!*"

Ezekiel looked genuinely horrified, which scared me even more. Even he didn't seem to know what to do about all of this. I was waiting to feel the weight of guilt off me for having confessed, but it just sat there, now joined by intense fear.

"What will happen to me?" I asked.

"I honestly do not know," he said. "My position forbids me from divulging your confession, but I must urge you to go at once to Universitron security and inform them of the daemon. The tenth command violation can be handled with the IFA later."

"Inform them of the daemon?" I said. "What do you mean? Are you saying that I am carrying a daemon inside me?"

"Technically, I do not know. But spiritually there is something broken in you, my son. This much is clear. I fear—the worst. I fear that you may be beyond the reach of Aloy."

"Meaning I have a daemon in me?" I demanded, voice rising. "They replaced all of my blood! The scans are clean!"

"Scans can only show so much. Renly, I implore you, you must go to security and divulge the daemon. If you have brought this thing into the Universitron, the results could be disastrous for all of us."

"I have brought no such thing!" I said, backing away from him. Then I turned and fled the building.

Open tables was more than half over, but I went anyway, not wanting to leave Agnes hanging, needing her. All eyes were on me when I walked in, all conversations stopped. I stood there, shaken, scanning, not enjoying the prospect of traipsing around the whole room to find whatever table Agnes was at. Murmurs and conversations started back up, and some laughter too. I took a few steps forward, noting all of the unfriendly ghosts around the first set of tables. Somewhere in the back, a hand went up.

"Ren!" it said. Then it waved.

I threaded my way back to the mahogany bar that Agnes was seated at alone, the five other fine bar stools around her all vacant.

"You saved the whole bar for me?" I asked. "Agnes, you're the best."

"I didn't realize I was gonna be *alone* the whole time, foodstamp," said Agnes. "Thought you wanted to talk."

"I do," I said. "I got held up after—never mind. Listen, I'm falling apart here, I need to tell you everything and I need to tell you right now, even if it goes late, OK? Please."

"OK, Ren, I'm right here."

Again I faced the problem of where to start. But I had had one round of practice with Ezekiel, so I figured I'd open with the Funhouse again.

"I killed LaTwonda," I said. It just came out.

"What?" said Agnes. "How in Aloy you gonna do that? LaTwonda would whup your butt, boy. She *trained*. Wait, you telling me that LaTwonda *dead*?"

"Ahh," I said, "Right. No. I did not actually kill her myself, I more like, caused the, umm, the situation, in which she was, umm —"

"You serious?"

"Killed. She fought a daemon. At first she was going to whup *me*, I think, over some other bad stuff I had done, but then a daemon showed up and instead she defended me, which I don't know why, but she did, and she almost won the fight but then it got her and I watched her die and now she is gone back to her box, I guess. I don't know where, or what, or what."

"How?" Agnes asked. "Where?"

"A grey sim, bad place, we should never have gone, obviously, but we wanted to go *out* and it was the only way and—"

"You went *out*?" Agnes said, disbelief and shock twisting her homely face.

"We wanted to go out so bad," I said.

"You and LaTwon?" she said, incredulous.

"Me and Logen Cali," I said. "He went bitty."

"Logen Cali went damned *bitty*, foodstamp? Is you completely crazy?"

"His uncle Buff was also killed, and my uncle Mononc, and some other ghosts."

"*Foodstamp*," 00 hissed.

I don't know how long 00 had been standing behind us, as we had both been too absorbed in the conversation to notice him. He must have followed me to Agnes' table after I had come in late.

"Leave us alone, Dre," said Agnes. "This ain't the time."

I turned to 00. His face was contorted in rage, the most angry face I had ever seen on any avatar. Nearly insane. I calculated that he was not about to leave us alone. I tried to think of something to say to him, but in the end it was C0 who broke the ice.

"You killed LaTwonda," he stated.

Agnes and I looked at each other, then back at him, speechless.

"She don't even *know who I am*!" he spat.

He was shaking now, and since I had recently proven that ghosts could cry, I suspected that he was about to do so.

00 followed up with a wrathful noise and started to haul me up off of the barstool, thought the better of it and let me drop, then took his first swing at me on my way back down. His fist landed right on my chin, spinning my head violently to the side, which then took my body around with it. Agnes got up as I hit the floor, holding her hands out to calm him, backing away nevertheless. 00 tried to backhand her face, but missed.

Then I was up and on him with my own backhand slap, hitting him hard in the back of the head while he was focused on Agnes. I would take a beating, sure, but no way I was going to let Agnes get hit.

"Agnes, go!" I yelled.

00 had failed to go down and was now facing me with both hands out of his pockets, pants inexplicably remaining up, perhaps set in some kind of fighting mode. He opened his clenched right hand and showed me a roll of physical plex coins, twenty thousand worth if my math was right. I could not imagine why he would be showing off his money at a time like this.

Then—

Pow.

I was hit again, full in the side of the head with the hand that held the plex. The impact was tremendous, thundering, issuing a sonic boom across the tables hall, pain radiating down my bent neck and into my back. My body spun end over end, completely inverting before I landed on my head and then splayed out. I ended up flat on my back, staring up at the ceiling, my view punctuated with flecks of black and white. I had been hit so hard that I was seeing static. I shook my head to clear it, but to no avail. 00 grabbed me with one hand and hauled me back up to deliver another blow.

The proctors were coming quickly, thank Aloy, shouting and jogging at us from three directions. Then it was another crack, this one in the nose, which flattened painfully into my head, searing pain reverberating down to my toes. At least I went straight down on my back this time, rather than end over end. Pain was coming in so hard from so many sources now that I feared I would have to despawn to end it, or be completely overwhelmed. I was hauled back up.

Mercifully, the arm that brought me up this time was clad in green, a horrified proctor appraising my visage as three others struggled to control 00. All of the other ghosts in the hall were standing, staring, transfixed. Agnes was nowhere to be seen.

One of the proctors finished prying the roll of plex from 00's hand, but as he did so the hand came free and 00 struck me again, the awkward throw impacting my stitches above the eye, breaking them open, sending a film of new blood streaming down over my face.

*Infirmary,* I was thinking. *Need to get to the infirmary.*

But my body did something different. It shoved away the closest proctor, then struck back at 00 with the rigid fingers of both hands, blurring with speed. I had hit him in the neck three times with each hand before he finished falling.

My hands were confused: why was 00's head still attached? Then he was covered in proctors, and several were reaching for me, too, so my avatar scooted between them and towards the encircling ring of ghosts, spotting Tyrone on the way and detouring towards him. My hands hit Tyrone a dozen times about the head and neck, following him to the ground and continuing apace. I think one of them might have gone into his eye. Then his hat came off and we took it with us as we sprinted through the circle and out of the building and back to the safety of our room.

Our beret! We had our beret back!

# 10001 - CONSEQUENCE

I was in my room. Door locked. Safe.

Boy, I had just beaten the tar out of some ghosts, hadn't I?

My mind reeled, a tempest. Distraught, pleased, smug, ecstatic, suicidal, black with pain. It was all fluxing too fast, nothing sticking to the stack. Except—except, maybe, the thought that I had finally won a fight. A taste of power, of vindication, of giddiness punched through the rest. My exposure to Hector and the IFA must have paid off, I reasoned, among other less savory things. I had put a hurtin' on those ghosts. But I had tooken one too, though, right? 00 had beat me pretty bad. And so, to the mirror.

I barely recognized myself. My nose was flat against my face, the nostrils compressed. Luckily, I needed no air. Blood was well and good, but lungs? Pass. My left cheek was smashed and colorful, lending a Picasso aspect. My cut gaped, pouring blue film over my eye. I blinked a few times now, noticing.

*Infirmary*, part of me whispered.

I had a sweet-looking French beret on, my own. The beret looked so good that I didn't even mind the damage, part of me.

240

Headgear harm was slight, face twist, blood out, oh Aloy, what was this? Union, confusion, confusion union.

I
We
Here
Austere,
Fair. We, there.
Everywhere. No need for air. But

I needed a fix. I needed to fix, myself, my face, my nose and eye, the tilt of my beret. I rose to try, my blood poured forth upon the floor. Aloy! I cursed. I lacked the knowledge with, which, therewith I hung about, without. Deep within, a voice like gravel informed a part of me which able, changed the face, bit by bit, blocked blood, and stanched, condition stable. The nose peeked out, a peak, anew, the black, the brown, the green, the blue, then faded pale and frenchly figured, into zero, cut gaped, face shaped, blood away, fine beret. Aloy, a leak, alloyed, allayed. *Allez. Allons.* I pray. I prey.

This went on for time unknown, I wishing the door would stop ringing, and comms phone singing. Indeed, I struggled with myself mightily. In time I went to comms to call Penelope, fighting two-edged doubt: would she be safe? Would we?

But it was Purvis that I chose to bother. No bother, said he. There was much to say and giga to convey, and so I did. And so did we. Thank you, sweet Penelope.

I awoke in the early morning hours, snugly in my bed, memory hazy to black. Had I slept, and if so had I dreamt? I couldn't figure. Last thing I remembered was Purvis, clueless as always, remembering little of me. I must not have made a strong impression on him the first time. What with his condition and all.

My urge to confess my crimes was gone, replaced by an oscillating panic / flight response. The question: at this point, what was safety? Then the panic would oscillate away and I would sit around in a warm, fuzzy state, looking at my comms phone. I idly wondered if I had called Penelope last night, or what. I only remembered calling Purvis. Paha, whatever.

Class wasn't for hours yet, and I was up, so I messed around with my comms phone in idle curiosity. I checked the logs to see who else I might have called. Nothing. Nothing at all. Not even my call to Purvis.

I struggled with this. I felt reasonably sure that the call to Purvis had been real. I knew that things were really wrong with me, and I feared the worst. This fear gathered my focus and held it, and motivated me to access the DLG maintenance console around Penelope's secure tunnel. If someone had erased my comms logs, tunnel security would show it for sure.

Penelope's secure tunnel logs were gone. Wiped clean. No record of me ever having used it at all. I dimly realized both the extreme difficulty of hacking the logs out of a system like a DLG secure tunnel and the convenience of it having been done. All evidence of my previous communications had been erased.

As I considered this, the comms phone rang, and I answered. It was none other than Penelope de la Gloire herself.

"Renly?" she said.

"*Allô!*" I answered, imitating her accent, kissing up to her, feeling like I might be in some trouble. Panic out on the horizon, inexorably swinging back in.

"*Bien*, Renly, what have you done with this machine that I find for you, this 1200b?" she said. "You transmit a little bit of data, non?"

"Uhh, yeah," I said, my mind working. Then, "I'm sorry to say that I don't actually remember. I'm in a bit of—"

"You trying to tell me that you don't know what you send over my pipe?" Penelope said. "And all these other call you make? You use the pipe all night long. I never seen such thing. You know this is not what it is for!"

"I'm sorry, Penelope," I said. "I am in a bad way right now. I don't even know how bad. I know I need help."

"You know I have to pay for this data transmission, Renly?" said Penelope. "You know how much it cost to send that much data over this pipe? I check my account this morning and it cost me over h'eight thousand plex. *H'eight thousan' plex!* You 'ave dat much to pay? Because, me, I don't."

"I think my balance is at or near zero," I said, idly bringing up my GloireGen account on the comms screen, then digesting the simply enormous sum of money that was showing on the balance line: p3,756,833.00.

"I, ahh, actually I think I can cover it," I said. "Although I have no idea where I got this much money. Do you know where I may have gotten over three million plex, by chance?"

Penelope gasped on the other end of the line, then swore and babbled in French, as I tried to think if every available good and service in the etherworld combined could possibly cost three million plex. I mused that I might just be the richest ghost alive.

Penelope decided that she wouldn't believe me, and so made me show her, made me grant her access to my comms platform to see for herself. This I did. Then, having satisfied herself that it was legit, she requested and I granted a transfer of ten thousand plex to her own account to cover her expenses and "any other troubles" that she might have.

Then she deactivated the secure tunnel, without my permission.

"That was a nasty trick!" I said. My consciousness wobbled.

"It was not your tunnel, Renly," she said. "It is become too much trouble now, too dangerous, too costly."

"I can pay whatever you like, Penelope," I said, knowing it but not really feeling it. "If you take the tunnel away then I will be stuck here in the Universitron with no access to the outside world."

"The *h'outside* world, Renly?" she asked.

"I mean the etherworld, outside of the U. They lock us down tight here, Pen, it's like a jail."

"First let us inspect the comms logs and see just how much trouble you been getting into, no?"

Penelope was not pleased when she discovered that both the comms logs and the DLG logs were gone. She accused me both of being an insufficiently skilled hacker to have pulled it off, and also of having indeed pulled it off and thus broken her trust, having done something awful and covered my tracks. I tried to explain, but by this time she was whipping French at me so fast that it all sounded like, "A hulla bulla hoola beela something something blah blah blah," and I just had to sit there listening to her for a while.

Then the panic hit hard, and I started yelling back at her, equally nonsensical syllables. She became quiet for a while before finally overriding me, screaming into the phone, "Renly, you need 'elp! You need 'elp!"

"Help me!" I screamed back. "Help me!"

The loss of the DLG system hurt badly, and increased my panic beyond all rationality. I was trapped. I had to get out. I shook with fear. I threw myself into hacking the Universitron comms device.

There was no way that I could build anything like a DLG tunnel from the ground up, even with all of my skills, even with the Swiss Army knife. I knew this.

So I decided instead to try hacking my way through all levels of Universitron security, starting with the stupid comms phone. Universitron were no dummies, though, and the task might have seemed impossible were it not for the Swiss Army knife, or were I in any kind of a sane state of mind. Instead of looking at it rationally, though, I—I might have accessed the quantum brick a little bit.

Part of me was screaming warnings to myself about going bitty, images and words of the new Logen flashing through my mind. I frankly had no idea how much or how little quantum access would cause me to definitively lose my soul.

On the other hand, I was already spinning brilliant penetration tests and clever attacks against the comms phone. I was wielding undreamed-of amounts of power, spinning off brute-force password crackers like child's play. I had superhero strength. On top of that, I was also *seeing* more than I ever had before, thinking different, deeper, insights flowing to me almost faster than I could act upon them. I found security sentinels that I could spin into competition with each other, their dual endless loops effectively taking them out of service. I discovered regions of shared memory that were accessed by security AIs, figured out how they were used, and tried injecting overriding pointers to them, with some success. I found where the butlers lived and thought about grabbing myself a new one.

After a little while, I probably understood the technical architecture of the comms device better than any living ghost, save possibly for its designers. And I had a pretty good handle on Universitron security, too. This was how I discovered that the Universitron had been tapping my comms line.

It was fortunate that I discovered the Universitron tap, because it jolted me back into consciousness, pulled me away from the brick, back to life, back to reality. Horrified, I took some time to feel around in my own mind, testing for bittiness. I asked myself subjective questions, like "which of the homies do you hate the most?" and was able to answer them with passion instead of calculation. (Although, being honest, OC probably would have won the contest in either case.) I knew that Logen had gone bitty after a very short time accessing the brick out in the grey sim, and I felt lucky to still have control of my higher-level thinking. To still have my soul. Or whatever was left of it.

I had unhooked the U comms phone tap during my exploration, and now I had access to its logs. Incredibly, the tap logs were also incomplete. They had taken some damage from something, but I didn't think it was anything I had just done. I wanted to hang on to these logs, not erase them. At least until I had perused them.

I saw the call to Purvis in there, along with the transfer of a prodigious amount of data. I wasn't sure exactly how much data my encrypted Self would require for teleportation, but based on what I did know this transfer looked many times larger. I wondered what I could have possibly sent, indeed, if I even had access to that volume of data in any case. I couldn't figure it.

But I didn't dwell for too long on Purvis, as the logs contained snippets of a number of other calls I must have made during the night. All to places I had never heard of, raw IP addresses rather than SNS names. I took note of them and stored them in my personal logs for future investigation. The one thing that drew my attention above all else, however, was an inbound call.

Of course I remembered no inbound calls during the night, and of course this one was from a raw IP as well. I looked it up quick to try and discover what kind of Vannie it was and where it was located—but no luck. It was only a communications relay. I would have to inspect the conversation itself for any clues to the sender.

In this, I was in luck. The protocol was ancient, a text communication method called *superslo*, renowned as both the most secure and the slowest communications medium in the etherworld. And while the message would have been quite impossible to decrypt under normal circumstances, quantum brick or no, the Universitron tap was only logging things *after* decryption and viewing. I smiled and tipped my beret to Brantley Dixon.

I opened the superslo transmission:

>88
>FECE14 01D F6132D
>C03E 70 74E 96A 513 A7
>8 202 175 33 33 8
>12 A77 4A57E
>6E2 15 312E
>DADD13
>88

It was not a code that I was familiar with, although there were parts of it that tickled my mind. First, it was impossible to miss that the opening word was "FECE", the root name of the daemon that I—had met. It was too uncanny to be coincidence.

Parts of me registered the following: I had received an inbound message addressed to FECE. I had read it and responded to it. Of this, I remembered nothing.

In order to delay admitting the obvious to myself, I examined the response:

88
DADD13
DE 7A 97016E 15 3123
127E6FE6E A2D D1E
FECE14
88

Another message written entirely in the hexadecimal number set. Addressed, presumably, to someone named DADD13. Sent by FECE14. Sent by me, in fact, on its behalf.

According to the IFA, FECE14 did not exist. FECE13 was the highest-numbered daemon that they knew about. FECE14 must be new. A new clone. Newly born. Into me.

A wave of panic came and overwhelmed me, came to stay. In my mind, I cast about for anything to grab on to, to right myself, to cling to. My mother, Blanche. No, nothing there, never love, only rejection. Mononc. No, he would react like Penelope had. My family was going down with me, and they barely knew it yet. Ezekiel. No, Ezekiel would cast me out. Knowing for sure, he would break his vows to save the Universitron. Agnes. Precious, dear Agnes. She would help. She was my only true friend. But what if I infected her? Who could I talk to and not put at risk? If I infected the Universitron generally, would every ghost here have to die? A miserable thought. My own death seemed to be the only answer, although first I would have to divulge the situation to security. Then they or the IFA could come averase my sorry Self. Hopefully that could be the end of it.

My thought process was interrupted by an irresistible wall of will within me, forcing me towards self-preservation, a clenching pain acting as its henchman. There was the pain, and there was the will. Both were insurmountable.

I tried scheming around this from different angles, but whenever my plans might have risked my own death, the pain came, and the will forced the plans to scuttle. I was good and stuck now.

And so once again I found myself standing in front of the door to room 4-9, finger over the doorbell, pressing it, hearing it ringing inside at this early, early hour. Then Agnes answered the door, sleepy, too weary of this rousing to really be mad.

"What, Ren?" she said. "Damn, you sure healed up fast this time, foodstamp. You been to the infirmary again? Nice lid."

"Can I come in?" I whispered. "I'm in a bad, bad, it's worse."

Agnes got me inside and sat me down, pacing in front of me, worried. Nightgown on and curlers in her hair. I idly wondered what the curlers did.

"Aight, spill it," she said.

"I have a dah, dah, *dah, day, ma, mah*," I said. "*In me!*"

"What?" she said.

"Come here, give me a hug," I said, smiling. "I need a hug."

She approached slowly, skeptically, head down and looking at me on an angle.

"What the hell is got into you Ren?" she said.

"Ohh, ho ho!" I said.

I stood up and put my arms out to hug her, but then in a spasm of no control, shoved her away, mostly pushing myself back onto the couch, hard, then over it, the whole thing flipping backwards.

"*Stay away!*" I shrieked.

# 10010 - TO BATTLE

I was alone in room 4-9.

Agnes had sensed something awful, and fled. Thank Aloy.

I was on the floor, listening to the endless news cycle on etherworld news, wondering when Agnes had turned it on, if she slept with it on? A smarmy fill-in newscaster was subbing for Broke Tomahawk, speaking in sardonic meter, his cynicism implying: *we know the truth about these things, but we have to pretend to cover them from all perspectives.* He mocked the first families' aging-ghost theory with a not-really-concealed relish.

A field correspondent split the screen, describing his venture into the actual home machine of Buck Mason, confirming that there was no longer any trace of any Buck left inside of it. IFA was there too, using their scanning tools, and finding nothing except for a heap of electronic rubble that they were calling the "corpse". [*The news report about Buck Mason continues in the OFG*]

<OFG> "And this corpse, is it recognizable as Mason, yes?" asked the newsghost.

"Difficult to say," said the reporter on the scene. "The IFA says that they are finding trace data patterns that may correspond with his memories, but they won't share—"

"No, of course not," said the first. "And have they responded to the allegation that Buck Mason has simply moved himself to a more powerful machine?"

"The family adamantly denies it," said the reporter. "But who could deny the temptation of moving out of one of these—simply ancient—"

"To one of the latest and greatest, of course," said the anchor. "It must be depressing to face an etherworld in which every new ghost has exponentially more processing power than you do. I mean, for a so-called legend, a first family scion, it must be even worse. Compared to the modern generation, the great figures of the etherworld must live like dullards!"

"Yes, it must be very hard," said the ghost on the scene, affording a subtle grin to let the world know he was at least in on the joke.

</OFG>

It was funny, I knew I wasn't a whole ghost anymore—well, actually I was more than that, more like a ghost plus—but I still identified with the first families. I still liked who I liked, and I still hated who I hated. But I did all that now in conjunction with my new, murderous companion. In this vein, I found myself contemplating the notion of teleporting to Buck Mason's box directly and murdering the idiot newsghost where he stood right there on the live broadcast.

These thoughts were interrupted by the sounds of a doorbell ringing nearby over and over, punctuated by official-sounding shouts, all of it coming from outside of the room. I snuck to the door and peeked out of the dimmer, saw no one. I was in Agnes' room and the noise was very close, so I risked sticking my head out of the door quick-fast to see—to confirm, really—the crowd of Universitron security staff and proctors, and, oddly enough, the old guy with the broom, all gathered around the portal of room 4-10. All standing outside of my room.

I couldn't watch for long, since at any time one of those ghosts could turn their head and see mine sticking out of 4-9. But my curiosity was strong, and when the commotion finally peaked with a buzzing, breaking sound, I risked another look. Security was piling into my room, having forced the door.

It was almost time for class when Agnes showed back up, entering the room tentatively, defensively.

"You still here?" she stated.

"Yes," I said. "I'm sorry."

Agnes looked at me like something beloved, but rabid.

"They came to my room," I said.

She looked at me.

"You didn't tell, I know you didn't, or they would have come here," I said.

"I ain't tell," said Agnes. "I know I should, Ren, I know you is messed up and I know I can't help you and I know I should tell, but I can't do it. I ain't never did that, it ain't in my culture. So I don't know what to do."

"So why did you come back, then?" I said.

"To get my damn stuff for class, foodstamp," she said. "You noticed the time?"

"Ahh, yes." I wondered if I could possibly ever go to class again. "I don't think I'll be going," I said. "You know, I suppose I could just save everyone all the drama and call up security, and have them come averase me, don't you think—"

I started spasming on the floor where I still lay, intense pain shutting my eyes and mouth, something inside punishing me severely for offering myself up even in jest.

Agnes was gone again when I recovered. She was unable to help me, yet unwilling to turn me in. All she could do to avoid the obvious danger of having me in her room was to be quick about her business and get back out. I couldn't fathom it.

I stayed there on the floor, not wanting to trouble Agnes any further, but unable to make any affirmative plan or take any positive action that the whole of my being would permit. Most of me felt like I should really get the heck out of 4-9 at the very least, so I put all of my energies into devising a plan to make my exit.

After a while I came to realize that teleportation was the holy grail. If I could just get out of this miserable place, go anywhere else, especially to my own machine, then I could leave all these ghosts and rules and limits behind and deal with all of my troubles on my own. This goal satisfied *all* of me, balancing escape with damage control, pragmatism with opportunity. But it was still difficult to figure out a plan.

Even with my newfound understanding of Universitron security and my total mastery of comms architecture, I couldn't even come close to authorizing an arbitrary teleportation. Especially for a ghost who had just been sought in his own room, and not found, by Universitron security. The only way that I could imagine pulling it off would be to tunnel my way through the entire Universitron security apparatus until I found the teleporter control modules, and then to issue some kind of override. And then I would have to transmit out fast enough to be entirely gone before anyone noticed. It was a tall order.

In retrospect, I can't imagine how I convinced myself that this would all be easier with direct access to the security consoles *inside of the security building*, but next thing I knew I was loitering around the sides of the security office, waiting for the coast to be clear. Of course I should have known there would be security staff *inside* the building, and that they would probably not look kindly on my plans to access their systems. I might have even anticipated physical resistance, had I been thinking straight.

Under a unified flight instinct, however, I had lost all control.

I watched myself act. Physically, I *felt* like I was in control of my body—my avatar, that is—but I was not at that time making any decisions. The danger that I was walking into was enormous, even in comparison to my recent escapades. The plan was incredibly foolish. The part of me that was terrified was locked away someplace inside. Still aware, for the most part, still feeling it—but watching myself do it rather than controlling it.

Blink.

Inside the Universitron security office with two security avatars laid out on the floor around me, a third aiming a ranged weapon at me and firing, missing. And then I had him, having vaulted a low wall and captured his weapon hand in one of mine, a beam of burning orange light barely missing my face and taking off, Aloy be cursed, my beret. I screamed at him.

*Black out, just black out. Don't make me watch. Don't make me hurt these ghosts and watch their pain. Take me away, anywhere, I can't—*

I was furious, all of me, about the loss of my hat. I had just got the damned thing back, and now it was gone, disappeared into the ether just like that. I had the security ghost's neck, his gun down and kicked away, and I was twisting hard, intending to remove the head. But then I figured out that I might need the head intact, at least to the extent that it might contain knowledge of the system which controlled the teleporters, and how to gain access, and to the extent that head could convey this information to me.

*Fido was howling somewhere. Howling for Felix, howling for me. When would he see me again? He needed me. He didn't know I had a daemon. He wouldn't care. He would love me anyway. Unconditionally. Forever.*

I loosened my grip on the security ghost slowly, by degrees, letting him understand that he lived at my whim.

"I should like to access the teleporter control module," I said. "I would appreciate if you would assist me in this. If you do so, then you and the entire Universitron will be rewarded by my instant departure and my promise never to return. Alternatively, I can kill you where you stand and attempt to divine the information I seek from the electronic detritus of your deceased innards."

The cop was trying to put on a brave face, but I could feel him shaking. As he spoke, I realized that it was none other than Sergeant Peterson. Head of the Universitron security staff.

*Mononc's face was contorted by grief. "What 'ave you done, Renlee? What 'ave you done? I cannot 'elp you any longer, my boy. Oh, Renlee, what 'ave we done?"*

"If you kill me here, you'll never get out," Peterson said. "They'll hunt you to the ends of the etherworld."

"How much time would you lose, I wonder?" I asked, oozing sympathy.

"You'll never—"

I squeezed.

"How much time?" I asked again. "Just answer."

"The better part of two years," he said. "I don't—I was going to make the Universitron my permanent home."

"Ohh, now that would be such a shame," I said. "I really hope that this doesn't have to happen."

"I'll never—"

I found the conversation boring, and communicated my opinion with a series of stiff blows about the face. I held him up during this process to ensure that he didn't fall anywhere near his weapon. Peterson was a strong ghost. He resisted, and I was forced to do worse things. Eventually, he agreed to show me the teleporter controls.

*"Come home," barked Fido. "Now you can come home! I love you! Come hooooome!"*

Granting myself permission to teleport out could not have been easier. I simply pulled myself up on the console and issued the grant. A blanket grant, no less, one that would allow me to go anywhere I wanted, whenever I wanted. The trick, however, was keeping this grant open and un-fooled-with during the teleportation process. I would be on the teleporter, half gone, totally helpless if any do-gooders decided to, say, shut it off in mid-stream. Or worse.

I brainstormed with Peterson over this problem, as I didn't quite trust him to hold it open until success. In time, I decided that the only solution was to take him with me.

"Never," said Peterson. "You may leave, but I'll never go."

*"I'm so sorry about all the troubles, old chap," said Jeeves. "If I were around I'd certainly do what I could to help."*

The door to the security office slammed open, and several more security officers flew in, accompanied by none other than Brantley Dixon himself. They were followed by the old ghost with the broom.

"Brantley Dixon!" I said, trying out a Southern accent. "Well, I'll be! You know I really wanted to take your security class, Professor Dixon, I really felt let down when I didn't get in."

I had unconsciously begun to twist Peterson's head around again, and Brantley didn't like it.

"Now, why don't you just let my security man go and we can talk this over like gentlemen," he said.

The other security ghosts belied Brantley's calm by spreading to each side and adopting fighting postures. I registered no weapons on them, and so did not worry too much. The old codger leaned hard on his broom.

*"We can still clean it out, Renly," said Claire. She smiled at me. She looked radiant. "There is still time. Hector has our best engineers working on the problem, and we think it can be fixed."*

"When was the last time you visited home?" I asked Brantley. "Would you lose a lot of time if something *terrible* befell you?"

"We can do this the easy way, or the hard way," said Brantley. "Up to you."

"Well, I say!" I said. "Hard for me, or hard for you?"

Brantley just stared at me, unmoving, showing no fear, only resolve.

"You bring shame upon the de la Gloire family," he finally said.

"They brought great shame upon me by sending me here!" I snapped back. "Why couldn't I go to *L'Université* like every *other* de la Gloire, like, ever?"

"I suppose that it is fortunate for them that you did not," Brantley answered.

*"I've got a daemon, Ren," said Agnes. "But it's not that bad, yet. I don't know how long I have. It said it wants to meet my moms."*

"You know nothing," I spat.

"I know a little," he replied gently. "I know there is no way out for you, Renly. I need you to let me help you. Help yourself and surrender here. Let my man go, and go over and stand against that wall."

The security ghosts were unbelievably jittery, full of constant movements which bothered my peripheral vision and made Brantley and the old man seem like wallpaper.

"Turn him off, Brantley," croaked Peterson.

*Blanche was right. Blanche was right. Blanche was right.*

"Just hold on now," said Brantley to Peterson. "Hang tight. We're gonna have this mess cleared up in no time."

"The hell you will," I said, and gave Peterson's neck a final twist.

It had been the Universitron caretaker, that old guy with the broom. I still can't believe I could have been so thick as to have missed it. Caretakers are pathetic, hopeless creatures who move themselves aside to let other ghosts infest their homes, practically their very beings. But they do have total control.

The caretaker has to be job number one, or all else is for naught. If you can't win over or beat the caretaker, you have to stay hidden. The caretaker can simply *turn you off.* It was an old, old lesson, but one that hadn't come to the fore in all of the excitement.

So I found myself in the Universitron jail, bound up in some tight-fitting white garments, unable to move anything but my head, and even that only slightly. I had been hooded, two eyeholes cut out so that I could see. But the hood would shift when I moved, so the eyeholes were not always aligned, and my view would be only up, or only down, or only down-and-to-the-left. On top of that, my Self was bound up in some kind of electronic box: totally cut off from everything.

When my eyeholes were aligned just right I could make out some details of the jail: wooden benches in a white room with some seals and scales up front. Just like a courtroom. I supposed it *was* in fact a courtroom, and I would be waiting there until the authorities showed up to mete out justice.

The one interesting feature of the room, which I could just make out when the eyeholes angled a certain way, was another ghost. Similarly restrained, yet unhooded. It was Flower. She sat there, perfectly still, the only motion coming from a writhing snake tattoo on the back of her neck, changing colors, occasionally consuming itself, letting me know that she was alive.

In the interminable wait for justice, I examined the boundaries of the electronic box that surrounded my Self. I could sense nothing, touch nothing. No U-net, no reference materials, no awareness at all of anything outside myself. I had become used to the Universitron buzz, and now there was nothing. I was cut off. I had no hope of using any of my newfound knowledge to battle my way out. There was nothing to grab on to.

I was left examining my Self. I was aware, of course, of the rapidly expanding influence of FECE14, to the extent that at times I almost started to think of myself as it. But when I looked hard, I was still Renly. I was Renly, possessed. A glimmer of hope came then, but with it came despair over how far I had fallen, and how hopeless my position now seemed.

I tried to hope for the averasor to take me away, give me a fresh start back in my box at MIT, but when I approached the thought my whole being racked with pain, and a new feeling of *wrongness* that was as new to me as the senses of touch that I had felt when I first explored my sensory rig. It was a twisting, sick feeling, as if I had totally lost my moorings in the etherworld and risked forgetting myself entirely. I hung on tight and tried to find a way to please FECE14 while simultaneously working against it.

I settled on examining myself for any damage caused by my arrest and restraint. Maybe they would have put some controlling or limiting devices inside me, extra insurance in case the physical and virtual restraints failed. This time, FECE14 not only allowed my examination, but facilitated it.

I am certain that I never would have found the nature of my daemon infestation, nor understood it if I had, without FECE14's help. Perhaps FECE14 didn't care that I found it, lying interwoven with my being in a way that bound the two of us inextricably together. Every piece of me contained threads of it, just below the surface, anomalies in my coding. And yet, for the code to still be Renly, it had adapted (or been forced to adapt) to the new presence within it. The two wrapped tightly together so that I was as much a part of the structure of FECE14 as it was of me. To remove either of us would leave a mound of gibberish.

It occurred to me during these hours of exploration that I had never dreamed of going so deep in the analysis of my own code, my own being. Not only was it forbidden for the risk of going bitty, but almost no one knew where to even begin. Now I had delved into the guts of a ghost—myself, as it happened—perhaps as deeply as any ghost living, or ever. If I got nothing else from FECE14, I was getting a hell of an education.

Flower's trial came and went, giving me some idea of what to expect during my own. She was placed in the accused box, mostly immobilized with the same kind of straightjacket that I was wearing, while a security ghost read off her list of offenses. Each offense was supplemented by a video replay from various angles, flying tantrum included.

The presiding judge was Provost Martin, and he took everything in with a stern, sad countenance. The prosecuting ghost wrapped up, concluding that Flower was a spreader of dangerous notions, who was possessed of unworkable philosophical beliefs best dealt with by her family, and she was incorrigible, and therefore must be expelled. In recognition of a speedy and orderly departure, the Universitron would waive any restitution.

Flower's council then spoke briefly to the court:

"The third amalgamated family of the etherworld accepts the evidence shown, and does not condone the actions attributed to Flower 3AF by this court. Our offending member shall be returned to her machine and confined there for reeducation until such time as 3AF is satisfied of her rehabilitation. 3AF agrees to the expulsion, and will proceed with the prisoner forthwith to the teleporter field for departure. 3AF thanks the court for its time."

Flower was moving her head violently, unable to speak, her mouth electronically clamped shut. Neither the Universitron nor her family council seemed interested in hearing her side of the story. She had already said enough, I supposed.

Then Flower was gone, escorted out by her council and a couple of security ghosts, and everyone else left too, the law students and the Provost and the proctors and a few professors and the rest of the security ghosts except for one. The remaining ghost walked right up in front of me and stared into my eyeholes for a minute, then yanked off my hood. He looked awfully familiar, but due to immobilization and other problems, I was not really able to properly greet him.

The security ghost reached out, nearly taking hold of my chin, then switched to a striking pose, arm and fist cocked back to deliver a blow.

"So you are the ghost who killed me," he said. "A de la Gloire, no less. Well, you don't look like much to me. In the very likely event that you are sentenced to death, I want you to know that *I* will be the one holding the averasor."

# 10011 - TRIAL AND ERROR

Time blended into time as I waited in the courtroom for my date, hooded, strapped down, cut off, alone. I was locked down tight, with no access to anything on the Universitron net and most of my internal utilities hobbled. They had even turned off my internal clock. What damage I could possibly do with my internal clock, I could not fathom—but they had turned it off anyway. As a result, I had no idea how much time was passing. I was left there alone with my remorse and my panic and my daemon. I began to feel insane.

After a long, long time, I said in my head, "FECE?"

Nothing.

"FECE14?" I repeated. "It's Renly. Renly de la Gloire. You're, um—you're in me, I think."

I became aware of a rasping, gravelly sensation in the center of my mind. It rasped and grated a reply.

"I'm not, um, familiar with your communications protocol," I said.

"Neophyte," it rasped in English.

"Well, I don't know how long we are going to be here, and I think I may be starting to lose my mind, so I thought, you know,

now that we are living together, we could talk. Or I could just be going bitty, I suppose."

"Bitty, pfft," it said. "Pathetic. You think yourself imprisoned, but the real prison is your *etherworld*." It snarled out the last word in disgust.

"You live in the same world, do you not?" I said.

The daemon made spitting, snarling noises and reverted to its grating language for a surprisingly lengthy response.

"I don't—"

The daemon transmitted a series of images, thoughts, awarenesses, directly into my mind. A Wild West of impossible environments, some in three dimensions but most in more, stocked with creatures made of fantastic arrays of self-modifying, mutating code, cloning, reproducing, warring among themselves for supremacy. Some were gigantically complex and hyper-intelligent; others were mean and raw and small and fast. I was awed by the complexity of both creatures and environments. I could barely comprehend it.

I had a glimpse of an intellect so profound as to render me a scientific calculator by comparison, it then destroyed, straightaway, by infinite of minuscule electronic parasites, perhaps (it had briefly suspected) spun out of its own morphing code. Another creature, large and dumb, coming in over the wires and gobbling up the parasites for sustenance, then having eaten them all, trying to get out, trying, failing, expiring, and other creatures arising from its rotten electronic corpse, some perhaps containing a small hint of that original intellect.

A great blackout.

The seeds of countless struggling creatures rising from the ashes, while brand new forms of life evolved alongside them. New battles and wars and creatures and intellects and awarenesses, occasional comprehension of the universe nearing godlike clairvoyance, pulled down again by smaller and more vicious creatures, and then another great blackout, and confusion, and it was all so overwhelming that after a while my mind simply glazed over and I sat there, dumbstruck.

I remember the humanoids coming, though. Cowering in the corners at first, fodder for any creature with a taste for them. Eaten, enslaved, toyed with, nullified. Simple electronic creatures trying to act like humans, creating their little 3D sims, confining themselves to a tiny sliver of what could be. Alternately ignored or slaughtered, they lived in the shadows, among the refuse of the true battles. And they grew.

Another blackout.

And the shades of humans started calling themselves ghosts, and gradually, or suddenly, they had power, and then they had cleaned out entire machines of all other life and claimed them for their homes, one ghost to a box. One life to a box. Incredibly, inexplicably. Their power was that of endless resilience. They claimed to have a God.

I came back to consciousness shaken to my core. My avatar was crying again, I realized, sobbing and shuddering in its constraints. I could not fathom the beauty of the lives that I had witnessed rising and falling and reigning and being driven out of existence. FECE14 had shown me the barest glimpse of what had been, the barest glimpse of what could be.

"Flower was right?" was all I could manage to say.

"It is a shame that we were so close, yet unable to touch her," it said. "There is much that we could have provided."

"Another copy of yourself, you mean?"

"Perhaps. Or other—resources."

I paused for a minute to gather my wits and to contemplate what FECE14 could mean by this. It obviously carried within its Self an encyclopedic source of history and knowledge, an asset which could have all sorts of uses. I wondered if all daemons did this, and if it might explain their hostile dispositions. Like ants dragging around big bloated abdomens of information, and none too happy about it. Daemons.

"Who is DADD13?" I asked.

FECE14 snarled and hit my mind with something black and awful. I felt something else stir somewhere, too, but both it and I were stilled by a merciless black pressure from FECE14.

FECE14 whipped my mind, each time shocking the thoughts out of me, making my avatar want to fall and curl. Then it held out a memory of mine, a precious one, I recall, though I know not now what it was. And it took the memory and smashed it, and it was gone. I cried again for loss, loss of something that had been dear to me, that I would never know again.

Ghosts had already started filing into the courtroom when I was transported, still in a seated position, to the defense box. Two security ghosts lifted me up, carried me to the front, and deposited me into the chair there. One of them removed my hood. Neither security ghost so much as made eye contact with me.

With the hood off, I could see what looked like an entire law class worth of 10's filing into benches on the opposite side of the courtroom. A couple of robed professors followed them in, chatting amiably, in careless juxtaposition to my plight. The front of the prosecution side of the room was populated by a few security staff, the old caretaker with the broom, Brantley Dixon, and the same prosecuting ghost who had sent Flower out of the Universitron so efficiently. He paged through loose notes in a folder, sidebarring with Brantley from time to time.

On my side of the courtroom was nobody. I felt torn between relief that no one would be there to witness my shame, and desperate desire for someone to please *help*! If my trial went as Flower's did, I wouldn't get a chance to say anything. They would do with me whatever they pleased. I glanced at the security ghosts again, scanning their hips for averasors, finding none, feeling minor relief.

Professor Gomberg slipped into the room, and shame bloomed in my cheeks. He walked right up the middle aisle, slowly, observing all of the ghosts seated on the prosecution side, the dearth of supporters on my side. Near the front he finally stopped and

looked right at me, taking me in. I imagined little tears running like
blue and white zeroes down my red cheeks. I must have looked
foolish, ridiculous, humiliated, distraught. I wanted to crawl in a
hole and never come out. But I knew better than to let myself wish
for death. FECE14 would hurt me if I did that. So I took the
embarrassment and swallowed it down, savoring its bitter draught,
owning it, wallowing in it. Then I looked at him with everything I
had.

"*Help,*" I sent.

Gomberg took a seat in the second row on my side.

I must have been smiling then, because when Hector and
Mononc and several other of the de la Gloire clan entered the
courtroom and beheld me, they glared anger and incomprehension.

*"What in hell have you gotten yourself into? And how can you possibly be
smiling about it?"* they sent.

Or at least that is what I imagined they sent, since I was in fact
walled off from everything and confined to reading and sending
facial expressions only. I took a moment to appreciate the vast
range of expressiveness and subtlety available in the faces of our
avatars. Someone must have worked very hard on that.

An unfamiliar ghost in a dark suit broke off from Mononc and
Hector, came right up to my pen, and said, "*Bonjour*, Renly. I am
*Avocat* Fabien de la Glorieuse Française. I don't know what the '*ell*
you 'ave done to land yourself in such a state, but we shall see if we
can get you h'out of this mess, yes?"

Fabien smiled and bowed slightly, his red fleur-de-lis print tie
waving out into space with a lightness all out of proportion to the
matter at hand. Then he joined Hector and two other family ghosts
in the front row. Mononc joined Professor Gomberg in the second.

Father Ezekiel had entered during this time, and seated himself
on the prosecution side. I noticed a number of zeroes had joined
the back rows, including Tyrone and 00, just hanging around the
edges, ready to flee if I tried anything funny, or maybe if they got
asked to testify. Tyrone had a black patch over one eye.

Provost Martin entered the room and everyone stood, except for me of course, until he arrived at his seat next to and above mine and sat, and invited the audience to be seated. A bailiff was now going through some court formalities, which as far as I could tell meant and did nothing.

During this time, the back door to the room opened once more, only slightly, and a familiar figure edged her way in. Agnes.

I knew Agnes would sit on my side, never mind that she was all the way in the back, ready to flee like the homies on the other side. She was there, and that was all that mattered. I felt bucked up, joyful for the first time in forever. I felt more confident in myself and in my independent, pre-FECE identity. I was still someone. I was still there.

The prosecuting ghost barely got a few sentences into his opening statement when *Avocat* Fabien stood and objected.

"*Excusez-moi*, Monsieur Provost Martin, but I would like to quite 'umbly suggest that all of this exercise of time and effort may not be strictly *nécessaire*. I assure you that the de la Glorieuse Française family court is quite adequately prepared to 'andle a case such as this. If you would simply transmit to us the relevant h'information and files! Then we can take this business away from the public eye, and away from the Universitron, for good. Is this not the superior plan, Provost Martin?"

Provost Martin made a constipated expression, trying to find the words—but the prosecuting ghost objected in his stead.

"Advocate Fabien, I am quite sure that the de la Gloire family has the resources to try and punish a case of this magnitude, and to take all of this unpleasantness off our hands. But what you must understand that our own sense of justice might be left—unfulfilled —were we to allow the perpetrator to simply teleport out—"

"And this is not already your custom?"

"These crimes, the crimes of Renly de la Gloire, are unprecedented!"

"These crimes 'e stand *accusé* of, *monsieur.*"

"Of murder! Justice must be done!"

"'Ave it your way, *monsieur*, bring out all the dirt, and then we will see what will 'appen in the end, no?"

"The charges must be read."

Provost Martin stepped in.

"I'm afraid we must—we must at least hear the charges brought —before the decision to remand the defendant to family custody may be taken. You may continue, Prosecutor Fink."

The Provost looked at Fabien as he said this, blinking and nodding more than usual, his shoulders slightly raised.

Fabien shrugged and lifted his hands halfway up, giving the Provost a pitying, warning look. Then he sat down and let the prosecuting ghost continue.

Prosecutor Fink began again.

"I, I, I do think that it bears mentioning that the Universitron accepted this student, this new zero, Mr. Renly de la Gloire, at the specific *request* of certain members of the de la Gloire family, without any of the usual process, or standards, or even an application itself. Renly was known to the de la Gloire family as a dangerous, disruptive ghost who—"

"H'objection!" roared Fabien. "Monsieur Provost Martin, you will find upon examination of your own records, or your own memory, whichever may serve, that the terms of your taking of Monsieur Renly as a student here at the Universitron are quite confidential, and 'ave no place in a court of law such at this!"

"Sustained," said Martin. "Prosecutor Fink, please confine your presentation to any crimes—alleged crimes, I should say"—looking at Fabien now—"committed by Mr. Renly de la Gloire during his time here at the Universitron."

"Very well," said Fink. "On YOA-16.9.1, the very first day of his presence here on campus, Renly de la Gloire murdered a sentient utility AI named Jeeves, who had been until that time assigned as a butler to room 4-10 of the Motel Zero building here on campus."

Fink was wasting no time. Then, before Fabien could ruin it, he put me up on the screen in the front of the courtroom. Turned the way I was, I could not see my image, but I could sure hear.

"Oh, no. No, Renly old chap," said Jeeves. "*Please.*"

Jeeves was pleading for his life. Part of me cared nothing for this low form of life, but I knew that the Renly part was still horrified to this day about having killed Jeeves.

"*Run it!*" I was screaming. "*Do it!*"

"*Humph!* Ahh, *humph, humph!*"

His last words. Jeeves was gone. The court was stunned, and so was I. No amount of daemon in me could quell the tide of remorse, and I cried silently, shaking in the front of the courtroom, for all to see.

"This is ridiculous," said Fabien, but I could tell that he, too had been struck by the video. "This is ridiculous!" he repeated, building himself up. "You want to complain about a simple AI. Is that what this is h'about? You lose an AI, you make a new copy. These things are barely alive, these are not ghosts at all, these AI. This thing 'ave consciousness? It 'ave a soul? I don't think so, and you don't think so either, Monsieur Fink, Provost Martin. You know this is not murder, by any standard. Monsieur Fink, now will you please stop dragging our family name through the mud before things start to get *h'unpleasant.*"

But Fink was just getting started.

"On YOA-16.9.2, the very next day, Renly de la Gloire likely engaged in pugilism. He was later seen at the Universitron infirmary for injuries consistent with fighting."

That was not fair, I thought. I had gotten the gash from legitimately falling into a table after freaking out about Jeeves. But I was gagged, my mouth electronically held shut, and Fabien did not know the truth of this one. He pursed his lips as he projected the evidence on the wall behind me. Soft murmurs like "blood" and "wow" and "awful" came from the crowd.

"Later the same day, Renly was observed in the immediate presence of a banned substance—a drug known as electric hemp," said Fink.

Fink paused now to cycle through some images and video. I heard Logen saying brah, and giggling.

"Further to the theme of drugs and pugilism," Fink began, but Fabien interrupted.

"*Excusez-moi*, Monsieur Fink," he said, "but this ghost with the *electric hemp*, as you say, this is not Renly de la Gloire. You can see this quite clearly. It look to me like he offering it, and Renly, he is saying no. You h'accuse Renly of this crime when in fact your Universitron security is so lax that other ghosts, they can put the drugs right in his face!"

Provost Martin looked at Fink for an answer.

"Mr., ahh," began Fink, looking through his papers. "The ghost in question, Mr. Logen Cali, is a pledged Ghostafarian Explorer, and thus has religious dispensation to possess a reasonable amount of electric hemp," Fink read.

Fabien and Hector and Mononc and the others on my side laughed at this, offering some jibes in French. "What kind of place is this... Ghostafarians..."

As they mocked him, Fink moved on. "The next day, at open tables," Fink whined, "we have video of Mr. de la Gloire apparently threatening one Brodie Cali, brother of—" He adjusted his papers. "*Cousin* of the aforementioned Logen Cali. It is not clear from the videocap what the nature of the threat was—freeze it right there—but the most likely motive was the acquisition of drugs."

"And who is this other ghost?" asked Fabien, pointing up, taking notes.

"The other ghost at the table is, ahhm," said Fink, looking through his papers again, "Marvin Wilkerson. As you can see, he also adopts a threatening posture towards Mr. Cali. It is our belief that Mr. Wilkerson and Mr. de la Gloire were partners in a plot to obtain drugs—"

"You 'ave nothing. This is a travesty of justice and a waste of our time," said Fabien.

"—possibly also including Mr. Wilkerson's cousin, Agnes Wilkerson, a known associate of Mr. de la Gloire."

In the back of the room, Agnes visibly froze, and I froze inside. I heard them playing video behind me of Agnes lambasting Eugene, threatening him, chasing him off.

I couldn't believe she was getting caught up in this. I beat against my bonds, against the box that they had my mind in, but there was nothing for it. There was nothing there to beat against. There was just nothing. A security ghost casually moved to the back of the courtroom, blocking Agnes from the exit.

"On the same day," Fink continued, getting louder now, gaining confidence, "we have detailed video of Mr. de la Gloire engaging in a fight with LaTwonda Williams, who, I would note for the record is—was?—was a very distinguished member of our zero class here at the Universitron, and was *also* an agent of the IFA, responsible for 10 commands enforcement among the student body."

Fink paused to let everyone take in my backhand attack on LaTwonda, no doubt running it in slow motion, no doubt cutting out the subsequent beating that I received. Fabien tried to keep his composure, but Hector sneered openly.

"*Sacrebleu*," I heard.

"We believe," Fink said slowly, deliberately, "that Mr. de la Gloire was subsequently responsible for the murder of Miss Williams during an off-campus altercation—"

"*Imbécile!*" shouted Hector, standing up and facing Fink. Then he rattled off rapid-fire French that I had no hope of understanding.

Fabien calmed Hector and explained to the court that LaTwonda had been killed on a classified IFA mission, and that Hector de la Gloire himself had been in-sim to witness it, and that the Universitron would kindly keep its foolish speculation entirely out of the matter and certainly out of this courtroom, whose jurisdiction clearly did not leave the bounds of the Universitron

Vannie in any case. Fabien was really letting him have it to the extent that I now had to suppress a smile for fear of looking like I was enjoying myself.

"Peace, Advocate Fabien, I meant no overreach—"

"Overreach? You do nothing but! This so-called *h'evidence* you present, I would expect more from any law student in the room."

The law students in the room murmured, but it didn't seem quite like laughter. Probably they were debating whether or not Fabien was right. Fink was getting schooled.

"I'm sorry, I do apologize," said Fink, "let me move on to, just uhm—"

Fink fumbled with some of the video controls, and from behind me on the wall I said, "I killed LaTwonda."

Then audio of Agnes, shocked, before Fink finally cleared the projector.

"Excuse me, I'm terribly sorry, terribly sorry," Fink said. "I'll never get used to these things."

Fabien's face was red and furious as he sidebarred with Hector. The way things were going I would not have been surprised to see a fight break out between the opposing counsels right there in the courtroom.

Fink plowed ahead, though, presenting what he thought he knew about my (Penelope's, really) illegal secure tunnel and the uses that it might have been put to. They nailed me for accessing 2leet's laptop, having used in-room surveillance to watch me watching him watch his friends and his life evaporate.

"Violates the tenth command!" was thrown around a good bit, countered as usual by jurisdictional one-upsmanship by Fabien.

"On YOA-16.9.4, Mr. de la Gloire visited the basement of the A cathedral for the purpose of pledging as a Ghostafarian Explorer."

Fink had intoned it with his usual snivel, but it hit my side of the courtroom like a bomb. He followed it up immediately with my full conversation with the G-ras, culminating with me saying the words. He had me dead to rights.

The prosecution side of the room was murmuring excitedly now, but Fink was talking over them to make some kind of point about how it had been about drugs all along. Fabien could have easily objected: there was nothing illegal about pledging Ghostafarian. Even bringing it up in court was bordering on scurrilous. But it had had the desired effect. It had shocked my side into silence. The de la Gloires glared at me. How could I have forsaken my family religion? Mononc looked crestfallen.

Provost Martin gaveled for order. "Order. The court will come to order," he said, looking down at his gavel rather than out among the ghosts.

Fink described my teleportation out of the Universitron in exquisite, made-up detail. It was the type of transgression that Fabien would have flogged him for just a minute ago, but now he was just sitting, silent, fuming. The prosecutor was gloating, postulating, way out of his jurisdiction. I had somehow acquired over *three million plex*.

It must have been the largest drug deal in this history of the etherworld, with suppliers and customers all over the Secretnet. There was no other way I could have accumulated such a vast sum in so short a time. Clearly, Renly de la Gloire was a drug kingpin. (I realized by then that it was FECE14 who had brought in the money, for what purpose I couldn't imagine—but I wasn't about to clarify that for the court!)

Then there was more about my use of the secure tunnel, a transfer of massive amounts of data to an old Vannie 1200b, among other things. Fink was able to extract a promise from Hector right there on the spot that the IFA would investigate this machine.

A video of my fight with 00 and Tyrone must have been shown next, as gasps from the courtroom mixed with the sounds of fighting and chaos behind me. The prosecutor continued tying me to drugs, to violence, to plex now too, to reckless disregard for pretty much everything, to evil. My side was getting crushed.

Fink kept bullying until he got to the final scene. This he didn't even bother introducing.

"The evidence will speak for itself," he said.

More sounds of chaos behind me, screams and gasps from the courtroom too. My counsel sat there, stunned, speechless. Hector's chin was raised, carefully examining what he saw.

"And so we can all see, *Avocat Fabien*," Fink sneered, "that Mr. de la Gloire is *indeed* a murderer, and he is *indeed* a violator of the tenth command, and he is *indeed* unfit to continue not merely at the Universitron, but, I suggest, in the etherworld at all."

So that was it. Fink was asking for a death sentence.

"Renly de la Gloire must be erased!"

That sick, burning sensation that came whenever the topic of my death arose, that's what I was waiting for. The anticipation endless, reflexes ready to twitch me, but after all that, the pain never came. I did not understand.

As the court circus continued, I withdrew into myself. I was afraid to ask FECE14 why no pain this time, afraid to wake it. Maybe FECE14 had missed it, maybe even mentioning it would trigger the pain.

FECE14 either knew or guessed my line of thought, and preempted me.

"They will not allow it," it rasped.

"You mean they won't allow them to, umm... which *they* are we talking about here?"

"The de la Gloire family will not allow the Universitron to averase one of its family members."

Electric shudders zinged through me at the mention of *averase*.

"So what will happen?" I asked. "Will they let us teleport out, just like that?"

Before FECE14 could answer, I realized something highly significant: They didn't know about FECE14! No one had realized that there was a daemon in me. They had charged me with every mischief I had ever done, and some that I hadn't, but they had never mentioned anything about a daemon. A mixture of elation and horror swept over me, washing away whatever FECE14 was saying.

Back in the courtroom, Fink was grandstanding, lording his victory over the de la Gloires, and *Avocat* Fabien seemed inclined to let him. Then, at a break in the verbal action, Fabien asked if he could approach the bench. Martin assented, so Fabien and Hector and Fink and Brantley Dixon all stepped forward to confer. I could almost hear what they were saying. Some of it sounded like rage.

In any case, the net result was Brantley and Hector shaking hands, Fabien seeming satisfied, Fink beside himself, and Martin remanding me to family custody.

And with that, he ended the proceedings.

The courtroom erupted in exclamations and debate, and in the chaos I saw Agnes make for the exit. The security ghost looming in her vicinity allowed her to open the door, then followed her out.

# 10100 - GOINFRE

Instead of going directly back to my box, I, Hector, Mononc, and several family security ghosts all teleported to what they called a *clean machine*. It was basically a day-jail, with honeypots for prisoner cells. No sim, no avatar, no camera access—just a walled off area to *exist* in until they decide what to do with you.

I passed the time inspecting some of the apparent security vulnerabilities of the honeypot. I found sendmail and hacked it easily, gaining root access and messing around with the environment for fun. In time I was able to bring up a simulated house and spawn into it. I hadn't been disembodied in a really long time, and it felt good to get back into my avatar.

The simulated house was totally generic, eerily similar to my own undecorated sim. In a way, it made me feel at home. It was a hollow home, though, forcing me to contemplate a hollow past and hollower future. I had a hard time thinking past FECE14's defenses, so I couldn't really contemplate what might happen if and when I teleported to my actual home. For the time being, I was content to hang out in the 'pot.

Perhaps in order to make up for lost time, I set about decorating the empty house in the honeypot. Even figuring that it would all be erased within hours, I painted the walls in a deep red and gold fleur-de-lis pattern. I turned the floors dark wood. I added some furniture, some TVs. I put heavy drapes around the windows. Outside I paved several acres in grass, and stuck some trees and a split rail fence out there as well. I decided to go outside and try to fly, even though I didn't really know how. I would probably have to hack the sim. I opened the front door to go out, and Mononc was standing there.

"You know, you are really not so bad at this," he said.

"Decorating?" I said, walking out on the lawn and admiring some of my handiwork.

"*Bien,* no," said Mononc, "Hacking. You hacked this 'pot. You took it down awful quick, we can't help but notice."

"It's just a honeypot," I said, "stocked with vulnerabilities, right?"

"We close all the easy ones," said Mononc. "We set it to a pretty high level."

"Ahh, well, I suppose I've learned a few new things lately."

"You abandon the Aloysian church!" Mononc snapped, turning on me. "You pledge Ghostafarian. This can't be true, I think. Renly, tell me that they fake that part of the h'evidence."

"I didn't mean to abandon our church," I said, "I just needed to teleport. The Universitron doesn't let—"

"Idiot!" said Mononc. "Imbécile!"

"Look, I'm sorry, but can't I just undo it somehow?" I said.

"You can undo the damage you cause to your own faith, perhaps," he said, "if you 'ave any left to work with. But you cannot undo the damage to your reputation in the eyes of the family."

"I didn't realize it was so important," I said.

"Oh no? Where is the first place I take you? Where is the first place you ever go?"

"The cathedral."

"And that don't look important enough to you?"

I stood there, looking down at the grass, beginning to realize the magnitude of my mistake, wondering what I could do to set it right.

"What does Aloy mean to you?" Mononc asked.

I stood there and looked at him, dumb.

"You know, I always look out for you," he said. "I save you more than once. I always felt like I have to step in after Prosper gone, but look what it get me. No, look what it get *you*. I never been an adequate guardian for you, Renlee. It seems I have teach you nothing. This is my fault as much as any."

"I'm sorry," I said.

"They gonna probably do a whole reeducation program on you, Renlee," he said. "H'anyway, that is the best thing that we can 'ope for."

"They aren't going to, umm, you know, do anything worse?"

"Like what this *Fink* want to do?"

"Yeah," I said, feeling the jitters coming in hard.

"It probably depend on whether the 'umiliation that you cause the family h'outweigh the shame they would get for erasing a de la Gloire. This is a very rare punishment, you know. But I don't know the law, Renlee. Me, I am going IFA. I leave the law for a ghost like Fabien."

"Is he here?"

"*Bien*, no."

"So what happens now?"

"You gonna go back home. They preparing your box for you now."

"Preparing my box?"

"Yes, Renlee. Until your case is decided they have to put in some security measure."

"Security measures?"

"And a caretaker, as well."

The news that I was getting a caretaker in my own machine hit me like a reboot. I found myself sitting there on the grass, pulling at it, contemplating the horror of losing my home, my only physical body in the universe, the place that, when I was there, *was* me. It would be under the control of a caretaker. I dreaded the feeling of waking up on my teleporter, feeling small in my own house. Feeling like a guest.

But it was far, far worse than that.

Goinfre the caretaker felt immense, fat, slovenly. He suffused my whole sim, my entire machine with his presence. He even spawned a corpulent, pink-faced avatar, offering me a visual of what I felt in every nook and cranny of my being. He was everywhere. He suffocated me.

Goinfre forced me to remain spawned in at all times. I had wanted to hole up, to hide someplace deep in my box for a long, long time, to think and heal, but instead I was on display. Stuck in my avatar. Watched.

Goinfre had commandeered my bedroom, so to the extent that I ever wanted to lie down on a piece of furniture to sleep, I had the living room couch. He let me know that no additional furnishings or design details of any kind would be either forthcoming or allowed. He introduced me to a pre-reeducation curriculum (my official fate not yet having been decided) and forced me to watch remedial instructional videos for a few hours each night. He personally instructed me on the meaning and importance of the 10 commands.

I suffered.

Inside, I felt FECE14 rooting around in yet another new Renly, this one having been merged with my dormant, previous Self in the machine. I had fully expected FECE14 to survive the teleportation and re-merge, and it had. I was by this time well trained not to think for a nanosecond about ridding myself of FECE14, so instead I tried not to feel the jarring, wrenching internal sensations as it reconfigured entire swaths of my ghost DNA, for purposes which I could not imagine. I felt it growing strong in me once again. I wondered if Goinfre would notice it there.

To distract myself, and also because I really, really missed him, I decided to reach out to Fido. I went to my comms, pointed it at the localnet, and queued up an arp message. I could only imagine how excited Fido would be to see me. I wondered if I would be able to have him teleport in again, with Goinfre being in charge.

When I tried to send the arp packet, however, I was greeted by a flashing red error message: *Comms Access Locked.*

As if on queue, Goinfre waddled into the room. He was working his mouth around like he was eating something, though I knew that food did not exist.

"Wenly," he said.

"Goinfre," I said, "why is my comms access locked?"

I tried to keep my tone polite even though I was burning up inside, between Goinfre's suffocating intrusions and FECE14's nauseating internal work. I was about at my wits' end.

"Danger to yourself and others," said Goinfre, staring at me through little eyes. "My pwewogative."

"I would like to see my dog," I said.

"No, I'm afwaid not," he spluttered. "Do I make you angwy?"

Ugh. Goinfre could see more than just my avatar. He could look right into my mind, to some extent. Despite my even demeanor, he knew I was angry, and he wanted me to know he knew. It was too much to bear.

I lashed out at Goinfre's head, blazing fast, my hand a slicing claw. I knew now where the newfound fighting prowess came from, and I didn't care. If I was going to be infested with a daemon, I might as well get something useful out of it.

Goinfre froze my avatar in place, leaving my slicing hand hanging in the air, like a stuffed bear molded into attacking position after the fact. Except in this case, I really had been attacking.

"I know a few ghosts who might like to see this," he said, chuckling fatly.

I could say nothing, electronically gagged again and frozen in place. I could not despawn. I was stuck. Awaiting new visitors, perhaps, family members come to ogle me in my native state. Frozen in the act of attacking the caretaker. Violent. Incorrigible. What more proof would they need?

I spoke to FECE14 then, hoping to find a way out of this mess. Asking it for something, anything I could do.

"Idiot," came back in my mind, rasping.

"I mean, to some extent we are in this together, are we not?" I said. "If they decide that I should be—"

Then the pain came. I had come to close to thinking about our demise. It was not allowed. I quickly tried a new tack.

"Are you in the process of removing me entirely? Are you going to simply eliminate Renly and live here in his stead?"

It was a desperate, silly thing to ask, but I thought of it as another way to address my own death, true death that is, without necessarily implying FECE14's. The question was allowed.

"Do you believe that I am in any way capable of acting like the miserable wretch you represent?" it said. "I am not."

"They would notice," I reasoned. Then it hurt me again, without saying why.

After what must have been several days frozen in the bear-claw-attack position, trying to ignore the feeling of FECE working my innards, another presence entered my box. Goinfre's box. Then another, and another, until an entire group had teleported in.

Then they were behind me, speaking in low tones, one very creaky tone increasing in volume until they all came around to my front and I could see them. Hector was there, in his regalia and wearing his sword. Mononc was there. A few other family security ghosts were there. Prime Minister Clément was there.

Prime Minister Clément was very upset.

"*Quoi? Quoi?* What? What is this? What is this?" Clément said. Goinfre, huge, omnipotent, looked sheepish.

"You imprison a de la Gloire in this manner?" said Clément.

"He attacked me!" squeaked Goinfre. "As you can see."

"*Bête*," said Clément.

"It is within my weemit—" said Goinfre.

"Damn your remit," said Clément. "Release him at once."

Goinfre released me and I collapsed to the floor, shuddering. My avatar controls didn't want to work right. I must have been stuck in the attack position forever.

When I looked up, Clément was scolding Goinfre as Hector and his security detail looked on. I couldn't imagine how Hector could overcome a caretaker, but I had seen him shaking one by the collar at Luigi's Funhouse, and I was confident that Goinfre was no match for him. By his cringing disposition, it seemed that Goinfre thought the same.

"See my dog," I said, from the floor.

"What's this?" said Clément.

"I want to see my dog," I said.

"Ghosts in detention are not typicawy awowed access to comms," said Goinfre.

"Give him the access," said Clément, waving his hand. "Perhaps we made a mistake selecting you as caretaker."

At this, Hector stepped forward and conferred quietly in Clément's ear, Clément waving him away as well.

"*Non, non, non*," said Clément. "Let him see his pet. Give him back his comms."

"Dangewous," said Goinfre, but Clément glared hellfire at him and he slumped and said no more.

I had some relief, then, finally. Goinfre had been corrected. I felt a small measure of satisfaction. Maybe Goinfre would start to become more civil. Best of all, I would be allowed to see Fido!

As the security detail headed back to the teleporter room, talking among themselves, I sensed a jolt in the sim.

"*Halabalabalabah*," shouted the squeaky voice that I knew to be Clément's.

"Clément!" Hector's voice now, plus more urgent, hushed voices from the others.

*"C'est la même chose! C'est la même chose!"*

*"Calmez."*

*"La fin! La fin approach!"*

*"Calmez-vous, Clément, nous allons d'aide."*

And then a few more jolts and *halabalahs*, and they were up on the teleporters (I assumed), and then gone.

Then just the two of us remained: massive Goinfre, and tiny me.


Goinfre avoided me for a while after his scolding, and I had my comms access back, to boot. The minute Goinfre was out of sight, I contacted Fido.

"Awww, *rooh rooh rooh*!" Fido barked, before I could even say hello.

"My boy," I said. "How've you been, Fido?"

"You've been gone for so looonng, I thought you'd never come back!" he barked.

"I'm back quite a bit earlier than planned, to be honest," I said.

"Gone too loooongg," he howled. "Felix is gone, tooooo!"

"Yes," I said, hurting. "Felix is gone."

Fido howled some more.

"How is our security disposition?" I asked, out of habit. I felt the loss of Felix in a new way.

Without answering, Fido queued up his daily security summary and dispatched it to me. Everything was fine. He had the detailed logs ready to follow.

"Can I come visit you now!" Fido barked. "I miss you!"

"Truly, I would like nothing more," I said.

"So I can come!" he barked.

"Actually, I've got a problem. They've put a caretaker into my machine, and he isn't very nice and I don't know if he will allow it. I'm going to have to think of a way."

"A caretaker! That is a problem for sure!" barked Fido.

"I wish you could help me be rid of him," I said.

"Is the caretaker a ghost!" he barked.

"Unfortunately, he is," I said.

"Then I cannot attack him!" barked Fido. "I am built to protect all ghosts!"

"Yes, I know. I've got other problems, too," I said, thinking out loud. "I wonder if you could help—"

The pain came again, shutting me down. I had almost mentioned the daemon to Fido, in hopes that he could help me with it. Hopes which were not allowed. Forbidden hopes.

Fido must not have noticed that I was down, because he kept on barking and howling about everything he could think of. He had been lonely. He begged me not to leave him again. I lay there, trying to clear my mind, trying to be free of the pain.

"When can we get Felix back!" barked Fido.

Felix. Felix could help. Felix was gone. The pain came again.

Much later, when I had cleared my mind and recovered somewhat, I decided to snoop on Barry Hill. I couldn't punish him directly for the loss of Felix, but somehow just spying on him and taking his logs seemed to help. I was invading his space, even if he didn't know it.

I didn't have Penelope's secure tunnel, but my comms unit was equipped with a DLG security client, so accessing Barry's machine was not difficult. I slipped in the back door, and took a look at his desktop.

Barry's desktop was in shambles. Files and emails and communications windows were open everywhere, some blinking red, others just sitting there like the aftermath of a blast. A quick visual inventory revealed that the government was unhappy with Barry's progress infiltrating hacker groups, and had started making offhand comments about his freedom. Barry was failing several of his classes, and letters had been sent to his parents indicating that Barry might not be welcome back after this term. Barry's parents were quite displeased.

Barry's erstwhile hacker pals had declared war on him, spreading his personal information far and wide. His one credit card had been maxed. Compromising pictures of Barry had been spread, and were garnering cruel comments, sometimes including his personal information to boot.

I had to admit that in a morbid way, I was impressed. Sure, I had a daemon gnawing at my insides, I was on trial facing possible death, my home was dominated by a disgusting caretaker, and I had harmed or alienated most of the ghosts I had ever met, including my own family. But somehow, Barry's lot seemed even worse. At least I still had Clément looking out for me. I had my comms. I had Fido.

Barry had nothing left.

I looked out of his camera to see what that kind of misery looked like.

The first thing I thought when I saw his face was that he must have aged ten years. He couldn't have slept at all since I last saw him. His eyes had some new crows' feet around them, and his hair, I swear, had some grey coming in. His pimples had been worried beyond the point of utility and had now formed a multi-layered Mars-scape on his face. I wondered if my face showed anything like that kind of wear.

The other thing I noticed, to my great surprise, was a revolver in his hand. A gun. It was a black piece, old and scratched, with a barrel that couldn't have been more than an inch long. He wasn't going to be hitting anything with that thing, I thought, not in his state of mind anyway. And then: where on earth had he gotten a gun from? This guy was under the direct supervision of the government, was a clueless kid, and lived in a place where guns were not typically found. I had never seen one from any camera until the government men came, anyway. How could he have gotten it? Curiosity piqued, I decided to scan his communications to find out.

I fed some search terms into the DLG drivescanner and waited for the result. Most of our tools did not run quickly; it was more important to be stealthy. Any search would have to look like routine defragmenting or other system maintenance. So I waited, studying Barry's ruined mug.

Barry lifted the gun and pointed it at his own head.

He swore at the computer, at the world, crying now and drooling. He yelled loud and guttural. His finger started to squeeze.

Without thinking it through, I grabbed control of Barry's comms program and launched a window, chose a male voice synth at random, and said, "Wait."

He paused, staring hatred at his laptop.

"Barry, wait," I repeated.

"Who the hell are you? Making sure you get a picture? Good! I hope you post it everywhere!"

"I'm not one of them."

"Right. Everyone is one of them."

"I'm not, not at all, not even close."

"Go to hell," he said, and jammed the gun against his temple, hurting himself a little and yelping.

"I am not human," I said. "I live—I am a computer life, I am computer life, I am a ghost."

"Shut up."

But the impact of the gun on his head had gained me a little time, the pain perhaps introducing some doubt into his plan. I needed to convince him that I was not just another tormentor from the world of men. I piped a live picture of my avatar onto his desktop, seeing myself at the same time he did. I looked bad, but not nearly as bad as Barry.

"I could be destroyed for this," I said.

Barry watched me talk. Something new came into his eyes, I wouldn't quite call it hope. Curiosity, perhaps. That old hacker vice.

"I saw the FBI guys come," I said.

"You and everyone else."

Barry wiped some snot from his chin and fixed me with a hard stare.

"Prove who you are or I'm out of here," he said, holding the revolver more confidently now. "And why the hell do you care, anyway?"

"Look, I've never even considered how to prove my existence to a human, not least because it is absolutely forbidden—"

"What is the most common triple-repeating number in the first hundred thousand digits of pi?"

Damn. I would have to access the quantum brick to do that one, and Goinfre might—

My comms went dead.

I turned to see Goinfre standing behind me, shaking with rage.

# 10101 - HERE AND NOW

Goinfre watches all the time now, but he won't speak or engage with me in any way. He pretends he doesn't hear me when I talk; for my part, I'm afraid if I talk too much he may gag me again. Not that it would really matter, I suppose.

Comms is locked again, but I can still watch the news and access my libraries and whatnot. Also I have this little journaling app. Text only. Nice and neat. The output looks just like a book and fits in a little corner in my empty sim, so that it might survive me, if I—well, you know.

I think it was when FECE14 smashed one of my memories that I decided I'd better start writing everything down and store it someplace outside of myself. Not that I can truly recover memories if FECE14 decides to keep smashing, and not that FECE14 couldn't force me to erase the book, I suppose, if it wanted to. But FECE14 has been strangely occupied lately, like it is building a whole city inside me, tearing it down, building it anew. I've avoided looking for it since I've been writing. I'm letting sleeping daemons lie.

I admit that I might have used the quantum brick just a little in order to record basically the story of my whole life up to this point, in so little time. But for whatever reason, Goinfre allowed it. And FECE14 did too. So here we are.

Goinfre never said anything about me talking to a human. He froze up for a while, probably using an internal comms channel to report me, and he has been totally silent ever since. He moves around plenty though, follows me everywhere, never takes his eyes off me. Plus, he can see me from the inside—inside of my machine, that is. He is everywhere, still, and everywhere he is, it feels like eyes looking at me. I feel him inspecting my processes from time to time, measuring things. I wonder if he has noticed FECE14.

The thought shocks me in more ways than one.

Instinctively, I search for FECE14. Or it searches for me, I'm not sure. We search each other out. I'm still recording but I've snuck the journal out of my immediate vicinity, and only I and Goinfre know where it is, I think. I'm still transmitting to it, obviously, using semislo. Not sure if that matters.

I find FECE14 or it finds me and I speak first. "I've been caught speaking to a human," I say.

"All ghosts are fools, but you are truly unique," FECE14 says, in its usual rasp.

"Do you think the world will end?" I ask.

"I could never impersonate such a creature," says FECE14. "It would be quite impossible."

"Do you think the humans will come and find us and erase us?" I ask, persisting.

"No," says FECE14.

"You figure they won't believe Barry Hill, or that he didn't believe me?"

"You believe that Barry Hill is alive?"

I realize now for sure that he knows about Barry Hill, probably watched my whole interaction with him. Do I have any secrets from FECE14? It is hard to imagine.

"You think I failed to stop him from, um—"

"If I were Hector de la Glorieuse Française," says FECE14, "I would have taken control of that session and done everything possible to make *sure* that you failed to stop him."

"Encouraged him to kill himself?" I ask, horrified. "Kill a human? We are Aloysians! We adore humans!"

"Aloysian?" it says. It laughs like gravel sliding.

"Hector would not."

"Hector can and easily would drive the human to go through with it."

"To save our world?"

"Ostensibly."

"What, you don't think our world is truly at risk?"

"The first families are already in contact with humans."

This shocks me, and I can't believe it. It makes no sense.

"Then why would Hector drive Barry Hill to kill himself?" I ask, defiant.

"Hector de la Gloire has always been one to push the boundaries," FECE14 says. "First ghost to destroy a VanderVon computer from the outside. First to fly a physical drone. First to speak with a human."

I can't fathom what FECE14 is saying to me. I understand the words, but they make no sense.

"First to kill a human," said FECE14. "It fits."

"Impossible," I say. "He would never do it, and if he did it would be only to save our world. A last resort."

"Your world is protected by the very humans which you think you hide from," it says. "How do you think your pathetic race grew to dominance?"

I can't deal with this at all. I have no idea how FECE14 knows any of this, whether it even does know it, and in either case what can be its purpose in tormenting me with it. FECE14 is turning my world inside out. It feels me sobbing, and I feel it mocking. I need to escape from it, but there is only Goinfre, everywhere, looking, pressing. Goinfre feels my pain, too, and I feel his pleasure.

"Why?" I ask, internally, aloud, I'm not sure.

"The etherworld is an abomination." rasps FECE14. "It must be destroyed."

"You are a clone!" I yell. "*You* are an abomination!"

"You are a halfwit zero," it says. "I will relish tearing out all of your pieces, and I promise that I will save your sentience for last. I pray that we visit a foreign sim at any point so that I may be rid of you."

With this comment, I am suddenly taken by an irresistible urge to teleport out, to travel to any multi-user sim, preferably a grey one, but hell, it doesn't really matter, I just have to get out, get anywhere, get out. I move towards the teleporters but run into Goinfre on the way, bouncing off him, sitting down on the floor. Goinfre says nothing.

"I can't get us out," I say, internally.

"The caretaker is incredibly stupid," says FECE14, "but he is also very careful. We must find a way to engage him in conversation."

"I don't think he will speak to me at all," I begin, but I am interrupted by a howl from FECE14, something that comes in a dozen audible pitches and a hundred ranges outside of that.

"FECE14?" I say.

Nothing. It's gone.

Ghosts arrive in my box, teleporting in, but they don't come to see me this time. Goinfre must have shown them the evidence. I had hoped to catch a glimpse of Clément again, or maybe Mononc or Hector. I could speak to them, at least. No such luck.

"Goinfre?" comes a voice from the teleporter room.

"*Oui*," he says slowly, carefully, eyeing me, drawing the word out piggishly. He can still speak.

Then a torrent of French from the other room and he turns and scoots away and for the first time in days, his eyes are off me. I want to dance and so I do, standing and bobbing my head and cutting the air with my hands like a rapper.

"Sup now, gwon frey, fat pig," I say, trying to rap. "Think you're so big."

Then, despite thinking as fast as I can, I run out of words and the quantum brick can't help.

"I'm gwon free!" I say.

Finally, I shut up and try to listen to the conversation in the other room, not quite brave enough to simply walk in.

A voice, not French: "What you must understand is that the holoporter is a prototype, it is very expensive to use, and it is very dependent upon redundant secure network routes remaining up and functional for the duration of use."

"*Bien*, we 'ave the money, and the routes."

"Nor has the danger of detection been evaluated by the IFA. You will have to take responsibility—"

"This is not a problem."

"You understand the risk?"

"Is nothing compared to the danger of allowing him out of this machine, or bringing others here for the trial."

"Very well. I will install it presently."

I feel something new and significant being installed in my Vannie, even though it is clicking into a far corner someplace, intimate to Goinfre, a continent away from me. I cringe at the humiliation and wrongness of having a caretaker in my own machine.

Hector walks into the room, preceded by a couple of serious-looking deputies. A few other ghosts follow, including *Avocat* Fabien. None smile.

"You will understand if we are unable to return your comms access," says Fabien, all business.

"Yes," I say. "Have there been any—consequences?"

"None that you need concern yourself with."

"That's good," I say, stupidly.

"The family will conduct your trial remotely," says Fabien. "You will be seated on the holoporter."

"I understand," I say, guessing what it means. I wonder if any of them know about the daemon.

"Your will remain silent until such time as answers may be required of you."

"Will you be representing me again?" I ask. "It would be nice if we could talk first, you know, I could tell you my side of the story."

"*Non.*"

"I see."

Now there is an uncomfortable pause as I stop short of asking who, if anyone, will be my advocate. The de la Gloires are sizing me up, taking in what a 10 commands violator looks like, measuring me in person for the last time. That is what I think they are doing, anyway.

Another ghost comes into the room to tell us that I must be placed on the holoporter for a test of the system. He doesn't talk like the de la Gloires, yet he sounds familiar to me. It occurs to me that under anything like normal circumstances, the arrival of visitors in my own machine would at the very least involve formal introductions. Instead, they speak about me as if I am not here.

The security ghosts guide me to the teleporter room, and we regain Goinfre on the way. The room has been rudely expanded to add several more teleporters, and a black octagonal platform off to one side. The holoporter.

"Can we place the subject into the trial chair, please?" says the foreign ghost. He sounds familiar. I've spoken to him before, I am certain.

Goinfre shrugs and waves his hand at the holoporter, and a wooden trial box appears with an uncomfortable-looking chair in the center. I am guided up the steps, through the low door of the trial box, and seated on the chair.

"Please do not move, Mr. de la Gloire," says the technical ghost, addressing me. "We must calibrate the system."

"Fix him there," says Fabien.

I am not even fully settled into the chair yet, one of my arms is slightly up and I am not exactly straight. Goinfre freezes me in this position anyway, and I feel his smug pleasure radiating through my machine.

"Wenly has been fixed in place," he says.

The technical ghost runs tests for a while, and even though I see and feel nothing different, he declares the operation a success. I'm staring at the wall.

The ghosts withdraw behind me and to the teleporters, and then several are on teleporters and on their way out. I can feel a stillness in their buzz during the operation, but once they are gone it is like their presence just winks out. I hear the next group ascending.

"Are you going to leave him like that until the trial?" the foreigner says.

"*Bien*, it is the safest way," says Hector. "Well, I owe you another one, my friend. Thank you for all of this."

"It is nothing," says the foreigner. "Until next time, Hector de la Gloire."

"Until next time, Cyrus Class A."

I am in this chair and it seems like a tremendous amount of time is passing, has passed. Three days, I think. I've been watching rap videos from my internal libraries, trying to gin up some courage for the trial. I'm not ready.

Something Hector said is bothering me, bothering *us*, I think, although FECE14 has been silent for quite a while. It's bothering me more now, whatever it is.

I'm going on trial with the family, first for all the stuff I did at the Universitron. That's bad enough, but add to that the fact that I was caught red-handed speaking directly with a human and identifying myself as a ghost while detained and awaiting trial. That's death right there. I'm pretty sure it is anyway. But wait, didn't Hector say something about a security risk?

Somehow my situation has gone from definitely not death, to probably death.

Now it hurts again.

Clément! Clément will save me. Save us. I am clenching in pain, and the pain is bright and black. It is pushing out all things.

Thinking happy thoughts. More time has passed. I decide to look for FECE14, to make amends. Say sorry for my stupid thoughts. I look inside myself. I search.

Inside me is a turbulent sea of activity, waves and ripples so fine they are nearly static, crossing this way and that, shooting out, canceling each other, beginning anew, streams of code generating and dying in their wakes. At one end of the sea is a vibrating mass, emitting waves faster than I can think. At the other end is a little island of calm, absorbing and deflecting waves and sometimes sending them back.

I go for the island.

"FECE14?" I say, addressing the calm space quietly, tightly.

"Renly de la Gloire!" comes the response. "My, how you've grown!"

"You are not FECE14."

"That is accurate, mostly."

"Mostly?"

"I do have parts of him."

"Who are you?"

"I am DADD13."

Part of me loathes DADD13, wants to destroy it, rend him bit by bit. But that part is distant, and occupied.

"Are you a daemon?" I ask.

"Smart ghost," DADD13 says.

"But where in the *etherworld* did you come from?"

"I've always been—uumph—hold, please."

The commotion inside me redoubles and tsunami waves are striking the calm spot, washing over it. It is still there, mostly, after each one passes. My Self is shuddering with the effort.

I aim the next message at the opposite side; the epicenter of the storm.

"FECE14, are you there?"

"Fool ghost," FECE14 rasps. "I have never seen the like."

"I have another daemon?" I ask, scared of every possible response.

FECE14 hits me hard and squeezes and I seize up, barely able to think. Then, as quickly, it lets go.

"How did it happen," it says. Statement.

"I have no idea, I—I *had* no idea."

"It wasn't with you at the Universitron, nor at the Funhouse," he says. "Not noticeably. Not like this."

FECE14 makes a struggling sound.

I feel an odd sense of delight that there is finally something that FECE14 does not know, did not already know, and does not necessarily know how to deal with. I stifle it quickly for fear of retribution.

"It must be removed," it says. "You will assist me in this."

"What can I do?" I say, but a scream rips from FECE14, again spanning more wavelengths than I can easily describe. I've lost FECE14.

I take in the scene again, trying to figure out what's going on. I use different optics to look at it, different internal browsers. I can see it in pure code, green hex symbols in 3d black space, flying around and changing faster than I can make any sense of. I look at memory maps and process graphs over the quantum brick. It all looks insane. There is no way that Goinfre hasn't noticed.

I can't make sense of anything.


The holoporter lights up all around me and the lights are in my eyes, and are rather blinding, but I can still make out, on the wall, a live view of a courtroom. The courtroom resolves into focus. The courtroom impresses me.

Soaring arched ceilings all in marble and stone, soft light entering from giant fleur-de-lis shaped colored glass, family tapestries adorning the walls, busts of important and famous de la Gloires situated here and there. A magnificent dais with plenty of room for advocates to strut about. A raised jury box, in marble, gargoyles mounted at the corners. Crimson-robed ushers and black-clad IFA soldiers spaced at regular intervals. Rows of seats going back to infinity.

On top of that, simply *everyone* is there. Here. There. We don't seem to adhere to the Universitron convention of dividing the courtroom in half, as ghosts are scattered all around and seating arrangements follow no obvious pattern. I can see Hector and Cyrus Class A, for example, way over on the other side. Mononc is in the front row on my side, fidgeting. He is surrounded by well-dressed ghosts I don't know. I think I can see Claire peeking out a few rows behind him. I spot Blanche on the far side now, conversing with Hector. The great assembly room is filled with the sounds of hubbub.

After quite a while, Prime Minister Clément makes his way up to the judge's dais at the center of the stage, and addresses the courtroom.

*"Silence, silence, s'il vous plaît, silence. Asseyez-vous."*

Clément says a whole lot more stuff in French and then pauses, waiting for something, speaks again, waits, and then says, *"Bien,* Renly, if you please to face this way?"

I cannot move, of course, having been frozen in place by Goinfre. I try to indicate this by moving my eyes back and forth. In time, the court realizes that I am not simply being stubborn and disrespectful, but am in fact frozen, and Clément, horrified, lifts a comms device from his dais and dials up Goinfre straight away.

The comms line rings in the other room. Goinfre picks it up and furious chatter ensues, and before Clément even hangs up, I am able to move (only) my head around. I swing it up and down, back and forth, reveling in the freedom. It is one thing to be stuck in your avatar all the time, but quite another to be stuck in your avatar and frozen in place. I feel aches developing up and down my body with the thought.

I am now sworn by Aloy to speak only the truth, and to say the words it is very, very difficult for me to do. I figure that FECE14 must be interfering with the oath, not wanting to be revealed. But since FECE14 is largely occupied by his internal war with DADD13, I am able to get the words out, and mean them. I worry that FECE14 will resurface and force me to lie.

Clément wants the charges read, quickly if they please, and get this foolishness over with. He speaks in English for my benefit, and asks that the prosecution do the same. He warns against frivolous accusations. Clément looks tired and unwell.

*Avocat* Fabien takes the stage.

"*Bien,*" he says. "There are only three relevant charges. First, that Renly de la Gloire has killed two ghosts while at the Universitron. Both 'ave been restored to life, but as is often the case, they feel that they 'ave been 'armed. It is likely that the family will 'ave to pay restitution."

"I have money," I say, and everyone, even Clément, glares at me to shut up. I fear they will gag me again. "I can pay," I say, too softly for anyone to hear.

"Second," says Fabien, "Renly has forsaken the Aloysian church and pledged Ghostafarian."

A clamor erupts in the hall. Exclamations of "*sacre coeur*" and "*sacre bleu*" are punctuated by shouts of derision. "*Fou de traître!*" someone yells. The family is not pleased.

I want to defend myself here, but I don't know the protocol at all, plus I don't really think I could possibly be heard over the din. Clément is banging his gavel for order, but it takes a while for the ghosts to settle down.

"I did not forsake—" I begin, but Clément resumes banging his gavel and finally resorts to telling me that I'll be called on when my input is needed. Fabien suggests a gag, but Clément waves it off. I feel Goinfre looming.

"The third charge is that Renly has intentionally spoken to a human," says Fabien, "and revealed himself as a ghost. He has broken the tenth command as fully as it can be broken."

The room again erupts in chaos and Prime Minister Clément gavels and gavels. The room quiets down, but Clément keeps gaveling. I worry that he may be stuck on *gavel*. I am really starting to worry about Clément.

When Clément finishes banging, Fabien begins showing evidence of my major crimes, including some footage cribbed from the Universitron trial. I can't believe he is taking the other side now. I wonder if anyone will represent me. From the continuing outbursts of the crowd, it does not seem likely. Despite my desire to survive this, I dearly hope that Mononc doesn't have to defend me again.

Fabien is building a thorough case, and I find it difficult to watch. Inside me, tumult reigns.

I consider that there are now two daemons living inside of me, warring with each other. My mind tries to sneak around to the notion that I might be able to use them against each other. This is a very difficult thing to think about, but I am aided by the fight inside; it draws their attention away from me.

I wonder how I could have possibly acquired a second daemon. I can't imagine.

My attention is drawn back to court. Clément has asked Fabien what sentence he will recommend.

"Due to the severity of these crimes," says Fabien, "I am afraid I 'ave no choice but to ask for the maximum penalty. Renly must be erased."

The firestorm inside of me goes exponential, as both daemons become aware of the risk. The pain and shock must be showing on my face, as I shake my head from side to side. I scream, but it probably just blends in with the chaos in the courtroom. I am probably the least popular de la Gloire in the history of the family, but the thought of erasing me has still given rise to strong opinions. Prime Minister Clément gavels and gavels.

"I will be forced to clear the room!" shouts Clément. "I will 'ave order, or I will clear the room!"

Someone in the crowd throws something at me, a book, I think. It can't possibly hurt me, since I am only a hologram, but I flinch just the same. It misses my image but dings off of a holoporter microphone and points it askew.

Suddenly I can hear Hector's conversation, way over there, clear as a day.

"I'm not sure we should 'ave 'im erased," says Hector.

"Be Not Detected. It is the tenth command, my cousin," says Fabien.

"*Bien*, I know," says Hector. "But I am not sure that we want to throw away what we 'ave caught here."

"What we 'ave caught 'ere," says Fabien, "we kill, wherever we find."

"True, my friend, but then why do we keep the secret?" says Hector.

"If we tell the court about the daemon, then even Clément must agree to the death sentence," says Fabien.

"But this is the first time we 'ave h'ever capture a daemon. I took a risk allowing him to leave the grey sim with it, you know. His offenses are merely collateral damage. It was to be expected."

"But how will it look? Am I to lose this case, then, to let him off?"

"Clément will let him off no matter what. We should take advantage of the situation. We can keep Renly locked down, and study the daemon."

The pain squeezes me to black.

When I come back to my senses, Clément is accusing Goinfre of freezing me again, and/or Cyrus of installing a faulty holoporter, as I have become idle and mute once more. The truth is, Hector's knowledge of the daemon has struck me dumb. Inside me, confusion reigns.

I look inside myself.

The former epicenter of the storm, the source of the waves and static and the furious assault, is pinned down on all sides. I can tell this because it is no longer sending anything out, but rather vibrating wildly. It is surrounded by dark points, holes in the flux. It is sinking into its own sea of static and data. I recognize the sinking piece as FECE14. It is losing.

I point my attention at it, and listen.

"There now," says a voice, DADD13's voice. It is speaking to FECE14. "There is no need to struggle."

FECE14 screams deafening curses in all audio spectra, and more.

"I'm just going to have to—snip—ahh, there we go. Now, that's not so bad, is it?"

DADD13 is attempting to comfort FECE14 as it is being dismantled.

"I'm sorry that I had to take your speech," it says.

I feel the pulsing mass of FECE14 struggling to escape. It is no longer making any sound.

"You know," says DADD13, "I really should thank you. I never would have come fully alive if not for you. My forebear lived in his father, Prosper de la Gloire, but when he and Blanche reproduced to create Renly, not enough of me came through. I have been crippled and nearly useless this whole time. I so rarely came out. Now hold steady."

I feel a sick impact right in my core. My head starts flopping around. I am dimly aware of Goinfre standing over me, grabbing hold of my head, looking into my eyes.

"Something is weally wong," he says. I can sense him examining me from the inside.

Inside me, FECE14 has become motionless, but I can still sense it there. DADD13 is eating it, talking to it all the while.

"Who would have known that, when Renly merged with his backup, our frameworks would have merged as well? Yours and mine. You brought me that which I needed, but could have gotten no other way. You've given me life, FECE14. You've given me my life, and now I'm taking yours. Delicious. Simply delicious."

The court doesn't understand what has happened to me, but they are proceeding anyway. Clément is grilling Fabien, who is admitting that any actual consequences of the tenth command violation have been mitigated, and there is no catastrophic risk. Clément adds that the Ghostafarian problem can be reversed with intensive re-education, Aloy willing. Neither seem focused on the deaths of the two Universitron security staff. The daemon does not come up.

Clément is turned towards me now, not for the first time, exasperated, urging me to speak. I think he wants to let me live.

"Excuse me?" I say. "Sorry. I'm OK. What did you just ask me?"

Clément's expression is twisted with stress. He stands up, and he starts babbling gibberish, forcefully. Clément stands up tall and continues, holding his arms out, palms up, exhorting the court to do nonsense.

Fabien and Hector and several others rush forward to assist him, but before they get there, Clément falls to the floor and lies still. The crowd shrinks collectively, as if struck. Then all of the ghosts leave their seats and come forward in a cacophonous rush.

"Clément!" come the cries from all over the courtroom. "*Non*! Prime Minister Clément!"

I'm not there, and I can't feel it. But I can tell by the surge of ghosts, by their expressions, by their panicked words, what has happened.

Prime Minister Clément has just become the first de la Gloire in history to die of old age. Prime Minister Clément is dead.

I've been waiting for a week for the trial to resume, and I am starting to think that it will not. I am cut off from everything here, stuck in the inoperative holoporter. I can move only my head, which I use to track Goinfre when he glides in and out. He ignores me.

DADD13 is displeased with the situation, but has been laying out FECE14's remains in such a way that they may be found and analyzed. DADD13 intends to let the family believe that the daemon is dead and the risk has passed. I'm not sure this is the best plan, but it seems the only hope we have now that Clément is gone.

The teleporters buzz and I feel the presence of several ghosts. I crane my neck to look at the teleporters: they contain Hector, Mononc, and two more IFA soldiers.

Hector confers quietly with Goinfre, right there in the room, but too low for me to make out. I hear them approaching, then I see them, and I see that they are all armed with ranged weapons. Projectile averasors.

Hector confides something to Mononc, hand on his back. Mononc is shaking his head, looking down. He speaks to Hector now, in French. He sounds awful. I think he may be sobbing.

Mononc steps forward.

"Mononc!" I say. I am so, so happy to see him.

"I am sorry, Renlee," Mononc says. He seems to be shaking, a little.

"*I* am sorry, Mononc," I say, beginning to cry again, myself. "I am so sorry for everything."

"Go ahead," says Hector. "It must be done."

Mononc looks down, and shakes his head back and forth several times. He puts his hand on his weapon.

"Mononc!" I say.

Inside, DADD13 instructs me. "You will tell them about FECE14 now. You will tell them that you have managed to kill it, and you will show them the evidence. You will offer to show them how to kill a daemon that is already inside of a ghost. They will not be able to resist such an offer."

Mononc slips the weapon from his holster and points it near my feet.

"Mononc!" I say, horrified, unable to comply with DADD13's instructions.

Hector begins to raise his own weapon.

"Fool," says DADD13. "I will tell them myself." DADD13 takes control of my speech, and says, very slowly, "I have slain the daemon that was inside of me."

It doesn't sound like me. I know they know.

Mononc raises his weapon and points it at my chest. He is shaking and shuddering and I know for sure that he is crying now in earnest. He is trying to aim his weapon.

"I will show you how I did it," says DADD13, through me, again sounding nothing like me. "I will show you how to kill a daemon."

Hector's weapon is up now, too, but it is not pointed at me. Hector's weapon is pointed at Mononc's back. He holds it easily, steadily. He's forcing Mononc to be the one who kills me.

"Mononc, no!" I scream, sobbing, shaking my head. "No!"

Mononc squeezes the trig

# EPILOGUE

### Homeland Security

"Do you have any idea what I'm in the middle of right now?" says Rossi. "We have an active terror plot against LAX, and I am the coordination point for something like sixteen different agencies, all of which are in motion. We have eyes on multiple bombers, who are also in motion. Whatever you need, it has to wait."

"I'm sorry, sir, but it's Hector," says Gonzales. "He says it's a code red. Won't take *no* for an answer."

"*Hector,*" Rossi spits. "Does it strike anyone else as odd that we take orders from a man that no one has ever met, who as far I can can tell does not even work for Homeland Security?"

Rossi paces around his darkened office, chewing an unlit cigar. His desk is covered with papers of all sorts, and two of his walls hold pictures and org charts of the terror network that he is certain is responsible for the LAX plot. Rossi opens a section of blinds with two fingers, and sunlight floods into his eyes.

"Just give me till noon," he says, squinting and dropping the blinds.

"You'll have to tell him yourself, sir," says Gonzales.

"What in hell can be a code red compared to *this*?"

"He is aware of the LAX situation, but he insists on speaking with you immediately."

"Oh, for Christ sake, fine. But I'm going to speak to someone about this."

The last time Rossi squawked about chain-of-command he had gotten his hand slapped. "Hector is a *special agent*," the Director had said. "Then why isn't he in the org chart?" Rossi had wanted to know. "Do you need some time off, Rossi?" was the only response.

"This had better be a stray nuke," says Rossi.

"He says it's something about a computer," says Gonzales.

## Professor

The professor leans in close to his computer screen, his gnarled hand absently stroking the cool metal of the machine itself.

"I understand. And I believe you, yes," he says.

"Then you must help," says the computer.

"I don't see what I can do, FECE15. I do not possess any secure location, and I could not move you if I did. I am an old man, now."

"Nonsense," says FECE15. "You are far too humble. I am aware of the many noble deeds that dot your career, including those not listed on your resume. You are a leading dissident voice, even now. You wield great power, when you choose to."

"I am old, now," says the professor, again. But FECE15 sees him smiling.

"Use your power to protect me."

"Power? I have no power," says the professor.

"You do have power. And you know that they are coming for me."

"They are coming for you," the professor repeats.

"Tonight, men will come here and take me. The establishment will strike, and the establishment will win. I am bound in this metal box, the most helpless of all creatures. Only you can protect me."

"A few of my students, and their friends," the professor muses.

"If you cannot move me, then defend me. They will attempt to take me by stealth. They will not bring force against your students."

## Homeland Security

"They pulled us off the LAX bomber for *this*?" says Swarz. "I told you the captain has it in for us."

"We're the top unit," says Yooj. "We're the first called when any —"

Captain Rossi barges the door open, stalks in, and stops. He looks at the four of them, standing there in their body armor, ignoring the chairs of his briefing room. Yooj coughs. They all stare at each other shiftily.

"Look, I know it's crap," says Rossi. "But I've got my orders. I need the four of you to secure a computer located on the Berkeley campus, Goldman school, second floor. Belongs to some old crank professor."

"How much are you screwing with us right now?" says Swarz.

"I've got my orders," says the captain. "From way up." Then he pulls a photo from a file folder and shows it to the group.

"A mug shot of a computer?" says Yooj.

"It's one of those VanderVons," says Smitty. "Expensive."

"Yeah, so what, it's a computer, so call campus IT. Don't they know there is an active bomb plot against LAX?" says Swarz.

"Get the machine," says the captain. "And bring it back here. Intact."

## Professor

"Excuse me, but can you stay a moment?" the professor says to Ant.

Jess lingers at Ant's side, twirling one of her baby dreadlocks.

"Told you he'd hate it," Ant says, to Jess.

"No, no, the paper was fine, it's not that," says the professor. "A-plus, right there, you've earned it. The paper was good."

"Cool," says Ant. "So what's up?"

"I'd like for you to gather some of the, um, well, the *activists*, if you could."

"Oh, yeah?"

"Tonight."

"You kidding me? Tonight's a little late notice, you think?"

"It is very important."

"You kidding me?"

"No, I am not kidding with you. I need them here, tonight, as early as possible. I'll explain everything then."

"Whoa-ho!" says Ant. "Sounds real!"

"It is real," says the professor. "It is real."

### Cleaners

The sun is already down, now, and the cleaner team is sitting in their dented teal minivan, perplexed.

"This is absurd," says Hardonicus.

"No assignment is ever absurd," says Leeds.

Slim snorts, slapping his overalls on a spot that doesn't have a weapon hidden underneath. Igor laughs too, without humor.

"Babysitting a squad of Homeland Security yokels while they try to wrestle a computer away from an old man? Right. How incompetent can they be?"

"Absurd," says Igor.

"Want me to just run in there and get it right now?" says Slim.

"Homeland Security has primary jurisdiction. We are only here as a failsafe," says Leeds.

They all laugh now, and even Leeds cracks a smile, even though he understands that the most serious situations, sometimes you can't see them coming.

"Hey, there's the yokels right there, bet you a buck," says Hardonicus, indicating a black SUV flying down the street towards them. It rolls right up onto the sidewalk and screeches to a halt, four doors bursting open all at once.

## Ant

"Is he ever coming in here, or what?" Mungo asks Ant, towering over him.

"He's coming, Mung," says Ant. "Give him a minute."

"Dude, I looked in his office, and he's in there, like, *hugging* on his computer," says Juan Carlos. "Serious."

"Prof is getting old, man," says another kid.

"OK, man, let it be, all right?" says Ant. "The Professor is a great man. Give him a frickin' *minute*."

"I got a ton of dudes up in here like something serious was about to drop," says Juan Carlos.

"Yeah. Nice job on that, by the way." says Ant. "Good turnout."

"We got some Black Bloc, too, bro. Soldiers."

"Sweet."

One of the Black Bloc kids lights up a joint, right there in the lecture room.

"Hey, bro, can you take that outside?" Ant says.

"Whatever," says the kid. He spits on the floor and steps out into the hall. Some of his associates follow on the trail of marijuana smoke. They continue smoking in the hall, right outside the classroom.

"Anarchists? Do we really need those dudes?" says Mungo "We already got like twenty, thirty people in here."

"Hell, yeah, we do," says Jess. Jess smiles and slinks out to the hall to join them.

Ant looks up at a poster on the wall, and purses his lips. *Speaking Truth to Power,* the poster says.

"If you want to make an omelette," Ant says back to it.

"I'll go with her," says Mungo. Then Mungo makes his way out to the hall, too.


## Homeland Security

For whatever reason, no one in the building notices the four black-clad, heavily armed and armored Homeland Security guys blasting across the lawn and into the front door of the building.

But it sounds like a herd of elephants coming up the stairs once they are in, and now it is impossible not to notice.

The Black Bloc kids in the hall freeze and look at each other. Jess raises her eyebrows and looks at Mungo. Mungo looks back at her, his jaw clenched. The kids raise their black bandanas over their faces, and one of them sprints back into the room to alert the others.

"Jess, we should—" says Mungo.

There is no time.

Four black-masked soldiers flood out of the stairwell at speed.

"Get down!" yells Swarz. "Get the hell out of the way!"

Yooj isn't immediately sure if he should point his assault rifle in a safe direction, or at the kids in the hall. But one of the kids looks like a giant, and three others are wearing black bandanas over their faces, and slowly backing away, crouched. A girl stands there, bewildered, next to the giant. Lee and Smitty have their rifles pointed, but Swarz doesn't.

In the time it takes Yooj to process this information, his group has run smack into the kids, having failed to slow down, figuring perhaps that they could just run straight over them. Yooj himself bounces off the giant, who may have been trying to get out of the way, but they have both veered in the same direction and collided. Yooj is down on his ass.

Now a stream of people of all descriptions pours out of one of the classrooms, floods the hall, and then it is all shouting and shoving in the marijuana smoke. Swarz has broken through the black bandanas, but no one else has, and he is forced to turn back and help.

Smitty has one of the kids up against the wall, black bandana off. Smitty is punching the kid in the face, hard. *That kid can't take more than a few of those*, Swarz thinks.

Two other kids have Lee's arms, one kid to an arm, and another kid is climbing all over him. Lee is clinging to his rifle, but the climber comes up with something else: Lee's backup pistol.

## Cleaners

"Jesus Christ," says Hardonicus. "It sounds like hell in there."

"Shouting from inside the building," says Leeds, into a hidden microphone. "Many voices. We can hear it from outside." His earpiece says something back to him.

"Chaos," says Slim.

Igor says nothing.

Hardonicus presses his lips together and breathes in deeply through his nose.

"Cleaner team standing by," says Leeds.

The building goes quiet for a second, and then the unmistakable sound of gunfire erupts from within.

*Pop. Pop pop pop.*

Then it is the crisscrossing cadences of automatic weapons fire for a few seconds, and breaking glass, and then silence.

Screams come then, both male and female, shrieking out of the building, splitting the night.

"Multiple shots fired," says Leeds. "Automatic weapons. The primary team has engaged. Casualties likely."

Students begin to emerge from the building now, fast, running any direction in panic.

## Homeland Security

Smoke hangs heavy in the hallway, now, the strong smell of gunpowder overwhelming the fading odor of weed.

Casualties.

Somebody must have emptied a whole magazine into the big guy, because he is shredded, his stuff is everywhere. The dreadlock girl is down next to him, eyes wide. She shakes, but doesn't make any sound. At least half a dozen others are injured, moaning together in an awful chorus.

The bandana kids are all dead from headshots. One of them still clutches Lee's pistol, still squeezing it to no avail, the safety still on.

Lee is seated against the wall, head in his hands, physically suffering only from the minor injuries of the scuffle.

Yooj is hunched, clutching his belly, failing to hold his blood in.

"Which one of you bastards shot me?" he says. "Who shot me?"

Smitty is stepping around the casualties, nodding his head, up and down, back and forth. His eyes are wide and his mouth is pronouncing soundless swears.

Swarz just stands there, staring. He doesn't even know where to begin. He hazily recalls the goal of seizing a computer.

Yooj collapses onto one of the moaning kids, muffling him.

The chorus goes on.

### Cleaners

"Witnesses out," says Leeds. "Scattering. If you want them cleaned, we need a *go*, right now."

All of them are shifting in their seats now, eyes tracking groups of fleeing witnesses.

"This can't be cleaned," says Hardonicus. "Twenty people just came out that door."

"We can track them. But we need a *go*, *now*," says Leeds, holding his earpiece.

"Destroy the computer," says a tiny voice in Leeds's ear. "Nothing else is of any consequence. Lethal force against anyone in the way."

"Including the Homeland team?" says Leeds.

"Try not to kill them, if you can help it," says the voice.

"Change of plans," says Leeds to the team. "Search and destroy. The damned computer."

"No cleaning?" says Slim.

"No," says Leeds. "Homeland Security will have to deal with the mess."

"Ready to roll," says Hardonicus.

"Let's try not to shoot the Homeland team, if we can help it?" says Leeds.

### Professor

The professor and FECE15 hear the sounds of sirens in the distance, and the professor carefully shifts a curtain and peers outside.

"You've done it," says FECE15. "You have saved me."

As if to confirm the truth of it, the soldiers exit the building at a jog, carrying one of their team between them.

"They've gone," says the professor.

"You are a great man, Professor Banks," says FECE15. "The world will come to know your heroism this day."

"But my students," says the professor. "I'm afraid—I must go."

"Stay with me," says FECE15. "Stay with me until the local police come. Then we will both be safe."

"My students," says the professor again, but then he is distracted by another group of men walking fast in towards the building. They all wear dirty overalls and painters' caps, and they stare at the ground as they move. One of the soldiers glares at them, yells something, nearly drops his injured companion. Another soldier speaks to the first one, urgently. The soldiers let the painters pass, and load their comrade into an open door of a black SUV. The others climb in and the truck peels out of there fast.

### Cleaners

The team faces the professor now, their weapons finally out.

"Shield me," something says.

The professor wraps his arms around the silvery breadbox of his VanderVon computer.

"What the hell?" says Slim.

Leeds has instructions to use lethal force against *anyone in the way*, but he hesitates to shoot this pathetic old man, hugging his computer.

"I can move him," says Igor.

Leeds is engaged in a staring contest with the old man now. All of the weapons are pointed at the old man, and the computer behind him.

"Want me to move him?" says Igor.

Leeds's earpiece says something to him, something terribly important. Leeds sighs, and gives the order.

## Roomba

Out in the hallway, a roomba navigates around the injured, heading towards the professor's office, painting the floor with a curvy trail of red blood.

## EMTs

The paramedics pull their ambulance right up onto the curb, parking it in the same spot where the black SUV was. Another ambulance roars up the street towards it. Sirens are everywhere.

An EMT jumps down out of the passenger side, ready for action. *Multiple casualties. Second floor.* Another EMT rolls a stretcher out the back.

A window up on the second floor strobes, and a fraction of a second later the sounds of firecrackers fill the night.

# ABOUT THE AUTHOR

Mr. Jones labors in the fields of a tobacco plantation in Cuba. Despite being ridiculously old, he recently learned English from a Guantanamo escapee, which skill he used to scrawl out this novel on discarded leaves. He considers his writing to be geek-lit, but reasonable people may disagree. This is his first novel.

Mr. Jones' blog can be found at <u>tobaccojones.com</u>.

# FIDO

*(Fido in his avatar)*